TH

H

PARTY

THE HANGING PARTY

A TEXAS LIGHTNING NOVEL

WILLIAM W. JOHNSTONE

AND J.A. JOHNSTONE

PINNACLE BOOKS
Kensington Publishing Corp.
www.kensingtonbooks.com

PINNACLE BOOKS are published by

Kensington Publishing Corp.
900 Third Avenue
New York, NY 10022

First Kensington Books hardcover printing: September 2024
First Pinnacle Books mass market paperback printing: December 2024

ISBN-13: 978-0-7860-5062-8
ISBN-13: 978-0-7860-5063-5 (eBook)

10 9 8 7 6 5 4 3 2 1

Printed in the United States of America

Chapter 1

"Hey, I know you—ain't you the one they call Texas Lightning?"

The trim, dark-haired man at the bar sighed and looked at his half-empty glass of beer, wondering if he'd get to finish it.

"Hey, I'm talking to you!"

The dark-haired man sighed again, louder this time, and looked over his left shoulder. It was a task not as easy as it sounds when you'd been shot in your right shoulder. He'd been looking over his shoulder a whole lot these past few years.

"Do I know you?"

The man who'd spoken first stared at the dark stranger in town.

For his part, the stranger took in the man with a quick glance before turning back to his beer. He'd seen the same man, or a near-enough version anyway, in every town from his birthplace of Sourwood Springs, Texas, to here, wherever here was. Some little mining town in the eastern foothills of the great spine of the Rockies.

And every time, the stranger saw the same thing—a fat-faced, sunburned idiot with a look of wet-eyed, drunken glee on his red face. He almost always wanted the same thing—to become instantly famous for killing the world's deadliest gunfighter. That'd be the stranger in town. Most folks knew him by his killer name, the one he had worn with smug, audacious pride for years. Until . . .

These days, getting recognized happened a whole lot less often than it used to, back when he was still supporting his reputation with gunplay.

"Don't you turn your face from me, mister! I asked you a question and I dang well want an answer."

The gunfighter flicked his eyes up from his glass, caught the gaze of the barkeep, who looked a little alarmed, but was doing nothing to calm the situation, save for standing with his chubby hands gripping his bar towel too tight above his big, aproned belly.

The barkeep had been a decent sort and the stranger didn't think he'd do anything foolish. Not that he cared one way or the other.

The stranger's gaze followed around once more, this time to the man who'd addressed him, who had moved and now stood a half-dozen feet from him at the bar, facing him. The promise of the unknown, of the expectation of some vague victory, hung within his grasp, mere moments away. The stranger had seen the look far too many times before.

"My name is Gage. Jon Gage," said the stranger in a

low, even voice. Then he once more turned his attention to the glass before him.

"I knew it! I knew it! You are him, you are Jon Gage, Texas Lightning! One and the same! I know all about you!" The man held his hands on his own gun belt. And he took a step closer.

The stranger named Gage ran his tongue over his teeth, then, without looking up, crooked his right index finger at the man, beckoning the hopeful fool closer.

The man swallowed and did as he was bade. When he was but a foot from Gage, he bent his head down as the gunfighter said, "I am who you say. And I won't be prodded." His voice came out low, cold, and grating— pitted, rusting steel sliding on pitted, rusting steel.

The red-faced man swallowed and pulled his head back.

Gage said no more. A few quiet moments passed; then the foolish, hopeful man turned, still wide-eyed, and hustled on out the door.

Gage sipped his beer. He knew he'd not seen the last of the man, who would, soon enough, blather to all his friends about the close call he'd had with Texas Lightning. Then they'd all gather and wait for him to leave the saloon. Maybe they'd challenge him, maybe they would just stare and shiver and try to look bold. It didn't much matter to Jon Gage what they did.

He'd leave by the front door anyway. And then, come what may, if they chose to shoot him, fine. He could not do much to defend himself, as he wore no guns.

But for now, he would sit in the otherwise-empty little saloon and enjoy his warm beer.

"Another?" said the barkeep.

Gage looked at the man a moment. "Sure. Why not?"

The barkeep filled a new glass and set it before Gage. Then he cocked his head to one side. "Why didn't you just say, 'No, that isn't me. Sorry, you don't have the right person'?"

"Because that would be wrong."

"Huh?"

"Dishonest," said Gage. "It'd be a lie, and I won't do that."

He looked at Gage as if the gunfighter had just gutted a kitten with a wooden spoon.

Gage knew the reason and the logic behind the sideways look. A gunfighter who won't lie? To most folks, that'd be like a lion that eats oats.

The barkeep shrugged and worked his rag in slow circles down the length of the already-gleaming bar top, leaving Jon Gage to once more walk his way through the stump field that was his mind.

Far from the first time, Gage ruminated on the fact that life was an odd affair. Most folks start off in much the same way, with a big future wide open before them. And almost as soon as you begin to draw breath and yelp and gurgle, you begin limiting yourself and narrowing your future by making choices, good ones, bad ones, downright vile ones, but all choices, nonetheless.

As odd as many of those choices and the lives surrounding them might get, very few folks wake up one day and say, "I'm going to kill people for a living."

Very few, indeed. But he did. In a roundabout way, that is.

And with that thought, Jon Gage, a slender, broad-shouldered, dark-haired man, with the beginnings of early gray dusting his temples, sat at the bar in a little mountain mining town in the eastern foothills of the Rockies, with a fresh glass of beer before him.

With that, Jonathan Gage, aka Texas Lightning, levered himself, like a boulder freshly unearthed, and sent himself toppling and rolling, crashing and careening downhill, back into his past.

Chapter 2

Twelve years earlier than his present day

"You will marry and you will take over this here ranch and you will take care of me as I have taken care of you, by gaw!" The rangy, raw-boned man who bellowed this did so from a swaying, spraddle-legged stance, sunken chest working like a bellows, paunched gut slopping.

His veiny face and bulbous red nose shone with sweat, his eyes glistening and wet and reddened. His skin's gray pallor looked as if it might be more at home on a dead man.

Jonathan Gage stared at this swaying man, Jasper Gage, his father, a bullying, brawling drunkard, who, despite spending most of his life upending one bottle of whiskey after another, still stood half a head taller than his son.

Both men regarded each other, open contempt pulling their features into sneers. Then Gage the elder turned and looked about him for his bottle. He finally realized it was clutched in one of his clawlike hands. He hoisted it and glugged back a couple of swallows.

"If Mama was here, you'd not act this way."

The older man swung around, his latest bottle arcing wide as he spun. "What? You dare mention your sainted mother to me?"

Jon Gage snorted and shook his head. "Now she's sainted? Seems to me you should have thought about that before you drove her to her grave."

"Me? Why, you whelp! I'll show you a grave!" The big man lunged, clearing half the room in two bold strides, upending chairs and a small table. "Ain't no way no child of mine is going to talk to me that way. And in my own home, too!"

Nothing his father was doing much surprised Jon Gage, as they'd plowed this same ground many times in the past.

"I told you more times than a man can count," said Jon, sidestepping his wildly lunging father, "that I am not a child and I am not afraid of you."

The older man pulled up short, realizing with a headshake that his son was not in front of him, but standing to the side, arms folded over his chest. The younger man continued to speak. "I am dang sure not going to marry to please you. And I am not going to take over this snake-infested sand pit you call a ranch! Heck, even the cattle we got don't know it's a ranch! It's no small wonder they look more like mangy coyotes than beeves, and light out for anywhere but here all the time anyway. No, sir." He shook his head. "I won't do any of that."

Jasper Gage leered, his lips pulled back tight over

his yellow teeth. He was about to launch into the familiar bellow that, in his whiskey-addled mind, he was perennially convinced would finally, finally convince his useless, fool-minded boy he'd best do all the things his father told him, without question, and right quick.

But as happened each time the topic came up, at least once a week now that the boy was of marrying age, Jasper Gage's volley of words had been preempted by the young man's usual final protest of the night.

Once more, Jonathan Gage stood his ground, tall and bold, chest filled with air, broad shoulders squared, and outthrust finger pointed at his father. "You pathetic old drunkard! You honestly think I'd take any advice from you? You honestly think I'd take care of you? Way you're going, it wouldn't be a long-term job, I'll grant you that. But ha to that, I say. Ha!" He snorted and shook his head, the smile on his mouth a brief, tight one, the rest of his visage hard-set in scorn and disgust.

That's when the old man did something that surprised them both. He whipped his right arm around, the one ending in a balled fist clutching the nearly empty whiskey bottle.

The thick fingers released the vessel, which spun end over end, spraying the amber liquid about the room, the bottle aimed right at Jonathan's head.

The younger man, blessed with a sober mind and the reflexes of youth, was able to jerk his head to the side in time to avoid a full-on, direct hit to the face. But not quick enough to prevent the bottle smacking the side of his head, just behind his left eye, before glancing off and smashing on the flagged floor.

Jonathan's temple throbbed with eyeblink speed and

his fingertips patted the spot. No blood, but it was already swelling. The younger Gage had spent much of his life under the man's thumb, and hated his father for being who he was: a bully; a domineering, loud-mouthed braggart with a ready, brutal word, and an even quicker taste of knuckles across the teeth.

Despite all this, and so much more, at that moment young Jonathan knew he was too much like his father in so many other ways. His hair-trigger temper was the most prominent of them.

Granted, it took Jonathan a whole lot longer to touch off than it did Jasper, but when he did, he was a whole lot like the old man, but a whole lot younger and quicker, too. And stronger, despite the fact that Jasper was an old bull with a lot of ranch-built power still backing his walloping, ham-size hands.

At that moment, the leeching color of blood red drizzled down before his eyes, not from a cut, but from within, fueled by rage, Gage rage, and he set his jaw and met the old man.

Jasper barreled at him, growling low and deep like a bull grizz. The two men met in the midst of the mess of the room.

It was Jonathan Gage's hard, quick, solid, slamming fist that made first contact between the two men, father and son, that night. It was not the first time they had come to blows over this threadbare topic, but neither man knew it would be the last.

Jonathan's big fist slammed hard into his father's once-broad chest, square and true. The blow stopped the older man as if he'd run smack into a stone wall. He jerked upright to his full height, eyes pulled wider than they had been since he'd begun tugging on the bottle's mouth that day, and they looked straight at the younger man.

Jasper's mouth opened in a big O and a thin, wheezing, scratchy sound came out, the only sound at that moment in the low-line ranch house.

Jonathan stood before the rigid man, his eyes also wide, his breath also stoppered, and his leading fist still balled and held before him, as if he were hoisting a lantern by the bail.

Jasper remained rigid, then swiveled his rheumy eyes up at his son and they narrowed. A low growl rose up from the depths of his once-mighty chest and a slow grin spread over his mouth. He tried another sloppy swing, but his eyes once more went wide and he stiffened, seemed to see something beyond Jon's right shoulder, and spasmed as he dropped to the floor in a sloppy heap.

"Pop?"

Jon remained immobile, his fist held before him, and he eyed his father sprawled at his feet.

"Pop!"

The old man remained motionless, curled in a heap on the scarred plank floor. His son's fist sagged, then dropped to his side. He knelt and felt for the man's breath. It was there.

"Lousy drunkard." Jonathan turned and walked away.

Chapter 3

"Yes, sir, Monty, I figure what I am best suited to is tending to the cards at the baize goddess over there, and dallying with the pretty ladies in this wind-stripped border town. And"—he smacked his empty mug on the bar top—"sampling the fine beer you serve here at the Top Palace! And speaking of, what say you top up that glass, huh, Monty?"

"You've about had enough, ain't you, Jon?"

Quicker than it seemed a man was capable of, Jon Gage shoved back and upright, sending the tall stool he'd been perched on stuttering, then pitching backward. "You going to tell me what I am and ain't capable of, Monty?"

"Oh, heck, Jon, set yourself back down." Monty barely blinked, accustomed as he was to the hair-trigger reactions of the Gage men. He drew another beer and set it before the still-sneering Gage.

Jon Gage eyed the beer, then smiled and stood his stool up and settled himself once more.

"Aw, you know I'm funning you, Monty. I'm just worked up about the old man."

"What's new?"

Gage nodded. "Yeah, we had ourselves another session. He won't listen to reason. He wants me to take over that rank little ranch and get married to some brood cow and tend to his sorry self so he can spend all his time drinking. Which he does anyway!"

Monty nodded and poured a shot for a newcomer who'd just sidled up to the bar. Gage glanced sideways at the man. "I know you, stranger?"

The newcomer sipped his whiskey, without looking to his right. He was an average-height man in a low-crown black hat, with more than the usual scatter of lines about his eyes and mouth, and a day's worth of peppered whiskers on his hard-lined jaw. And he wore a tied-down, double-gun rig hanging low beneath his short, rawhide brown vest. "Doubt it."

"Huh," said Jon. "You sure do look familiar." He sighed. "All right, then, since we don't know one another, and since my sainted mother always said folks you ain't yet met are just friends waiting to happen, or something like that, let me buy you a round of that rye whiskey you're nibbling on."

That finally drew the stranger's attention enough for him to turn his gaze on Gage. "Why?"

"Why what? Why would I buy you a drink?" Gage looked at Monty, smiling, but only with his eyes. "This fellow is a character, all right. Suspicious of someone who'd buy him a shot of rye!" He smacked the bar top and then knocked back a shot himself. He refilled it, held up the glass, and winked at the stranger. "Here's to you!"

The stranger seemed to relax, perhaps even smile a little, and finished off his drink, then had himself another.

Monty moved on down the bar, shaking his head, to serve other customers. The stranger nodded once at Gage. "I thank you kindly, son," he said.

"You bet . . . Pops!" Gage let loose with a burble of laughter and tucked into another shot of rye.

He did not notice that the stranger had lost the meager beginnings of a smile he'd tried to conjure. Now he looked cold and hard once more.

Several long minutes passed as Jon Gage felt the familiar but welcome roar of heat from all that whiskey in so short a time, sending pleasurable flames up his throat and warming his chest and face.

Finally he said, "I will say that you are the touchiest old fellow I ever did meet hereabouts. Oh, oh, wait a minute!" Gage poked skyward with a finger. "I take that back. My old man is by far the prickliest hereabouts. But you are a sour close second—yes, sir!" He nodded and knocked back another round.

"That's it!" The older stranger spun, both hands on the butt ends of his revolvers. "You have insulted me for the last time, you wet-nose pup." His words had a drawl to them, not local, as far as Gage could tell.

But at that moment, he did not think much about the man's accent. Nor did he hear the rest of the sounds in the well-filled, smokey room stutter to a stop.

The piano player, a garter-armed old soak named

Benny, spun in his stool, facing the impending scuffle with a ripple of glee up his spine and a grin on his face.

All the gamblers at the baize tables paused, too, their cigars and pipes clamped in their lips, eyes wide, cards held in midair, chips no longer clinking. Even the two women cavorting with cowhands stilled their twittering ministrations.

Only Monty, the barkeep, spoke up. "All right, you two. Enough of this. You have a complaint, you take it up with each other anywhere but in here. I have no doubt you two could wind up killing one another."

"Outside, then," said the stranger, and pushed past Gage, notably not knocking into him as he did several other men no less far from his steam-fueled swagger.

"I reckon not," said Gage in a low, cold tone.

The stranger had just about reached the double doors. He jerked to a halt; those who could see him saw a slow sneer spread across his stubbled features. He half turned. "That mean you are too yellow to fight me . . . pup?"

"Benny!" shouted Monty to the piano man. "Go get Marshal Wickham."

The piano player didn't move.

"Benny!"

He relented. "Aw, Monty, I'm going to miss all the doings!"

"You'll have plenty of time to miss things when you're out of work. Now get gone!"

Monty's exaggerated threat struck a note of humor with everyone there, despite, or perhaps because of, the drama of violence unfolding before them. Several folks giggled and others used the moment as a means of releasing nervous chuckles. The moment did not last long.

"Shut it!" growled the stranger, presuming he was in charge.

Monty palmed the bar top and vaulted over, landing hard on his backside on the polished surface to skitter coins and clatter glassware. He did not stop, but shoved off and, though a large man, bounded between Gage and the stranger and held up both arms wide, one big hand aimed at each. "No, sir! Not in my bar! No, I say!"

"Fine," said Gage, shoving past Monty's arm and knocking into the stranger's shoulder as he kicked on through the door and onto the planking of the board-walk out front.

"Gage! Don't do it!"

But the riled young man was beyond hearing.

A dozen folks spilled out behind him, whispering and jostling each other to get out there, eager for a close-up spot to what was looking like it might well be an honest-to-goodness shoot-out right there on the mangy, dusty, little main street of Sourwood Springs, Texas. Who would have thought it?

The stranger strode out, once more shoving past Monty, who, still holding a bar towel in a balled fist, turned back to his nearly empty establishment and threw it down hard onto the floor.

His gaze flicked up to the one person in the bar, an old drunkard named Jubal, who swamped the place for Monty now and again. He wasn't up to tasks any more menial than emptying spittoons and sweeping because he'd all but pickled himself through long years of guzzling booze whenever the opportunity presented itself.

Such as it was doing at that moment.

"Oh, for heaven's sake, Jubal!"

The old soak smirked and shrugged his shoulders as he guzzled back whatever remained of the drinks Monty's patrons had left behind as they hustled out front.

"Knock it off, now, and get out there. I don't trust you any more than I trust a cat to guard a jug of cream."

Jubal dragged his feet as he trailed along the bar, keeping his eyes on Monty.

The big barkeep turned away for a moment to glance out the doorway at the proceedings and Jubal took that moment to claw a half-filled bottle of rye whiskey and snatch it back as quick as his trembly old limbs would allow. He had just gotten it snugged beneath the ragged front of his rancid-smelling coat when Monty glanced back at him.

The barkeep had seen the theft, but let it go. He reckoned Jubal was close to ending his days anyhow. A victory now and again to think back on might comfort him when the time came.

Both men were almost to the door when over his shoulder, old wobbly Jubal said, "All I know is I wouldn't want to be in no gunfight with Lightnin' Shiller."

Monty grabbed the old man by the shoulder and spun him. "What's that you say?" He ignored the bottle of rye Jubal had already palmed and was fishing out of his coat.

"I said that stranger yonder in the street fixing to gun down young Jon Gage is none other than Lee Shiller from Arkansas. Course most folks know him as Lightning Shiller. But you knew that."

He'd gotten about half of that out when Monty shoved him to the side and barreled on through bystanders thronging the porch before his bar. By the time he reached the steps, two shots cracked the near-silent, stifling Texas air. One shot gnashed its teeth at the heels of the first.

Monty looked left, then right, and saw astonishment on the faces of both men.

Chapter 4

It hadn't taken the two riled men, strangers to one another, very long to make their way out to the dusty street.

"You called me out," shouted Gage, standing in the midst of the dusty street, facing the other man some fifty feet from him. "Get to it!"

"You heard him," shouted the stranger to the crowd. "I am defending myself here! This young pup has threatened me!"

"He did no such thing!" an irate fellow shouted from atop steps across the street.

Both gunmen ignored him, and just as the stranger's right arm began to tighten and flex, drawing itself upward, a voice from the western end of the street shouted, "Hold there! This is Marshal Wickham! Hold, men!"

But it was too late.

From Marshal Wickham's vantage point, more or less aligned with the two shooters, he could see both, and knew the name of one—young Jon Gage, at the far end. The other, a stranger to Sourwood Springs, was unknown to him.

But as the last of his bellowed commands to cease this madness were clipped off by double gunfire, what he saw was the stranger jerk as if gripped by a brief bout of ague.

Blue smoke drifted upward, obscuring Wickham's view of Gage, in the distance. Closer in, with his back to the lawman, the stranger followed up his jerking motion with a sideways step, showing him in profile to the lawman.

Past him, through the clearing smoke, Marshal Wickham now saw Gage, still holding his own six-gun at gut height, his tall form bent forward in a slight crouch, his gun-free right hand slightly raised as if he was about to bat away an irksome bluebottle.

The lawman realized that he'd neglected to draw his own weapon, so shocked had he been at seeing this, and hearing the fool piano player tell him there was about to be a gunfight in Sourwood Springs, his very town.

Marshal Wickham snatched at his gun and tried to jerk it free of the holster, but the rawhide thong was tied over the hammer. He fumbled with it, without lifting his eyes from the scene before him.

And then, before he could do anything else, the stranger, still holding his six-gun in his right hand, completed his turn and stared now at the lawman.

Wickham drew and cocked, aiming at the stranger. "Drop it, mister! Now!" But even as he said it, he saw the reason for the man's jerking and sloppy turn—the stranger had been shot, just below the chest.

His shirt sported a dark stain leaching outward from a puckered, smoking hole between the wings of his unbuttoned rawhide vest. For a flash of a second, it looked to the lawman as if the man had spilled wine on himself. But no, this was no wine stain.

As if to prove the lawman's assessment, the stranger's left knee buckled forward and the man dropped as if time had slowed, falling face down on the dusty street.

For a long moment, still stretching out that sliver of slowed time, or so it seemed to Marshal Wickham, the entire town of Sourwood Springs, Texas, fell silent. Not a rooster could be heard crowing from one of the many coops behind the houses and businesses lining the dusty street. No children shouted, no steers bellowed, not even a fly buzzed.

Everyone on the street merely stared—and that turned out to be most of the residents of the town proper, plus whoever happened to be in town shopping or otherwise engaged. And what they stared at was the face-down, dead man, a stranger in their midst, a stranger who would never leave. Indeed, he would become enmeshed in the town's history, its folklore, forever.

Beyond the dead man, also in the street, half crouched, the man who had shot him, young Jonathan Gage. He, too, was staring.

At the impossible.

Chapter 5

Four minutes earlier

There was some part of Jon Gage, some bellowing but dim voice deep within him, that knew what he was about to do was foolhardy. That he should know better, that he was about to die, and die foolishly, and far too soon. There was still so much to see and do in life.

But despite hearing that voice shouting deep within him, and knowing it made more sense than anything else at that moment, Gage had shoved on through that saloon door.

Despite the warning, or perhaps because it reminded him of his father's annoying voice always shouting in his ear, young Gage ignored it and plowed through the gathering crowd.

Once on the street, he felt oddly calm. He watched the hotheaded stranger stomp on down the west end of the street some distance away. Gage saw all this and even though he knew he was about to be part of a gunfight—a genuine, honest-to-goodness gunfight—he did not feel unease. On the contrary, he felt as if he had all the time in the world. In fact, it felt as if he had not a care in that very same world.

While he had stomped on down the steps, he had casually unhooked the keeper on the hammer of the revolver that hung on his left side. He was a left-handed man, always had been, something he'd been proud of, mostly because his blasted father always mocked the fact, and told him he would never amount to a thing because left-handed men were liars and thieves and cheats and scoundrels. Young Gage had always wondered why, then, was his father not a left-handed man.

The gun was loaded fully and cared for as if it were a beloved child. And the time he spent drawing and flexing and shooting at imaginary outlaws and rustlers was also something his father had mocked.

But young Jon did not much care. Never had, once he gained a certain age. No, sir, once he reached his early teenage years, he had come to see what sort of man his father really was—a bellicose drunkard who was seen as such by his fellows in town and elsewhere, and what's more, seen by them to be a fool.

Despite feeling calm and at ease, Gage also felt that same old, red-raw rage creep up on him, inside him, and grasp him tight from within. It was a trait he shared with his father, something that when in the grip of it, he could do little about. It overtook him, and he could do nothing but obey his anger.

But this calmness in him at the same time, this was something new, a combination within him that did not war, but somehow worked together. He did not know how this fight would end, but he did not care. In that moment, he was accepting of it. What the two men had disagreed upon was now of no consequence. There was a fight and he was in it, and that was all there was to it.

And then he, Gage, shouted something not worth recalling. And then the stranger shouted something in response, also not worth remembering. And then the stranger flexed his arm.

And that was all young Jonathan Gage could or would remember of that fight. The first of what would be many, many gunfights in which he would participate in his long and storied life.

He would only come around and out of his strange, placid stupor when Marshal Wickham, always a kind man to him, placed an arm on his left shoulder. Gage, with his revolver still gripped tight and held before him in his hand, blinked his eyes once, twice, and looked at the lawman.

"Jon. Jon, can you hear me, son? It's me, Marshal Wickham, son. Let go of the gun now. It's all over. You're all right."

Gage did as he was bade and relinquished the revolver to the lawman. It would be the last time he would ever give his gun willingly to the grasp of another.

"Marshal?"

"Yes, son. It's all right now. You're fine. Now, why don't you come with me so we can talk. Okay?"

Another voice, from one of the many faces to crowd around him there in the dusty street, said, "Aw, for heaven's sake, Marshal, let the man alone! We all saw what happened! He just killed a man in a fair gunfight. He was called out and he defended himself. What's this world coming to if the law goes poking its sniffer into every situation to come up in life?"

"Yeah!" said another, and another, until the chorus of voices, men and women, drowned out the lawman's own increasingly irate shouts.

Soon the crowd pressed in and pinched off Gage from the lawman, hustling the still-mystified young man with it and on into Monty's Top Palace saloon, leaving Marshal Wickham standing in the street, holding the young man's revolver.

Soon, save for a few curious souls poking and prodding the dead man's corpse down the street, he was alone. And wondering what in the heck had just happened to his little, docile town of Sourwood Springs, Texas.

"Marshal, Jon Gage may be a whole lot of things, but he sure isn't a killer." Monty shook his head. "That Shiller character riled him in the bar. Gage tried to make nice with him, but Shiller was . . . Oh, it was as if he was looking for a fight. Oh, if I had known, I'd have told Jon to hush up, back away, give the man room. But that rascal wouldn't simmer. Finally Shiller called out young Jon and, well, you know the rest." Monty shrugged and walked back to his bar, still shaking his head.

He found Jubal back in there, leaning on the bar, his pilfered bottle of spirits at his elbow, crying.

"Jubal, what on earth are you sobbing for?"

"'Cause it could have been young Jon Gage laying out there dead in the street."

"Yeah," said Monty. "Yeah, it could well have been. But it isn't."

"I know, I know. But look, young Jon, he's always been good to me, you know? Always bought me a drink when other folks would shove me away."

Monty sighed. "Yeah, I know. He's a good one. Not like his father, thankfully." The big man tidied up the bar and waited for the inevitable rush of folks who would want nothing more than to drink and talk about this for hours—no, make that days, weeks, and more to come.

Monty shrugged and wondered if it was all right to profit from such a situation. But within minutes, he had no chance to consider this notion further, for the Top Palace filled to brimming. He was busy without letup for hours and hours. And though he tried not to, he was smiling about it.

"That there was quick as a lightning strike, I tell you what!" The man who spoke guzzled back a third of his fresh beer.

Jubal, his companion at the bar, recognized the man as a German farmer who came to town not infrequently for supplies, and always spent a few hours drinking beer before departing for home, a wind-stripped patch of land some miles out of town, where his plump, dour wife and six children would be waiting for him, keeping busy doing all the chores while Pap drank beer in town.

"Well, now, that's just the thing," said Jubal, hoping to keep the story fresh. "See, that there fella he shot out yonder in the street was none other than Lee Shiller from Arkansas."

"So?"

"So! So you'd know him better by the name Lightning Shiller, don't you?"

"Oh, my word. Oh, my word! You mean our very own young Jon Gage, him the son of Jasper Gage, went and bested a famous gunfighter? *Nein,* naw." The farmer shook his head and quaffed another inch of his beer. "Naw, I say. Can't be."

"I know it, I know it, but it is," said Jubal, the swamper, eyeing and judging his new companion's thirst, coin purse, and eagerness for conversation.

If I tease this out, he thought, *I might well earn myself another free round before I run out of story. Then again, I could always make up various bits and bobs.*

"I saw the entire thing," Nedley Madewell said to a small cluster of folks gathered about him before the bar. "From the first prodding by the stranger to that same man's pathetic crumple and drop to the dusty street! Why, his face smacked hard, I tell you! Hard, a pinch after his hat brim pecked the ground. I've never been so impressed with any act by a man in all my days. Not the stranger's dropping dead, mind you, but the shooting itself."

He guzzled back half a glass full of beer, hoping he could retain his audience before he ran out of story. "Oh, both men shot, and Shiller's bullet whizzed by Gage's right arm, about midway up, harmless as a bee passing through."

He nodded, sipped, and continued. "But it was Jon Gage's shot that was delivered first, and it was Gage's shot that did the job it was intended to. For that bullet from his six-gun drilled square into the dead center of that man, Shiller. Distance was enough that I don't believe it left out a back door, so it must still be wedged inside him somewhere, likely lodged in the bone of the man's spine."

Ned said this all, while holding his hoisted, nearly empty mug of warm beer halfway to his face.

Two people were left listening to him, and they were doing that only because they knew that when Ned Madewell was in his cups, he had been known to be generous in buying drinks for whoever had the fortitude to withstand the latest round in his constant retellings of windy stories.

Those stories were frequently, as was the case now, recountings of events and occurrences that most other folks had also seen. This bothered him not a whit.

A couple of years before, a stranger, a drummer bearing a display case of sewing accoutrements, had asked Ned why he constantly recounted moments that everyone else had obviously also witnessed.

Ned had replied, with a straight, level gaze, "It strikes me as odd that you, a man of the road, a fellow I can only assume who feels he is quite skilled in assessing others, should fail to recognize the bald fact that each person is as different as he can imagine. And therefore each person's story, no matter how familiar the initial facts might seem to others, will be different, unique."

This little diatribe had been comprehended by roughly

half of the listeners, but it mattered little to them. Ned Madewell had settled in their town and opened a decent mercantile after the town suffered for years without one. And given that Ned made it known to anyone who talked with him, old or new acquaintance, for more than a few minutes, that he was a college-educated fellow, his dressing-down of the drummer was no surprise to those listening.

The drummer, red-faced, packed his wares and left town to try his fortune elsewhere. It being quite apparent by then that Madewell would purchase no sewing implements from him. All this, despite the fact that his wife, Martha, had taken a shine to a fancy sewing kit for use on journeys. It was her fervent hope that Nedley would one day take her back East.

Once there, her plan was to work him like a fireplace bellows, hoping to convince him that the civilized East was where they should be spending their time, and not the hot, dusty heathen lands of Texas.

She was unsuccessful, both at securing the coveted travel sewing kit and at convincing Ned to take her on a trip back East, or "home," as she had called it for the sixteen years they'd lived in Sourwood Springs, Texas.

Chapter 6

Jon Gage sobered up three days later—only because he had run out of his own money. Others had stood him for round upon round of whiskey and beer. He seemed to recall even trying something warm, made with cinnamon, and it hadn't been half bad, even if it wasn't the season for such concoctions.

He'd spent the nights upstairs in a borrowed bed, sometimes in the arms of one of several soiled doves who worked the bar, sometimes snoring away on his own. It hadn't much mattered to him.

On the morning of the third day after the shooting, he made his way on shaky pins back down to the bar and was sipping the first of the offered cups of steaming, hot coffee from Monty, who was trying to tell him something about being a legend. It made little sense to Gage.

He was still amazed that he had been in town this long and he knew he had to get back to the ranch. He had no doubt that his father would long since have decided he was going to meet the young man at the ranch gate, wearing a sneer and toting his old sawed-off shredder.

So be it, thought Jon as he sipped the hot coffee again.

Then something came to him. "What day did you say it was now?"

"It's Tuesday morning, Jon. You mean you really didn't know what day today is?"

Gage didn't answer. He was thinking, or trying to, between the hollow, wind-blown feeling that trembled his very fingers and toes and the thudding in his head from too much booze and no food and poor sleep.

He'd been down this lane before and he knew that the hair of the dog would work for a short spell, but it would only postpone the coming pain. But what was it he was trying to think about? Ah, yes, his father. Waiting for him with the shotgun.

But no, the old man would have made his way to town long before now. So, why hadn't he?

"Monty, any chance I could get a sip of whiskey? I'm good for it. I'll be out of your hair soon. Get myself back to the ranch; I have a little money there I can pay you with."

Monty looked at him with tired eyes and shook his head. He poured the kid a double shot and waved his hand away as Gage tried to thank him.

The bedraggled young man knocked back the drink, draining the last drop from it, and then carried his refilled cup of coffee to a table where he could sit down and rest his head a moment.

The next thing Jonathan Gage knew, he was still

seated at the baize-top poker table, his cup of coffee still stood before him, but this time Marshal Wickham was sitting there, too, holding his own cup of coffee and talking to him.

"Son, son? You listening to me?"

"Huh? Oh, sure, Marshal. Sure."

Wickham sighed and looked at Monty, then back to Gage. "Did you hear a thing I just told you, Jon?"

"I . . . I don't know. What did you say?"

The lawman sighed again. "I told you that I found your father, Jon."

"What's that now? Oh, hey, you don't think—"

"No, now I know, I know, son. You were here. Heck, if I didn't know your pap was a drunkard and a rager when he was full up with the devil's juice—you know I don't hold with drinking, don't you, Jon?—then I'd be forced to think you and him had one of your set-tos and that might well have been what finished ol' Jasper." The marshal fixed Jon with a long, cold gaze.

Gage did not know what to say to that. If he was hearing the lawman right, his father was dead. But that could not be. And yet . . . it would account for the fact that the old man hadn't sought him out here in town for what now? Three days?

Or had he?

"Monty, did you see my pap in here since I came to town?"

"You mean since you shot that man and then proceeded to drink my place dry?"

Jon grew silent. He'd not forgotten he'd shot the man they claimed was Lee Shiller. The one and only Lightning Shiller, if that truly was him. But . . . he'd killed a man and that was something he was trying to keep the thought at bay, but not doing much of a good job of doing so.

Monty must have realized what the comment had set off inside Gage, because he sighed and poured the kid more coffee.

The coffee's warmth and promise was good, but not nearly as nice as that of whiskey and the calm it would offer him, if fleeting. The thought forced Jon's tongue tip to run along his dry lips. "Ah, I'm fresh out of cash, Monty. I—"

Monty rapped his knuckles on the bar top. "Coffee, Jon. That's all. And this time, it's on me." He winked and turned away to leave the lawman and Gage to talk.

Jon sipped the coffee and closed his eyes a moment to let it work its way into him. It was precious little, but it would do; it would have to. He opened his lids and turned bleary eyes on the lawman, who was still staring at him and waiting. "It's true, Marshal Wickham, that me and Pap fight a whole lot. Always have. It's his way. Mine too, I reckon."

"When was the last time you saw him?"

"That's easy. It was Saturday, just after midday. Just had another fight."

"How was he when you left him?"

Gage half smiled and shook his head. "Like he is every time I leave him. Passed out."

"You're sure."

"Sure I'm sure."

Marshal Wickham sighed. "Okay, then. Seems pretty much as I thought it was when I rode out there."

"You rode out there?"

"Yep, wanted to try to get him to come on into town and fetch you back."

"I'm no child, Marshal. I don't need fetching by my daddy, or anybody else."

"Well, anyway, I rode out there, and do you know what I found?"

"Let me guess, let me guess. You found a grumpy old drunk doing his best to not work and a passel of cattle bellowing for feed and water. Am I right?"

"Well, son, in part. I found your pap all right, but, well, look, Jon, that daddy of yours, well . . . he's dead, son. I found him this morning, not but three or four hours ago."

For a long moment, nobody said anything; then Gage looked at the lawman. Jon could not make sense of what he'd just heard. Finally he said, "Can't be. He's too ornery to die."

"No, Jon. He's not. He's dead. Been dead for a few days, I reckon, but I don't know how to tell such things any better than that. Seems to me, he had himself a big ol' tirade, wrecked the place, and then his ol' heart just gave up the ghost." He nodded, agreeing with himself.

Jonathan Gage walked to the bar and stared at the cloudy reflection of himself in the mirror behind the bottles, seeing his face, staring back at him, wedged between the necks of two whiskey bottles.

He looked rough, eyes red and puffed, sunken and circled with gray-purple bruising. His hair was a messy tuft and his whiskers had grown out some. All in all, it was not a look he would have preferred to sport in town.

"You mean I'm an orphan now?"

"That's one way of looking at it. Little old to be calling yourself that, though. Anyway, you got a ranch now."

"And a reputation, too," said Monty.

"About that," said Wickham. "You clean yourself up, then come to my office. We got ourselves some talking to do. I still have your gun, too."

"That's where that got to."

"One hour," said the marshal. "Don't be late. And Jonathan?" He waited for the shaky young man to face him.

"For what it's worth to you, I am sorry about your daddy."

Chapter 7

It took Gage the full hour before he could muster the strength—still shaky and groggy, but propped with coffee and two more bumps of free whiskey—to make his way to the lawman's office.

He had started the short journey down and across the dusty main street of Sourwood Springs, but had been interrupted five times en route by townsfolk who pretended to be surprised to see him. The first, young Dilbert Mepps, was a gangly youth, with odd corn-silk hair and a stammer that launched him into blushes over and over again.

"Mi-mi-mister G-G-G-Gage?"

It took Jon a moment to catch on to the fact that he was being addressed. He spun and waited for the day to catch up to him. When his vision settled, he saw a slump-shouldered youth, with a slouch hat and suspenders, peering up from beneath the flop brim. Jon recognized him.

The funny thing was, this kid was not but a few years Jon's junior. And he was nearly as tall as Jon. But

Mepps always walked bowed as if searching for something he'd dropped in the dust of the street. His hunched shoulders, one got the sense, would never again stretch and straighten to full height.

At that moment, as Gage saw the youth before him looking up at him sheepishly, he wondered, *What is it in life that makes one strapping ranch lad walk with his head high, as if he were sniffing daisies on the breeze, and another curl himself inward, as if to keep out a bitter wind?*

"Dilbert, hey there. You okay this morning?" Jon did not know what to say to the lad. "I didn't know you were talking to me. My pap is usually the one who goes by Mr. Gage. In fact, I believe you might be the very first person to ever call me mister."

At that comment, the slouchy youth before him seemed to brighten, perhaps even straighten his curl of a spine a wee bit. "Y-y-y-you think so?"

"Sure I do. Sure of it. Put that down as a fact. Now, what can I do for you?"

Just saying it in such a strident tone, and keeping a smile pasted on his face, made Jon's head thud louder, harder, and his eyes felt as if they were about to pop out and hiss and crackle on the flames of the fire that threatened to consume him from within.

"Oh, I, I do-don't wa-wa-want to bother you, but I was won-won-wondering what . . ." Then young Mepps had to swallow and wet his lips.

"What was it you're wondering? Only I have to get on over to see Marshal Wickham."

"Oh, oh, I'm s-s-so s-s-sorry. I didn't mean to keep you."

And with that, young Dilbert Mepps took off running a gangle-legged gait, but covering a heck of a lot of ground, as only a ranch boy can, leaving Jon staring with the widest eyes he'd pulled all day so far.

"Huh," he said, shrugging and turning once more toward the marshal's office. He was welcomed in by the lawman, and once they were each seated, the marshal opened the ball.

"You know, Jon, folks have taken to calling you Texas Lightning. What do you make of that?"

Gage ran a hand across his stubbled chin and sighed. "Seems I recall hearing that a time or two these past few days."

"Given how much liquor you took in, boy, I am surprised you remember anything of the past three days."

"I am my father's son," he said.

The lawman eyed him hard. "That's what I want to talk with you about, Jon."

"What? The old man? Why talk about him? You already told me what I need to know. Besides, you know as well as I do, it'd be a waste of breath to talk about him with me."

"I know how you and your father got on."

"Or didn't."

"Okay, or didn't. But I want you to go out there with me. Right now."

"Now?"

"Yes. Now let's go to the stable. I've had your horse looked after, since you seem to have forgotten all about him during your celebrations and all."

Jon was about to protest, when the marshal handed him a cup of coffee. "Although how anyone can celebrate the killing of another person mystifies me. Now drink that down and then we're riding out to your ranch."

Gage did as he was told, beginning to wonder what they would find. Surely, the old man was alive when Jon left the ranch. Had to be. They'd had fights before, and come to blows, too. But a thought nested deep in Jon's mind that perhaps this time it was different.

Maybe the blow Jon landed to Pap's chest had . . . *No, don't think that way,* he told himself. *My old man was too tough to die that way. Must have had an accident or some such.*

The ride out from the ranch was a too-long trip when he was trying to get to town, and far too short whenever he had to go back to the ranch. But on this day, riding alongside the lawman, normally a chatty man, he found the road to the ranch was a long one, and felt as if it were taking forever and a day.

Chapter 8

In his present day

Gage sat at the bar, staring at the glass of beer before him, mired in remembrance of the twelve years from that first gunfight until now, dozens of gunfights later. He'd long since lost count, mostly due to the haze that liquor left him in for weeks, months at a time.

He could not say now, without lying, that he had never sought the fame, attention, and, yes, fortune at times, and in various forms, that had come his way because of his skills with the guns. It had been a heady time, especially early on.

Seven years earlier than his present day

He'd lingered around Sourwood Springs, uncertain of what to do with himself, not wanting to run the ranch, but not wanting to make the decision that needed to be made. He began spending more time in town and not tending to the beeves, so he hired young Dilbert Mepps to oversee the place.

And then one day, while he was at Monty's bar, someone came in, a pumpkin roller from New Hope, a town about fifty miles away. That farm boy was nervous but pesky, pressing him, crowding him, and would not back down, even though Gage would have none of it.

After a half hour of this foolishness, Jon settled up with Monty and left. The pumpkin roller followed him out into the street and called him a coward.

Jon thought, too late, that he should have kept on walking, kept his back to the fool. But, in truth, he had walked right past his horse and needed him to ride back home. So there Gage was, right in the street. He turned, hands folded over his chest, and eyed the farming youth.

The main street hushed, save for the smith Sammy and the clang of his rhythmic, metallic ringing.

"What in the heck are you doing, boy?" shouted Gage, keeping his arms folded.

Jon was a tall fellow, he knew, and was well built with wide shoulders and sizable hands from years of setting posts and building and repairing and wrangling. Most of the time, he put in double duty on all the ranch work, as his father was prone to slinking off to the house in midchore for a few drops. It never ended there. The result was always a whole lot of extra work for Jon and a whole lot of muscle.

And now he was hoping that this lanky but rugged young man from away might see he was in no hurry to play the gunfight game with him or anyone else.

And then the kid did what Jon was afraid of. He went for his gun. Right there and then. No warning.

Somehow Jon knew, just knew that the fool was going to make his play. Perhaps it was the twitch of his right eye, the quick lick of his lip beneath the peach fuzz moustache he was trying to conjure on his young farm boy face. If nothing else tipped off Gage, it was most assuredly the skillful, practiced grab the kid made with his right hand for the loose revolver nested there in his tied-down holster.

Gage had hoped his attempt at appearing large and menacing and shouty to the fool might be enough to intimidate him into backing down and going away, back to his own life. But it was not to be. And so, Jon Gage, for the second time in recent memory, was forced into a gunfight, right there on the main street of his hometown, Sourwood Springs, Texas.

He had no idea how his gun's hammer thong loosened, or how his left hand conjured the gun into place nested right there in it, as if born to hold it. No idea how it thumbed back the hammer as he raised it and aimed and . . .

This time, the blast ripped Gage from his lull as sudden as one of Pap's backhands across his jaw when he'd done something, anything, that displeased the old man. As the blue smoke drifted and cleared before him, Jon saw the farm boy, the cursed pumpkin roller, flat on his back in the dusty street, facing skyward, his hat some feet away, arms wide and his revolver also some distance from him.

Gage's bullet cored a hole low on the kid's neck, in the hollow where it rises from the shoulders. Gage saw this within moments of shooting, because he rushed forward to look down at the fool youth.

He shouted, "Why? Why, curse you!"

The kid could not reply, for he was dead, likely before he slopped to the parched earth. But Marshal Wickham replied. He walked right up to the trembling, red-faced Gage, determined to not let the townsfolk bustle him on out of there and make a mockery of the law this time around. No, sir, not ever again in his town.

"No, sir! No, I say!" Wickham, no short man, either, poked a ramrod finger into Jon Gage's chest.

The startled, staring younger man backed up with each hard jab from that finger. He did not try to raise the gun, which he still held in his left hand, but he did shift his gaze from the dead pumpkin roller to the enraged lawman poking him in the chest.

"Never again, Gage! I have had it and more from you and your dead father! This town doesn't need your kind here. You are not welcome here any longer. Now get out, get out, I say! Sell off your ranch, burn it, I don't care what you do, but I want you gone. And if you don't take this one chance I'm giving you, I will arrest you and I will hang you! Myself, if need be! And don't think that I can't and don't think that I won't!"

"But, Marshal, I—"

"No! Get on your horse and get gone! Now! I give you two days to clear up your affairs and then I'm coming for you. And I won't soften my thinking on this, you . . . you . . . cursed gunfighter! Useless! Turned out just like your father!"

Jon Gage had always known Marshal Wickham. Heck, he and Pap had once been friends, card-playing pals who'd visit each other now and again. And Jon had, over and over through the years, been the recipient of little kindnesses on the lawman's part toward Jon. Friendly chat, soft advice, encouraging words.

Jon had always tried to respect the man and his position, and to thank him in whatever ways he might. He'd never wanted to take advantage of the man's kindness. But now he realized that any friendship they'd had was long gone. With finger-snap speed it had evaporated like rain in the desert.

After that day of his second kill, after that dressing-down by Wickham in front of the whole scowling town, his own hometown, Jon Gage up and gave over to the reputation he seemed to have earned.

No, he thought, that's not quite right. It was a reputation he never sought, but that was draped over him, nonetheless, like a wet wool blanket. It hung heavy and he did not know what to do about it, but he knew he had nothing else going for him in life.

Turned out Pap had borrowed in no small amounts

against the ranch. Any goodness they had built up in it had been sipped away by Pap. And there wasn't a thing Jon could do about it.

The bank, which really meant Junior Haskell, owned most of the ranch. After all that work, Jon thought, the only thing he could do was sign over the farm to young Dilbert Mepps and tell him that though Haskell owned most of it, he was welcome to try to work with Haskell to resume the payments and make a go of it. Who knows? Maybe the kid had gumption enough to do it. He sure seemed keen.

Jon wrote a note, had the kid sign it, and then he signed it. He had two witnesses sign it, the kid's father and a neighboring rancher, Paco Sabatez. And then Jon scavenged the house for anything he might need in his upcoming, unknown life. In truth, there was precious little he wanted from the place.

But what he did take, aside from his horse, decent tack, and the best kit of clothing and camping supplies and food he could locate, was a small wooden box his father kept under his bed. It had always intrigued Jon, but he'd been so fearful of retribution by the old man that he'd never asked about it, let alone tried to peek inside.

Turns out, even though it had a locking clasp, that it was unlocked. He flipped open the lid and found a small locket, hinged, that contained two small tintypes, one of his father as a young man, and one of his long-dead mother. She'd been a beauty and, if Jon had to admit it, his father, ol' Jasper, had been a good-looking fellow, too.

Inside the box, there were also six letters, bound with a faded blue silk ribbon. Jon slipped them into his inner vest pocket, along with the locket.

Then he took the last thing he'd been looking for, from atop his father's chest of drawers: a new, unused, two-blade Barlow folding knife. He recognized it as the very one he'd bought his father years before. He'd saved for a year, vowing that by the time his father's birthday came around in October, he would have enough saved for it. And he had, by hiring himself out to neighboring ranches for any sort of paying work.

When the old man's birthday came around, Jon gave him the present. And there it sat, unacknowledged and unused. If Jasper ever liked the gift, or at least the effort that went into buying it, he never said.

"Well, Jon, my boy," said Jon Gage to himself, slipping the knife into his trouser pocket, "at least you have good taste in knives."

He made one last tour of the small, bedraggled home, and then stepped outside, closing the door behind himself. "Let Dilbert have the rest. Maybe he can build a life here free of frustration and anger. The Gages sure couldn't."

He strode to the barn and repacked all the gear and food he thought he might need, arranging it all on his horse, Rig. Then he saw old Cobby, their stalwart mule, and he gave brief thought to loading him up with a pack frame, but decided it would be too much for the old gent.

He gave the slow-moving beast an extra dose of feed, and scratched his head and ears. Then, with a tight throat and a sigh, Gage mounted up on Rig and rode on out of the Gage ranch, vowing to never return to Sourwood Springs, Texas, for as long as his life lasted.

The way things were headed, he thought as he passed through the far gate and made his way northward, it might be as short as a few days.

Jon Gage still didn't know what to make of the two killings he'd been backed into. But he knew one thing: he was going to do his level best to avoid any more such fights. He would ride north and get himself hired on at a ranch somewhere, maybe far enough away that they hadn't heard of the Gages of Pagosa Springs.

That first day, he rode for a good six, eight hours before drifting to a stop. He'd not pushed it, and had walked a number of times, letting Rig set his own pace.

For some reason he'd not given thought once all day to looking at his back trail. He would come to regret that decision.

As he dismounted and scouted a likely spot off the roadway to set up camp, he glanced southward. The sun to his right offered a warm glow, still hot, but promising to be a cool evening, and as he looked, it cast a shimmering dark hue to everything southward. Including the silhouette of a rider appearing to be in no hurry, but definitely making his way northward, too.

"Wonder who that might be," said Jon, tugging off the saddle. He regretted not putting more distance between himself and the roadway, but he'd been tired and, he knew, sloppy in his choice.

"Nothing for it," he said, and proceeded to construct

his meager camp. He'd been looking forward to making a small pot of coffee and frying up the last of the bacon they'd had in the house.

Instead, he checked his weapons and then sipped water from the canteen and nibbled on a hard biscuit as he waited for the stranger to approach.

It didn't take long.

The man rode straight toward Gage, as if he hadn't a care in mind. Despite the fact that Jon knew it was a well-traveled public roadway, and that he hadn't done a thing to ask for trouble, a cold, prickling feeling slithered up his spine, nonetheless, and nested atop his head as the man slowly closed the distance between them.

When the fellow was roughly thirty feet from him, he eased his mount to a stop.

The fellow was in his early twenties, and had the look of a farmer, complete with shoulder braces, slouch hat, and tall, too-worn, flap-ear boots. The thing he did wear that marked him as anything but a farmer was a bandolier of brass-cased shells and a large revolver nested in the waist of his belted trousers.

Jon stood where he'd been, beside Rig, his hands resting seemingly comfortably on his waist.

"Howdy."

The man on the horse nodded, but said nothing. Jon could not quite see his face, as the man's hat brim was tugged low.

The prickling, cold feeling pulsed in his neck, his shoulders, and his head. Something about this situation was not right and Jon knew to pay attention to the feeling.

"Passing?" Jon asked, knowing how stupid it sounded, but, man alive, this fellow hadn't said or done much of anything and he'd already wormed his way beneath Jon's skin.

The man stared at him a long moment more, then shrugged, though barely.

Jon knew that the only thing he was not going to do was turn his back on this man. He'd stand here all night, if need be.

About when Jon was ready to say something else, anything else, the man on the horse said, "You . . ." and then casually slid down out of his saddle. He let the horse's reins dangle.

Once the man had both feet on the ground and stood facing Jon, assuming a casual pose with his arms folded over his chest, he finished his thought. ". . . killed my brother, a few days back in Sourwood Springs."

For a long moment, thoughts warred in Jon's mind. Should he deny it? Try to talk this fool out of the revenge he obviously had in mind? What else might he do to avoid another gunfight?

But as quick as such notions came to him, he dispensed with them, knowing the only road available to him from here on out was the truth. He was who he was, and so far he'd done nothing he was ashamed of. Regretted? Sure. But he'd defended his life twice, and he was still kicking.

Someday he would not be so lucky, but he vowed to

himself in that very moment that he would not die a coward or a liar.

"If you're talking about that farm kid from New Hope, then yes, that was me. And I am sorry for it. But he drew on me. I had no choice in the matter."

Gage's voice sounded to him as one carved in stone and intoned from a distance. He did not sound like himself. He sounded . . . older, maybe wiser. Certainly more decisive than he'd ever been. And more tired, too.

"You . . ." said the other man once more.

This time, Gage detected a thin, hard edge in the voice. It had been there before, but Gage had mistaken it for coolness. Now he realized what it was— rage, seething rage. This man was beyond angry and Jon could hardly blame him. But the fellow was also not in any shape to pick a fight. He was too blinded with anger.

The man unfolded his tightly crossed arms and they hovered rib height, each hand ready to descend to the man's waist.

The pistol's butt was curved to the man's right, so he would most likely snatch it up from where it rode in his belt with his right hand. Gage walked to his own right, away from Rig, and the man did the same, to his left.

Each man sidestepped with deliberation until they were in the roadway.

"You . . . killer!"

For a long moment, Gage said nothing in reply. He was about to shout something, anything that might jar the fool from his reverie of rage, when he noticed the man's hands begin to shake. They continued to do so, increasing until they made visible, jerking motions.

Without warning, the man turned away, his shoulders working up and down, his arms once more hugging his chest.

Gage kept still, poised, ready for trickery. But soon it became apparent that the young man was not going to shoot him, at least not at that moment.

He spun back, still hugging himself tight. His face was red and his eyes wet. "You . . . killed my brother, curse you!"

"I had no—"

"Shut up! You lie! We all have choices!"

Gage swallowed then, a hard lump in his throat. It was bitter, all bile, doubly so because the man spoke the truth.

Once more, they stood facing each other for long moments. The man slowly calmed, but he kept his hands wrapped tight about himself, as if he had to in order to remain upright. "He was hotheaded. Hated the farm."

Gage listened, but said nothing. He reckoned hotheadedness ran in the family. His too, he mused.

"I will not try to shoot you myself. I cannot do that to Mama and Daddy. Who else will they have?"

The man turned with decision, then, and in two quick movements mounted his horse once more. He turned the beast and pointed at Gage, who still stood in the street, poised and ready for deceit.

"I will not shoot you." The man wheeled the horse to face southward once more. He looked over his left shoulder at Gage as the horse danced. "But I will save my money and hire someone who will one day best you and kill you deader than dead, Texas Lightning."

With that, he jammed his worn bootheels hard into the horse's withers and galloped back toward the way he came.

Gage relaxed, then walked back to his horse and gear, feeling as though he were sagging inside.

"This is your life now, Jonathan Gage," he said.

The horse whickered low, as if in agreement.

Chapter 9

As Jon Gage's reputation as a sure-shot gunfighter grew, outsizing him as all legends will that bloom up around mere mortals, his proper given name and family name were all but forgotten in favor of the name the legend had earned: Texas Lightning.

Early on, he despised it, and did his best to avoid it and the reputation he'd earned killing men. As time wore on, however, he came, if not to accept it, at least to resign himself to the fact that no matter where he went, and no matter what name he used, he would be found out as Texas Lightning. He was not happy about this, but he could not seem to shake it.

He would drift from job to job, usually at ranches, and all would be fine for a few days, perhaps for a few weeks. Once at a ranch in Utah, he worked for nearly two months before he was recognized. In all of these instances, the result was the same.

The other men—men he had moments before been guardedly chummy with—now distanced themselves from him and gave him looks of distrust and fear. And he could hardly blame them.

It was after the Utah ranch episode that Gage did what he always did when he had a pay packet in his pocket—he made for the nearest bar. There, he knew he could buy a bottle or two, buy time with a woman, and forget who he was and what he'd become.

If only for a short time. And only if he wasn't goaded into a fight. But that happened with increasing frequency.

And though he knew from experience that spending all his money on fleeting distractions would result in a draping of dark dread and sadness that he would wear for days, he did it anyway. Any relief, even that as wispy as smoke, was better than none at all.

But then an interesting thing happened—instead of drifting from ranch to ranch, threadbare and with an increasingly tired horse, Jon Gage had begun, albeit with reluctance, to enjoy the sordid benefits of being famous.

And saloon owners saw the benefits of keeping a fellow such as himself around for a while. He was an attraction, a curiosity to many, mostly so they might say they had seen him, or bought a drink for him, talked with him, shook his famous hand.

Every once in a while, a young man, almost always from a small ranch or homestead or farm somewhere, from far and wide, would show up, down a round or two, and then call out the gunfighter. Gage always ignored them at first, but as the evening wore on and he sampled more whiskey, his temper would rise.

This trait became known to the bartenders and to the other patrons lusting for blood sport. It also became known to the young bucks doing the goading.

It was also known to Gage. But he could not help himself. He also knew he was acting just like his dead pap. But he just could not help it.

He began to win at cards and other games of chance, but not because he was good at any of them. Oh, he wasn't so bad, but no better than most of the other men at the tables. But his reputation for having a quicksilver temperament was well known enough that men who bet against him did so with caution, and then often backed out of the play, just in case.

In this way, Gage was able, for a time, to accumulate enough money to keep him in whiskey, women, and fine duds for long stretches, all without having to resort to looking once more for ranch work. He always made certain to take care of Rig first, treating him, when he was able, to the best stables in whatever town he happened to have drifted to.

And so, killing after unprovoked killing slowly built up his reputation, and with each one, the local law would run him out of town. Sometimes he was dogged for a day or two by posses of self-righteous men, who sought to rid the land of such evil as he represented. He could not blame them, but neither did he linger and let them lynch him.

Twice in those years, though his shot ended the life of his antagonizer, so, too, did their shot reach its mark. Or at least partially. Twice Gage felt the brute sting and punch of a bullet piercing his hide.

The first time it had been, he was certain, a lucky

shot by an unlucky kid, the last thing the fool ever did. It had slammed into Gage's shoulder and spun him halfway around.

It was also the thing that likely saved his life, for after that, he began to take his situation in life with more care and caution. He realized, as he stood there with blood dripping in a steady run down his numbed, useless right arm—not his gun arm—that lately he had been living his life assuming he would always come out victorious.

And he realized—as did all the other folks watching this grotesque act play out on the main street of whatever town that had been—that Texas Lightning could bleed, could be damaged, could perhaps be killed. He did not change his ways wholly, but he did cut back on his drinking of hard liquor. And for a while, it seemed to help.

Nearly from the start, there was a bounty on his head, added to now and again, when he cared to check with a jittery lawdog, or, as was more often the case, when he was told by some zealous saloon owner or half-drunk barfly eager to witness a killing.

Often they would get their wish, for the mounting bounty drew men desperate for money and eager to build their own reputations.

Seven years earlier than his present day

It came about that yet another man was once more laid low by Gage. It had been in Woody Glen, and the man was no youngster, but Gage's age, or a bit older. He was a workingman, a man of the land, with the clothes and the muscles and the large ham hands to prove it. And though he was nerved up, he would not be dissuaded.

He'd not gone into the saloon, but shouted him out into the street, a nervous bellow masked by volume and fear and a rising distaste in his gorge for what he was about to do.

That man, Gage realized, as he had with nearly all of his opponents, truly believed he was going to be the one to best him.

He had not been. Instead, he had died a quick death in the street, Gage's bullet coring a neat hole in the middle of his forehead. It was the only thing that Gage could give the men—a quick death bereft of long suffering during which the men would cry like children and beg forgiveness, and there was little the town doctors could do for them.

Gage had long ago decided that whenever possible he would make the ends of his prodders quick. And he was good at it. And he hated himself for it. But the cold comfort he could offer himself was that he never once sought a fight.

Gage's father had told him once, when Jon came home weepy, with a buttoned-up eye from a fight with a kid from town, that he should never start a fight in all his days, for then he would be branded as a bully.

"But when someone else picks one with you, boy," said Jasper, "you best be the one to finish it." Jasper had eyed him hard and then shook his head, as if ashamed of what he was seeing.

And what he was seeing, as young Jon well knew,

was a son with a split lip, a bloodied nose, and a right eye puffing with each second that passed.

Jasper had stomped away from him then, shaking his head some more. "Never thought I'd see the day when a son of mine would take a beating."

That memory had stayed with Gage through the years and he counted it as one of the few shreds of a legacy his father left him that had actually been of use to him.

Some years after he shot his first man in a gunfight in the street, and a week after killing that farmer in Woody Glen, Jon Gage found himself not far away, in Akin, Colorado, a little hill town in Onion River country.

As with so many such settlements, it had been established some years before when silver was found in the surrounding hills. Those veins had largely played out, but by then folks came to realize that the land thereabouts wasn't too bad for raising crops and critters, so they stayed on and became subsistence farmers long after their dreams of silver faded.

Gage had stopped there, despite the fact that after a killing he liked to put more distance behind him than this. But as he was on his way north or east or west, he really didn't care which, he figured one night wouldn't hurt.

He was headed wherever he might find a far-off sizable town at which to top up his flagging funds with a few rounds of poker, and perhaps hole up with a woman and a bottle before continuing on. He might as well spend a night here, and get a jump on the funds part in Akin.

He'd heard of Akin days before while in Woody Glen, some miles southward. It sounded like a decent enough place to spend the night before moving on. The town turned out to be more bustling and larger than he had been led to believe, so he settled in at the largest of the town's four saloons.

The main street was busier than he expected it to be; then he remembered it was Saturday, a market day.

He watered his horse at the trough and tied him on the shady side of the street, intending to do the same for himself—a glass of beer, warm or cold, would help ease the dusty itch in his throat, and a little shade would do no harm, either. Then he'd take the horse to the livery, and settle in for a day and a night, perhaps longer.

The beer was cooler than he had any right to expect, which pleased Gage. He kept his hat drawn low and said few words. He figured his quiet ways and plain, dusty garb would serve to keep him from being recognized, especially in a somewhat-small farming town such as this.

He was wrong. But it would take another day before he was recognized. The next day, at nearly ten o'clock in the morning, Gage was seated at one of the barroom tables. Not yet halfway through his first cup of coffee, and anticipating the plate of steak and eggs and beans he had ordered, he heard shouts from the street.

At first, he took no notice. But the shouts continued. A slight quiver of fear, as it always did when truth began to dawn on him, tickled his guts. He ground his teeth hard, working his jaw muscles as he set down his crockery cup.

Within seconds, boots stomped across the boardwalk and someone opened the door wide.

"Hey!" shouted a man. "Man outside says Texas Lightnin' is in here and that he should come on out!"

Gage, who faced the door, a pose he always adopted for the sake of self-preservation, did not look at the man. He reached once more for his cup and sipped, suppressing a curse and a groan. He would not, could not, avoid this. But experience had told him that if he waited a bit, the town's lawman might, just might, call a halt to this mounting madness.

Gage had already settled up with the hostler and had rigged up his horse, intending to leave the small town after breakfast. The thought came to him then, as it did in each town he stopped at: Would he leave this town? Alive and whole and not dead, slopped and draining out his life's juices into a bounty man's wagon?

Gage looked over at the barman; at the same time, the barman looked at him. Gage was the only other man in there besides the moustachioed, oil-haired barkeep, who looked old enough to be Gage's father.

"You him?" said the barman, pausing in stacking pastries under a screened dome.

"Might be."

Gage flicked a quick glance at the second man to speak, the one in the doorway. He wore a look Gage had seen countless times through the years. His eyes were wide and bright, his face pinked with anticipation. Sweat stippled his forehead, and he breathed in short, heavy gasps.

Gage wanted to tell the man to calm down, take a few breaths, enjoy his life, and, for heaven's sake, stop lusting for the blood of others.

The man in the doorway spun as the confirmation settled into his mind and he bolted, the door clunking in the frame, the glass rattling.

The entire time, the shouting voice from the street—a high-pitched, angry voice—howled for attention. Unlike before, there were now no other sounds competing with it. Missing were the ringing of the smith's hammer, the clack and rumble of hooves and wheels, squeals of children and yips of dogs, and the low, but near-steady, murmur of townsfolk and those in town for the day, making purchases and selling farm goods. All these normal sounds had abated.

Gage knew exactly what it meant, for he'd heard it more times than he cared to recall. And all those fine and normal sounds had pinched off because of him, because of his very presence in their little market town.

Jon Gage smoothed his moustache with the linen napkin, folded it, and laid it atop the dishes before him. He sighed and stood, shoving back the chair. It stuttered on the wood floor. He smoothed his shirtfront and vest, then walked toward the door.

"Mister."

Gage stopped and looked to the barkeep. Instead of seeing someone wearing a sneer, or worse, fear on his face, Gage saw the older man's face had softened.

"You look tired."

For a long moment, Jon Gage let the words, and the look on the face that had uttered them, sink in. It was a

pected him to be. And the kid's bullet found its mark, not fully in flesh, but boring a deep chasm high on his left side, between Gage's raised gun arm and his ribs. And that's what proved the kid's ruin.

Although he'd been quicker than Gage, his quick shot had altered Gage's aim, and as the kid's bullet sliced Gage's rib cage, he flinched, pulling his shot back to center.

As always, Gage's bullet fulfilled its last foul task, driving like a cold chisel straight into the center of the youth's chest. Gage watched this through a quickening scrim of lancing pain. He staggered, managed to shove his gun back into its holster, and felt the wetness leaching down his side.

He staggered forward, the townsfolk already crowding around the foolish challenger far down the street.

Before he got there, he heard gasps, moans, and screams, both men and women. He staggered forward, managed to shake off the tremors, and walked slowly, but upright, at the crowd. The people parted as he came to the body, lying face up in the street.

First he spied the boots, large, ungainly things for someone so thin. The legs were decked out in raggedy, worn canvas work trousers, also too large for the slender frame. The shirt was the same, the oft-mended brown work coat lay flung open, and the gun belt cinching the waist was built for a wider man. Everything the kid owned was handed down, it seemed.

But what Jon Gage saw next changed everything about his life.

The large slouch hat that had been shadowing the

young man's face had fallen off when the youth had hit the dirt. The chest wound was a dead-on shot, not what Gage had intended.

The entrance hole was not large, but he saw, from the blood seeping out beneath the shoulders and up about the head, that it had caused brutal, fatal damage.

But all this Gage barely comprehended, for it was the young man's face that staggered him more than any bullet wound could.

He saw long, long hair the color of corn silk in the midday sun splayed out about the face, blood leaching into the gold of it. But here, dead at his feet, lay a beautiful young woman, such a pretty, pretty young thing.

As Gage looked down at her, he saw the life flee from her perfect face and death film her open, bright blue eyes. He might well have been the last face she saw. And he realized he could as easily have fallen in love with this young fair maiden instead of killing her.

"Oh no! No, no!" He heard the shouts, the gut-tearing deep grief-riddled sobs, but did not know they were coming from himself. He stood shaking, trembling in fear and revulsion at what he had done, at what he had become—a thing, a monster from a foul place where there was no redemption. None.

Jon Gage had no idea how long he had been there, but when he came back to himself, he was kneeling over the woman, one hand on her shoulder, the other clasped over his mouth. He was whispering, "She gave me no choice."

A voice across from him, coming from beside the girl's left side, said, "There's always a choice, mister."

It was an old woman with a shawl wrapped about her head. Her old gray eyes glistened with tears. "You should have let her kill you." She turned away.

He looked around him then, and saw that the rest of the townsfolk had also widened back away from him and the dead girl. And on their faces, he saw not the awe and fear and incredulity he had grown accustomed to seeing, but revulsion and disgust and hatred.

And it was directed at Jon Gage, as if he had been seen for the first time by others for what he truly was. And what he knew they saw sickened them. One by one, they turned away from him.

"All right, mister. Stand up, stand up."

It was a lawman, seizing his gun arm tight and hauling him to his feet. The man's voice was solid as stone, but beneath it, Gage heard contempt and rage ready to boil over.

"Where were you?" said Gage, looking at the man. "Why didn't you stop her?"

"Tending my wife . . . cancer. Not that it's your business."

"Lock me up. Oh, lock me up."

The lawman eyed him through slitted lids, regarding him with coldness. "No, I don't want your kind here. That'd just force good, angry folks to do a lynching on you. And they'd never forgive themselves. No, sir, I don't want your kind in my town. Nor anywhere hereabouts."

"But . . ."

"You were goaded into it. Not without cause, though. Her pa was a good man, foolish and desperate to try for the reward money on your head some days back in Woody Glen. Different town, same results. No, I don't want you here. Get gone. Now."

Jon Gage looked at the man, then at the girl, and reached into his inner pocket for his cash, all he had. "For . . . for her burial," he said in a low voice.

The lawman took it with a sneer. "Won't carry her four young siblings very far," he said, then turned away and walked to fetch the undertaker.

Gage walked to his horse, the townsfolk still seething, barely holding themselves back. He was unaware of them. He untied his horse from the rail and, ready to mount up, looked down as if seeing his double-gun black leather rig for the first time.

He winced and unbuckled the thing and let it drop to the dust at his feet. Then he mounted up and rode off, northward, though he had no idea of the direction.

The only thing he could think of was that girl's face. Her beautiful, dying face, and the life leaving her eyes as he watched. He vowed, over and over as he rode, that he would send money to the lawman for the girl's family. He had to, had to.

Gage rode for hours, and was still in the saddle when he realized his horse was no longer moving. He had no idea how long poor Rig had been that way. It was nearly full dark and he had no notion as to where he was. He didn't seem to be on a roadway, but he thought he saw the dim winding trace of a trail.

"Okay," he said. "Good enough." As he stepped down out of the saddle, a wash of illness drizzled down over him and he fell backward, landing on his left side in the dirt. And it hurt, like damnation had come specifically for him.

That's when he remembered he'd been shot. It had been a long time since he'd ever felt so bad, maybe never. All he could do was lie there. Eventually he fell asleep or passed out, he knew not which. But as he did, he dreamt of that pretty girl's face.

But this time, her dead eyes popped wide and a sneer crossed her mouth and she turned into that old woman in the street. He heard her cracked voice saying, "You should have let her kill you!"

And as he once more lost grip of his senses, he thought that perhaps the girl had actually succeeded.

Chapter 10

His present day

It was the coldness of the air that woke him. Cold and . . . the dream, that's right. He'd had it for so long now, it was no longer unexpected. It was not ever once welcomed, but it was endured. It had to be. And he felt certain that long after he was dead, the dream would be something he would long for, instead of the licking, searing flames of hell, where he felt assured he would one day end up.

Gage lay awake, soaked in his sweat, knowing the coldness of this early middle-autumn morning would soon wrack him with chills and force him to get up and move about. Despite the cold, and the dread that was blessedly slipping from him with the departure of sleep, this was his favorite time of the day, had always been, in fact.

As a child, he had often lain awake for hours in this predawn time, with only the faint but constant sound of his father snoring his way through another bout of drunkenness to accompany Jon's thoughts. And even then, he could, with effort, lose himself in thought and not hear the snoring, and just lie still. Those were good memories, the quietness, the calm, the peacefulness of it.

And then dawn would leak in through cracks in windows and doors and dusty, torn curtains, the sunlight would bloom in the front room where Jon slept and reveal the ugliness and squalor in which they lived, and nothing would be the same again for another whole day and night.

All those years later, in his frigid blankets, Jon Gage shuddered and sighed and tried to forget the dim past. Then flashes of blood in dirt and the echoes of screams and the begging of men dying and the hateful stares, always the eyes of strangers, even in wakefulness, stole from him. The last thought he had before he pulled his arms out from beneath the thin wool blanket was once more of his father, red-faced and intoxicated and shouting at him to get up and get to the barn. Of course, the old man would never go out there himself that early.

Jasper would grumble and stagger and slam things in the kitchen and end up splashing whiskey, if there was any left over from the night before, into a grimy tin cup half filled with tepid coffee. That would fortify him enough to make his way to the barn, where he would rummage in one of his many hiding places for another bottle that might have a little something left in it.

By then, Jon would have chores well in hand. Never well enough, however, to satisfy Jasper.

Jon shook his head and ran a hand up and down his face. "Even in death, you vex me, old man. My punishment, I guess."

And then, while he lay there, summoning up enough courage to shed the blanket and rise, he heard a distant rumbling. Far from him still, on the roadway, he thought, from southeastward. It was the lane he'd taken, and would, come full morning, continue on into the mountains.

The sound was too steady to be thunder, something he did not expect anyway at this time of day and at this time of year. And it increased as it gained on him. Or, rather, on the roadway to his right. He'd chosen a spot well off the lane, hoping to avoid anyone he might come across.

It was an odd time for a wagon to be on the road. Nonetheless, someone was up and about. Given the slowness and deep thickness of the sound, perhaps it was a freighter. In the old days, what he thought of as his dim, grim past, he would have readied himself for the possibility that these strangers might somehow get the better of him.

Now he no longer cared. Let them come. Let them stop and dismount and seek him out and shoot him in his blanket. Then he'd be done with it.

It had been a long two years since . . . the girl. And he had expected, hoped with each new day, that someone from his past, an enraged family member, anyone, would seek him out and shoot him and leave him for dead. And he would oblige them by dying.

But it had not yet happened. And so, he had made a deal with his own soul in the dark days following that time when he'd murdered the girl, for that's what he regarded it as. He had vowed to not pursue his own death by hanging himself, shooting himself, riding off a cliff, anything of the sort. But if someone sought him out for his past deeds, he would not avoid them.

By then, the wagon was almost to him. He heard it creak and groan, heard the plodding steps of what sounded like oxen. Slow and sure-footed, those beasts could drag a load of ore up a scree slope, reach the top, and lumber on down the other side. Such fortitude was their nature.

Soon, laced within the rumblings and creakings and squeakings of the heavy work wagon, which he knew with certainty now to be a freight load, he also heard the low talk of men, two of them, though their words were too muted and worked within the wagon noises to be picked out.

Gage lay still, listening, as the sounds faded and the wagon rolled, step by step, deeper into the coming hills.

He would not rush his morning. He never did, but on this day, he had no particular wish to catch up to the freight wagon. He wished to avoid the annoying habit most folks had of pausing and sparking conversation with strangers.

He was always a stranger everywhere he went, and though he had grown a full beard, diminishing the possibility of being recognized, he did not wish to chat with anyone until he had to. And that would happen soon enough, for he had to find employment, at least for a spell, if not for the winter.

He figured one of these old mining towns in Wyoming's Rocky Mountain foothills might suit him. Better yet, if there was a nearby ranch where he could hole up at a line camp for a time.

It took another twenty minutes before he smelled coffee beginning to warm in his old pot on the flames of his modest fire.

He'd already risen, stretched, wincing as he'd stretched. The two-year-old wound on his upper left rib cage reminded him of who he was and what he'd done. It did its job well, and with frequency.

After that he'd urinated away from camp, then tended his horse. Rig was still with him, despite Gage's past. He was the one thing, that horse, that could still induce a slim smile from the man. As he'd aged, Rig had developed more of the personality he had had even from his days as a colt.

He was never a biter, but he was not above showing his teeth and arching an eyelid in a way that Gage had never seen another horse do. At other times, he was downright chipper, trotting as if he were carrying a fine gentleman through a cosmopolitan parkland and showing off before the other horses. Yes, Rig was an odd one, but a more solid, dependable horse Gage had never seen.

As he poured his coffee, Gage wished fleetingly, as he did most mornings, that he had whiskey to pour in with it, just to cut the edge off the morning's chill. And then he shook his head, chiding himself.

He had given up drinking hard liquor one year back, after a year of living as a brutish drunkard. Nowadays, only occasionally in summer's heat, did he allow himself to have a glass of beer, rarely two. He could no longer stomach the thought that he might end up like

Pap. Too many awful things could happen and he'd dealt enough of those on others. No more.

With the coffee, he warmed griddle cakes, left over from the previous morning. To this, he added dried apple slices, which he shared with the horse, and topped it with his last slim slice of jerked elk meat.

All this took time, plenty of it, perhaps too much, now that he saw the sun in the sky had marked its way well beyond dawn. He saddled Rig, broke camp, drizzled the last of his coffee on the fire's dying embers, and gave the site a final look in case he missed retrieving one of his few possessions. Finding none, he mounted up.

It took him mere moments to see the wagon tracks. They were deep and wide, the steel rims grinding and crushing small stones into smaller stones, the hoofprints of the oxen—he'd been correct—revealed a single pair. And while Gage knew that the wagon itself was a heavy thing, it had not been loaded with freight that taxed the beasts. Likely, the teamsters had driven so slowly only because it had still been dark.

It took two more hours, but nearing midday, Gage saw the raw edges of a settlement emerge out of the landscape. Here he passed shanties, not many, but the state of them told him they were still lived in, though by folks who had long since given up on showing the passing world they cared about much.

Curtains were in tatters, the earth was rutted, a roped cur bared its remaining teeth at him, but looked too old and infirm to follow through with its intentions. Gage saw various broken and discarded tools, namely shovels and picks and mattocks. These indicated mining. Or at least prospecting at some time in the past.

Of humans, he saw none. Not until they rode a few minutes farther, passing more shanties, with dirt tracks leading off into the rocky hills behind them. Then the landscape ahead opened up and the roadway rose higher than it had been. They crested the rise and he saw below, a town nested tight to much larger hills, at the feet of the rocky crags he'd been riding toward for what had felt like days.

He paused there and surveyed the scene ahead and slightly below them. Despite the sour flavor the decrepit shanties had given him, the town, as they rode closer, still in no hurry, appeared to be tidy, not too big, and yet not too small.

The hills behind and all about the basin the town occupied were laced with roadways, donkey trails, and footpaths that led up, and then disappeared into trees and, he knew, ravines, where miners lived and worked. And the larger trails, likely roadways, led deeper into the mountains, winding up and into smaller working mine camps.

Once more, Rig drifted to a halt. Yes, this would be a town with work, Gage thought as he sat in the saddle, perusing the scene before him. But from the pillaged landscape, not much in the way of ranch work.

Still, he thought, heeling Rig into a walk once more, it would buy him time, time to outfit himself, perhaps, for a venture he had only begun entertaining of late. Perhaps the place for him was deep into the mountains, alone—save for Rig and a pack animal. There he might become one of those "mountainy men," as he'd heard them called.

The market for furs was always up and down, but surely he could figure out how to earn enough to keep himself alive? Then he remembered who he was and why he was out here in the first place, roaming and aimless.

That's right, Jon Gage. No matter where you go and what you do, you cannot outrun yourself or your past.

He'd suspected he'd be riding into a market town one of these days, because he'd seen intermittent but increasing signs of silver and gold camps, given the roadways lacing up into the hills hereabouts. This made the freight wagon no mystery.

Gage took his time moseying on into town and, soon enough, at the eastern edge of what looked to be a main street, he saw what he'd hoped to see—a sign in white script on a black double-planked background, proclaiming the town's name in pretty, yet bold, lettering: NEWEL, COLORADO.

"Okay, Newel," whispered Gage. "Nice to meet you."

"Rhymes with 'jewel,'" said a voice to Gage's left. He turned, reaching for his hat brim and tugging it even lower.

His eyes settled on a thin old-timer, half clad in buckskins. His top half wore a faded crimson, rough-spun shirt. At his waist, he wore a big sheath knife. And atop his head, he wore a black slouch hat, moderate brim, with an old, haggard feather tucked in the narrow fur band.

"What's that?" said Gage, his voice low and even.

"The town's name. It's *Newel,* rhymes with *jewel*."

"Oh, I see. Yes, I assumed that."

"Good. Too many folks don't. That's where they get in trouble."

Gage wondered how anyone might mispronounce the word, but he didn't say anything more.

"Well," said the old-timer, smoothing his ample gray beard, "since you're so chatty, I'll leave you to it. Got work to do." He walked toward town, the same direction Gage was headed. Without looking back, the older man offered a brief wave over his right shoulder.

"Nice meeting you," said Gage, wondering, but not really caring, if he'd offended the man.

"Yep," said the codger.

Despite himself, Gage had to smile. The fellow was like so many other broke-down miner types he'd met over the years—no-nonsense and straight to it, though friendly enough in the end when engaged in conversation. He reckoned he himself was much the same. Except for the friendly part. He'd never allowed himself to become chummy with anyone in a friendship sort of way.

He rode on in, careful to let the welcoming committee stay ahead of him. The town proper appeared as if conjured, as did so many such towns throughout the West. Buildings rose to either side of him, false fronts hiding canvas tent interiors on a few at the near end. The rest looked to be erected of hewn logs, and a good many of lumber.

He passed a cabinetmaker business, with wide double doors revealing a dim interior from which a lean man, about his own age, emerged wearing a leather apron and carrying a plank in one hand and a tool of some sort in the other. It looked to Gage to be a plane. He saw leaning against the structure freshly constructed crates and what he took to be a tall pantry cupboard still missing one front door. He guessed that was what the man was working on.

To the other side of the big double doors, Gage saw three coffins arranged right to left, large to small. That would be serious, but grim, work. Far less grim, he reminded himself, than being the one who filled those boxes with corpses bearing bullet holes.

He rode on and saw, two shops down from the joiner, a sign above a loading dock running the width of the business: DELANO FREIGHTING. The name was familiar, but he wasn't certain why.

Parked alongside the loading dock sat a freight wagon with two oxen standing as they do—at ease and looking as if they were in a deep doze. Gage imagined that they were sleeping, having just arrived from the same direction he'd taken. He also imagined that was the very wagon that had rumbled by his camp, but a few hours before.

The wagon's bed was still loaded. It contained a lumpy load covered in a thick tarpaulin and lashed down with ropes. There was no sign of the drivers.

He rode on, doing his best to avoid direct looks by anyone. He was not particularly worried that he was going to be recognized, though it had happened in recent months. His full beard, a bit bushy, had helped quite a bit in avoiding surprise encounters of that ilk.

The fact that he was not overly well-off financially

was evident in the quality and repair of his clothing. He was dusty, his old dandified clothes had long since been swapped for a rough spun, brown wool coat. He'd bought it secondhand, as he had his black wool trousers.

The gent in the mercantile had told him they had belonged to a man who'd become tangled in the traces of his team and had been dragged to death when they'd spooked. The clothes he wore were his second set of work garments, traded at the store by his widow on her way out of town the day after the funeral.

The merchant had seemed keen to reveal this information, and grinned, no doubt expecting a reply.

"Clothes are clothes," Gage had said. "And we all die one day."

That had not been what the man had hoped to hear, but he'd made the sale, knocking a dollar off the asking price for both because the coat needed buttons, which he said he'd sell Gage.

The somber Texan had refused, saying he had time before the cold weather came to whittle himself a set of buttons. And that is just what he had done.

Carving small, useful items had been something he had always enjoyed, and now, since he no longer gambled or drank, carving was something he did in an evening about the campfire, or if he were fortunate enough to land a ranch job, he carved in a bunkhouse.

He'd tried to learn how to darn his socks from an old-timer cowboy, but it was a skill Gage had yet to master adequately. His attempts left his heels sore and his socks feeling too tight.

Now he took his bearded, old-clothed self atop his old horse and rode, in no hurry, toward a sign he spied down the street, near the far end, flapping and painted on canvas. It was an establishment promising HOME-MADE FOOD. The phrase struck him as funny, but more than that, it reminded him that it had been weeks since he'd had a real, decent meal.

He knew he had enough cash for such an indulgence, as well as a bit left over, too, for foodstuffs for the trail, should he fail to find paying work.

He made for it, but paused once at a water trough, where Rig drank his fill.

Before Gage reached the restaurant, which turned out to be an open-faced tent with three tables out front, he passed another depot, this time on the right side of the street. This one also bore a sign over the loading dock: R. SHIERSON, FREIGHT HAULAGE.

Made sense that a hub town among so many mine camps would have at least two hauling outfits, perhaps more. This one, however, though the big sliding door was open and he thought he spied a person inside the warehouse within, looked all but out of business. Then he noticed that there were fresh horse and wheel tracks before the dock.

He made it to the food tent and dismounted, tying Rig to the flimsy rail. There were few people about the street and no other customers inside, but it looked as though he'd arrived after the noon meal rush, because tin plates, bowls, and cups were stacked at the ends of the tables, as if awaiting someone to fetch them. Then he saw a portly woman at the back, a stove to one side of her, and to the other, a table with two steel basins atop. She was washing dishes, and Gage detected the aroma of something toothsome in the air.

He stood that way a long moment, sniffing and trying to place the smell. Stew, perhaps.

"Hey, you!"

Gage snapped out of his reverie. It was the stout woman staring at him.

"Yeah, you—make yourself useful and fetch those dishes on over here!"

He stood still a moment longer, uncertain if she was addressing him, when she said, "Something wrong with you?"

"Me? No, I—"

"Good, then bring me my dishes!"

This time, he did as he was bade and soon had all three stacks plunked in the near-full, soapy basin on the left. As soon as he finished, she said, "Thanks," then raised her head and sniffed, much as he had done not a minute before.

"Uh-oh," she said, spinning and nearly knocking him over. "My stew's burning on the bottom! Didn't you smell that?"

"No, no, ma'am," said Gage.

She busied herself at the stove, muttering and sputtering and stirring and dolloping what looked like dumplings atop the stew.

He licked his lips, then saw the dishes still unwashed. So he tugged off his coat, unbuttoned his cuffs, rolled up his sleeves, and set to work washing the dishes.

He'd nearly finished when she hurried back over. "Hey, thanks, mister. I love cooking and I hate washing up after. Especially after the savages hereabouts. Honestly, just because you're a miner doesn't mean you were raised by wolves! Some of them surely had mothers with sense enough to teach them manners. Honestly!"

Gage smiled and said nothing. They worked side by side for a minute longer. Once the dishes were washed, rinsed, and set to dry, she said, "I suppose you didn't do that just for fun."

He looked down at her, and for the first time since he'd made her acquaintance, she was smiling. "Come on, sit down, then. You can be the first to sample the stew and dumplings." She half turned, then looked back at him. "That is, if you're hungry."

"Yes, ma'am."

"And none of this 'ma'am' business. I'm Gerty. And I'm far too long in the tooth for anyone to call me that."

He nodded and sat down, setting his hat on the bench next to him.

She ladled up stew and dumplings and set it before him, along with a spoon and a blue calico napkin, then poured two cups of black coffee and set them down, taking a seat across from him.

He had hoped she'd stay busy, but she was showing him a kindness, of sorts, so he could hardly refuse her company.

"Ain't seen you here before."

"Nope," he said, blowing on a spoonful of stew. It looked rich, thick, and swimming with hunks of meat, likely mule deer, as well as carrots and potatoes, maybe turnip. "Passing through. Unless I can find work for a spell."

"You from Texas?" she said, sipping her coffee.

He paused, then shrugged and continued eating.

"Sounds like it. Anyhoo, sure there's work hereabouts. Two sorts that I know of. But one's digging for rocks in rock, which sure seems like a fool's game to me."

"The other?"

"Oh yeah, well, that's driving for Delano." She shook her head and pulled a sneer as if she were about to spit out a fly that had landed in her coffee.

"Delano? That the freighting outfit at the other end of the street?"

"Know of 'em, huh?"

He shrugged. "Rode by and saw the sign."

"Well, if you can jehu, you'll likely get hired. But working for Delano ain't a long-term task, if you know what I mean." She nodded knowingly and sipped her coffee.

He neared the bottom of his bowl, spooning up the last of his stew and dumplings, and regretted that it was soon to be over.

"I'll fill that for you."

"Oh, thank you, but–"

"Bah, no charge for your dinner today, mister. You helped me with that onerous task of washing up. I'm grateful." She winked at him and returned to the stove.

When she'd set down the second bowl of stew before him, he said, "Thank you. What about this freighting outfit over there?" He nodded to his left.

"Oh, Shierson's? Nah, they ain't hiring. Ain't likely to, neither. Just hanging on. Delano moved in a while back and rode hard right over poor Shierson."

"You're not a fan of Delano, I take it."

"Ha!" She offered up a wide, false smile and then shook her head. "Find me anyone who is." She leaned forward, and in a lower voice, she said, "Man owns freight outfits all over the region. I'd say he's successful, sure, but not by being kind or making any friends in the process. And there's some would say he got to where he is by doing anything, and I mean *anything,* to make his deals."

Then she leaned back and sipped her coffee, watching him eat, a satisfied smile on her face seeing him enjoying the food. "But if it's short-term work you're wanting, you could make a few runs for him, then get out before he turns on you."

"Sounds bad," said Gage.

"Oh, it's true. Patrick Delano ain't good, not a bone in him guilty of that, but he'll pay you. Not a prime wage, mind you, but he'll pay you. Then he'll find fault and send you packing. Or if you have sense, more than likely you'll come to your senses and leave him wanting."

Gage finished his stew in silence. She took the hint and sipped the last of her coffee, looking down the long road. When he'd finished, she rose, cleaned his place, and said, "Sure was nice to see someone with manners take his time and enjoy the food. These savages hereabouts, honestly!"

"You're sure I can't pay you for the meal, Gerty? It was excellent. Truly."

"Naw, but thank you just the same."

He rose and tugged on his coat and hat. "Thanks again."

"Sure. I'm here all the time. Come on back and do the dishes!" she added with a laugh.

As he threaded his way through the benches, Gerty called out, "Hey, mister! Good luck with Delano. And I mean it." With that, she turned back to her stove and to her muttering and sputtering.

She'd given him food for thought, recalling a phrase he'd heard an old-timer at the mercantile say once, long ago, back in Sourwood Springs. Now he knew he had to pay a visit to this Delano character. Mostly out of curiosity. Could a man be all that bad? Doubtful.

As he rode back down the street, Jon Gage realized he himself was the living embodiment of a truly bad man. How could anyone be worse?

Chapter 11

Ten minutes after his most excellent stew and not unpleasant chat with Gerty, the proprietress, Gage realized he never offered her his name, but then again neither did she ask it—he found himself stepping into the cool interior of the office at Delano Freighting.

A thick-faced man, in a bowler tilted back on his head, sat behind a raised desk dead ahead of the door. Gage stepped inside and waited for his eyes to adjust to the dim light. The man still hadn't looked up from whatever he was writing in, but what looked to be a ledger book. How he could see what he was doing was a mystery to Gage. He waited.

He knew the man was aware of his presence, because he'd glanced up briefly when Gage stepped through the doorway. Finally the man emitted an elaborate sigh, smacked his dip pen down on the ledger, and looked up.

"What?"

That annoyed Gage faster than just about anything

else might. Still, he tried on a forced smile. "You treat all potential customers that way?"

The man narrowed his eyes and looked him up and down. "You don't look like somebody who has enough of anything to hire an outfit like mine."

"So you're Delano."

The man sighed again. "You didn't answer my question."

"You didn't ask much of one." Gage kept staring the man down.

"Are you a customer, then?"

"As it happens, no. I heard you might be hiring drivers."

That made the man smile. "You did, did you?"

He rose and walked around the chair, descended two steps, and emerged before Gage. The man was shorter than Gage had assumed, but he looked to be one of those runty, chunky men with more confidence and bluster than anything else. As annoying as such folks were, Gage had to admit a number of them he'd met had been effective at their occupations, usually business of some sort. He guessed that was because they felt they had something more to prove, given their height.

"Well, now, I don't know, I don't know. Might be I could use another man, might be not."

Gage regarded the man a moment longer, then nodded. "All right, then. Thanks for your time."

He turned, and when he was nearly through the door, a voice behind him said, "Now hold on, you hold on. Never let it be said that Patrick Delano don't give a man a fair shake. I reckon I can do you a favor."

"Don't want a favor, just a job. Labor and skill for money. It's a business agreement."

"I knew I liked you! Come on back in here already."

The man rounded the desk once more and sat in his creaking chair. "Now, you got experience as a bull-whacker?"

"Some."

"You know the region? All the little towns and camps? Mountains hereabouts are filled with folks and mines and whatnot looking for their goods or looking for me to drag their rocks on out."

"I don't know the region well, but I'll learn."

"Yeah, well, I don't know, I don't know. I ain't got no time for learners. I need doers. I haul all manner of goods—food, hardware, hard and soft goods, livestock— you name it, I haul it." Delano's exclamation turned to a groan and he rubbed his face as if his stubbly beard annoyed him.

"That's fine. I understand." Gage was not liking this man one bit. So little, in fact, that he would have pre-ferred to walk on out of there, maybe try the next town. But he'd already put himself forward for a job, so he figured he'd let the conversation unroll for another minute or two before he took his leave.

"Oh, all right, all right! But don't you let me down, you hear?" Delano pointed a finger up at Gage.

Gage didn't move, then said, "Or what?"

"Or . . . or, well, you just wait and see." Delano popped on that false smile and shook his head.

"Don't threaten me, Delano, and we'll get along just fine."

Gage hoped that was enough for the man to continue flying into his odd little rage and send him packing. But Delano must have been more desperate for drivers than Gage guessed, for the little freight owner laughed, a cold, raspy sound.

"I like you . . . By the way, what's your name, did you say?"

"I didn't. But it's Gage."

"Hmm, Gage, Gage . . ." The chunky, smaller man leaned back in his squeaking chair. "You know, you look familiar to me. What do you say to that?"

Gage shrugged. *Here we go,* he thought. "Nothing to say. You aren't familiar to me at all."

"Fair enough. Okay, then. I got two men who come in earlier with a load. You can make yourself useful and unload it. Warehouse is yonder." Delano jerked a thumb to his left, toward a door, beyond which Gage already knew he'd find the firm's storage space.

"On second thought"—Delano tapped his teeth and regarded Gage a moment—"I think we might as well lob you on into the pond, see if you can swim or not. Those goods, save for three sacks of meal laid atop, just under that tarpaulin that's stretched tight on the load? Well, them three sacks go inside. You'll see the other sacks of meal and such in the front right corner. All be hauled out in a couple of days anyway.

"But once you do that, you lash that cover down tight on that load again and haul it out the west end of the street, past that awful dining tent. That old hag who runs it ought to be arrested and hanged, but what are you going to do?"

"I met her already. Excellent stew."

"Now there's folks who can do most anything in the kitchen and it'll appeal to some people, not to others. I am of the latter group there. But then again, I have what you might call refined taste. Course, if folks want to like something, it's none of my business if they don't."

"What is it you're trying to say, Delano?"

It was the businessman's turn to shrug. "Nothing, nothing. So you make for the far end of town." He pointed, then let his arm drop as if the effort had been far too much for him.

"Then you keep on rolling, for about four, five miles, and the roadway will fork. What you do then is you take the right road, make for the cleft in the hills. It's a steep one, you'll be driving a two-horse team, not them oxen. They're good, but they're slow. Only reason Trigg and Axel was using the oxen is they hauled ore on out. The horses will get the job done quicker."

"When do I leave and when do you want me back?"

Delano grinned and narrowed his eyes. "I like that you are keen, man, but I ain't through talking yet. Nobody interrupts Patrick Delano. Be wise of you to commit that fact to mind.

"Now," he said, leaning forward on his desk, "it's all . . . all about money to me. You understand? Course you don't, otherwise you'd be in my position and not staring at me in your threadbare clothes and all, wanting money." He shook his head, still grinning as if he knew the secrets to all the magical things in the world and Gage was a dim-minded child.

"You insulting me, Delano? You don't even know me."

Delano giggled. "It's just my way. You work for Patrick Delano, you got to learn to get used to it, man."

Several minutes later, after further negotiation, Gage found himself busy with rejiggering the load of goods. He was also chewing over the encounter with Delano. It left Gage cold and feeling as if he'd just wrassled with a diseased dog. But he needed the money and the amount Delano finally agreed on, after more than enough haggling and complaining, would carry Gage nicely for a couple of months.

It would be enough, if he was cautious with how he spent it, to keep him in food and even buy a new pair of woolen socks and maybe even a new, heavy, cold-weather shirt.

As much as Delano's comment about his threadbare clothes had rankled and stung him, he knew the little tyrant was correct. He was looking ratty about the edges, as one old-timer on a crew he'd been with a while back had said about a no-luck bum in a cattle town as they passed through.

He'd also negotiated with Delano that he keep his horse in the company stable and yard, though the feed and use of the barn would come out of his wages. He'd keep an eye on how much that figure was going to work out to be.

As for his saddlebags, he'd take them with him, and leave behind in the tack stall his saddle and other gear for Rig. He had no desire to leave anything personal behind, not that he had much for a stranger to rummage through.

But in his experience, there was nothing less trust-worthy than a stranger who had looked at him as if he had a deep-down gut feeling that he might be some-body they'd heard about. And that deep-down gut feel-ing had urged many a person to sniff through his belongings. It had happened at two ranches he'd worked at, and perhaps more.

Once he'd settled Rig in his new home, at least for a few days, and hayed him, he walked to the nearest mer-cantile, one of two he'd learned about, and bought basic provisions. It would be an overnight trip, and he was expected back at the depot in thirty minutes. He had just enough time to stow his gear beneath the seat.

It looked like he'd just make it—the sky had dark-ened and, unless he was sorely mistaken, and he didn't think he was, the rest of the day and evening were going to be wet ones.

That made him groan to himself because the rutted mountain trails he was headed for, often near impass-able at the best of times as they were gouged and washed out and rutted, were going to be a real treat during, before, and after a rain.

Gage was aware, too, that Delano was watching him like an eagle and would be until he and the team rolled on out of town and out of sight. He didn't give the re-pugnant little man the satisfaction of seeing Gage glance back. He knew there would be eyes on him and that was enough.

He also had to admit that Delano's likely trepidation regarding hiring Gage, a raw stranger, was not un-founded or unjustified. He owned a business—a thriving business, if Delano was to be believed—and he was trusting Gage with a whole lot of goods and a hefty investment in a wagon and team.

The horses, two big, muscled brown geldings, looked somewhat rested and up to the task, though Gage thought they could use with more meat on their bones, particularly in making frequent runs into steep, rough terrain. He didn't doubt that Delano shorted them on feed when he could, in order to save himself money.

Gage figured that if he could, he'd haul up for the night somewhere the big beasts might be able to graze amply. In his experience with high country, even late in the season, there were always open spots where a horse might nibble its fill.

He had to make it as far as he might today, then camp; then first thing in the morning, he'd make his delivery to Clabberville, the mine camp expecting him.

Gage worked the team harder on the road leading out of town, then into and up the foothills, knowing that the going was only going to become more difficult. He was right. After four hours, the horses' strength began to flag. He'd stopped them twice to let them drink, not their fill, as they'd get in trouble with guts full of water, or at the least become sluggish and not want to work.

But now that the terrain was steeper and the switchbacks were becoming more frequent and tighter in the turns, they were slowing, straining at times, and beginning to show signs of real fatigue. They shuddered and blew, frothing from their mouths when they were hard put to drag the wagon lurching and slamming over the rutted, rocky roadway.

They leveled off atop a ridge. It was the first real ridge he'd come to, as Delano had told him, and it was to be the first of two. Somebody had cleared a patch of trees wide enough for him to gaze out northeastward. He saw the next ridge they had to conquer, and apparently Clabberville sat "like a muddy mess," as Delano had put it, on the other side of that second ridgetop, not but a ten-minute wagon ride down.

He eyed the lane ahead. It kept level for some time, then disappeared from sight. He waited for the horses to blow and catch their wind. If they could make it down a ways, they might be able to find that mythical sweet location where he could hobble them and let them graze.

"Get up thar! Hee yaa!" He laid into them far less than they were used to, he'd bet money on that. He'd never been able to stomach whipping on a beast just to get it to do the thing it was doing in the first place.

That's when lightning, like a critter seen from the corner of your eye, caught his attention. It was a flash to the north. Soon enough, he heard thunder dogging it, both far off yet. It was too soon to tell if the storm would make it to him or travel elsewhere.

The sky, which had already been filled with low, dark, oppressive clouds, had become darker still, in part because the day was aging. But he didn't like the look of the low, churning cloud mass rolling southward, at him. Indeed, it looked as if it had singled him out to torment, for it rolled and churned closer as he watched.

He urged the beasts on, not wanting to be atop the ridge when the storm visited.

The last glimpse he had of the sky northward was not encouraging—daggers of silver like claws or teeth of the encroaching sky beast flashed once, twice, and the thunder clapped hard and quick, sending a sudden gust of cold down at him.

He urged the neighing horses down the first steep grade, too fast for his liking. Although he had to get them down as low as possible, he did not want to end up below some loose-bouldered slope, where they might get crushed by tumbling stones. He'd not experienced such a thing himself, but had heard tales told by men who had no reason to stretch the truth about such things. He'd seen the fear in their eyes.

"Curse money," he growled through gritted teeth, hating the idea that he had to earn it in such a way. And to put these poor horses through this was an added vexation. The terrorized beasts thrashed and lunged, unable to do what they wanted, which was to bolt in the only direction they could, downhill.

He had to hold them back, lest the wagon, already creaking and jostling more than he liked, slide too far to his left. Not six, seven feet from his near front wheel, the roadway sloped at times at a dangerous angle. The earth beneath his wheels still looked solid enough, but it was a rum spot to be in.

Gage willed himself to give it as much as he could. With the lines gripped tight in his gloved fists, he half stood in the driving well, his right leg jammed forward, his boot wedged beneath something up under there, and his left leg and thigh angled outward to give him a better stance.

"Hee yaa, get up there! Go! Go!"

That's when the first hard, lonely, cold raindrop smacked his arm. He saw it hit his coat sleeve and he knew it wasn't his sweat, though there was plenty of that, too.

Whoever built the roadway had done a decent enough job—he hoped. But the thing that pleased him most at that moment was the long stretch of it before them. It appeared that the lane widened at the end of that particular run, flaring out into what he hoped was an ample safe spot to stop. Because the rain was coming.

That first drop seemed to be a lone wolf. Or so he thought for a time as he drove that team on down that long stretch. But that notion, that wish, did not last for long. The rest of its raindrop friends, when they arrived, did so with a fury that Gage did not expect. It was as if someone had sent a pail of water skyward over him. It sluiced down, driving into him as thousands of stinging drops—and it didn't let up.

The horses' backs looked as if they were being raked by some rogue beast. And then the rain came down so hard and so fast and the rain drops were so dense, they looked as if they were emitting steam or smoke, and through the sizzling wall all about them, Gage found it difficult to see the roadway. Then he lost sight of it completely.

He gave the horses their heads and on they thundered. He hoped their instincts kept their footfalls from the downside slope. They began to come out of their long, slow descent across the hillside and leveled off, instead. At the same time, he felt, more so than heard, the wagon slow, and the crashing and slamming, up to now so sharp and sudden-sounding, lessened, and then they stopped.

He sat there alive, panting, though he knew he had no reason to do so, at least no reason close to what his horses had, and hunched, cursing himself for not tugging on his slicker. It was an old thing, uncomfortable once heat crept back in, but it did serve to keep him somewhat dry.

Just like him, though, he thought with disgust, that he waited and waited, preferring to save the task of untying his lashed gear and freeing the garment. Now he was paying for his laziness.

He shook his head and thought, *Jon, man, you are a fool and a half, and no mistake.*

Ahead, two dark, humped shapes told him the horses, too, were hunched and not enjoying the rain one bit.

"Better than dead," he muttered from beneath his drooped, dripping hat brim as he set the brake and held tight to the lines. And then, as if summoned by his foolish utterance, thunder pealed and lightning crackled at the same time.

It felt to Gage as if his world had exploded. He screamed, the horses screamed, and not one of them was heard over the brute sounds from on high.

The earth pulsed beneath them, the air about them vibrated and hummed. It felt thick, as if he were under water. It pressed in on him and he could hear nothing, save his own heart hammering in his chest.

What he could still do was smell, and what he smelled was not anything he had ever sniffed before. It was not unlike the stink of the wagon brakes when tested rumbling down a steep grade, or the steely, singed stench of a train going too fast and trying to brake to make its stop at a station. And yet it was not like these things at all. It was the smell of the very heavens on fire.

As he looked behind them, while holding tight to the lines to keep the dancing, flailing horses from dragging them to their deaths, he saw what he had just envisioned—fire. But this was no heavenly thing and no damnation spawn, it was genuine flames licking and dancing and leaping up and down the length of a now-downed tree.

Less than fifty feet behind them, lying across the roadway they had traveled not moments before, the large tree, which had been upslope of them, had been smacked by the lightning. The bolt had snagged it at the top and slithered its way down the great trunk, or so it seemed to Gage.

The mammoth pine, larger around than he could grasp with both arms, was one of many that Gage had not noticed in their frantic scramble forward. And now it lay split lengthwise, its hairy head of needled branches crushed and flaming, even in the pelting rain, as the trunk sputtered and billowed.

The smoke would almost have been a welcome scent to Gage, and the heat might well be needed soon, if the fire managed to stay alight. He looked ahead and found that he could see past the dancing horses.

"Simmer down! Simmer down! Here now!" he shouted, and could barely hear his voice.

All about them, the storm slammed and snarled and slashed and spewed. Despite all that, he was tired, bone tired, he realized. And yet, the foolishness of the horses kept him from dozing, because he spent the time waiting out the storm eyeing the still-burning tree behind him and keeping the jumpy, nerved-up horses before him barely under control.

It seemed to take a month and more, but as he sat there, shivering and eyeing with hunger the few flaming spots left on the steaming, smoking pine carcass, the tail of the southbound storm passed over them and left him sodden, the horses played out, and with just enough light to see where they had ended up. They stood in the midst of that flared-out, widened spot at the end of the long laneway he'd spied before the storm hit them.

Behind him, a big tree still burned in a promising spot in its middle, conveniently right in the midst of the roadway. In front of the shaking, head-hanging horses, a landslide appeared to have rendered the lane to the long, wide, curving switchback down all but impassable.

He broke out in a haggard laugh, tying the lines as he realized he'd expended all that effort and the horses couldn't have gone another thirty feet anyway.

"Gage," he said aloud, stepping down and surveying the scene in the dim twilight, "it appears you are trapped." He reached into the wagon and hauled out his somewhat-dry bag. "Looks like a problem we can deal with in the morning, eh, horses?"

They shook their heads as best they could in their rain-soaked harnesses and seemed to give him a hard look. Or so he imagined.

It didn't take the rain long to dwindle to a random scatter of drops that he thought, given that they were largely in the trees, were rattling down from the soaked pine needles and bare aspen branches above.

There was only one thing he really wanted to do from the moment he climbed, stiff-jointed, down from the wagon, and that was to capture the fire while it still burned in the cleft tree.

It had been a quick storm, but a real soaker, and it would be far too much work to scratch for duff and dry wood. If he could keep this guttering fire alive, he might be all right. Heck, he might even be able to dry his clothes.

"First things first, Gage," he muttered. "Keep this fire going, but not too much, lest the forest burn. And then see to the horses. They've had a harder time of it than you did, after all."

He glanced back at them and they were still there, shuddering and chomping. He would want to sluice off that water from their coats soon, get some good food into them. He'd been shown where to fetch the horse feed and where on the wagon to store it—in one of the two ample storage boxes riding beneath the wagon's sides.

He walked to the tree and eyed the flame. Then he held his hands before it and enjoyed the warmth it gave him—enough to smile. That was a feeling he could take more of, yes, sir.

He walked to the side of the roadway, where the uphill slope and the road met, and shoved and drove with his heel at the earth, gouging out and clearing a depression a foot and a half wide and a few inches deeper than the road's surface.

That uphill slope to his left looked promising, as it was a scatter of dropped branches, needles, and twigs—all wet on the surface. He dug a finger in and rummaged beneath the surface, shoved and brushed aside the damp bits. He found, beneath a large, long, fallen pine bough, dry matter—leaves and needles and twigs, brittle and stone dry.

This he scraped up and then carried a couple of two-handed scoopfuls to his new fire pit. For wood, he figured to snap off the fire-dried branches along the trunk. They were sooty and some still smoked and smoldered. Twice he felt the heat through his leather gloves.

In this manner, he methodically built up a fire along the roadway, then made three twists of duff and larger materials and transferred flame with them as small torches from the tree, setting them on the scorched trunk beside the flames. He lit one twist and let it consume the ragged end of his newly built fire.

He added snapped branches, then more, and soon had a crackling little fire in danger of consuming the wood as fast as he could lay it on. This did not worry him, nor did the effort bother him. He quite enjoyed the simple task of laying in a store of wood for the night's use.

At last satisfied the fire would be self-sustaining for a spell, long enough to allow him to feed the horses and tie and hobble them for the night. He had to take the extra precautions. He was in country unfamiliar to him and he wasn't in any mood to chase after fool horses that might take a notion to wander or spook.

While he rummaged in the less-than-tidy, but decently stocked, storage boxes, he discovered a solid axe and honing stone. "You will be useful," he said, hefting the tool, smiling because he was talking to himself. Sure, the horses might hear him, but what of it? They weren't looking too eager to laugh.

Once the fire was in no danger of sputtering out, Gage spent the remainder of the daylight tending the horses. He watered them from the canvas waterskin they carried on board the wagon, which seemed laughable, given the amount of water they'd just endured from above. Neither horse was too thirsty, but they tucked in to their feed and a few scant snatches of hay he'd managed to roll up in a smaller scrap of tarpaulin.

He tied them to the rear of the wagon and rubbed them down one more time each with a wool saddle blanket. They seemed not to mind the attention, dozy as they were.

He found a lantern in one of the boxes, but unless he really needed it, he preferred to leave it alone. Besides, if it was tended as well as the rest of the gear he'd rummaged through, it wouldn't work worth a bean. The small can of lamp oil was not topped up.

There were things Gage told himself he would make certain to attend to when he made it back to Newel. If, that is, he decided to continue working for Delano. The man was a pompous fool and a blowhard, and he ran his business poorly, in Gage's estimation. That said, the man did own the business and Gage did not, so there was something to that.

He lugged his bag over to the fire. It was chill and growing cooler, so he shucked out of his wet togs, and hung them on the crude branch drying rack he made with help from his belt knife and the axe.

The air hastened his re-dressing. He was glad he'd had the foresight last year to purchase a new, long-handle suit. That and the dry pair of socks would suffice until his other clothes dried.

He found he needed more wood than he'd first thought, so he set to work with the axe on the big, sappy, sundered pine beside him. He'd have to hack it apart in the morning anyway, since the road was likely the only out or in to the town of Clabberville he'd yet to see.

It seemed unlikely that anyone might venture on down after him. But if they did, he'd hear them and figure it out from there. With that thought in mind, he set up the lantern and checked his bag for dry matches. He had a half dozen left. Another thing to purchase, once he was paid for his efforts.

He gnawed on two strips of jerky and a short stack of hardtack biscuits as he waited for the coffee to boil. It took a long, ol' time and he felt himself nodding off while he waited. So he forced himself up to his feet and gathered more wood.

The clothes were steaming and hissing, a good sign, but they would need a lot more fire warmth to be dry by morning. Or at least wearable.

Finally he smelled the tang of brewed coffee and sat down on his blanket, stretched his now-soiled, damp socks to the flames, and poured a cup of too-hot coffee. He burned his tongue and did not care. Never had any cup of coffee tasted so good.

He sighed. "Just right."

Chapter 12

The next morning, Jon Gage shivered long and hard before he opened his eyes. It was cold, awfully cold. This sort of bone-deep cold didn't happen in the part of Texas he was from. Not that he thought much of that place anymore.

It had been years since he'd even set foot in the south of Texas, and if he had his way, he never would again. He'd grown fond of experiencing the fullness of four seasons.

He cracked open his eyes and winced. The morning sun was up and shining. He'd been more tired than he thought. He usually woke before dawn, and had for years. The horses still stood where he'd left them, though they were looking around themselves as if planning an escape.

"Not if I can help it," he said, stretching and yawning. His words came out as vapor before his face. "Great."

The fire was out, had been for quite some time. His

intention of staying awake for hours to prod it and add to it and get his clothes and boots dry never happened. Sleep had knocked him cold, even after his second cup of coffee.

He rose, massaged his stiff knees, and gingerly rubbed his side wound, doing his best—and not succeeding—to not think about the beautiful young woman who'd given it to him.

After he'd tended to his morning needs, Gage yawned his way over to the horses, fed and watered them, and stepped wide of the piles they'd delivered in the night. The fire proved to be simpler to revive than he'd suspected, as he still had three small, but promising, coals with a faint glow about them.

It wasn't long before he had the blaze crackling once again. He set about gathering more firewood and soon had the coffeepot back on the fire, sooting up, sure, but bubbling coffee, too.

His clothes needed more time before the fire, so he flopped them around a bit on the makeshift rack he'd built, and then made his way around the wagon to the far side to assess the one thing he'd avoided looking over the night before—the landslide he'd seen before them.

It was indeed a slump of dirt and rock and two small trees from the steep, uphill bank to his right. But it was not as bad as he'd initially suspected.

He sighed and went back to the fire to set himself and the horses up for the day. And it looked as if it was going to be a day of grunt labor just to free them from their odd, storm-induced mess.

* * *

"Hey there!"

Gage, fed and dressed in his mostly dry clothes, and still-damp, but usable, boots, was working on the big lightning-dropped pine, sending chips flying from the edge of the decent axe he'd found in the workbox. He'd honed the blade to a keen edge with the stone and it really paid off. The tree's flesh was giving way beneath his powerful blows.

The shout, between strikes, was well timed—sent forth by a man who himself had used an axe and knew that a man wielding one wasn't to be interrupted lightly. Gage, with the axe not yet raised, spun, crouching low, his left hand reaching for a gun that wasn't there.

From around the leading edge of the gravel and soil landslide strode a slender, slouch-shouldered man, with dark hair and drooping moustache. In the roadway, he held up a hand in a wave.

"Hey!" he said again.

Gage stood and returned the raised-hand gesture. "Hello there."

The man advanced, smiling. Gage noticed the fellow wore no visible guns. His garb was more that of a workingman—patched brown wool coat, trousers the same, faded blue work shirt, and braces. Atop his head rode a much-abused bowler.

"How do," said the man as he drew nearer.

Gage nodded, but hesitated, the axe still in his hand. He wore no guns, hadn't since that day, but he did own a small-caliber rifle, snug in its canvas and leather sheath. He used it solely for bringing down game. And there was a shotgun that Delano had handed him, along with six shells. "For defending my goods and my team and wagon. You hear?"

Gage had wondered what the man thought he might do with the thing if not use it to scare off would-be thieves.

Gage leaned the axe against the tree trunk and walked forward, wiping his neck and face with his kerchief.

Before he could speak, the man said, "That there's a load of work." He nodded past Gage toward the tree as he halted a dozen feet from Gage.

"You bet. Nothing for it, though."

"That's for certain. Same with that." The man hiked a thumb over his shoulder toward the slumped earth. Gage had saved that mess for later, uncertain how to deal with it. He had no shovel, something that the wagon really should have on board, and it was something else he'd have to mention to Delano. He was not going to be looked on with much kindness by the annoying pudgy man on his return to Newel.

"I figured I'd tuck into that next."

"You got a shovel?" said the man.

"As it happens, I don't."

"No worries, then. I do. Two, in fact. And a mattock."

"You travel prepared," said Gage with a grin.

"I do when I'm checking the road after storms."

"I'm guessing this isn't the first time this has happened, then."

"No, sir. About every big whipper that rolls through, we got to work on the road. Only one in or out."

"So you're from Clabberville, the town back in the hills there?" Gage asked.

"Right in one." He offered his hand. "Morton Reilly."

"Gage," said Jon, hesitating, then taking the offered hand.

"Yeah, we're concerned because we been expecting a load of goods, the first of two before winter strands us back here." He smiled, but Gage thought he could see a little worry in his eyes.

"One of the hazards of living out here, I guess."

"You sure are right, Mr. Gage. Say, I ain't seen you before. You a Delano man, or can I assume you to be from Shierson Freight Haulage?"

"Shierson?" It took a moment for that name to sink into Gage's brain. "Oh, that's the other outfit in town. But it's not looking too good for their business, I'm afraid."

"Yeah." The man eyed him through slits, then swung his head to the side and sluiced a rope of brown spittle to the ground and dragged a hand across his mouth. "Chaw. Rough habit, so says the wife. Me? I like it."

He looked behind him as if there might be someone there, lurking, then said, "Dumbest thing I ever did was invite the missus and the squallerin' bairns on up here to this place. I kept telling her it was awful, just about a hell on earth, but she wanted to come. She missed me, so she says. As did the chilluns. Well, when she got up here and saw how wonderful it is, she hit me on the arm, right in front of the other men. Can you imagine?"

Gage cleared his throat. "Well, yes, it is very pretty up here, I'll grant you that."

"So, Mr. Gage, which outfit you say you're working for?"

"Delano. Delano Freighting."

"Huh, now that's interesting. See, we didn't contract with Delano Freighting. We contracted with Shierson. Good folks, them Shiersons."

Gage nodded, relieved to be back to the topic on which they began their conversation. "I expect Mr. Delano has bought out the contracts for Shierson, taking over their business, but I don't know that for certain."

"Yeah, well, we actually know a bit about this Delano fellow up there in Clabberville. You see, he's a rascal, and I don't much care if you are a friend of his or not." The man paused and Gage read his face, something he was good at. He saw that tightening around the mouth, the slight narrowing of the eyes.

Gage shook his head. "He's no friend of mine. I just hired on because I need the money. I have a little coffee in the pot, if you care to tell your story. Then maybe we can work together to free up the road from its load of dirt yonder."

Suspicion eased itself from the man's features and his smile returned. "Well, now, that's mighty kind of you, Mr. Gage. Mighty kind. Been a month of Sundays since I had coffee, to be honest. We been making do with ground nuts and pine bark, making pretend it tastes like coffee. But it don't."

It took a few minutes, but Gage had a fresh pot of coffee on the boil and the two men sat by the fire, toasting their palms despite the growing warmth of the morning.

"Ain't much to tell, really," said the man, almost fearfully. "Hardly worth the price of a cup of coffee."

Gage smiled. "No worries there. I brought plenty. If there's one thing I need on the trail, it's hot coffee in the morning. And sometimes in the afternoon as well."

Reilly eyed the steaming pot. "I hear that."

"So . . . Delano?"

"Yeah, yeah, well, one of the men used to be in town, he's moved on since, fella by the name of Rinks, he used to work for Delano. He told stories of that rascal that would make your hair curl."

Reilly plucked off his hat and revealed a near-gleaming pate, with but a few wispy hairs atop. He laughed and shook his head. "I swear, I don't get to trot out that nugget too often, as everybody I know already knows me and has heard it far too many times!"

Gage chuckled at the meager joke and poured a cup of coffee for the man, then poured some into his battered tin bowl for himself.

"Oh, now, I can't be taking a man's cup!"

"You can if you're my guest. A vessel's a vessel. And a story's a story."

"Oh, right." Reilly sipped the brew with his eyes closed and smacked his lips. "Oh, but that's tasty. I am right obliged, Mr. Gage."

"My pleasure."

"As to that Delano fella, I warned you it wasn't much of a story, as stories go, but the fella Rinks, as I said, used to work for the man, but not in Newel. No, it was back in Utah someplace. And he said that Delano would fire men for offenses that weren't even there. He'd make up lies, and because Rinks and others like him was strangers in town, newcomers looking for work, and because Delano's pal was the marshal in town, why, he'd get away with it. Never ended up having to pay those fellows!"

Reilly sipped again. "So, if I was you, I'd be careful where I step around that little viper. He's liable to sink fang."

Gage drank his coffee. "I appreciate the warning."

Reilly nodded. "Behavior such as his can only earn a man enemies. Most folks don't forget when they've been wronged. That's why even though Rinks has moved on from Clabberville, we didn't use Delano to haul our goods. The other outfit in town, Shierson's, was always good to us. Man was a decent sort, always treated us well and vice versa. You could trust a man like that. But this Delano . . ." Reilly shook his head and sipped his coffee.

"You said 'was.'"

"Sure I did. That's because Roger Shierson, who ran the outfit, was killed. Nobody knows for certain by who, but there's rumors aplenty." He sipped.

"Killed how?"

"A blow to the head. Out here somewhere, in fact." Reilly waved a hand in a gesture that seemed to take in the entire range.

Gage thought a moment. "And you say nobody knows by who?"

"That's correct."

"But there are suspicions?"

"That's also correct."

"And would those suspicions include Delano?"

"Now, now," said Reilly. "You're backing a man

into a conversational corner and I don't know as I can get on out of that one. But I think you're a trustworthy sort, so I will say yes, that Delano has been considered to be behind Shierson's death. But you didn't hear it from me."

"Understood."

They chatted together for another twenty minutes, sipping fresh coffee, and then Reilly stood. "Well, I got to get this roadway cleared or we'll never get our goods, and you'll never get back to Newel!"

The two men set to work with the shovels Reilly had strapped to the back of his mule, a beast he rode in an awkward pose, so he told Gage, because of the modified pack frame he'd outfitted it with. The mule appeared resigned to its dismal fate and sulked, untied, along the side of the trail, nosing small stands of brittle grasses and trying to crib bark from trees.

It didn't take nearly as long to shift the dirt and debris from the roadway as Gage had suspected; then he remembered he had to finish lopping the log, but Reilly shoved past him and snatched up the axe. "No man who shares his coffee deserves to work while Mort Reilly stands by!" He winked and set to finishing the cut that Gage had begun. It didn't take the man long to work his way through it.

Gage had whacked away at the trunk in such a spot that little of it jutted into the road. And because of the springiness of the branches and the greenness of the tree, they were able, with effort, to shift the remainder of the tree sideways. Then, with a few roped tugs by the mule, who Gage learned was named Mule, the rest of the tree slid, then rolled, well off the downhill side of the roadway.

All in all, it had taken a couple of hours, but it was time well spent. He offered Reilly hardtack, jerky, and more coffee. The miner accepted, and they tucked in with gusto to the modest meal.

By then, the sun had begun its journey past the high point of the day.

"We have a few hours of daylight to us," said Reilly. "We can make it if your team's up for it. Rest of the road was fine when I come through it this morning."

"Let's do it. I'll spend the night in your town and leave first thing in the morning."

Reilly nodded. "You best—don't want to get in deep with Delano!" He raised his eyebrows and pitched in to help Gage rig up the team.

The horses were well rested and fidgety. And not a little hungry. But work, Gage knew, would tickle that urge and make them keener in the pulling.

They made tracks, and though Reilly kept an eye on his back trail, it was all Gage could do to keep up with the man on the mule. He reckoned the lanky miner had cause to keep them rolling hard. And he wasn't wrong. For all their pushing, darkness fell and Reilly shouted back that they still had a couple of miles to go.

Since he knew the way, Reilly offered to hold the lantern aloft to give Gage something to aim for, and in this manner, they moved along at a decent clip, despite the lack of light.

A half-dozen folks were waiting for them, one lantern held up between them. Gage figured that was to save lamp oil, for the cold, dark months were coming.

Mine camps, such as this, were all but cut off from the outside world for weeks and sometimes months, since the snows could be so deep that a man could barely shove through, even on snowshoes. And then only to ferry news back and forth, or to lug and drag what gear and goods he could pull behind him on a sled.

"Where have you been, Morton Reilly?"

It was a woman's voice, and it sounded big and sharp-edged. Gage guessed it was his missus. And he wasn't wrong.

"Oh, Ma, now don't get all worked up. We're fine, just fine. Had to clear a landslide and a tree out of the way is all."

"Supper's gone cold, but I'm heating it. And there's enough for the driver, too. If you say it's all right to invite him on in."

"All right?" said Reilly. "Why, of course, it's all right. This here fella's salt of the earth, I tell you. Good man all around."

"Then quit jawin' with me and get busy. You got a wagon to unload and the rest of these men have suppers to get home to, don't you, boys?"

A chorus of "Yes'm's" rippled through the small assemblage.

"Where should I park the load, Reilly?" said Gage.

"Yonder by that log barn, the open-face bay will be fine. We'll back her in and light her up and divvy the load."

As they worked, Gage thought that his first visit to Clabberville was going rather well, despite the storm that crippled his momentum for half a day, at least— perhaps longer.

By the end of that long day with all its labors, he didn't much care about Delano or what the man would think when Gage returned. Time enough to worry about that in the morning.

Chapter 13

"Where in the heck have you been?" The chunky little man circled around from behind his desk, a cigar stump jutted from his teeth and he began pacing, casting hard looks up at Gage.

Before Gage could reply, Delano said, "I was close, paper thin close, to selling off your tack and horse. Figured you took off on me with my wagon and team! Wouldn't be the first time that happened to me, I can tell you!"

"Hold on a minute there, Delano." Gage felt himself brewing up a temper, and in recent years past, when that feeling overcame him, he quelled it, learned to work his way through it in his mind before saying or doing something he'd regret.

But not this time.

He pulled in a deep draft of air and stomped up close and tight to the boss man. As he looked down at him, his voice slid out of his mouth, a low, cold, grating sound, as if gravel were being crushed by steel.

"You're doing two things that don't sit too tight with

me, little man. The first is accusing me of theft, and the second is threatening to sell off my personal goods."

"I never did either of those two things, mister man!" Delano, instead of being cowed by Gage's barely controlled rage, surprised the big man by leaning closer to Gage, as if daring him to keep pushing.

"What makes you think you can go through life making such accusations, Delano?"

"Because I am king of the heap, you low-pay drifter! And if you know what's good for you, you'll shut your yapper and tell me why you're late."

"Not even possible."

"What?" Delano's eyebrows met above his soft nose. "What?"

"First you tell me to shut my mouth and then you tell me to tell you what happened. Make up your mind."

The boss narrowed his eyes and slowly grinned, that cold, humor-free look once more writ large on his face. "You're a pain in my backside, and you're a wise man, too, eh?"

Gage said nothing, but continued to glare down at the man. Delano was, as the old-timers called it, a vexation to him.

"Out with it! Tell me why you're so blamed late. We got work to do."

Gage felt the tension tighten, but that was only within his mind, he knew that. For the moment, he knew he had to either shut his mouth and walk away before he punched the man flat, or just go ahead and do it.

But knowing Delano, he'd put Gage in jail. Probably had the law locked down in this town, too. And then

Gage might well be discovered for who he was, a has-been gunfighter with a cold, dark past filled with dead bodies bleeding out in the dust and sunlight.

Delano made the decision for him. He turned and walked back to the desk, hefting the weighty canvas sack Gage had set there. "What's this gold nugget and dust for?"

"It's from the folks up in Clabberville. They usually gave it to Shierson to deposit for them in their bank account. Then on the next run up to the hills, which they figure will be their last before snow flies. But they expect to send someone down to town in a few weeks."

"Oh, they will, will they?" Delano hadn't looked at Gage as he spoke, but probed among the smaller sacks nested within the larger sack. "Hmm. Well, that's partly why that sap, Shierson, left his fool widow about on death's door with that business of his. Wish she'd up and close the doors and be done with it. It is a burr in my backside, and I don't mind saying it. But we'll deal with them. Always have, always will. It's the Delano way."

"How's that?" said Gage.

Delano was in a chatty mood; the color rose on his face and he fingered and probed the dust and nuggets within. Delano looked up at him briefly, a childish smile on his fat face. "Shierson. He was a fool and so is his widow. She's still trying to compete with me! Can you believe it? What a fool." He shook his head.

Gage realized Delano hadn't answered the previous question and wasn't about to, and so he followed up with another. "What's put them out of business?"

A dark scowl replaced Delano's glee and he looked

back up at Gage. "What are you saying? You talk to somebody? Because you'd do well to keep your mouth shut in this town. You're a Delano man now. That means you shut your mouth and do your job and don't question me, you hear?" The fat man stuffed his cigar back between his lips.

"Hang on a minute, there, Delano."

The runty man looked at Gage, his cigar jutting from his moist lips, his eyebrows raised. "Last time you say that to me, Gage. I don't take much prodding and you have shoved me about as far as any man ever has. I hope to all that's holy that you are hearing me, Mr. Gage. 'Cause ain't nobody talks to Patrick Delano as if they are equals, especially not a worker, and gets away with it.

"Now, where was I? Oh yeah, yeah, counting my takings. Those poor fools up yonder in Clabberville. My word, they are far too trusting."

Gage sighed. He had to let this back-and-forth fool-ishness die or he was going to drop the man. "You know, Delano, I know exactly how much money is in that sack."

Without missing a moment of counting, the little chunky man said, "Oh, I just bet you do. Pulled right over halfway back here and tucked away a goodly amount. Can't say I blame you. But don't you worry about a thing. I'll deposit the money on behalf of the fine citizens of that rathole of a mine camp, don't you fret over it. In the meantime, you go unload that ore and tend to my stock. Then I want that warehouse tidied. Trigg and Axel, they're okay workers, but, man alive, are they slovenly! Never have I seen the like."

He shook his head and grunted as he hefted the sack of gold and carried it to the safe. The door was open and he swung it wider, then glanced at Gage. "You waiting for permission to leave my royal presence or what?" The fat man brayed and turned back to the safe. "Now git!"

Gage simmered and stewed as he unloaded the sacks of ore onto the loading dock, then led the team around the building to the stable. Rig was there, and perked his ears when he saw him. "How you doing, boy? Huh?"

Gage walked over and smelled it before he saw the stink of manure and urine in the horse's stall. He'd not been let out once, as Delano had promised. "Why would I even believe him?" muttered Gage. He patted the horse's neck, stroked his muzzle, and said, "I have to tend these two chums, and then I'll be back. We'll get you out of here. All right?"

"You busy, boy?" said a voice behind him. Gage spun, his left hand reaching, only to find nothing there but the handle of his hip knife.

The man, silhouetted against the open doorway, laughed—a wet, craggy sound. Gage suspected it was Trigg or Axel. They were similar in stature and appearance and sound. Both braying, coarse men. If he didn't know they worked for Delano, he'd guess they did. Same type of character.

"Matter of fact, I am," said Gage, straightening and walking toward the man.

Trigg, he thought it was. He seemed to recall when they'd been pointed out to him by Delano that Trigg had been the one with no hat covering a head of greasy, stringy hair the color of mud. He also smelled as if he hadn't washed in a good, long while.

"You'll excuse me, I have to tend to these horses."

"Aw, no rush. They ain't going nowhere. Here, I wanna talk to you. You're the new fella, ain't you?"

This must have been Trigg's way of trying to be chummy.

"Yep."

"So, where you been at?"

"I just got back from a run up to Clabberville." Gage suspected the man knew this already.

"Oh yeah, that's right. You got stuck with that one. Ha! Me and Axel took bets on if the boss man was going to make us do that awful run or what. Lucky you come along. We'd still be up there, I reckon, fighting rocks and who knows what else. That's one nasty place to get to."

Gage shrugged. "No difference to me. Work is work. As long as I get paid, I don't mind."

"Paid, ha! You'll be lucky if you see much of that pay you're expecting. Ol' Delano, he's tighter than a spinster's mouth!"

His braying guffaw was annoying, but the information he was relating set Gage's teeth together. "Why's that?"

"Well, 'cause—"

"Yes, Trigg, do tell us, why it is that I am, how did you put it? 'Tighter than a spinster's mouth'?"

Trigg spun and saw Delano leaning against the doorframe, arms folded. "Oh, boss, I was only funnin'."

"Yes, I know, Trigg. Now go finish getting the other wagon ready, will you? And tell Axel to lay off the liquor until you're out of my sight. I have a little chore for you two to do before you lurch on out of here in the morning."

"Yes, sir." Trigg slumped his shoulders and took small steps as he slunk by his boss. Delano watched him walk by.

Gage followed, at his own pace, and not cowed in the least. Delano eyed him as he walked by; then Gage paused. "As far as my pay goes, we agreed before I made the run that you'd pay me on my return."

"Yep, we did. But I did not say how soon after you returned."

Gage's eyebrows rose.

"You ain't taken care of my horses yet, have you? That's part of the deal, in my opinion. And as I am the boss, my opinion is the only one worth hearing. You get me?"

Gage shook his head and continued on toward the horses. He unhitched them, and when he looked up again, Delano was nowhere to be seen. He put away the tack and rubbed down the once-skittery horses with sacking. Soon after, he doled out ample feed to the team, and then some.

They'd more than earned it, considering the work they'd put in on the run up to Clabberville and back. The longer he stayed in Newel, the smellier everything seemed. Delano was vermin, and Jon knew it before he signed on with him. Gage knew it was nobody's but his own blamed fault.

As he rubbed down the tack, something he suspected had not been done in a long, ol' time, Gage mused on the fact that his life had largely been one of poor decisions, one after another. Ridiculous that he kept on doing that, landing himself in situations such as this.

"Time to think harder, Gage," he told himself, sighing. First things first—he'd endure this fool a bit longer, get paid, and then get on out of here. Whatever problems the people of this town had with Delano and whoever else, it was their own fault for letting him run ramrod over them.

As for himself, Jonathan Gage figured with another run, maybe two, he'd have earned just enough cash money to outfit himself with a meager poke. And maybe with careful spending, it would be enough to buy him the winter clothes he needed, the food, and a small assortment of the traps and other bits he'd need to try his hand at winter trapping up in the high country.

Maybe he'd find himself an abandoned trapper's cabin nobody needed for a few months, lay in some wood, make some meat, and call it good. That would be all right with him. He'd had enough of civilization anyway. Plenty, and then some.

Gage finished tending to the tack, then checked again that the horse team was in decent flesh after their foray into the hills. He fed them more hay, and headed for the front door once more. He made his way around to the warehouse and set to work untying and then lugging in the remainder of the load.

It took him the better part of an hour to shift it all into the dimly lit warehouse. When he was finished, he drank a few swallows of water from his canteen, then splashed and rinsed off his face, arms, neck, and hands.

It was a quiet afternoon, no human sounds, save for the random squeaks of a wagon wheel passing in the street. To the west, a somewhat-steady *ring-ring-ring* on the air told everyone in town that though they may all be tired from their day's efforts, the smithy was not. He was also not a man to trifle with, should anyone be fool enough to try their luck at doing so.

Gage had seen the man as he'd ridden in. He was a large, bulky Black man, with a long, ragged-edged scar that began atop his crown and led down over his left eye. It continued beneath the eye, then down the cheek, and faded beside his chin.

Nobody had ever asked him what had happened, but that didn't mean that Gage suspected everyone in town wasn't curious. So, what? The man had nodded and smiled and from the poorly spelled rate sign out front, he didn't charge much money for his services. And Gage had seen a few examples of the man's work, and it had looked to be among the finest he had seen in some time.

On this day, Gage surveyed the length of the nearly empty street. He had learned it was this way because a good amount of the folks in Newel didn't live in town, but were miners who didn't mind tramping on in, in the morning, or for a noon meal. And especially in the evenings to drink.

The rest of the town seemed to like to nap in the afternoon, or hole up and enjoy a beer or three in the heat of the day. Gage suspected that even though the cooler weather had arrived, they still followed that summer routine.

He led Rig, with his saddle and other gear draped

atop the horse and lashed down lightly. The stable he'd seen the day he'd arrived wasn't far on up the street. When he knocked on the big double doors and shouted, "Hello? Anybody in?" nobody answered.

He spied a number of empty stalls to the right, just before a second set of double doors at the rear of the barn, which led to a paddock. He tied Rig in one of the stalls for the time being, unburdened him of the saddle and other tack, and hoisted it to rest on a rack alongside the stall.

Just about then, he heard a long, luxurious yawn rise up from the dark to his back. He turned to see an old man emerge from a small doorway. The room beyond was boxed off, with a window hole looking in on the barn.

The old-timer smiled and wagged a thumb over his shoulder toward the room behind him. "Yep, yonder's where I sleep, eat, read books, and drink, too, if I've a mind."

"I'm sorry if I woke you."

"Why? It's my place, ain't it? And you just showed up with your horse. Works for me."

Gage nodded. "Fair enough. I'd like to stable my horse here for a spell. I can pay, of course."

"Of course." The old man nodded.

"I want to make certain he gets a good feed. Maybe a rubdown and time outdoors. He gets along with most other horses."

The old man nodded. "What's his name?" He stepped into the stall and smoothed his hands along Rig's neck and back. "Good fella, good boy. Handsome, ain't you? I got the same trouble myself."

"He's called Rig."

Again the man nodded. "Good name. Rates are on the placard yonder." He aimed with a jerk of his head toward a wall behind them. Gage walked over and read them, nodding. "Sounds fine and fair to me."

"You get along with your horse?"

The question was an odd one, unexpected, and it took Gage a moment to think of a response. "Yes, I suppose I do. Why?"

The old man shrugged. "Seemed like it, though you'd be surprised how some men will ride a horse for years and not get to know them. Strange way to live, if you ask me. I spend that much time with a critter, man or otherwise, I'd sure like to chat now and again. You know?"

Gage nodded. "I do. As much time and as many hours and days and weeks and years as we've put in together, I think I know Rig pretty well. Guess that means he knows me, too."

"Oh, you bet he does. Horses are among your smarter animals, I tell you true."

Gage had to smile at the man's emphatic manner. "I won't argue that point, mister."

"Call me Charles. It ain't my name, but it's what I answer to." He bent over with a wheezy little laugh and Gage smiled a bit more, nodding. "All right, Charles. You can call me Gage."

"Fair enough. Now, as I say, if you want, you're welcome to hole up here and bunk in with the horse, seeing as how you two get along and all. I got no problem with that. Also ain't got many horses in my care at the moment."

"I appreciate that. I think I will take you up on the offer. I'm between runs, but I don't know when the next one's coming, or if there will be another."

"'Runs'? You a freighter, by chance?"

Gage nodded, noted the man's hesitancy.

"For Delano?" He said it with care, but Gage could tell that to the man, the word was like a hot coal in his mouth.

"Yep."

The old man stepped backward once, and looked Gage up and down. "You don't look like a fool, but then again, I don't much know you yet."

Gage grinned. "I could say the same. And you're not the first person I've met to have that response when my employer's name's mentioned."

"And for good reason, too." The old man squinted and moved closer. "Why'd you do that to yourself? And willingly?"

Gage shrugged. "I needed the work and didn't know much about his reputation before."

"Well, good luck, Gage. You have my sympathy. Just you be careful. He chews up folks and spits them out as if they tasted like poison to him. The only thing he likes is money, and he will do anything to get more of it. *Anything.*"

Gage nodded. "Thank you, I understand. And hopefully, it won't be for long. I have plans."

"Good, and the sooner you get on out of here, the longer you'll live."

Gage tidied the rest of his gear. "Okay if I bunk down right here?" It was a spot just outside Rig's stall in soft hay.

"Sure, sure. Grab yourself a few of them saddle blankets from the rack by the door if you get cold. My bones tell me it's fixing to be an early winter."

"Thanks, I appreciate it. Well, I thought I'd go scare up some food, then get back to the depot, see what Delano has in store for me."

"Only food you'll find this time of day is at the Big Strike Saloon. You can get bread and cheese and soup. Gerty, at the tent by the end of the street, she ain't serving now. Not until four or so. She'll be working to get ready for the supper folks."

"I met her when I first got to town. Best stew and dumplings I've ever had."

Charles nodded. "Truer words ain't never passed the lips of a man before. She's a wonder in the kitchen. Newel's lucky to have her."

Gage touched his hat brim. "Thank you, Charles. I'll see you later."

The old man had already turned and made for the feed. "Yep. I'll be here. Always am. Except when I'm not!" He worked up one of those wheezing laughs and kept it up as Gage left.

He stood outside in the full light of the afternoon and reacquainted himself with Newel's main street. He finally located the Big Strike. Its demure sign topped the porch of a two-story building that sat across the street, catty-corner, from Delano's depot.

"Convenient," he said, making for the other side of the street.

He looked to his left as he stepped up onto the board-walk and into the shade. Down the street, on his side, he spied a thin, shapely woman with dark hair done up atop her head. She stood on a depot loading dock in the sunlight, her eyes closed, her hands on her hips. She arched her back, stretching, rolling her head slowly on her shoulders. She wore a long, printed blue calico dress and a work apron. Over her shoulders, she wore a cream shawl.

Gage stood watching her, forgetting that he was intruding on what was obvious to him to be a private moment, as if she were taking a break from whatever work she'd been at. Then she turned to walk back into the depot and saw him watching her. She stopped and stared at him, then pulled her shawl tight and hustled on in and away from his sight.

He felt bad about being seen, as if he had been a child caught nipping hot cookies off the table. But not that bad. She was a beautiful woman, that much he saw, even from a distance of what must have been one hundred or more feet, and he wondered if she might be Shierson's widow, given the fact that she'd stood on the dock of the very building he knew was occupied by the town's other freighting outfit.

He mused on this as he strolled down the boardwalk toward the saloon.

Inside, he let his eyes adjust to the light and eyed the room. There were a half-dozen men throughout the space, including the barkeep. Several occupied tables, one man by himself and two others seated together.

Given the empty bowls and coffee cups, they appeared to be finished eating and were playing cards in a carefree way. Gage saw no money on the table.

The man by himself sat toward the back of the room, spooning in soup and dunking bread in the bowl, too.

He looked to be in no hurry, but he concentrated on the task without looking up. The lighting was dim, but he seemed familiar to Gage.

Two men stood at the bar, down at the far end, and he recognized them as Trigg and Axel. When he walked in, they looked his way, as did the bartender and the two men playing cards.

Gage took off his hat and leaned on the near end of the bar. The bartender walked down from chatting with the two men. Gage set the hat atop the bar and smiled. "Afternoon. Any chance I can get something to eat?"

The man did not offer a full smile at him, but appeared to want to try one. He took his time in replying, and finally he said, "Yeah. We got soup, bread, cheese. Cheese is a little off, but it don't seem to slow up folks much from eating it."

Gage nodded. "I'll have soup and bread, please. And a glass of beer when you get the chance."

"Yeah." The barkeep took his big, bulky, brooding self back down the bar and resumed talking with Trigg and Axel.

He kept this up for a good minute before Gage said, "Any chance I can get that food today?"

Everyone in the place looked at him then. He didn't need to look around to know. Having all eyes in an establishment stare at him was a feeling he'd become familiar with. *But, man,* he thought, *I am hungry.*

Once more, the man said, "Yeah," and moved off, disappearing into a back room.

As soon as he did so, Axel scooted around the end of the bar, tiptoeing as if he might make too much noise otherwise, and snatched up a nearby half bottle of rye.

He giggled, and so did Trigg as Axel handed it to him. Axel stuffed it into his coat pocket. Axel resumed his place at the bar and looked at Gage.

"He's a friend of ours."

"Then why steal from him?" said Gage.

The wet-eyed glares he received in reply confirmed what he suspected—these two were well on their way to be liquored up and they needed to be given a wide cut around, or else he'd find himself in a fight with two large, drunk men. Not good odds, even if he was sober.

Trigg looked as if he wanted to respond, but the bartender swung back in through the door, a deep bowl filled with steaming soup in one hand and a plate on which sat two thick slices of bread, as well as a hunk of hard-looking cheese.

The man set the food before Gage and actually attempted a smile.

"That looks good, thank you," said Gage.

"Yeah, my wife, she's a decent cook, all right." He smacked his ample gut and grinned.

"Um, do you have a spoon?"

"Oh yeah, sorry." The bartender rummaged in the pocket of his apron and pulled out a spoon and a wadded napkin. He smoothed it and set the spoon on it and slid it toward Gage. "I'll get that beer."

"You know, on second thought, I'd prefer coffee, if you have any on the boil."

"Sure do. That's all I drink these days." He leaned toward Gage. "Liquor made me do a whole mess of dumb things I still don't quite recall."

"Yeah!" barked Axel. "Like buying a saloon!"

That set the two fools braying like donkeys. The bartender rolled his eyes and turned to Trigg and Axel. "No, worst of them all is chumming up to the likes of you two."

Trigg set his jaw. "Just so you don't forget who it is we work for. You hear?"

Though it appeared to pain him to do so, the bartender nodded. "Yeah, yeah, yeah. I hear you."

Just then, the man seated by himself eating at the back of the room got up, his chair squawking a pinch as he shoved it back. He made for the back door, a painted sign reading GENTLEMEN, with a pointing finger, told Gage the man might not be done with his meal.

As soon as the door closed behind the man, Trigg and Axel whispered together, heads bent close. Gage heard bits of words: "him" and "Delano said" and what sounded like "once and for all."

Gage spooned in the thick soup, not as toothsome a hot dish as that made by the woman from his first day in town, but pretty tasty, nonetheless.

He eyed the two men as they knocked back the last of their drinks, then shoved away from the bar and weaved their way toward the back door, giggling and whispering together. Axel, behind, flexed his big ham hands as if in anticipation of using them for some sort of labor.

Gage looked to the bartender, but the man was busying himself tidying bottles that didn't need it. He kept glancing toward the back door, then to his work.

"What are they up to out there?" said Gage.

"Huh? Oh, them two? Nah, they're . . . I can't say."

"Can't or won't?" Gage stood and wiped his mouth on the napkin.

As he neared the back door, the bartender said, "It ain't as easy as you think."

Gage nodded, thinking something about Delano and the barman being beholden to him. He opened the door and found himself on a small landing half stacked with crates. But it was the commotion down the three steps and to his left that caught his attention.

What he saw in the few moments that he paused to take in the scene was the backs of Trigg and Axel hunched over something, their arms driving alternately down as if they were pistons. Gage caught a glimpse of the object of their attention. It was the lone dining man from inside, as Gage knew it would be.

The man was down on the packed earth, his arms jerking, slapping, trying to get a purchase on his attackers. He was not having any luck.

Beyond them, the outhouse door swung open, then closed, then opened again, as the man's milling arms struck it in his frantic efforts.

Gage bounded down the steps and tapped the two hunched men on the shoulders. "Hey," he said, stepping back enough so that if they swung around on him unexpectedly—and anything a drunkard did was unexpected—he might avoid a raking fist to the face or chest.

His tapping did not hinder them. He tried it again, with more forceful digs of his fingertips. They both paused and looked at him.

"What?" said Trigg, his face a mask of savage glee. Axel looked much the same, and was breathing harder.

"I'm trying to get to the outhouse," said Gage.

"You joking me?" said Axel.

"We're busy." Axel looked at his companion. "What did Mr. Delano call it? 'Eliminating the competition'!"

"That's right," said Trigg. "Now get outta here, Gage!"

During the interruption, the man they were pummeling had tried to scoot away on his backside, but Axel had his shirtfront grasped tight in a big ham hand. For the first time, Gage got a good look at their victim and he was startled to see that he recognized the man.

It was the old fellow who'd talked to him that first day as Gage had ridden into town. Gage recognized the ample beard, now blood-matted, the crimson shirt, and the buckskin trousers. As to the man's distinctive black hat with the feather in the band, it lay crown down by the latrine, probably where they had grabbed him.

No matter who it was, this lopsided pummeling would not stand.

He stuck out his left leg behind Trigg as the men resumed beating down on the shouting older fellow.

At the same time, Gage snatched Trigg's collar and jerked him backward so that he fell over Gage's leg, then landed on his back with a hard thud. He was stunned for a moment, long enough for Gage to dole out much the same maneuver to Axel.

Axel, the larger of the two fools, went down harder, and seemed content for a few moments, at least, to stay that way.

Gage glanced at the old man again, and saw that his face was bloodied and already swelling. He was trying to roll away, but one of his arms stuck out at an odd angle. Then Trigg was on Gage and he had all he could do to keep away from the brute's big, swinging fists.

Gage bent low and drove forward, delivering a solid blow straight into the man's paunch. It was like hitting a sack of meal, and the owner of that sack wheezed and folded forward. Gage smelled the rank stink of whiskey and sweat and raw-man stink, and he sneered as he readied himself to dole out another blow.

Trigg's big face swung down at just the right angle for Gage to deliver a hard, sharp left to the side of Trigg's head.

Trigg groaned again and pitched to his left, landing on one knee that did not hold him.

Gage watched him a moment too long, because behind him Axel, still ground-bound, wrapped his arms around Gage's legs and upended him. Gage spun as he dropped and managed to land on his backside, though his elbows slammed hard against the hard-packed latrine path.

Jags of hot pain lanced through both upper arms, and his teeth came together hard. Dazed, he was late in reacting to Axel's renewed attack. But not late enough to let the big brute overpower him.

Gage shook his head and raised his arms as Axel, up on his knees, raised his clasped fists high, prepping to bring them downward toward Gage's bent head.

"Look out!"

The voice was garbled, wet with blood, but clear enough and loud enough for Gage to hear. He canted his head to the left, caught sight of what was about to drive down on him, and shoved to his right.

The blow smacked the ribs on his left side. The old wound felt as if it had exploded and burned anew with a blazing fire. It hurt more than anything Gage could recall in recent years, but it also served to snap him out of his daze. He rolled, gained momentum, and jerked himself to his feet as Axel, drunk and riled and growling, struggled to shove back to his knees. He was too late.

Gage drove a hard left fist straight into Axel's right temple and the fool wheezed, then collapsed in a heap face-first in the dirt. Chest heaving, Gage looked at the three men on the ground before him. He grunted, staggered sideways a step, then righted himself.

"Hey," he said, "you okay?"

The victim of Trigg and Axel lay on the ground, on his back. His chest moved up and down, so Gage knew he wasn't dead, but he sure looked like he would be soon.

"If . . ." said the old man; then he licked his lips and began again. "If you're talking to me, well, no, I ain't okay. But then again"—he cracked open his eyes and Gage thought he saw a thin smile beginning on the man's bloodied face—"there's folks who say I ain't been right for some time now."

"I recognize you," said Gage, bending down to the man's side. He had to hold still a moment while his head swam.

"We met a few days back when you rode in. I was the welcoming brigade."

"Yes," said Gage. " '*Newel* rhymes with *jewel*.' "

"That's me."

"Let's get going." Gage eyed the other men. "These

two won't stay out forever. And I don't think I can go through that twice."

"Me neither. Help me up."

Gage stood himself, bent at the waist, and fought through gritted teeth to steady the spinning in his head. Then he grasped the old man's raised left arm and lifted.

The man hissed and groaned as he was raised up by Gage, who got an arm behind him and steadied him.

"I'll get you back inside."

"No! No, not in there. Take me to the depot. Shierson's, not that other one. And go behind the buildings, down the path yonder, behind that shed."

Gage hesitated a moment. He had to pay his lunch bill, but as he thought it, as if reading his mind, a voice behind him said, "Go, do as he says. I'll take care of these two."

Gage looked up to see the bartender. He held a bucket of water. "I won't dump it on their sorry hides until you two are good and gone."

"My lunch. I didn't pay you," said Gage.

"No worry there. Neither of you owes me a thing. Just take care of Cooley. This here ain't right. And it's that blasted Delano's doing."

Gage nodded and helped the old man to turn. The gent took a few steps, then leaned against Gage's arm. "Hold a moment, hold on."

"You're in no shape to walk. Lean back."

"All right, all right, but fetch my topper, will you? Ain't fitting for a man to be out of doors without a hat on his pate."

The barkeep shook his head as he retrieved the

man's hat from the dirt by the latrine and set it on Cooley's head.

Gage bent and lifted the codger as if carrying a napping child. The old man's useless right arm hung and swung. The man's face went gray and his eyes widened.

Gage reached quickly over the man's bloodied tunic and lifted the battered limb by the sleeve, laying it atop the old man's gut.

The codger didn't make it to the back fence before he passed out. Gage saw he was still breathing and did his best to move doubly fast to his left, toward the depot the old man had said.

It took but a minute or so before he saw it ahead, the back side of the very depot where he had, not too much earlier, seen the pretty woman in the sunlight out front. Two unused freight wagons sat parked neatly, side by side, and a paddock beyond hosted four stout horses eating hay.

About then, the old man came around. He leaned his head up a bit. "That's it. Up them steps. Mrs. Shierson will be in there working. Shout for her, she'll come."

Gage reached the steps and though the old man was light, he'd taken a beating himself and raising his boots to each of the six or so steps to the landing took extra effort.

He didn't have to shout because the mysterious Mrs. Shierson emerged from inside the darkened building and looked at them, her eyes wide. Gage saw that she was, indeed, the pretty woman he'd seen earlier.

"What has happened to Mr. Cooley?" Her words were directed at Gage, but her eyes were on the old man. Already she was stepping aside and pointing in-side to the warehouse. Gage carried the once-more un-conscious man in and found himself in a well-lit space. The timbers glowed honey colored from the two oil lamps hanging on arms jutting low from beams.

The place was not like any depot he'd ever been in—it was, for one thing, nearly empty. And for another, it was spotless. He saw no dirt or debris on the plank floor and no cobwebs spanning the spaces between beams. The double doors at the front were open wide and the afternoon light lit much of the rest of the space.

Behind him, the woman swung open an identical pair of big doors leading to the rear dock. "Put him on that table and help me tug off his boots."

"Yes, ma'am." He did as she bade him and then stood back as she shoved him to the side. She fluttered about the still form of the old man, washing his face, tending his wounds and bruises with a mint-smelling lotion from a squat jar.

Then she groped his right arm. "This is broken, but the bone doesn't appear to have moved. I'll need to wrap it tight and put it in a sling so he doesn't injure it further before it has time to mend."

Gage watched her the entire time, standing about eight feet away, but ready to assist, should she ask. He knew it was wrong, but he could not keep his eyes from her. Up close, everything about her confirmed what he had seen and suspected from a distance earlier when he'd seen her stretching and taking in the after-noon sun on the front loading dock. Before she had seen him, withering and embarrassing him.

As she finished tending the still-sleeping or unconscious old man, she spoke. "Am I to assume that you, sir, are Mr. Cooley's savior?"

"I wouldn't go so far as to say that, ma'am," said Gage, his dry voice cracking. "I happened to be there when he needed a hand."

"Judging from the abuse he withstood, it would seem to me that you could have lent that hand sooner." She looked at him with an arched eyebrow.

Once again, she withered him and he felt like a schoolboy. "Yes, ma'am."

She looked him up and down. "You appear to have taken a drubbing yourself. Sit down over there by the woodstove."

"No, ma'am. I'm fine. I should be going."

"Nonsense. Sit." She pointed toward a straight-back chair by the fire. Beside it, he saw a small table with a book and an unfinished knitted garment in blue. Threads of yarn trailed from it to a basket on the floor holding a ball of yarn with needles stuck in it.

She poured hot water into a bowl and fetched a clean scrap of cloth from a shelf. As if reading his mind, she said, "This depot is my home, hence the personal items."

He didn't know what to say, so he kept his mouth closed. She approached with the hot water and rag, dipped it, wrung it out, and said, "Tilt your head to the left." Then she grunted and retrieved the nearest lamp and set it on the little table. "That's better."

She dabbed at his own bloodied, bruised face and he winced.

"Oh, please," she said, her face close by his as she

squinted in the low light to tend him. "It's not that bad. Honestly, men," and then she grew silent.

He wanted to laugh, but she didn't seem to be in the mood for such a reaction. Still, he couldn't help himself and smiled.

"Do I amuse you?" she said.

He didn't respond for a long moment, because just then, her breath touched his face. He closed his eyes and let her continue dabbing him and applying her minty ointment to his burgeoning bruises. It had been so long, far too long, since he'd been this close to a beautiful woman.

A moment later, he realized she had finished. She cleared her throat and he glanced to his right and saw that she was staring at him.

"Are you quite comfortable, mister?"

"Yes, ma'am. Oh, I mean, no, ma'am."

He made to rise, but she shook her head. "Sit still." She moved to the shelves again and retrieved a teapot. "Time for tea. You will take a cup, mister?"

"Yes, ma'am. Thank you. And the name is Gage."

"First, last, or only?"

"Oh, last. It's . . . Jay. Jay Gage."

He did not know why he lied to her. He rarely referred to his given name anymore these days, but he had felt the need to answer her question. Still, he hadn't really lied, he told himself. Plenty of people went by their first initial, and the name Jay could be construed as that, sure.

"Pleased to meet you, Mr. Gage. I am Mrs. Shierson."

"Ma'am," he said, reaching to touch his hat brim. It was then he noted he had failed to retrieve his own hat from the fight. No, that wasn't true, he didn't think he'd worn it out there. Perhaps it was still in the bar.

He told himself he'd stop in there later, when he went back to Delano's. The thought of that man made him cold right away and he shook off the feeling.

"Perhaps you were hit harder in the head than you think, Mr. Gage." He saw her smirk as she poured hot water from the gray enamel kettle into the brown teapot. Within moments, he smelled the tea, a warm, nutty scent that filled the air between them.

She carried a chair over to the other side of the stove. Though it had been a warm afternoon, the day was waning and the season's coldness had crept in. The stove's warmth felt good to Gage. She handed him a fancy china teacup on a saucer and he held it in one palm and steadied it with the other. It rattled, nonetheless. She smiled, likely at his awkwardness, and carried a cup and saucer to her seat and sat down.

They both sipped, though he waited for her to do so first, uncertain of himself in the presence of a refined woman. He was afraid he might do something wrong, or unintentionally damage her cup and saucer. It looked so small in his hand.

She gazed at the still-sleeping Mr. Cooley.

A sudden thought came to him and he was afraid she might ask who it was who attacked the man. So far, oddly, she hadn't, and he did not want her to.

"Is he a relative of yours, ma'am?"

"Mr. Cooley? Heavens no, but he might as well be.

He's very dear to me and has helped me through some recent difficult times."

"I see." He nodded and sipped his tea. He did not know what else to say, not being overly chatty anyway. He had always figured that he was better off holding his tongue than blathering on without a thought as to what he was saying, as so many folks seemed to do.

And then he did know of something to say. He cleared his throat. "Ma'am."

"Mrs. Shierson, please."

"Yes, Mrs. Shierson. Do you think he'll be all right? I ask because he took some hard knocks to his head."

She sighed. "I don't know, Mr. Gage. I certainly hope so. The arm should mend. The cuts and bruises, the same. But inside his head? Time will tell all, as a wise person once said."

"I believe that was me," said a feeble voice from the dimly lit table.

She got up and went to the old man's side. "Mr. Cooley. I am relieved you are once more with us. And no, the wise person I spoke of was not you. But I'll grant you it is something you may well have uttered at one time or another."

Gage stood, setting the cup and saucer, which he had emptied, down on the small table beside the chair. He joined them at the table. The old man looked up at him. "You! Oh, now I recall. Them two what beat on me. Yep, that's right. They was Delano's men."

Gage glanced at the woman. She held her face rigid, but he saw her cheek muscles bunch and flex. And he knew why, if what Gerty had said had been correct.

But as bad as Delano was, and Gage knew the man was a stunted seed, there had to be more to it than that. A fellow didn't just ride all over an entire town, not without some resistance.

And then he bet he knew—it had been this woman and her husband who had provided that resistance in Newel. And in addition to owning the only local competitive business, they were unafraid to call out the man for what he was.

Trouble with that, thought Gage as he watched her, was that they not only made Delano even more of an enemy than he might have been, though that was unlikely, but they also caused a rift between them and some of the townsfolk. Likely, they were the residents who were looking for the paying work that Delano promised, which, Gage guessed, he surely did in every town into which he intruded.

"I suspected as much. But as Mr. Gage is a newcomer to town, I didn't want to burden him with smut and gossip. Patrick Delano will get his comeuppance someday."

"Well, don't hold it against him, Mrs. Shierson."

"Who?" she said. "Delano?"

"No," said Cooley, waving a feeble few fingers at Gage. "This fella here. A man has to take work where he can get it these days. Don't mean he's a polecat. Though I will say, mister, that if you lay down with dogs, you'll most often than not wake up with fleas. So mind how you go with that mangy cur." Cooley winked at him.

The woman looked at Gage, her brown eyes harder than they had been since he'd brought Cooley in. "Is what Mr. Cooley says true, Mr. Gage? Are you in the employ of that . . . of Patrick Delano?" She did not suppress the sneer on her pretty mouth.

He pulled in a deep breath through his nose and nodded. "Yes, ma'am. But I can assure you, I am not of his mind—"

Redness rose up from her collar and colored her cheeks. Her nostrils flared and her eyes narrowed. In an even, but hard, cold voice, she said, "I ask you to please leave my place of business, Mr. Gage. *Now.*"

"But, ma'am, if you'd listen—"

"Wait, hold on there, Mrs. Shierson," said Cooley, rising up on his one good elbow, wincing with the effort.

She pointed a finger at him and it nearly touched his nose. "No, Mr. Cooley. You be quiet. You have no say in this matter."

"I guess the heck I do!"

"Quiet!" she said again, her voice truly raised for the first time that Gage had heard. He did not think it was something to which she was accustomed.

He saw fear and anger and exhaustion warring for dominance on her pretty face. She would shout at him next and he didn't want to vex her further.

"All right, ma'am," said Gage. "I'm sorry to have troubled you."

He walked out the open front doors and into the sunshine on the loading dock, and kept going, crossing over to the short run of steps off to the side. He felt his face heat up, and though he knew he had done no real wrong, he sure felt as if he'd just killed a kitten right in front of her.

What he really wanted to do was fetch his horse and ride out of this little town of Newel, and never return. But what he knew he had to do was go see Delano, draw his tainted pay from the cursed man, and then head on out. Or something along those lines. He wasn't quite certain what to do yet.

Despite all the filth that a man such as Patrick Delano brought to the situation, Gage liked the town. He was certain it had something to do with the fact that the widow he'd just met was a comely thing, sure. But more than that, she had been wronged, was still being wronged, and that did not sit well with him. Especially not when she regarded him as part of the problem.

He walked as smoothly as he could down the boardwalk, past the handful of folks who'd come out to shop or stroll from one place to another along the main street. But each step reminded him that he'd had a beating, and he wasn't twenty years old anymore. He'd take some days to feel right again.

Poor old Cooley, he thought. For all the man's bluster, he was an old-timer and had been savaged quite badly. He was the one who would need a good many days, weeks, perhaps months, before he was anything close to his usual wiry self again. Gage silently wished the old man luck.

To his left, he saw the bar he'd had lunch in and decided to stop in for his hat. He opened the door, keeping an eye for any movement close by, in case Trigg and Axel were waiting for him.

"Come on in. Nobody else in here, mister. Got your hat on the counter."

Despite what the barkeep said, as Gage entered, he kept up his caution. But it appeared the two sidewinders were nowhere in sight.

"Thanks," he said, lifting his hat from the bar, just where he'd left it. His lunch was gone, but he wasn't hungry anymore anyway.

He pulled out a couple of coins and laid them on the bar. "For the lunch."

"No, I told you not to worry about that. Me and Cooley, we go way back. He's a good sort. I didn't know they were going to go that far, see."

"But why put up with them at all?"

"Well, they're not actually my friends, just so you know. They're, well, it . . ."

"Has to do with Patrick Delano?" finished Gage.

The bartender nodded. "Yeah. He owns a stake in the bar. Made business tight when he moved into town and disrupted everything. Then he went around the region, offering to buy in here and there, said he was bringing in all manner of new workers. Said Newel was going to be 'a hub of commerce.'" The man nodded. "Yes, sir, those are his exact words."

"But it hasn't worked out that way."

"No." The big-bellied bartender chuckled. "Not by half." He leaned forward and spoke in a low tone. "I think ol' Delano's having troubles of his own. I think money's not so good for him, as it used to be. Talk is, there's been trouble dogging him from other towns and he's running out of places to run to. Everybody knows him and what he really is."

Gage nodded. "A man's past has a way of catching

up with him. It's the one thing you can't outrun in life. Maybe not even in death."

"Sounds like you're speaking from experience."

Gage looked up at the man. "Oh, me? Well, sure, sure." He turned toward the door. "What man hasn't done things he wished he could change."

He kept on going, still uncertain what he was going to do, but knowing more than he did a couple of minutes before.

Chapter 14

"You what?" The portly little man looked up from his desk. "I must be getting hard of hearing. Say that again."

Gage sighed. Games, he was tired of games. "I said I want my pay for services rendered. Then I'm done working for you."

"Oh." A thin grin spread across Delano's face. The man stood and walked around the desk, his thumbs hooked in his braces. "Oh, I see what's happened. You're taken with the pretty little widow woman. Uh-huh, I see it all clear now! Clear as a fresh-washed windowpane!"

Gage regarded the man a moment.

"Yep, that's just what's happened. Well, I'll tell you a thing or two about that woman, Gage. She's a two-bit floozy who's shacked up with the old fool Cooley. Why, he's old enough to be her pa!" He offered up a fake snort and smacked his thigh.

"You're an idiot, Delano."

That pulled the false smile from the man's face.

"Now you look here!" He walked toward Gage, with a pudgy index finger trained on him. "You got no call to up and leave my employment! Why, you've barely begun as a freighter! I've hardly taught you what you need to know about this business. What you don't know is that Delano Freight is perched right on the edge of making a fortune off these rubes in town and their fool friends in the hills! Won't take long at all."

He fidgeted, spittle flecked his lips, and his eyes shone as he mused and warmed to his subject—a topic, Gage had learned, that was more important to the man than any other. It was money, and Patrick Delano's ability to procure it, by any means necessary.

"Why, you saw those poor backward folks up in the hills at Clabberville. They're sending their hard-dug gold on down with us. Trusted me with their earnings—can you imagine?"

He leaned forward, a piggy little smile on his face. In a lowered voice, he said, "I peel some off the top, purely for the extra work and trouble they have caused me, and nobody's the wiser. You get me?"

It was all Gage needed to hear, if only to verify his decision. "First off, you can't teach me a cursed thing about freighting. I've done more real freighting work than you have, I reckon. Secondly, if I hear those folks from Clabberville have been cheated out of their money, I'll hold you responsible and I will get all the missing cash from you, coin by coin, nugget by nugget, flake of dust by flake of dust. You hear me?

"If you're having a tough time with your financial situation, that is a problem of your own making. And not one I care a bit about. And if I hear you are responsible for harming Widow Shierson or Mr. Cooley or anyone else in or out of this town, by your own self, if you can muster the strength to lift a fist, or if you hire those other idiots of yours, Trigg and Axel, no matter— you'll answer to me, you hear?"

Delano glared and stared and grew redder, but he did not respond.

"And lastly? Lastly you better dig deep and find that money you owe me. I'm not leaving until you do." He stood tall, arms folded, and stared as Delano squirmed like a live moth pinned to a specimen board.

"I demand . . . a reason!"

Gage advanced on him and snatched him by the shirtfront. He must have grabbed chest hairs, too, because the pudgy man flailed and shrieked, clawing at Gage's hand, but Gage was taller and wider and fitter and younger than Delano. *And,* thought Gage, *I'm right.*

He didn't try to lift the man, as that would not have worked and made him look foolish, but he did back the man fast, slamming the back of his legs against the front edge of the desk.

Delano yelped and yipped as Gage tipped him backward, guiding his every action with a viselike grip on Delano's front.

The man wore a shirt, a long underwear inner shirt, and a wool coat. Plenty to grab. And Delano, try as he might, could not do more than flail as if he were a crab on its back on the beach.

"You useless weasel," growled Gage. "You pay me what we agreed on and I won't peel your fingernails off, one at a time, with my sheath knife."

That elicited a yelp from Delano, and the little annoying man nodded once.

"Was that a nod of agreement?"

The pudgy man nodded again. "Yeah, yeah."

"Good." Gage dragged him back upright and marched him, backward, until he hit the chair, then shoved him hard into it. "Now spin around in that chair of yours and open your safe and get me my money."

It took the man a few scant moments to produce the agreed-upon amount. He shoved his way around the desk and faced Gage.

"Now get out of my way." He did not wait for Delano to move, but pushed past him, sending the chunky man stumbling backward. He sputtered and slammed into a tottering stack of empty nail kegs. They wobbled and toppled, but Delano managed to stay upright and he growled as he surged forward.

As Gage reached the top step, he saw Trigg and Axel emerge from the shadows behind Delano. This seemed to puff the man's annoyance and he shouted, "Nobody quits on Patrick Delano!"

Gage stopped and eyed the man for a moment. What he saw was a sagging, red-faced man with a gut and soft pink hands and eyes that bugged out as he gritted his teeth and growled.

"Nobody!" Delano yelled.

"Yeah?" said Gage, not bothering to suppress his smile. "Well, there's always a first time, Mr. Patrick Delano."

Gage didn't look back, but he did hear the various blue parting words that Delano uttered, now that he was somewhat assured that the big, brooding man had left him for good. Plus, he had Trigg and Axel by his side.

Delano looked at them, both aching from hangovers that had visited them far too early, for they were surely still inebriated and suffering, if looks were to be believed, from ailments far worse than what booze might induce in a man.

"What ails you two? Why are you so bruised up? And how did Gage know so much about Cooley? He came in here blaming me, and convinced I was the mastermind of such a lie! Can you imagine?" Delano shook his head as if he actually believed he was innocent and had been wronged somehow.

"Um, boss?"

"Yes, Trigg."

Neither man looked at each other when he spoke, which was fine with them. They each knew that when Patrick Delano fixed his eyes on you, it felt as if you were being looked on by somebody twice as big and a whole lot more frightening.

"You did tell us to clobber the old man Cooley."

Delano sighed and looked at the big oaf beside him. "I know that, and you know that, but nobody else in the world is going to hear you ever say that, you get what I am telling you, you idiot?"

"Uh, yeah, boss. Sure."

"And you?" Delano fixed an eye on the still-silent Axel, but the man had apparently dozed off leaning against the doorframe.

Delano sighed again and wondered, not for the first or last time that day, how he had gotten himself into this fix. All the depots he had set up in all the other towns in two states and a territory, and this was what it had all come to.

All gone, save for a team of horses, a brace of oxen, two wagons, two idiots who couldn't manage to stay sober for ten minutes at a stretch, and this lousy little depot in this lousy little town. He cast a glance up and down the street, watched the tall, dark figure of the man called Gage turn into the stable up the street, near the far end.

"Jewel, indeed," he muttered, recalling vaguely the words old man Cooley himself had told him with a smile when Delano had ridden into town that day. When was it? Two years or more ago?

He'd still had hope back then that the remaining few other depots in other towns that constituted the Delano Freighting empire might still hang on. But he'd burned too many bridges, even then, and knew that the likelihood of that was slim.

What he needed was a big wad of money to right the ship, to bring back the glory to the name Delano, which he'd once had. He didn't need friends, he needed money, that was all.

And then Patrick Delano thought of the four small sacks of nuggets and dust that Gage had brought to him from that silly little mine camp up in the hills. A thought came to him, a seed, a nugget—yes, that was the very word for it! A nugget of a word had just come to him; and for the first time, in a long time, Patrick

Delano smiled, a true, honest smile. Well, as honest as he was liable to ever get, he thought with a chuckle.

He was going to come out of this all right, yes, sir. All right, indeed. And the brutish Gage was going to be the one to have helped him do it.

"Perfect," he muttered, staring down the street. "Jewel of a town, indeed."

"Huh?" said Axel, rousing from his brief doze. "What?"

"Shut up," said Delano. "You two." He spun on the men. "Follow me. I have work for you to do."

Despite their fear of the man, they groaned, partly because they hated the word "work," for it meant they had to perform some, but mostly because they were sore from tangling with that cursed Gage, and the fine feeling of being drunk in the middle of the day was beginning to wane.

Chapter 15

After sunrise the next morning, Gage left Rig, after sharing a cup of offered hot coffee with Charles in the midst of the soft smells of the warm stable.

Then he'd made for Gerty's and had himself a modest breakfast of elk steak and eggs and biscuits, and, of course, coffee. All of it was delicious. Then he pulled in a quick draft of cool morning air and mounted the steps of the Shierson depot. He knocked.

Mrs. Shierson answered the door, looking, once more, remarkably pretty, despite her lack of a smile. "I expect you are here to check on Mr. Cooley's progress," she said, and stepped aside to let him in.

Gage was surprised, but he held the hat he'd taken off before he knocked, nodded to her, and stepped into the warmly lit depot. As soon as she closed the door and walked over to her stove, he came right out with it.

"I quit working for Delano, ma'am."

She regarded him with those same hard eyes she'd had when he left her the afternoon before. Finally she said, "Is that so?"

"Yes, ma'am."

"Why are you telling me this? Shouldn't you be drifting on elsewhere, looking for work?"

"In a manner of speaking, that's what I'm doing here, ma'am."

"I don't understand."

He swallowed and turned his hat brim in his big hands. "Well, ma'am, you'll pardon me for speaking plainly, but with Mr. Cooley down for a spell, and you with a wagon that needs filling and hauling, and with me out of work, and with little mine camps all over these hills needing supplies and whatnot, why, I thought—"

"You thought? You thought? You are not capable of such a maneuver, Mr. Gage, I see that now. Anyone who works for that murderous criminal Patrick Delano is no thinking man, that much is plain!"

Before he could wedge a toe into the conversation, she turned, no doubt gathering more words for another assault, but she was stopped by Cooley, who'd been leaning against an upright piano, in the shadows.

"Look here, Mrs. Shierson, Gage here is a solid fella. Brought me here, didn't he?"

"That doesn't mean he's not the enemy. And you should be resting."

"Oh, bother!" But Cooley didn't let her angle in there and shout him down. "And what's more," he said, "Gage helped the folks up in Clabberville. And Delano didn't like it one bit, but this fella, he didn't care. Come back and him and Delano had it out. Delano's desperate, missy."

She narrowed her eyes and glanced at Gage once.

"I might well be wrong," continued Cooley, "but I

reckon that if we can get a few more runs in, we might get an edge over him in this freighting game. We was on top before he come here, and everybody liked us. Still do, but he's threatened them all. Only now, he can't get help, see?" Cooley nodded toward Gage. "But we can."

"But one man alone, that would never do."

"*Alone?* Who said he was going to be alone? I got one good arm. That's all I need to ride shotgun."

"Oh no, that's not acceptable, Mr. Cooley. You need your rest."

"Pishposh! I'm going flat-out bedridden in here from all this rest!"

"Look, ma'am," said Gage. "I'm not the enemy here. I hired on with him, yes, but I was new to town and he was hiring. I was told by Gerty at the diner that you had all but closed up shop. Well, I was wrong, apparently. I've made one run for the man, as Cooley said, up to Clabberville."

Her eyes brightened. "Did you meet Morton Reilly and that Nate Willy? Oh, and how is Mrs. Reilly?"

He sensed a chink in the stern woman's armor. "They're all well, ma'am. Judging by the flakes and nuggets and dust and ore samples they sent down with me, they are doing very well up there. They were disappointed that it wasn't your wagon that brought them their requested goods, though."

"Yes, well, I had to make the decision to close up shop, as you put it. I am sorry about that, truly. But their gold, did you hand it over to Delano?"

"I'm afraid I did, ma'am. But I take responsibility

for it and I will get it from him and to the bank, some-how."

"Yes, well, it's a nice sentiment, Mr. Gage, but I doubt your success with that notion."

"Well, now," said Cooley, rubbing his busted arm gingerly, "that gold aside, from what Gage here has been telling me, there's still time to make all this freighting right. We got us a chance, see."

"What sort of chance might that be, Mr. Gage?" Her weary tone matched her suddenly tired-looking face.

Gage cleared his throat. "I was told, and then I saw with my own eyes, that Delano's business is not in good shape."

She snorted. "So, what? Neither is mine. In fact, I don't even have one anymore. Nor do I have a husband."

"I'm sorry, ma'am. I know this must be painful, but I believe if we can make a few runs, cut into his business, we stand a chance of getting you back on your feet."

"And with any luck," said Cooley with a smile, "we might run Patrick Delano right on out of town! Heck, we might end up escorting the rascal right into the jail cell that he's been nibbling his way toward for years now."

They both grew silent and watched her. She'd half turned back to them and ran her long, slender fingertips over the surface of the worktable. Her hands, Gage noted, were reddened by work and the sewing that she took in to make a little money. Somehow, this seemed a shame to him.

That a woman of obvious refinement, and likely used to finery in her life, should be reduced to living in an otherwise-empty warehouse, living like a pauper, taking in other people's mending, all to keep body and soul together was wrong, plain wrong.

And if what he'd been told since he arrived in town was even partly true, and he didn't doubt that it all was true, then she deserved better. So much better.

And the man who'd caused it all, Patrick Delano, was the one impediment to making her life better. Perhaps somehow, someway, Gage could see to it that Delano paid for it all. Somehow.

But how, Jon Gage? he thought as he watched emotions conflict on her face.

"All right, gentlemen," she said, turning to face them. Her eyes were hard and narrowed, and she still looked weary, but at least, thought Gage, she was agreeing to something. And at least she hadn't succeeded in throwing him out of her establishment once again.

"All right, what?" said Cooley, fingering his beard.

Gage thought it rude at first, and then he remembered that they were old friends. Indeed, Cooley lived apparently on a cot somewhere in the depot, too. In part, because he had nowhere else to go, and in part, because he viewed himself as her self-styled protector.

Even with one arm in a sling, Gage imagined, Cooley was a pretty useful guard dog. Not one Gage would underestimate, particularly with that nubbed-off shotgun Cooley toted.

She sighed. "I'll agree to resume trade. We still have horses and decent wagons. That is, if Mr. Cooley feels they are in working order. The horses and the wagons, that is."

"Sure they are! Been keeping them greased and fed. The wagons and the horses, that is." He winked. "They're all ready to work. Same as me."

"Oh no, Mr. Cooley, I'm afraid that's out of the question. You are far too ill to resume your duties as a driver."

"Pishposh again, I say!" His rooster neck craned and his voice grew reedy as his face reddened. "I'll show you ill!" He hefted his shotgun and cradled it, somewhat awkwardly, but in a serviceable position. "I already told you, I'll be the shotgun rider."

"And a driver?" she said, not looking at Gage.

"Oh, Mrs. Shierson," said Cooley, shaking his head, "you are a hard one. You got a man right here willing to work for no pay, ain't that right, Gage?"

The question surprised Gage for the briefest of moments. "What? Oh, of course, yes. That's fine."

"I knew it," she said, shaking her head. "Work for free—ha! You're like all the rest. You just want money and then you want to be gone from here, while the rest of us have to live with our choices and the consequences of them. Stuck, as they say, for the rest of our days."

Gage was about to protest, but his eyes fell on Cooley, who gave him the slightest of headshakes, which told him to let it go, let it pass. She'd come around. Somehow Gage could interpret all that from the man's quick look. He nodded once and followed Cooley out the back door and into the sunshine.

Once they were down the steps and away from the building, making for the paddock with the well-fed and well-rested horses, Cooley said, "You mustn't mind her. She gets quick spells of these dark moods, you see. Been that way since her husband died. They were quite a team, so happy, so devoted to each other."

Gage glanced toward the building, some hundred feet behind them. "Any children?"

Cooley took his time in answering. Finally he said, "Was going to be one, yes."

"Was?"

He sighed. "Yes, when he died, she was with child. The shock of it, I guess. Doc said there was nothing he could do for her. Poor little bird lost her husband and her child all at once."

"Why on earth did she stay on here in Newel?"

"Had to," said Cooley, resting a boot on a low rail and overlooking the horses. "No choice, no money, same thing. Except what money she could make with the business. We had a few men then, good men, solid workers, and I was ramrod of the outfit, by sheer luck, I guess. I been with the Shiersons from the start, so I knew them well, knew the business, the routes. All of it. And for a spell, it looked as if it might all work out. But she held on, wouldn't think of selling. She'd say, 'One more haul, Mr. Cooley.' That became one more month, then one more season. She felt beholden to all the folks depending on her, the workers and the customers."

Cooley sighed and shook his head. "Well, you know how that goes. Winter passes into spring, summer comes, and on and on, and the business expanded with the bursting of folks into these hills. Little mine camps everywhere. Well, we had a lock on the freighting to all of them. Couldn't hardly keep up. We hired on more men, bought more mule and horse teams, the works. It was something, them days was. She even smiled now and then, too." The memory of it made him smile.

"And then?"

Cooley chuckled, a weary, dry sound. "You know the answer already, pard. And then Patrick Delano rolls on into town. With money and promises that, looking back, sound ridiculous. But there you have it. Folks see something shiny and exciting hanging there in front of them and they chase it. Trouble is, it keeps just two steps ahead of you all the time. Then you've run so far after it, you got no choice but to keep on chasing it. Before you know it, you're up to your armpits in debt and being in debt to a fellow such as Patrick Delano ain't no thing a level-minded fellow or lady would want."

Gage shifted his boot on the same low rail and regarded his big hands hanging limp across the top rail, then the grazing horses beyond.

"Just how did her husband die, Cooley?" he asked, sensing this was not only something the old man knew, but something he wanted, or, perhaps, more to the point, felt he needed to share.

"Well, sir, it was odd, I don't mind telling you. 'Twas more than two years back, when Roger, that's Mr. Shierson's given name, he was on a run up in the hills. Matter of fact, I think he had two stops to make, and one of them was up to your town of Clabberville, you know, where you and Mort Reilly hit it off so well, and had such a time clearing the roadway.

"Anyway, Mr. Shierson, he was to be gone for two full days, though he told me he was going to make it in one, on account of him being fearful of leaving Mrs. Shierson all alone with the bairn on the way and all. I can understand that."

Cooley paused and regarded Gage, who nodded his agreement.

"Sensible thing for Mr. Shierson to think, sure. Though that's a mighty lot of hauling for a one-day trip," Gage commented.

Cooley nodded. "Yep, and I told him so. Tried to get him to leave it to me. Said one day wouldn't matter none to them folks up in the hills, and one day was what I needed to get my own run done. But he wanted me on that one, said it was important that I do it. A southern trip to two towns to pick up goods, drop them off at another depot for moving on elsewhere.

"But that was the problem, see. I knew, and he knew, that my run was the easier trip. He give it to me and wouldn't let me convince him different, only because I'm what you might call long in the tooth. But I can still scrap plenty, don't you worry about that!" Cooley puffed in his old red shirt and flapped his good upper arm like a bandy-legged rooster working up a mighty morning crow.

"I don't doubt that, Mr. Cooley."

"Good. You best not. Other men have tried and have lived with the gimpiness to regret it! Now, where was I? Oh yes, yes, so, no matter how I tried, I could not convince him to let me take the harder run up into the hills. So he went off, determined to get back soon. Well, sir, he got up there all right, and delivered the goods, but on the way back, near as we could tell, he got himself waylaid by bandits. Or so we thought at the time. Well, they were bandits, sure, just not the sort who wait for somebody to come along and then rob them."

"What sort were they?" said Gage.

"I'm getting to that. Now, when he didn't come back when I knew he wanted to—and if ever there was a man who was determined to keep his word, I ain't met him, save for Mr. Shierson. He was true to his word. So him being later than he said was a warning to me that something had gone wrong. I saddled up a stout mule, Molly, that one there, named after Mrs. Shierson." He winked. "Both of them is hardheaded, but kind at the core. Course it takes a while of knowing her to get to that."

Gage nodded, but said nothing, especially not now that Cooley was getting to the meat of the matter.

"You know yourself that the going can be rough for a lone rider, let alone a team tugging a wagon. But luck was with me that day. Molly rambled on through. Not the quickest beast in the bunch, but she'll get the job done when others are curling up to die. I was half a day up, maybe a pinch more scouting the trail sides for sign of anything amiss.

"Some of those ravines can hide a whole lot of heartache and sin. But I never did see any wreckage of a wagon down there, for which I was heartily grateful. But as I said, along about early afternoon, I see in the roadway ahead a sight that at first I was glad to see. It was a team with what looked to be a wagon dragged behind. But they was stopped dead in the roadway.

"I knew before I could get a good look at the beasts that the outfit was for sure one of ours. I shucked my shotgun and loosened the thong on my hip blade. Then I stepped down and walked on over, curious-like, and slow stepping.

"At first, I saw nobody around. The horses were standing there, flicking flies with their ears, snorting, looking at me hopeful like, and I knew they hadn't been there all that long. But who knows with a horse, could have been half a day! So I walked on up, my head looking left, then right, fore and aft on the roadway, nothing did I see. No sign of Mr. Shierson hunched up in the bushes. Didn't mean he wasn't in there, responding to an urgent natural call. But I shouted for him just the same.

"'Mr. Shierson?' I waited. Nothing. I tried again. 'Mr. Shierson?' Nothing. 'Roger! Roger! Come on out now, it's Cooley, Mr. Shierson. It's me, Cooley. You okay?' I waited, holding still like a deer in the woods will do. One of the horses, Ned, I think it was, yonder, that big brown horse over there. He shook his head as if to tell me I was being foolish, and so I heeded that call. Horses are smart folk."

"So I've heard."

"Mm-hmm, I know. You been talking with Charlie, over to the stable." Cooley winked. "Me and him, we're pals. We sit and palaver and sip whiskey of an evening. Good fella, is Charlie. Anyway, I walked on, closer and closer, and do you know what I saw? A boot, the sole of a boot, the left one. I hustled on over to the wagon.

"That boot was attached to a body and it was Mr. Shierson, slumped down in the boot well of the wagon. He was in there all right, tucked half under the seat! I leaned my gun against the wagon, all caution gone, and grabbed him by the shoulders.

"'Mr. Shierson!' I shouted. 'Roger! Roger!' I lifted him. He was a good-size fellow. Like you, he was trim, but wide of the shoulder. I had a time yanking him on out of there, but I did, and got him so he was sitting up. But it was all my effort that did it. He had no steam left in him. Not responding at all to me. I got an arm around his shoulders and grasped his face with my other hand, but his head flopped to the side, his eyes half open.

"I seen my share of dead folks, I tell you, Gage, and it's not something you're likely to forget. You know what I mean?"

Gage stiffened. He knew all right. He well knew it.

"Gage? You all right? Some folks get squeamish when we talk of the dead. I won't go on if you can't handle it."

"No, no. Keep going, Mr. Cooley. I'm fine."

"Well, sir, I knew in that finger snap of time that nothing was ever going to be the same again. And it wasn't, as you know."

"How did he die?"

"Well, now, that's the thing. He was clubbed in the head." Cooley pointed to the right side of his own head. "Right along here. Crushed part of his skull. 'Twas a mighty blow by something that left a dent. I hope it was an instant death for him. There was blood, but I suspect there was a lot more inside his pate." He tapped his own head again, and shook it.

"Sorrowful, it was. I kept trying for far too long, trying not to sob, but I'm afraid I did. Here was a man, a kind man, about to be a father, too. And with a woman who loved him more than anything else, as you well know."

"You said it was bandits? But not the sort who'd waylay a man."

"Right." Cooley nodded.

"Well, how did you know that?"

"I didn't, not right away. But I got my wits about me and poked around, and everything was in order. There were a few things in the bed of the wagon, all lashed down nice and neat, like Mr. Shierson was apt to do, so I don't believe anything was taken. Still don't. That was my first clue that something was amiss.

"Who'd kill a man who was well liked and not take a thing from him? His guns were there, the hip gun he carried only on runs, 'cause Mrs. Shierson, she's not one to go in for guns or gunplay."

A coldness, familiar to Gage, clawed through his guts.

"So I got my wits gathered, as much as I could, then I scouted hard up and down the road and up and down the slope to either side of the wagon. I found a few tracks, a jumble of hoofprints. Now, I'm no tracker, but it seemed to me that there were maybe one or two sets of horse tracks that angled off, up the hills. It was steep, so I suspect they switchbacked up and out of there. But if I was a killer, I'd not dawdle around waiting for somebody to come along and gander at my handiwork and then find me. No, sir, they was long gone. Or so I thought."

"What did you do then?"

"Well, sir, it was too far to make for Clabberville, so I dragged Mr. Shierson over the seat and laid him out in the wagon, took the spare tarpaulin we always carry behind the seat in the box of gear and supplies and covered him over and secured him well. Then I tied my mount, Molly, to the rear of the wagon, climbed into the driver's seat, and checked my gun again, and kept a sharp eye on the roadway up and down. And then I got that wagon rolling.

"It was a frightening time, not knowing who was out there, but knowing what evil they had put upon my friend. I was touchy and the horses sensed it, for they were jumpy, too. I kept glancing back at Molly behind, but she was the same as you see her now, just walking along, minding her own."

"So, what you're leading up to is . . . what?"

The old man pulled his head back and stared at Gage with drawn brows. "You must have been an annoying child."

"What makes you say that?"

"Because you have no patience. Now let a man tell his story. Precious few moments in life as it is to sit and listen to someone for a spell."

Gage nodded. "Okay, you're right. I apologize."

"Good. Now, where was I? Oh yes, so there we were, me and Mr. Shierson and the horses and Molly, we were getting along that road as fast as I could make the team go without risk of sliding off the steep parts, nor fetching up a wheel on the confounded ruts and rocks.

"I had all I could do to keep my eyes on the road, you see, but I happened to glance to my left, on the uphill side, and caught a glimpse of blue. Not sky, mind you, because it was down lower, blue like you see on bright new cloth at the mercantile."

"Blue?" said Gage.

Cooley nodded. "Blue. And it was moving. I know, I know, so was I, but this was traveling, I tell you, in the sparse sort of woods up there, heading in the same direction we were. So I looked back thataway again, when I could, but then I saw nothing. Might well have been making noise, too, stomping duff and branches and such, but we were kicking up enough of our own fuss that I couldn't tell."

"Did you investigate?"

"I was not about to slow down, let alone stop to investigate, you whelp!"

"All right, all right." Instead of feeling offended, Gage had to suppress a smile. This man was not unlike so many old-timers he'd met through his years of travel. He'd grown accustomed to, and had even grown to like, the surliness that masked a kind heart.

"Now, where was I? Oh yes, the blue. So I swiveled my head like a fool after that, you can bet your last dollar, but as you can see, nobody bushwhacked me on my way back to Newel with my woeful news and my grim passenger. The day was awful, as were the days that followed. Still are, in some respects, what with Mrs. Shierson losing the child, and then not wanting to live herself. Why, I think she still pines so much for her lost husband and babe that she wishes she was with them. She's as much as told me so. I understand. Had hard times of my own through the years."

Cooley fell silent, and Gage did not think it wise to interrupt the man yet again. Perhaps he'd get the rest of his story at some time down the road.

After a few moments, Cooley resumed. "But that's another story for another time. Right now, I aim to tell you what-all I learned about the color blue." He laid a finger aside his nose. "'Twasn't but two days later that I was making for the far end of the street to fetch tinctures at the mercantile for the doc who was helping Mrs. Shierson, when I saw that the new fella in town, a loudmouthed braggart laying down all manner of cash since his arrival a week or more before, had set up shop officially. You can probably guess who that might have been."

Gage nodded. "Your description left little for the imagination. Patrick Delano."

"That's the one and the same, yep. And what do you think I saw? None other than two other strangers to town, two fellas I later overheard at a bar, from Delano himself, that they were what he called his 'associates.' These two were new arrivals, but word had it that they worked for him doing all manner of jobs. Right then, when I saw them on the street, they were loafing in the shadows of Delano's loading dock, but not so far in the shadows I couldn't see what they were wearing." He nodded, and Gage tamped down his urge to say the word "blue."

"One of them was wearing a bright blue shirt. And I

didn't see anybody else wearing such in that town before or since. It was bold and distinctive. The rest of the man's attire was in keeping with that snappy shirt of his. Fancy-man boots with silver conchos trailing down the sides and a hat with similar hardware on it. Striped trousers and a gun rig all shiny and duded up. And how did I see all that, you ask? Well, for one, I slowed my route to a walk, so as to take in the competition. And secondly, that blue-shirted rascal sauntered on out to the edge of the dock and folded his arms over his chest and tipped his hat back on his head and smiled at me! *Smiled,* I tell you!"

"So he knew who you were and he knew that you knew who he was," said Gage.

"I guess. Now you're just talking to confuse the situation. But you bet he knew who I was, and I sure knew him."

That's what I said, thought Gage, but he kept his mouth shut and merely nodded.

"So that there is how Delano is involved. I have thought much on this, and I have come to the notion that Delano hired Blue Boy and his pal to eliminate the competition so he could set up and there'd be an immediate need for his freighting services."

Gage nodded. "Makes sense."

"Course it does. And since then, Delano has been a whole lot more plain as day about his actions and his intentions in this town. I vowed right then and there to make certain he paid for his filthy ways. And Blue Boy was going to topple first!"

"And did you?"

"Nah, not Blue Boy anyway. He and his compadre

lit out for other business affairs of Delano's not long after that. Off to kill folks somewhere else, I reckon."

"Does Mrs. Shierson know all this?"

"Nope, not about Blue Boy. But word leaks out, you see. These so-called associates, they blabbed when they was in their cups, mentioned how they should be named the 'eliminators,' instead of associates. 'Cause they were hired to eliminate the competition, and that they were good at what they did."

"But they weren't, were they? Because you and Mrs. Shierson held on."

"Sure we did. I kept things rolling, as I mentioned, and for a spell, it looked as if there might be plenty of room for two freighters in town. Truth be told, it was useful to have another outfit around to help us as we got back to full running order after Mr. Shierson was killed."

He smiled. "Folks were moving into the hills hereabouts, like there was no end to it. We had a silver strike and two smaller gold strikes. Once that word got out, my lands, folks come pounding on in from everywhere. China, Ireland, Poland, and back East, too!"

For a while, no man said a thing; then Gage spoke: "So, Mr. Cooley, where does that leave us?"

The old man looked up at him from beneath his bushy eyebrows. "You really sure you want in on this mess? I played along in front of Mrs. Shierson, but you ain't committed, you know. Me, I got no choice."

"I have more reason than you could ever know, Mr. Cooley, to see folks like Delano pay for their misdeeds."

"Good. Then here's what I think we need to do."

Cooley smacked his good hand against the hand jutting from his sling and winced, then turned an alarming shade of gray.

"You all right?"

"Will be, sure." Cooley gulped, shook his head, then said, "Don't never get old, son. Takes too long to heal."

"*Heal?* It just happened."

"Yeah, but I'm tough. Not half as tough as I used to be, though. Was a time I would have licked both those men with one hand, just for fun. Still"—he winked—"you gave 'em some good shots, I saw that, all right."

Gage shrugged, thinking of how he wished he had done the same to Delano. He tried to imagine hiring someone to kill off his business adversaries, and realized he had no business, and so no need to have adversaries. And yet, there was Patrick Delano, as much an enemy as Gage could imagine.

"All right, then. Where's our first run going to be?"

"That's the thing. Ain't got no orders just yet." He snapped a finger. "But I do happen to know that the folks up in Bewley, sort of north and west of Clabberville, where you made your one and only run for that rascal, will be needing their goods ferried down to town. We got a safe and a warehouse that we can keep locked."

"Do you have anyone to keep an eye on things if we're both out on runs?"

"I think you're underestimating Mrs. Shierson. She's fierce, and has, at least in her eyes, nothing to lose."

"That's good. I assume she has a weapon handy."

"Yep, two shotguns, a brace of revolvers, and two rifles. She kept all her husband's things. And she's a good shot, too, for a woman not fond of guns. Roger, he taught her. They were a curious pair, he was from farming stock up in Vermont, I think it was, or Maine, or some such spot off the map up there. But he moved to the city of Boston early on and met her while he was studying to be a schoolteacher or some such.

"She wanted to write books, of all things. Can you imagine anyone wanting to do that? And she was raised with servants and such. But love is a wonder, and they up and moved out West because he had the wandering ways. My old gran always said you beware of men with such a notion, for they will never be happy anywhere. And it's true—I'm the same way, myself. Been here in Newel longer than I been anywhere, all because of the Shiersons, mind you. Elsewise, I'd have been hither and yon for years now."

Gage knew from the man's chatty tone that he wanted to hear Gage's story, where he was from, what he'd been up to. Gage decided he would oblige him, to a point. He'd also made himself a promise he would never shy away from truth, when he could, stopping short of revealing he had been a common street killer for money.

"I'm from Texas," said Gage.

"That much I know. Could tell by your accent. You just saddle-tramping your way through life, son?"

Gage knew by Cooley's squinted eyes and hard stare that the man was giving him an easy way to keep himself to himself. And he appreciated it.

"Something like that, yeah," said Gage.

"Worse ways to spend your time, I reckon. Good, honest work and clean air. Only rum part about it is all them beeves. I rode drag once on a drive. Never again. I like myself too much to put up with that silliness in a steady stream." Cooley chuckled. "Okay, back to the haul. See, I do believe we can make a run up into them hills. The wagons are greased, workboxes are sorted and tidied, and the critters are well fed, maybe too much so. But they like the work. They're bored doing nothing, same as me."

"We ride to the mine camp you mentioned, no contract, huh? You think they'll welcome us or need our services?"

"Bewley? Oh yes, we go way back. Headman up there is a fellow named Blanchette. A Frenchman from Quebec, if I recall correctly. He's a good one. Course they've all been forced to deal with Delano for some time now, but I know that most folks in those camps would prefer to have their fingers gnawed off by wolves if they had the choice, but they ain't."

"Well," said Gage, standing up and looking beyond Cooley, "they will soon, if we have anything to say about it." He nodded toward the depot. "Here comes your employer."

Cooley spun and caught sight of Mrs. Shierson walking toward them with an unreadable look on her face.

"Your employer, too," said Cooley just before she reached them.

Both men shucked their hats and nodded.

She regarded each of them in turn, then settled her eyes on the old man. "Mr. Cooley."

"Yes'm?"

She paused, as if in thought, then said, "It seems to

me that, given our lack of recent endeavors, that we should resume freighting operations by offering our services to a mine camp with which we have had agreeable relations in the past."

Now it was Cooley's turn to descend into thought. Gage could see him chewing over the words Mrs. Shierson used. Then the old man's face brightened and he stroked his beard—something Gage had noticed the codger did when he was getting worked up about something.

"Now, that's a good idea, ma'am. I like it. Any particular camps in mind?"

She nodded without hesitation. "Bewley. And then, perhaps, Clabberville."

Cooley nodded and glanced at Gage. "That'll do. Yep, good choice. Bewley and then Clabberville will do nicely."

"Good," she said. "You, Mr. Gage, will command the wagon."

"I will do my level best, ma'am." He nodded with as much solemnity as he could offer in such a simple gesture. She did not offer him a smile.

"And you, Mr. Cooley, since you are too thick-headed for your own good, will, as you intend, ride shotgun. But I must have your word, Mr. Gage, that no harm will come to Mr. Cooley."

She flashed a quick glance at Gage, then back to Cooley. "He is indispensable to the operation of Shierson Freight Haulage." She said this, but her eyes had softened as she gazed on the old man. Then she turned away and walked back to the depot. She had not gone a dozen feet, when she stopped and half turned, saying, "I expect the wagon to be ready first thing in the morning."

"Yes, ma'am!" shouted Cooley. He turned to Gage with a smile. "You heard the lady."

"You were testing her."

"Me testing her? Naw, I just wanted to make certain her thinking skills are still sharp as carpet tacks. And they are."

"All right, then," said Gage. "I have a few things to tend to at the stable, and then I'll be back to rig the wagon and tend the team. I figure I'll need about an hour. That work for you?"

"Make it two hours," said Cooley. "Give me time for a spell of shut-eye. I ain't as young as I used to be."

"None of us is." A last thought came to Gage. "Say, Cooley, just how did you know all that about me and the folks up at Clabberville, and my arguments with Delano?"

"You think I'd tell you all my secrets?" Cooley grinned and touched his nose with a fingertip. "Ha! I may be old, but Cooley sure ain't deaf or dumb, neither!" He grinned and hefted the old, but well-tended, shotgun with his left arm.

"Can't blame a man for being curious." Gage returned the smile and saluted him with a couple of fingers off his hat brim. He strode away, skirting the depot and emerging onto the main street from the alley, to the east of the building. He worked his way on over to the stable, thinking that a nap would be all right with him as well. He was still sore from the fight and all the turmoil these days were bringing him.

Honestly, he thought, *if I had known this seemingly sleepy little town would dole out this much headache, I would have gladly kept right on riding, not through town, but far around, and into the mountains.*

That thought brought his eyes to bear on the foothills to the west of town that rose into bigger rises, then finally, in the distance, snow-topped peaks.

His gaze lingered there a moment, then drifted back down to the street view, and there, at the end of Main Street, sat Gerty's restaurant.

That is just what I need, he thought. *Another good, hot meal. No telling when I'll get the chance at another.*

But first, he needed to make certain Rig was going to be all right with the old stableman Charles. He smiled as he walked, wishing he had told old Cooley he'd see him in three hours. Of course, then it would be getting on into dark before they were finished.

Chapter 16

The next morning, dawn found the men well on out of town, hoping in large part to avoid prying questions and stares from nosy locals. From the number of folks making like prairie dogs as they rolled westward, rumbling on out of town, it hadn't much worked.

Right away, Gage saw that, though there was definitely a lot wrong with Cooley, including a broken wing, and the fact that he was well on in years, the old fellow had something not a lot of men Gage had worked with had. It was something he hoped he had a smidgen of himself. That elusive trait was grit. He'd heard some men call it sand. Whatever cute word folks cared to use, it was a quality in abundance in old Cooley.

Here he was, aged enough, Gage guessed, to be his grandfather, and Cooley was tough. He was stringy like an old rooster, bowlegged and ambling with a slight limp, but he was quick with a joke and free with his curses, though never in front of women. Gage liked him and, despite the broken arm, he felt a bit of comfort having him along, because the man was confident and capable with the shotgun.

And he was chatty. Gage had never minded chumming with a fellow who could tell a good story. He was not much for small talk himself. And when he was alone, which he was much of the time, he tended to brood over his past. This never failed to put him in a dark mood. So having Cooley tell him of the man's past exploits as a range scout, a swamper, a military man, and a trapper sat all right with Gage.

They rode along, taking the west road out of Newel, the same road Gage had traveled on his one and only run for Delano. This time, he was intrigued, not wholly because there was high risk and little reward—though that was, if he had to be honest with himself, some of it. But he was pleased because he didn't have the specter of a grubbing, greedy man as his boss hanging over his every move.

This time, his boss was a woman who was a stunningly beautiful creature to look upon. He knew he could and would never do anything more than admire her, but a fellow could indulge in warm thoughts, and for spells here and there, he would let his mind wander into the territory of *what if*?

And then, for a few moments, he would be happy, thinking of what a life with such a woman might have been like. Then, of course, his mind would click back to the face of the young, dying woman in the street, equally as beautiful, perhaps more so because life's travails had not had a chance to really sink their fangs into her and drag her down. And then he'd done it, instead. He'd gunned her down as if flicking away a fly from his plate.

"Gage. I lose you with all my palaver?" Cooley looked at the quiet, large man beside him on the seat.

"Me? No, I like it fine. Just thinking."

"Uh-oh. I tell you what, I didn't get to where I am in life by indulging in much of that!" The older fellow winked. "Say, you're not much for guns, are you?"

Gage remained silent for a moment, then said, "No, not much these days. More and more, I think there should be a way for a man to think his way out of a gunfight."

Cooley nodded. "I reckon I understand your aim there, but a fellow will want to be mighty quick with his thinker"—he rapped a gnarled old finger to his temple—"if a bullet's on its way toward him, huh?"

Gage smiled and nodded. "Sometimes it's unavoidable, I agree. I'm trying to keep those moments few and far between."

They rode for a while; then Cooley said, "Gage, now don't take this the wrong way." He glanced at him with a smirk on his face. "But you are an odd duck, no mistake. A good one, but an odd one."

Gage didn't say anything for a spell.

"You offended?" said the old man.

"No, no, just the opposite, in fact. I like being the odd one, unless it attracts attention to me."

"That it might, but it ain't like you're famous or some such silliness. Why, I knew a fella could drop a buffalo at a thousand paces. No lie! Somehow he got himself notoriety just for killing something innocent like a big old buffalo. Course he laid low a whole lot more than one of the poor beasts. Can you imagine? Folks getting all worked up over somebody who kills other creatures, not in a fight or for food, but for, well, I just don't know." He shook his head.

Gage said nothing, but if Cooley had looked over at him, he would have seen the big man with his jaw clenched, the muscles of his cheek flexing and bunching, and his hands gripping the lines far too tight.

Two hours later, they decided to give the horses a rest. They weren't hauling much of a loaded wagon, after all, just the men and their required gear, but the beasts had been lazing about in the pasture for a few months and had not been worked. No sense in risking them fouling a muscle before they rolled deeper into the coming hill country.

The slopes ahead were far less forgiving than those they had already trudged up. Gage steered the team into a wide, level, shaded stretch with a clear, shallow brook burbling not far away. He halted them for a breather.

The spot had been used by other teams for much the same purpose, as evidenced by the trampled earth and the well-used firepot with convenient rocks and log butts for seating.

Cooley maneuvered himself down out of the wagon before Gage could make his way over to offer help. The old-timer might have just the one useful arm at present, but that didn't mean he wanted to be treated like an old and frail man. Gage and Cooley both knew this, and each man did his best to not get worked up in either direction about it.

The old gent walked over to the fire pit and palmed the coals. "Cold, damp. Been a while."

Gage nodded and unhitched two leather straps holding the wooden bucket to the side of the wagon. He wound his way down the path to the stream, angling through clawing rabbit brush, and came to a brook. When the bucket was filled, he knelt and then stretched out prone, his face poised over the run of clear water. He looked at his reflection a moment, then grunted and sipped and sipped.

It was good, cold runoff from the high peaks above. It would not be this way for much longer, he knew. For the water would seize up and cease to flow with the coming cold.

As if the thought were more than he could bear, Gage shuddered, his lips and teeth and mouth numb from the delicious drink. He fetched the bucket and walked back to begin ferrying what he suspected would be a series of buckets of water for the horses. He'd let them drink their fill, though he knew there would be other streams higher up as they traveled.

But they were soon to depart from the trail he had taken to get to Clabberville. The new road would lead them northwest, to Bewley, and then, if they had the time and the room, they would take a ridgeline connector road eastward to Clabberville, and then back to Newel.

Cooley and Mrs. Shierson had said both towns were peopled with folks sympathetic to the Shierson Freight Haulage concern, and not impressed at all with Delano. Despite how those townsfolk felt about Delano, they were forced to deal with him and his rogue men because there were no other active freighters near enough, and they were not yet ready to haul their own goods.

Until they decided to pool their cash and make runs to town in their own wagons, they were stuck with Delano.

"About time you got yourself back here."

It was Cooley and he was poised in a half crouch, whispering and pointing across the roadway. Out of instinct, Gage also bent low and squinted toward where the older man pointed. At first, he saw nothing, and then he spied movement, erratic and barely visible, as if something were toying with them, perhaps, ducking down and then popping up again, only to dip back down.

What could it be?

Whatever it was, Gage decided, it was not overly large. And given the random, erratic actions it took, perhaps it was nothing more than a bird feeding on late seed heads of wispy brown stalks of grasses.

"Might be a bird," said Gage.

"Might. Might also be an Injun laying in wait."

Gage had not had much to do with any natives in his years of roving, but he'd certainly seen a number of them, often from a distance. Once, perhaps three years earlier, he had stopped a gang of town boys, none older than twelve or so, from attacking an old Indian woman who'd come into the town to trade her dead husband's goods for food.

Normally, he did his best to stay out of the affairs

of others, in an effort to keep from drawing attention to himself. But that time, he had to intervene. The woman, who spoke no English, was grateful, but frightened and confused.

The children were well-fed town brats with no common sense, and no one about to keep them from harming others. It seemed to him that they should not have needed anyone to tell them that attacking an old woman was wrong.

Gage had wondered back then, and continued to shake his head when he thought back on the incident today, over where the parents had been and why they were raising such miniature moppets.

He walked to the wagon, fetched the other shotgun that Mrs. Shierson had suggested they take along and that Cooley had insisted on. The uncomfortable feeling, however fleeting, of hefting a large firearm, even if he intended to use it for defense, shuddered through Gage and left him as it always did, feeling tired and cold.

He indicated to Cooley that he would go investigate and that Cooley should stay with the wagon. The old man had already sidled up to the wagon and leaned through the boot well, giving him a clear sight line across the narrow roadway toward the mysterious object.

Gage checked the barrel and patted his coat pocket, where he'd stuffed in two extra shells. He cut to his right, up the road, and angled across, figuring to come at the odd thing, whatever it might be, from the north.

He catwalked low, keeping the shotgun poised and

even, not intending to use the cursed thing if he could avoid it. The only thing that might induce him to shoot a gun at another person is if that person happened to be in the act of trying to take Gage's own life.

He could have left it back in the wagon, but that was not smart, if only because he had made himself, if not indispensable then, at least much relied upon by Mrs. Shierson and Cooley. They needed him alive and well and not acting the fool.

"Here goes," he muttered as he stepped over the berm on the far side of the road.

The black thing was not visible from where he stood. He was also mindful that he was stepping into tall grass, and while it was getting cold enough that snakes were likely starting to hole up, this was one of the warmer days they'd had of late.

Nothing for it, he thought, and waded on into the grass.

He did not feel the whip-crack strike of a snake, or the jab and sting of its tooth as it punctured and then slid into his leg. What he did feel was an urgency to get the next few steps over with, even if they exposed him to whoever might be lurking roadside. He leapt, holding the shotgun tight in his left fist, and landed with a thud and a dust cloud; then he dropped down fast to his right knee, the gun up and ready.

But he saw no one, as he sort of expected. What he did see was the back side of the black erratic, wagging thing. He walked slowly toward it, keeping the shotgun's barrel aimed at it.

When he was four feet away, he saw it clearly for

what it was—a large black feather. He straightened and waved an arm to Cooley, who had kept his old eagle eyes on Gage for each moment of his funny little foray.

"Okay?" shouted Cooley, walking around the wagon, hefting his shotgun, too. He walked on over, though still with caution, and with the shotgun's butt wedged awkwardly, but soundly, against his gut, his fingers not on the trigger, but ready to slide there.

"Yeah. A feather."

"That all?"

Gage stepped closer to the thing. "Yep." He reached with a worn-leather-gloved hand and gingerly lifted the feather and eyed it from all sides.

The old man ambled over, his bristling somewhat quelled by Gage's slowness. "It's a feather, as you said. So, what's taking so long?"

Gage kept looking at the thing, then at the length of the shiny black feather. "Doesn't look as if it's been here too long. The feather's not raggedy and beat up."

"Again I say, so?" Cooley straightened and looked around, stretching his gun-toting arm. "Likely off a raven or buzzard. Huh, just now had a thought."

"Oh?" said Gage.

"Yeah, this feather reminds me of something. Remember when I told you about them two fellas, one wearing the fancy blue shirt?"

"Yeah."

"And there was his compadre, who I didn't mention much. Well, he was quieter, stocky built, wore a buckskin tunic, and I'd bet a dollar and a half he was at least a half-breed. What flavor of tribe, I don't know."

"Well," said Gage, uncertain if he'd ever need that

bit of information, but glad to have it just the same, "good to know."

Cooley smiled and smacked his leg. Dust rose up from his own buckskin trousers. "Don't that beat all! You running for a fancy political office or something?"

"How's that?"

"Oh, I'm kidding with you. For a second there, the way you said, 'Good to know' reminded me of a mayor or some such from some big, fancy city. Or worse, one of those useless rascals in Washington."

Gage heard him, but that got him thinking about the blue-shirted man and his trail mate. And those hired killers were the last thing he needed to think about.

"I don't know much about politicians, but I do know if we don't get moving soon, we're going to be out here in the dark with feathers in the weeds and no ground gained," Gage observed.

"Agreed."

Gage eyed the odd thing one last time. "You want this for your hat, Cooley?"

"Nah, thanks just the same."

Gage let it slip from his hand. He cut wide, uproad, figuring he'd minimize any sign of himself or Cooley he might have left there. He had no clear reason for doing this, but he figured it was a gut thing, as he'd heard instinct called. And gut things, no matter what name folks gave them, rarely steered him wrong in life.

Ten minutes later found them rolling on. They had each anticipated making coffee and resting for a bit, but there was an oddness about the spot that somehow left them unsettled.

They'd been riding for a half hour when they came

to their first incline of the day of any note. Gage guided the horses right, to take the switchback with as easy an approach as possible.

"Cooley, have you been thinking about Blue Boy much lately?"

"Yeah," said the old man, stuffing a lint-covered knob of chaw from his pocket into his cheek. "You bet I have. Not certain why. Feels like something's in the air. Can't explain it any more than that. For whatever reason, seeing that feather brought to mind that blue-shirted rascal, and the rascal's part-Indian pard."

Gage kept silent for a bit, save for urging the horses on with barked words and quick whistles. The team, when they started their journey, had been full of pepper and ready for action, but now they were tired and the climb was but the first in a series they were expected to make today, and then more the next day.

"This doesn't bode well."

"Nope, but they'll get a new wind, you rest easy. It'll come, oh, another hour or so. Once they know we won't be turning back for their home pasture today, they'll wade in and give it their all."

Gage was skeptical of this, but said nothing. He kept doing what he could—urging the beasts forward and keeping them to the best side of the increasingly rough trail.

"This roadway gets better up ahead. It also levels out a bit. I recall there are at last three good campsites along that stretch, and more beyond. I expect we'll make it to them just fine. Give Tom and Tim a chance, you won't be disappointed." Cooley winked and resumed swiveling his bearded head in all the directions he could manage from his perch.

Gage said nothing, but did manage a weak smile and head nod.

True to Cooley's word, the road did level out between the first hill and the next. The horses seemed to maintain and perhaps speed up their efforts. They did so again, in another two hours, once they rolled on up their next big rise. This time, they were working up a higher foothill, giving it their all. Cooley said nothing, but his grin spoke volumes to Gage.

"All right, I admit it," said the ex-gunman. "You were right. They seem to be more spry and lively."

"Course they do. I instructed them, didn't I?"

Now it was Gage's turn to grin. He nodded as they rolled along easier. He was about to ask if Cooley thought they ought to keep an eye out for a good site for the evening, when a buzzing snaked by his right ear, right between the two men.

Both of the freighters jerked aside, instinct overriding reason for a brief moment. But as they jerked in reaction, the sound of a sharp crack, like a single, far-off hand clap—or a rifle shot—reached them.

The direction of the shot had been back behind them, and to the southwest, off trail, Gage knew from his memory of the terrain they'd just rolled in and out of.

"My rifle," barked Gage to Cooley. "Use it, instead of the shotgun. They're far off. And keep low."

They both knew they were in a bad spot, too exposed from all quarters. That was all the time for thought they had, because another buzzing sounded, followed by the cracking smack of the gun. Gage knew by the sound that it was a different rifle. It also sounded as though it came from behind, but from the southeast.

Had they ridden right between two gunmen? He had no time to dwell on this, because a third shot zipped and then cracked, this time from the direction the first had come in. This was followed by a fourth, as he expected, from the second gun's direction in the southeast.

Whoever was doing the shooting was either slowly closing in on them, adjusting for distance and terrain with each shot, or they were playing games with them. Because even though it sounded to him as if the shots had come to them from quite a distance, they were not hitting their marks. That felt intentional to Gage.

"Cat and mouse!" yelped Cooley, agreeing with Gage's thoughts.

Gage nodded and shouted the team onward, toward what looked to be a tree-lined dip in the roadway, perhaps an eighth of a mile ahead.

"Good cover ahead!" growled Cooley from his kneeling position in the boot well. He faced backward, doing his best to balance the rifle atop the seat back, wedging it tight to his shoulder. His bound arm flapped, and he must have jarred it hard against something, for in the brief moment Gage stole to glance at him, he saw the old freighter's face turn gray, but he kept his consciousness and gritted his teeth. Cooley squinted back behind them, the rifle ready to deliver a shot.

They were closer to their destination, and still the shots, spaced almost as if timed, kept driving in, parting the air between them. A couple of them whipped by to the outside of each man.

If this was all intentional, Gage was impressed. Any idiot could crank off a shot and have it travel quite a ways. But accurate distance shooting was a real trick to do well.

The horses, lathered and with heaving barrels, thundered onward, urged by the strident tickles Gage delivered to their backsides, and by the fear and urgency washing off the two men in the wagon behind them. It boiled outward from them as if it were a visible thing.

"Here! Here!" barked Cooley, jerking his head to his left, the right side of the roadway.

Gage saw what he meant, because though the spot was low, it was well protected and would give them ample cover, while also offering protection from most sides for them and for the horses. From there, they might be able to wait out whoever was doing this. And Gage had a solid idea of who was behind it. Time for thinking about that later.

Gage guided the team into the sizable lay-by, set the brake, and looped the lines. No time for further securing the team. He followed Cooley's lead and bailed out of the wagon, and joined the codger on the inner slope side of the wagon. No more shots sizzled in as they hunkered, waiting. The wagon shotgun sat propped in the boot well, a foot from his right hand.

He snatched for it, thinking that moment might well be the one when the shooters decided to get serious and stop toying with them.

But no shot came as he drew the heavy gun back toward him.

"Grab mine next," said Cooley, nodding toward his single-barrel shredder. It made sense that Cooley would use it, since it was lighter and less cumbersome, good points for him most of the time, and certainly now that he had one useful arm.

Gage did so and handed it to him, and Cooley returned Gage's rifle. It was his meat maker, as he called it, in grim homage to not only his despised past, but to the gun's sole function in his life.

Neither man spoke for long minutes, peering instead up into the landscape above them. They were high in the hills, but had descended into a small cleft that would wind its way down into the larger valley separating this foothill from the next.

Not far off, down the road a ways, Gage saw the mouth of what looked to be an abandoned digging. The gaping black hole in the hillside was shored up with stout log uprights and similar crosspieces.

It might do as a hidey-hole if they were pressed from all sides. That meant leaving the horses to fend for themselves. Few men killed horses if their real quarry was a fellow man. But there were a good many, Gage knew, who were not above coring a horse's brain with a lead pill if they thought it might help them in their zeal to keep the man they hunted from escaping.

This attack felt as random as did their discovery of the silly black feather snagged in the grasses earlier.

"What do you reckon?" he said, not looking at Cooley.

"Hmm, I'd say we got us two men. They're off behind us a ways, and they are good shots. Good enough to let us live, but not so great that I care to meet them, unless it's with me or you standing over them with a gun." Cooley nodded, the finality of his statement convincing enough for Gage.

"The same," Gage said. "But we can't sit here all day and wait for them to grow bored with us."

"No, no, we can't do that. While we still have daylight, let's secure this spot as best we can. I don't mind saying I don't like it one bit. Feels as though we're being waited out. Then when they're good and ready they're gonna strike harder and faster."

"And with more accuracy." Gage nodded in agreement. "But we have no choice, really."

"Could go on toward Bewley. Nothing else for it, really."

"I wondered about that. They haven't shot us yet, for a reason. I'm thinking it's to get us to do what we did, which is to pull over, so they can rob us. Otherwise, if it's Delano's men, why not kill us and be done with it?"

"That's grim thinking, Gage."

The former gunman shrugged. "Grim times."

"True, true. So you think we might as well move on?"

"I'm leaning that way. Heck, I don't know. And I hate not knowing."

Cooley smiled, eyeing the now-silent terrain. "I knew there was a reason I like you. You're a man of action, same as myself. Sitting around doesn't sit right, if you catch my meaning."

Gage nodded. "I do. So?"

"So let's get back on the trail, keep low, and hope we get to Bewley before those bullets get lonely and look for a home."

"Hope, in my experience, has never worked out too well as a plan."

"Can't argue that. But sitting on my thumbs has had the same effect on me."

Gage kept low, walking around the horses, checking them over and taking the long way back to the driver's seat, by way of edging around the front of the team, the farthest from the direction the shooters had been.

Gage also decided he needed a better plan. But there wasn't one. If they sat there in the lay-by through the rest of the daylight hours, and on through the night, weren't they inviting whoever was firing at them to climb down and make themselves at home right in their own camp?

No, Cooley was right—there was no way around it, except through it.

"I've heard no branches snapping, no footfalls of horses, no nothing," said Cooley. "Now I'm not saying we're safe, but it's a sign anyway."

"A sign of what?" Gage asked, also peering from behind the relative safety of the wagon's thick side planking. He regarded the weathered, slivered wood, noted how at one time it had been painted a deep green color, the wheels red. "When they started the freighting company, the Shiersons must have had a good bit of money to invest, and high hopes."

Cooley nodded. "They had a bit of both. As I believe I said, they come from back East. There was some money from family, and Roger, he thought he might be able to make his mark out here, maybe do just what Delano has been doing, namely set up a hauling business with depots all over the West. He told me he thought Newel seemed as good a place as any. Maybe even more suited to it than some."

"How's that?" Gage asked.

"Oh, all the mining hereabouts. In that regard, he was right. Since we set up shop, it's only gotten busier. There was a time when it seemed like everybody from the East was moving on into the town and the hills in these parts. No wonder nobody hits the big strikes anymore."

"No?"

Cooley smiled. "Bah, nothing grand like the old days, but then again, that's the fun of it, I expect. You dig and you dig and you cling to that dream that you just might be that one lucky fool whose spade and pick sink into a million-dollar deposit of gold or silver or tin or who-knows-what."

Cooley shook his head. "Me? I'll take good friends and work here and there over banging away at rocks and sweating out my days hoping for money. All these fools do that, and look what it gets them—nothing but a broke-down body and misery, dawn to dusk. Meanwhile they've left their wives and children and fathers and mothers and brothers and sisters back East somewhere!

"And those folks are still back home doing all their own work, and that of the folks who left. Plus, they're worried sick with fear, since they haven't heard from the gold hound who up and abandoned them a year or more before!"

As he spoke, Cooley's voice rose in volume and his cheeks bloomed pink above his white beard.

"Seems to me you've put a lot of thought into this," said Gage quietly, in hopes of influencing his companion to do the same.

"I have, at that. Seen too many folks lose everything just to say they're pleased with making a little something now and again with flakes or nuggets. And they're the lucky ones."

It was a curious thing to Gage to learn more about this man, since he had not known him all that long. He had assumed that Cooley was a typical old fellow who'd seen it all and done it all—or at least that was the impression men such as Cooley always seemed to want to give.

But not so with Cooley. He was a thoughtful, fiery spirit, and not quite like anyone else Gage had ever met. Not that anyone could truly be like anyone else, he thought, focusing his gaze on an unmoving darkness by the base of a wide ponderosa pine far up the slope to their southeast.

"What do you make of that?" Gage asked, not taking his eyes from the spot.

Cooley followed Gage's sight line. "That black bit yonder by the pine? Could be a killer with a brace of pistols." He narrowed his eyes. "Or it could be a shadow off that boulder just behind the tree. Mind where the sun is."

"Good point," said Gage, not quite willing to let go of the notion yet. But even when he let his eyes drift to either side of it, a better way of seeing something than staring at it dead on, nothing changed. Might well be a shadow, he thought.

He continued onward to his right, assessing as much of the route up and across the hillside as he could. On a whim, he glanced back to the dark spot behind the ponderosa. And it was not there. He grunted.

So much for trusting others with what I see, he thought.

This cautious skittishness continued on their part for another few minutes; then Cooley said he had to "make water," as Cooley referred to relieving himself. Gage kept watch on the hillside; then when Cooley returned, he told the old man of his paltry plan.

Cooley agreed and kept a gun trained on the hillside while Gage worked.

He flipped up the wagon's bench seat and dragged anything in the storage area beneath up over the upraised seat planking and stuffed it all in the back of the wagon, save for their three guns—Gage's rifle, the wagon's shotgun, and Cooley's shotgun—and ammunition.

Then with the help of the hatchet from the toolbox, Gage knocked the front boards of the box free. He cobbled the two planks, with the help of a length of shim stock snapped in half, to the upraised seat planking.

The result was a raised panel that, if the two men crouched in the more commodious seat area and boot well of the wagon, would hopefully protect them from bullets delivered at them from their back trail.

It would do little to shield them from shots sent in from the sides, and nothing from the front. But it was a decent hasty solution and made them feel as if they just might with a pinch of luck and kindness from on high, they might just make it through to Bewley without leaking blood from bullet holes.

It was a thin plan, but it topped sitting there waiting for their attackers to circle around and take them from the sides or from the front.

"Keep them behind us and we stand a chance," said Cooley, snugging his knife back in its sheath.

The new, enlarged space was cramped, particularly for Gage, who was not a small man to begin with. And with Cooley, still crampy and stiff from his beating, they were quite a pair trying to climb into their freshly cobbled spot with haste.

"Think they're onto us?" Cooley's fluffy raised eyebrows and earnest tone made Gage smile.

"Nah," he said. "Not unless they're deaf and blind."

"Great," said Cooley.

"You ready?" said Gage. "We have to get out while we can."

"Let us roll, then, Mr. Gage!" Cooley smacked a hand against his bent knee and offered a smile.

Gage nodded, released the brake, and snapped the lines, urging the teams into quick motion. He guided the team back onto the lane and was thinking they might well be shed of their tormentors, a foolish wish, he knew, but neither had they been attacked while building the makeshift shield behind them.

He did not have long to pursue his line of wishful thought, for a shot buzzed in close, smacking into the planking barely a finger snap of time before they heard the crack of the shot. That told Gage that whoever was shooting was still far enough away that they were not certain to make a dead-on shot. But that said, he knew they were good just the same.

"Hee-yaa!" He slapped the lines on the rumps of the team and they bolted, charging hard and sending the unsteadily perched Cooley flopping backward on his rump.

"Easy, boy! You fixing to kill me before they get the chance?"

"That's not possible," growled Gage through gritted teeth as he worked to keep his head down, his rifle from jostling over onto its side, and the team on the track. It was a rutted affair and the smooth rolling proved short-lived.

They descended and a switchback showed itself as the steep sides of the road revealed the curve ahead. Gage pulled back on the lines and the jouncing team slowed enough for them to make the turn. It bore them to the left and both men knew this might well put them in plain sight of anyone from above.

As they feared, and suspected, once they made the turn, pelting and snapping sounds drove down at them. None of the bullets caught them in the flesh, nor did they strike the horses, but it was unpleasant and unsettling for all ahead of and within the slamming, clunking wagon.

They rolled on through the curve, a tight one but manageable enough at their slowed speed. Neither man dared to speak or to do anything to interrupt their doubled concentration and efforts at trying to stay as low and hidden as possible in the wagon.

This running from danger did not sit well with Gage, who, despite his efforts over the past years to avoid fights, still did not like to show his back to any ill-intentioned prairie rat. Least of all, men who sought to kill him. Or, as this case seemed to be, who sought to frighten him off.

But to what end? None of this made much sense.

They had been easy targets, and their pursuers had free and open shots at them, if they so chose.

The bullets snapped in with irregular frequency, pocking the boards behind them, the sides of the wagon, the planking in front. They tore furrows, plowing up ragged, splintered trenches, unearthing the fresh, raw wood beneath, and with each one, Cooley offered a growling yelp as if counting them.

Gage could tell the little old-timer beside him wanted to trade shots with the rogues as much as he did, but whenever he dared a glance uphill, Gage saw no one.

And then they leveled off and came to a rutted, but somewhat straight, path, still angling downward and with another switchback at the end. It looked as if it would drop them to the final stretch along the little valley's treed bottom.

It took a full minute before Gage realized they were no longer being shot at. That caused him to glance up and to their left, to the steep slope above, just before they reached that next switchback. Cooley was doing the same.

"Don't question it!" snarled Cooley with a half grin.

"Think about it later," said Gage.

"Exactly!"

They rolled on into the curve and leveled off as they slowed, out of necessity, as the road was all but washed out. Each pop and crack of gravel beneath the steel rims of the wagon's heavy wheels as they ground slowly along the rutted, pitted roadway caused each man to wince and hunker deeper, still not trusting the lack of shots as anything but a calm before a big blow.

But because they had been forced to slow, they

heard more than the clunking, thrashing, pounding of
the horses' hooves on the graveled roadway. And instead of the zinging and slamming of bullets, they
heard laughter.

From far off and up above, they could hear the sound
of a man laughing—a big, hearty guffawing sound, as
if the man were an actor pretending to laugh in a play.
Soon after, a second laugh joined the first. The second
was higher in pitch, but also that of a man. And as with
the first, it, too, sounded forced. But both were loud and
intended for them—Gage was certain of that much.

"What do you make of that?" he asked, eyeing the
slope the same as Cooley. The trees, while not growing
close together, were still thick enough, and hazed with
the late-autumn gray of leafless rabbit brush, that the
men had to look hard left and right to make out possible shapes that might be their tormentors.

They were not disappointed in their surveying.

"Look at that!" yelped Cooley, forgetting his predicament for a moment as he pointed with his good
arm upslope and slightly westward.

Gage followed the man's arm and finger up to a
now-easy-to-spot figure standing with intention beside
a dark horse in a tree-free spot. The man was easy to
locate because he wore a bright blue shirt. He also held
a long gun, not thick like a shotgun, but rather a rifle.

It was not held at the ready, but canted with the
stock's butt resting on his hip, the barrel jutting up and
away. It was a casual pose, and if it was meant to mock
them, Gage felt it was doing the job.

Most assuredly, Blue Shirt was one of the shooters.
And one look at Cooley's snarling face told him that

the old man recognized the man in the blue shirt, even at this distance, as the murderer—one of two, anyway—of his former boss and friend, Roger Shierson.

"The raw nerve of that . . ."

Gage rested a hand on the old man's shoulder to simmer him down, lest he be tempted to crack off a wild blast from his gun that would do nothing but rile their horses, deafen the two of them, and rip through bushes. And likely elicit more fake laughter.

"I know how you feel," said Gage, "but—"

That was all he got out, for Cooley had seen something else, upslope, and to the left, eastward. Again he pointed.

And Gage followed the man's arm to see another man, a fellow staring in much the same pose as the first, leering down at them. This one wore buckskins, and though shorter than Blue Shirt, was a swarthy character with darkish skin and black hair splayed out about his shoulders from beneath a brown slouch hat.

"That's the other rascal! You see them? They're the killers who work for Delano! Give me your rifle!" Cooley spun on him, crazed eyes set in his white-whiskered face.

"No, Cooley! That's what they want. You shoot at them and they'll finish us off. At least now we stand a chance of getting out of here and then tracking them down later."

For a long moment, neither man spoke, but stared hard at the other. It was not what Cooley wanted to hear, not by a long shot, but it was the only logical response.

Finally the old man sagged and returned to stare at

the two far-off men, who were still laughing and mocking them.

Throughout this brief, shocking discovery, the wagon had slowed to a stop, mostly because the horses were faced with a gully washout. Gage risked leaning out and took a peek at it. It was not too bad, but without momentum, the team might have a time in pulling the wagon through.

"Of all the times . . ."

"Yeah," muttered Cooley. "Lady Luck has winged off somewhere else."

"Maybe not," said Gage.

"How you figure that?"

"Could have been shot by now."

"True!"

Luck was indeed with them, though, for not far to the left side of the wagon, Gage spied a half-rotted log, just long enough to span much of the roadway. He slipped from the wagon's boot well and grabbed the log at one end, making to lift it and grunt it the two feet up onto the road, then maybe kick it into place to help fill in the washout.

Being a Texan and having spent much of his life there and in areas close to the hot, unforgiving desert, he knew that one of the few things that seemed to thrive there were snakes. And, in particular, rattlers. And as a native of that state, Gage knew enough to not grab on to logs in the woods in snake country. He knew this, and yet he did not keep it in mind.

Despite the slamming and clunking close by, nothing had roused and frightened off the slumbering timber rattler that blended so artfully in with the mottled sand-and-buckskin shades of the decomposing log.

It sat curled atop the log, but a foot and a half from Gage's grasping hands that he held extended forward from his crouched body. All he wanted was to drag the log onto the roadway and roll it into the shallow ditch to ease the passage of the wagon. But he froze now as he stared at the wedge-shaped head with its flicking tongue.

The head sat rigid and raised atop the tightly curled body; the only other part of the snake that showed it meant to defend itself was the raised length of its rattling, buzzing tail tip.

"Gage."

It was difficult for Cooley to get through to the man. He tried again. On the third attempt, Cooley, smiling once more, said, "I'm closer to death's door than you are. In years, that is. Have some sense and back up." He smiled. "Don't do it sudden-like, though. Snakes are not partial to quick movements."

No kidding, thought Gage. He did not dare utter anything more than a shallow breath, and even then, he was not certain if he was breathing or holding it in.

"I'll shoot the thing with the shotgun, but I'm afeared that those rogues up the hill will think we're toying with them."

Through all this, Gage kept his mouth shut. He also hadn't breathed in the few moments he and the snake had begun to face off. Without warning, he jerked himself backward, his arms pulling tight to his belly as his powerful legs shoved, propelling him away from the log. He hoped that he would be out of danger when the snake decided to strike, for he well knew the fearsome viper would attack.

And the thing did not disappoint, but kept coming, and Gage kept churning his legs backward. Then his boot caught on a half-sunk rock at the edge of the roadway and sent him sprawling on his backside. He scrambled, even before he could locate the snake.

He didn't have long to wait. He also didn't anticipate what was happening at the wagon.

Cooley had slid down out of the protection of the boot well and had managed to slam the butt of his shotgun down, apparently to smash the viper.

By that time, Gage regained his feet and had moved to slick out his sheath knife. It was a twelve-inch-long, thick- and wide-bladed brute of a weapon he'd bought in a mercantile in Kansas a few years back. It had belonged to a mountain man of some repute who had been found, or rather parts of him had been found, and buried by another of his kind.

That man who'd done the finding had scavenged up the dead man's gear and had lugged it with him and sold it to a traveling merchant, who had then sold off parts and pieces here and there as he hawked his wares. And so the knife had come to be for sale days before Gage happened along.

It was one heck of a knife, useful to him on far too many occasions to count. It had served as a hatchet to chunk up kindling and larger bits of wood when used with another piece he whacked against the spine of the blade.

The steel was of the finest quality, best he'd ever come across, in fact, and he counted himself fortunate to own the knife. The handgrips were of a hardwood, solid and seemingly impervious to abuse, and riveted with thick brass pins through the tang. He'd made himself a thick leather sheath, buffalo hide, with a double-laced thong at the top to keep it from jostling free.

The downside of this setup was that he found himself fumbling to untie the lacing holding the knife securely in the sheath. Though Gage found himself in unpredictable situations more often than he cared to recall, he'd rarely, if ever, found he needed the assistance of the big knife at those times. And not using it on another living creature suited him just fine.

Now, though, a riled rattler was making its way toward him, none too slowly. And he couldn't free the blasted blade from the sheath.

And Cooley, despite his best intentions, was doing little, save for putting himself in dire danger with every slam of the gun's butt closer and closer to the advancing snake. Another slam or two and Gage figured the old man was going to get a face full of newly distracted viper.

When the snake was but a foot from Gage's boot soles, and coming on strong, and with a fumbling, one-armed Cooley close behind, a sizzling sound parted the air followed quickly with a snapping boom.

Gravel spumed just before the snake, distracting it but a moment from its single-minded attack.

Gage knew it was a gunshot, but had no time for any further thought, because he'd just crabwalked backward into the ditch. He slopped in, his boots now elevated a bit above his head, and the bottom of the ditch still funky with damp gravel and muck.

Just then, the snake's head crested the edge of the ditch, and whipping back and forth as if the creature were seeking him, it paused, as if it had eyed him, and began its quick plunge down.

Another sizzling crack sounded then and the snake's clublike head whipped upward and flailed in the air as if it had been gripped from behind by a demon. And perhaps it had. For an eyeblink of time, Gage assumed Cooley had finally landed a solid blow on the snake, something that caused this seemingly agonizing flailing. But then Gage realized the crack had been another gunshot.

His mind finally snapped from its full fixation on the snake and he realized both sounds had been gunshots, yes, but not from close up, and not from a shotgun. They had come from a rifle. The same rifle, no doubt. All this ruled out Cooley . . .

The men on the hill?

And then he had no more time for such thinking, for the full, long, girthy body of the thrashing, flailing rattler whipped up in the air before him, its ample girth arcing high before tumbling down on him.

Even as the thing whipped upward before him, skylined against the brighter gray-white clouds and patches of blue, Gage was on the move, abandoning his scrabbling attempts to free his blade from its safe sheath— too blasted safe, he thought with a snarl. He rolled to his right and pulled his head back last, just in time to see the big snaky head, with jaws parted far too wide, he thought, to be anything but seething with rage and bent on sinking fangs into Gage.

He rolled again before he dared to try to scramble

away on all fours, then raked gravel as he tried to stand. All the while, Gage kept his gaze pinned on the big, writhing body of the snake.

Up close, it was far larger than he had first assumed. The thought came to him that perhaps the snake he'd originally seen coiled atop the log had been a different, smaller one, and this one was its mother. Its angry mother.

But no, this had to be the same one. And then the old-timer popped up, well away from the edge of the shallow embankment, and peered in.

By then, Gage was well away, making once more for the roadside, perhaps a dozen feet along, and moving. He gained enough distance between the roiling snake and himself that he glanced up at the hillside and saw, closer than they had been, the two tormentors up the hill.

They were still a good distance away and up, but now they were closer together. And they both had their long guns leveled on Gage and Cooley.

During all of this unexpected hubbub, the horses had jerked and stomped, working their big heads up and down on their thick necks like pump handles. Gage had not set the brake and they had rolled the wagon forward toward the ditch, until they stopped but a foot from it. They didn't dare step into it or try to step over it, the width varying from a foot to two along its crumbled edge.

He looked back to the snake and Cooley. Both were moving, Cooley because he'd gotten far too close. One of the more dangerous things a fellow could do was to mistake anything dead or dying for something that was incapacitated or harmless.

Gage saw the snake in full once more and saw that it had indeed been shot, for part of the thick meat of its body, a third of the way back from its snapping, striking head, had been chewed away, leaving a ragged, bloodied, pulped wound, blood and white meat and stringy bits slapping the earth and rising up again.

The beast, witless in its bloodied agony, flailed and seemed to want to sink its knifelike fangs into something, anything, and the nearest something was Cooley.

The old gent jumped as if dancing on a well-fired skillet, his sling-borne arm flailing up and down as if it were a featherless wing. He'd lost his hat somewhere in the proceedings and his bald dome and white fluff of beard pumped and wagged as he howled and stomped. All in all doing a poor job, Gage thought, of retreating from the snapping snake.

Gage scrambled up and out of the end of the ditch and clambered back up to the rutted roadway, his big blade now finally freed.

He chose his moment to lunge, and with finger-snap speed, a gout of blood sprayed as he delivered a quick, low, arcing swing from right to left, then back again, from left to right. He needed do no more, for his brutal, keen blade left behind a foot-long length of snake, the popping, snapping jaws showing no sign of letting up in their quest for blind vengeance. The severed thing bucked and writhed, sand and gravel pasting to the steaming, clotted stump.

The other stump also flailed atop the snapping,

whipping length of snake body, the rattles sounding as if they had waited a long time to sing out their final, shrill song.

Gage cut wide around the gory sight and closed in on Cooley, who now leaned against the wagon, panting, his chest working like a bellows.

"You all right?"

But before he could answer, both men realized there was a sound neither had paid attention to for the past busy minutes, though it came to them that it had been there all along. It was laughter, again, and it came from up on the hill overlooking their weird little scene.

Cooley raised his good fist and shook it at them, then shouted, "Come down here, you rascals! I'll give you something to laugh about!"

Gage had had about enough of those two tormentors himself and reached into the wagon for his rifle. They had cover behind the wagon now and he felt like he needed to begin defending himself against them.

Whatever their game was, he found it beyond unnerving and confusing, and he was sick of it, even if they had saved him from a potential snakebite.

He looked back up the hill, over the head of the riled old man, and saw the two still-laughing men, retreating westward, then south, cutting up the steep embankment.

He lost sight of the one in buckskin first; then the blue-shirted man passed behind the dark trunks of ponderosa pines and the brief glimpses of blue blurred into shadow and they were gone.

The last thing to leave was their hearty laughter.

A long, quiet moment passed; then Cooley said, "Well, I am glad we could supply them with something to giggle like little girls about." He cast one last, long sneer up at the now-vacant hillside, then looked at the scene before them.

Gage reapproached the snake log, kicked it a couple of times, then dragged it over and rolled it into the ditch, as he had originally intended. Then he led the hesitant team, with a few hard tugs and harsh words and rump slaps from Cooley, over the awkward bridge and onto the other side. They walked along with the team for a few more yards, and then Gage paused.

By unspoken agreement, they decided to call it a day and set up camp right there. Each man hoped the two men on their tail were no longer a threat. It made little sense to assume that, they knew, but they did just the same. They knew the spot was one where they might be able to defend themselves more easily than if they resumed their trek.

Their stretch of road was widely cut into the upper side and bermed by a natural blockade of boulders. It would provide ample cover from above and to each side. And their wagon, parked before it, would confound possible attackers from below. It was a decent spot to stop.

"You like snake, Gage?"

"To eat?"

"No, to play dollies with. Course to eat!"

Gage shrugged. "I've had my share over the years."

Cooley shook his head. "That ain't what I asked, but

that less-than-excited response of yours tells me what I need to know."

"Why? Are you thinking of frying up that beast?"

"I am. Skin ain't much useful now, all shot up and such as it is, but the meat'll be good."

"Well . . ."

"Aw, you eat my share of the beans and bacon. I'll tuck into this here snake meat. It's free and tasty. And besides"—he tapped his nose—"my old friend Running Boy, him of the Sioux Nation, told me that you never dishonor a fellow critter by killing it and not making of it what you can. You take in some snake, you get yourself a few more traits that just might stand you well next time you find yourself in a scuffle."

"Do you believe that?" Gage asked, pausing in unfastening a brass harness buckle, not trying to sound doubtful, but thinking he might have.

"Course I do! Ain't a thing in this world that don't have a deeper meaning than humankind gives it stock for, nor more value than we care to give it."

Gage looked at Cooley and nodded. "I believe I understand you. And I agree. All right, then, let's dine on that big ol' snake."

"Good man! You bet you agree! Knew you would. You're a smart fella, Gage, and quick with that knife, to boot!" He went back to slicing the snake's skin off its meat. "Besides, it's not like the snake asked to be bothered. That beast was just a-sunning itself when we happened along."

"True," said Gage, smiling at the old, wily codger. He certainly held up his end of the conversation, and much of Gage's, too. Good thing, thought Gage as he tugged and slid the harness off the second horse. For with each passing hour, Gage felt less prone to chat. Not when there was so much trouble about.

They spelled one another twice during the night. Gage tried to let Cooley sleep through his second stint, but the old man popped open an eye. "You had best not be thinking of doing what I know you are thinking of doing, mister." He sat up and rubbed the upper part of his wounded arm. "Let kiddies be kiddies. Me? I'm a man, not an old man, just a man, so treat me like one."

Gage nodded and lay down, tugging his blanket up over him.

Cooley poured himself a cup of cooled coffee from the tin pot. "Don't mean I don't appreciate the thought." Then he ambled off into the dark to make water and take over watch.

Despite—or perhaps because of, thought Gage—their attention to the comings and goings of the creatures of the night, it was a quiet, if not restful, night. They called it good just before dawn and rubbed warmth into their shivering limbs, stomping about the campsite.

Gage had been concerned that the rattlesnake, which he ate an acceptable portion of last evening, might not sit well with him. But Cooley had probably had the same thought and had fried it up until it was decidedly dead and gone.

Just to be certain, Gage had followed it up with two biscuits and plenty of coffee. And then later, he chased it with a couple of hunks of hardtack, for good measure.

"You want to finish off the rattler for breakfast?" Cooley held up the fry pan, in which he'd left the remaining hunks, already fried to a crusted crisp.

"No, no, you go ahead. I'm still full."

Cooley laughed. "I hope you don't play much poker, Gage."

"That obvious?"

"Pretty much, yep. As bad at lying as you are, you're liable to lose your hat, boots, and everything between."

Gage grinned and sipped a fresh cup of hot coffee and sighed. No matter how much of it he had in a day or a night, or both, there was something enjoyable about a cup of hot coffee most anytime.

Cooley joined him and they firmed up their already-decided plan for the day. They would make tracks for Bewley, which, by Cooley's reckoning, was another ridge away. Gage drove the team, but they both swiveled their heads around as they rolled, doing their best to keep a tight eye on anything that might not feel or look right to them.

The remainder of the journey, over a road that at times looked to be anything but passable, remained free of men in buckskins or blue shirts. Or any other humans, for that matter.

They did frighten two fat grizzly cubs and rolled fast on by as the twins scampered thirty feet up a tree, because their mama showed up. She was a thick-necked and full-bellied sow, and offered plenty of jaw popping and head shaking and low, chesty bellows.

Their horses were not impressed with this, but Gage was able to keep them lunging on ahead, not without applying a few choice cracks with the whip's tip to tickle their rumps.

Once they were safely past the real danger the mother bear could well have delivered to them, Cooley grinned. "Reminds me of a woman I knew once, back in Ohio somewhere. Big gal, and fun as all get-out. Until it came to her children. Then she was business and nothing but. If them kids didn't turn out to be tycoons who took care of their mama for the rest of her days, I will eat this hat."

"Not really the sort of thing a fellow can follow up on now, is it?" Gage was beginning to get a read of Cooley's temperament, and he knew he could poke him a bit here and there and he'd take it well enough. It was fun to get him riled.

"Now you look here, Gage. I get the sense you think I'm a fibber!"

"No, no, not you, Mr. Cooley. I could never think such a thing."

Their banter went on as such in spurts and lags until past noon. They were closing in on Bewley, and when they could see a scrim of low-hanging smoke, from chimneys and campfires, they knew town was close.

Cooley had begun recalling landmarks and way-points—an abandoned miner's dugout, several dark shaft openings leading who knew how deep. And he took pride in pointing out a stone as big as a wagon that looked to have stopped its steep mountainside descent at the very edge of the roadway.

Cooley would not agree to Gage's notion that perhaps the builders of the road had cut around the huge tumbledown a whole lot of years after the thing rolled to a stop at that very spot.

Before he could argue further, a dog came at them from a bend a bare hundred feet up the road. It was a gray-and-black hound cross and looked to have last been fed some years before. But it stood its ground in the roadway and bayed as if they were raccoons he was determined to tree.

"I do believe the welcoming committee has arrived."

Gage smiled and nodded. "Shall we wait for the human version?"

"I think we ought to. The folks up here tend to get a little odd in the noggin about strangers showing up."

"And you didn't think to tell me this earlier?"

"Nah, they know me. We'll be fine."

As if prompted by his comment, two figures, men, also emerged from around the bend and stood in the roadway, each cradling a long gun.

From their stopped position, Gage regarded the duo. Cooley squinted.

"Too far for me to recognize them, but I'd say it might well be Horace Haskell on the right. Taller man. The other, dunno." He raised a hand and waved once, wide and slow. "Howdy! It's Cooley. You recall me? Been a spell."

The two men didn't seem to respond; then they leaned their heads together, conferring. Finally the tall one, who Cooley thought might be Haskell, said, "What you want?"

That response caught Cooley short. "What do I want?"

he said to Gage in a low voice. "It is Haskell. For pity's sake, I thought we was friends."

"Don't tell me," said Gage. "Tell them. I'm the stranger here."

"Oh yeah." Cooley pulled in a breath, fluffed his beard with his free hand, a trait Gage noticed the man indulged in when he was nerved up about something. Cooley fluffed often.

"I say it's Cooley! From Shierson Freight Haulage! Come to see about business!"

The two men stiffened a bit, and then, as if on cue, they looked in opposite directions, to the slopes around and beyond Gage and Cooley.

"What are they looking for?" Cooley, too, looked around.

"Not a what. I bet it's a who."

"Huh?"

"I wonder if Delano's men visited them."

"Oh," said Cooley. "Hmm. Well, they haven't taken aim at us yet. I say we roll on in."

"All right, but keep that gut shredder of yours ready. We may need its persuasive powers."

"You bet."

And with that, Gage snapped the lines lightly and the team began its slow plod forward. How they might ever pull a full load, he wasn't certain. But at the rate they were going, it might not be a point of consideration anyway.

They rolled ahead, and when they drew to within fifty feet of the men, the tall one, Haskell, brought his rifle around, and though he kept it aimed downward, he could as easily lift it quick to bear on them. Gage cast quick glances to either side of them, lest they ride into an ambuscade.

"Now look here, Haskell, don't you see me, man? It's Cooley! Why, we hoisted the jug a few times, not all that long since."

"I know it, Cooley. I know it. But . . . well . . ."

"Then what's got into you, man? What's going on here?"

Gage wasn't certain, but it looked to him as if the man turned red and squirmed as he stood there. Finally he hefted the rifle and laid it on his shoulder. The other man, shorter and with more of a swarthy face and thick features, but not sour-looking, glanced at Haskell.

The taller man shrugged and the swarthy man nodded and he, too, laid his rifle over his shoulder.

"Come on in, closer," said Haskell. "We're good."

"Now, you're talking," said Cooley, grinning.

Gage thought that even if his shotgun rider was satisfied, he wasn't. He pasted on a mild look and clucked the team onward, until they drew up to about eight to ten feet before the two men.

They looked to Gage to be no different in appearance than most dirt farmers and miners he'd ever met or known—worn out and haggard before their times. But likely decent, solid men, all the same.

"Cooley." Haskell nodded.

"Haskell," said the old man. Gage noted that Cooley fluffed his beard quickly.

"Who's your friend?" said the tall man, looking at Gage.

"Could say the same to you," said Cooley.

"Oh, this here's Roberto. Come here about, what was it?" Haskell looked at his swarthy companion. "About a year back?"

Roberto frowned, scrunched his eyes, and nodded. "Just, yes."

"Good to meet you, Roberto," said Cooley, nodding. "This big lug here's Gage. We convinced Mrs. Shierson to get back into the trade. Been long enough for grieving that bills need to be paid. And besides"—Cooley leaned forward as if to tell them a secret—"Newel ain't big enough for two freighters. Leastwise not when one is Delano."

Gage watched the two men during this exchange. When Cooley mentioned the unscrupulous freighter's name, Roberto and Haskell both tensed, their eyes widened, and they once more glanced about them, as if they had heard some danger and were now on their guard.

"Good to meet you both," said Gage.

Roberto and Haskell nodded and, glancing once more to the hillsides, they turned, with the taller man raising a beckoning hand.

Gage complied and Cooley leaned close. "What do you think that's all about, Gage?"

The big man was silent a moment, then said, in an equally low voice, "Not certain, but if I had to guess, I'd say Delano has somehow put a fear into them. Maybe threatened them somehow against using any service other than his."

Rather than crow and fret, as Gage had expected him to do, Cooley nodded and fluffed his beard some more. Once in a while, he muttered something that wasn't a kindly word, but a word that Gage bet he was using with Delano in mind.

Then the man's face brightened. "Well, we're here now and we can do our best to put their minds at ease, eh, young fella?" Cooley winked.

"You bet," said Gage. But inside, he was thinking of those looks the two men ahead had given to the woods and the hills about them. Raw fear was what he had seen there. And Cooley knew it, too.

Chapter 17

The little, plump, pink-faced man looked up from his meal at the two men standing in the doorway staring at him. Delano's cheeks were filled with food. "Huh. You're back. You do as I told you?" A platter laden with steaming tender beef and buttered boiled potatoes, all topped with thick, dark gravy, sat on his desk before him.

"What do you think?"

It was the one in the blue shirt, Pierce, a man Delano did not like in the least. And no better was his estimation of the smaller man in buckskins, Nob.

"Not sure I like your tone, Pierce," said Delano.

What happened next was something Delano would never forget. Pierce moved fast, one, two steps, and then he was right there, before the desk, standing over Delano, who had just spooned in a wad of potatoes and gravy. Pierce's hand snatched fast, grabbing Delano's shirtfront, undershirt, and loosened string tie and lifted the porky man up, using his other hand to drag Delano higher, then across the desk.

The freight boss's belly smooshed flat atop the steaming food and it oozed out and down his shirt. Pierce kept on dragging, smiling the entire time, with Nob behind him hoorah-ing and smacking his leather trousers. "Give it to him, man! Give it!"

Pierce backed up and dragged the chubby freight man completely over the top of the desk and held him up before him, jerking him close enough that their noses nearly touched. "How do you like my tone now, you little pig?"

Nob howled louder and then set to grunting and shouting, *"Sooey! Sooey!"*

With his gagging, pooched lips, through his mouthful of potatoes and gravy, Delano spluttered and windmilled his arms. "Wha-wha . . ."

"What's that, Delano? What? Can't hear you quite well enough. Could be all that food you jammed in your fat face. Now swallow it or spit it out and then talk. Didn't anyone ever teach you manners?"

Delano, despite the situation, could not bring himself to waste food by spitting it out. Instead, he swallowed the potatoes and spluttered some more. Finally he said, "Thought we was friends, Pierce. Business associates."

"We were. Until you decided to summon us here, knowing full well you don't have the money to pay our fee."

"But—"

"But nothing, Delano. You made a promise, a business promise, by hiring us, and you are trying to back on out of it. And that"—Pierce began to shake the chunky fellow in time with each word he uttered—"is unacceptable! You hear me?"

The entire time he did this, he smiled, a wide, leering grin. Then he dropped Delano at his feet in a heap of mewling, slobbering man.

"Now let's see." Pierce turned to his pal. "Nob, did we do as the man asked?"

The man in buckskin grinned and scratched his chin whiskers as if deep in thought. "Dunno, Pierce. Dunno if we did."

Pierce snapped his fingers. "Oh, that's right. We did not actually put a bullet in Gage and Cooley, as you told us to, Delano. No, not that. But we did put a little fear into them. Yep, that's what we did."

Pierce looked down at the scrabbling man. "That's right. And we did the same with those vermin up in the hills. The ones in that mine camp they call Bewley. Ain't that right, Nob?"

"You bet, you bet, man." The fellow smiled and his head bobbed.

"Now, Delano, see, if you had paid us like we have always done, all up front, just like always, you would have been a smiling man right about now. But that there is not how this played out. And all because you played us false."

Delano had crabwalked backward, away from the looming, blue-shirted man. "I have money, I swear it. Look, look!" He half crawled around the far end of his desk and grabbed at it with his meaty, gravy-slick fingers to raise himself up to a standing position.

The man in the blue shirt backed away and, as if

cued, both he and his buckskin-clad friend whipped their sidearms free and had them aimed and cocked, pointing square at Delano as he hurried to get behind the desk.

"Don't shoot me! Oh, Lordy, no! I haven't done a thing wrong! I have the money! All in gold, even. I swear it! Just going to get the safe open. I swear it!"

Pierce smiled and they kept their guns pointed. "I bet you have. But I'm only interested in seeing that money, not in seeing you snatch up a handful of pistol, you hear, you sneaky slob, you."

"I wouldn't do that, Pierce. I swear it. Just let me get the safe open and you'll see!"

"Okay, then," said the killer, sidestepping so he could get a better view of the safe when it was opened. "But easy and slow, I got all day."

"Me too!" said Delano.

Delano wiped his shaking pink hands on his shirt-front, but that only made them filthier. He rubbed them on his backside, and Pierce said, "Easy now, pig man. Or you'll be covered in more than meat and potatoes and gravy."

"Okay, all right." Delano bent over, then dropped to one knee with a grunt before the safe. He fumbled and shook and small squeals came out from his nearly closed mouth. He tried not to make them, but he couldn't seem to help it. The noises only caused Pierce to smile wider and Nob to laugh like a demented child behind him.

Finally Delano managed to make the mechanism slide into that final position and he grabbed the steel handle and yanked down and outward. The heavy door of the small safe slowly opened. As it did, Delano had a truly frightening thought: What if somebody had robbed him? These two peckerwoods would gun him down right there, behind his desk, with food all over himself.

Oh, my lovely meal, he thought; then his eyes fell on the sacks in the safe.

He reached in and dragged the heavy sacks out; then, swaying a little with the effort, he set them atop the desk, on a clean corner.

"See? I told you. I got the money, all right."

As the two men crowded closer, and Pierce tugged open the rawhide thongs securing the mouths of the bags tight, Delano backed up a pace. A thought came to him then.

"Um, Pierce. How would I have known I was supposed to give the money to Nob?"

The blue-shirted man looked up from peering into the bags, his revolver still held a foot from Delano's sullied gut. "Why, whatever are you talking about, Delano?"

The fat man shrugged, and tried to smile. "Well, all the times before, you both showed up and I'd repeat to you what I wanted you to do. But this time, you sent Nob, but you didn't show up in town. He never said I should give him the money."

"Well, now, Delano. As we were coming in from the north, it didn't make all that much sense for us both to ride to Newel, then back up into the hills, now, did it? You said it plain enough in your note that the good folks up at Bewley needed a reminding that your freighting outfit was the only one they were allowed to use.

"So while my pard, Nob, here made his way to Newel to listen to you give us *orders*"—at that word, Pierce's voice rose and grew colder and his eyes narrowed—"I made darn certain those folks up in the hills at Bewley were good and scared."

"Yes, well, sure, that makes good sense. But that Gage fellow and the old man . . ."

Pierce nodded, running a free hand into a bag of gold dust, as if he were caressing a pretty woman's cheek. "I know, I know. You wanted them dead. But see, you sent Nob packing off after me without giving him any money. And that just ain't the way we operate, never have. You surely remember that, Delano." He gave the chunky man a hard stare.

"Sure, sure. I didn't know—"

"Oh, now. Don't insult the intelligence of my trail pard, Nob. Okay, Delano? He might not be the sharpest knife in the kitchen, but he sure can cut when the need arises. Ain't that right, Nobby?"

At that, the man in buckskins lifted free a big hunting blade swinging in a sheath by his side. "Uh-huh." He leered and waved the big blade menacingly.

It looked to Delano like a snake's head about to strike. He had to look away. "Oh, I didn't mean to insult him. No, no, what I meant was . . . he never asked for the money, you see."

"Never had to before, Delano. See, me and Nob, we operate on some basic notions. One of them is that we do a job right, no games, beginning to end. And another is that we expect, especially from folks we've worked with in the past, not to have to repeat ourselves every single time we are hired on. We just assume you know the score, being an old friend of ours and all."

"Oh, oh, we are friends, Pierce. I swear it!" Delano grinned as if he'd heard smiles could be traded for dollars.

"Glad one of us thinks that. Now, the problem is, as I said, Delano, you never offered my friend the money we always get when we start a job. Old hand like you, we have naturally extended the courtesy of paying us half up front and then the rest when you get proof of the job's finish."

"I appreciate that, Pierce. I really do. I—"

Pierce held up a hand. "Let me finish, you little pig. Now, despite the fact that you failed to uphold your end of our long-standing bargain, we still did half of the job. Namely, in putting deathly fears into those fools up at Bewley, and then instead of laying waste to the two men you whined about making their way up into the hills, trying no doubt to gnaw away at your so-called freighting empire, we shot at them, scared them right good, too, wouldn't you say, Nob?"

The shorter hired killer grinned and nodded and sniggered.

"And do you know what, Delano?"

"No, Pierce, what?" The soiled freight owner swallowed back a growing lump in his throat.

"Two things make me think we'll give you a second chance. And that's not something we ever do, right, Nob?"

The man in buckskins shook his head, a rueful grimace on his homely face.

"One, all this here gold will do us nicely. Just right, I tell you."

"But—" Delano fought back a rising case of screaming panic.

Pierce held up his hand once more. "You interrupt me again, piggy, and that'll be the last time you ever do that, or anything else, to anyone else, right?"

A wide-eyed Delano nodded, but kept his mouth clamped shut.

"Good boy. Now, number two, that Gage fellow. He interests me. Yes, sir, he does. And I tell you what, Delano. He should interest you, too. You want to know why?"

Delano, still afraid to speak, nodded quickly.

Pierce smiled. "Because he is none other than a wanted man, Delano. It's true, sure as the sun will no doubt shine down on all us sinners come tomorrow. That Gage is none other than Jonathan Gage. That ring any chimes in your fat head?"

Delano shook his head.

"No? Well, it should. Oh, maybe you heard of his other name . . . Texas Lightning."

The words Pierce spoke sizzled in the air between them, and slowly a scrim of confusion parted and Delano's eyes widened once more. "The gunfighter? But I thought he was dead."

"Naw, not dead. Just gone for a spell. But like all vermin, he poked his head up eventually. And we happened to see him. Now, do you know why that bit of information should interest you, piggy?"

Delano shrugged. He was beginning to tire of hearing this blue-shirted monkey call him names.

"Because if you drag your fat self on down to the local lawdog's office, you will probably find a Wanted dodger on that Gage fellow. And below the lousy drawing of the man's homely face, you will see a dollar sign and a number with a handful of zeros attached. You following me?"

Delano nodded and a smile crept onto his face. Things were starting to come together in his mind. Things he liked to think about, a whole lot of interesting things. "How much?"

Pierce canted his head to one side and regarded Delano through narrowed eyes. "Just how lazy are you, Delano? Does a man have to do everything for you?"

Now that he was back behind his desk, a well-worn apparatus he had come to regard as a shield, a buffer between himself and the buffoons who worked for him, and the fools who hired his firm's services, Delano felt more comfortable.

That his beloved desk had failed to shield him from the brutal attack of Pierce and his braying partner was something he could dwell on later—and Delano knew himself well enough to know that he would indeed brood later about the vicious assault he had endured. And this brooding would lead to him returning the favor in kind. He knew a few tricks himself.

Before that, he simply had to learn how to handle a gun. It had been something he had been meaning to do for some time, and it was a skill that would have come in useful a few times over the years. But somehow making money—and thus having the means to hire idiots who knew how to use guns—had always been of more importance. Until now.

He stood behind the desk, well behind, and closer to the far end, away from Pierce and Nob, who were still fondling the bags of gold. Delano stood straight, stretching to his full height, and trying to look dignified, despite wearing his meal on his belly and chest.

"Gentlemen," he said, waiting for them to look at him.

He had to say it again before Pierce glanced his way. "What?"

"I am willing to overlook the, shall we say, poor treatment of myself, in lieu of the fact that we . . . ah, well, got ourselves off on the wrong foot, you see."

He was talking too much, and not getting to the point. He knew this because Pierce was eyeing him with that annoyed look of his. Delano hurried himself along.

"What I mean to say is, I am willing to let you have those bags of gold. Full and free, provided you, ah, complete the job for which I summoned you here."

"Oh yeah? Well, what makes you think this here isn't just a down payment on what we have already done, never mind doing more?"

Delano had expected this sort of reaction. "I am confident of this, because it is of far greater value than any price we have agreed upon in the past for similar work, and because I will gladly share whatever reward I shall reap from the law once Gage is dealt with."

"Ha!" Pierce shook his head and smiled. "I'll give you this, Delano—you got a high opinion of yourself, no lie. I reckon that's what it takes to make a success of a man."

Delano smiled and nodded, accepting the compliment.

"Like you used to be anyway."

Delano lost his smile. That remark had pulled no small amount of wind from his sails, he didn't mind admitting. But he also knew he got what he wanted to see—he of the blue shirt interested in further work. In completing the task; in killing Gage and Cooley, too.

Then maybe that pesky Shierson woman would finally pull up stakes and hit the trail back East, where she belonged. Or to wherever she wanted to run away to, he didn't much care.

Too bad, too, that she was stone broke, though he guessed he had something to do with that. Because she was a fine-looking thing. Just think—if she didn't hate him, and if she did somehow still have money at her disposal, she'd be one dandy arm trinket to drag around to show the high-cotton moneymen back in Denver City.

The ones he owed so much money to. If Pierce and Nob ever got wind of that debt, not only would they never work for him again, they'd likely hire on to do to him what he needed them to do to Gage and Cooley. Namely, to render them dead, dead, dead.

Chapter 18

Bright the next morning, Gage and Cooley rolled back to Newel. But it took much cajoling and probing and arguing and, finally, convincing the skittish people of Bewley mine camp to let them haul a small load of their ore back to Newel with them.

In exchange, the townsfolk promised they'd not continue freighting with Delano, but only on the condition that Cooley guaranteed they would not be molested or harassed or intimidated further by Delano's beasts. They didn't want much to do with Gage, seeing as how he was a newcomer and all. But Cooley, they all admitted, was a true chum, someone they had all liked and relied on for several years. At least before the Shierson Freight Haulage firm began to fall apart.

"The most important information I got out of all that yammering was that those buggers, ol' Blue Boy and his buckskin compadre, were the ones who bothered those folks. Must have been them on their way out of here, and back to Newel to see Delano, when we ran across them. Or them, us."

Gage nodded. "I still don't know why they didn't kill us when they had the chance."

"Why do you think?" Cooley tapped his nose and rummaged in his tunic for his pipe and baccy.

Gage shrugged. "Likely, they haven't seen a dime from Delano yet. I don't think they will, either." And as quickly as he'd said it, Gage knew it was the most plausible explanation.

"I bet they pulled their shots just enough to scare us off."

"But they didn't get away with much, now, did they, Cooley?"

"Nope." The old man shook his head and smiled and set fire to a bowl of tobacco.

He might well be feeling in fine form, despite the deadly intentions of Blue Shirt and the other one, but Gage knew this was no time to let down their guard. Especially not now. He drove the team as hard as he dared. Given the threat of being gunned down, they would not venture to Clabberville on this trip, and they would not spend the night in the hills on the trail if he could help it.

Reversing their course through the switchbacks was the most hair-raising, nerve-wracking part, for much of the time they each had to look not so much at their back trail as ahead and upward.

It wasn't until they were close to the halfway mark on their homeward leg of the journey that Gage noticed Cooley was not looking too good, nor was he as chatty as he had been. Come to think of it, the old man had been a bit reserved since they left Bewley. He'd assumed it was because of the rigorous verbal workout he'd had to endure with the folks at Bewley, folks Gage had come to learn truly were Cooley's friends, and who were fond of Mrs. Shierson as well.

In fact, the miners had nothing off to say about the Shierson freighting firm, save for the fact that they had felt a little perturbed that they had been left high and dry when she'd had to close her doors and park the freight wagons, leaving them no option but to give in to Delano and his gouging, nasty ways.

By the time they rolled into Newel, it was an hour past sundown and Gage had had to let the horses pick their way along. His night vision was tested just enough in finding the edges of the track. Fortunately, this close to town, the roadway was wide and well traveled.

They had barely made the wide turn into Shierson's back lot, when a lantern appeared from within the warehouse and moved to the edge of the loading dock.

"Ma'am," said Gage, "we're back safe, but I could use help with Cooley."

"What's wrong?" she said, already setting down the lantern and making to jump down.

"I think he's fevered. Hasn't been as talkative as usual for some hours now."

"First time I heard somebody complain I ain't chatty enough." Cooley's voice was thick, the intended mirth clouded by fatigue.

"Hush now," said Mrs. Shierson. "I knew you were still too weak to make such a run."

"Oh, I . . ." But that was all the old man got out, because he slipped into a fretful slumber.

Mrs. Shierson laid a hand over his forehead. "He's

burning up." She looked over. "Mr. Gage, please carry him inside and lay him on his cot. I'll make up a nostrum to reduce the fever."

Gage did as he was bade, and within short order he realized the only thing he would be useful—or tolerated—for was to unload the wagon and tend to the team and gear.

He did so, and then, with sheepish caution, reentered the part of the warehouse that had been sectioned off as living quarters.

"Ma'am? How is he?"

She looked up, and though Gage could not see her face clearly in the dim lamplight, he thought she might not be too angry; though with her, it had been difficult for him to tell.

"Considering he is unconscious, and should not have ventured out in his condition into the wilds of this land in the first place, I would say that the fact that he is not dead shows that Mr. Cooley is as ornery and as difficult as ever."

There was a rattly cough from the old man. He tried to say something, but was hushed up by the doting woman.

"Blue Boy . . . Curse him . . . Blue shirt . . . devil!"

The old man's weak, but insistent, voice filled the silence and neither Gage nor Mrs. Shierson spoke. Cooley finally settled back to collapse into his bedding and appeared once more to slide into a deep sleep.

She stood and gazed down at him once more. Then she lifted the lantern and made for the small, makeshift kitchen worktable by her glowing woodstove.

"Mr. Gage," she said, just loud enough for him to hear. She did not follow this with words, so he walked over and warmed his hands by the stove.

"Ma'am?"

She turned and handed him a cup of hot tea. "Just made," she said, and nearly smiled. It shocked him a moment and he nodded his thanks, taking the cup from her.

"Am I that daunting?" she said, sipping her own cup.

"No, ma'am. Well, maybe a little." He risked a small smile. She did not reciprocate, but he felt good, as if they had somehow turned a corner.

"I have made soup and there is plenty for us all." Her gesture took in Cooley as well, looking small and old on his cot at the edge of the shadows. "Though I doubt Mr. Cooley will join us."

"Thank you, ma'am. I don't want to trouble you."

"It's not a trouble. As I said, it's all made. And fresh bread as well." She turned to her worktable and soon had a deep bowl of steaming, thick soup set on the small table between the two sitting chairs by the stove. She placed a small plate of bread there, and then handed him a spoon and a neatly folded, crisp flowered napkin. "Please, Mr. Gage, take a seat and eat. It will grow cold and it is not the sort of soup intended for that."

He wondered as he sat if indeed there were soups somewhere in the world that were served cold. Just might be, he thought. What a very small bit of the world he had seen, he thought as he waited for her to take her seat.

They ate in silence, save for the clinking of spoons now and then against the crockery. He was tempted to run a hunk of bread around the inside of his bowl to sop up the last of the soup, but he decided that might do the last bit of convincing she needed to show her he was the heathen she suspected he was.

"There is more soup, Mr. Gage, if you are still hungry."

"Thank you, ma'am, but no. It was quite tasty, but an old-timer I met years ago told me that a fellow should always leave the table feeling as if he could eat more. That way, somewhere in the world, there would always be plenty of food for others."

"A wise man, your friend. Where is he now?"

"Oh, that was some time ago, and he was no spring chicken then. I suspect he's gone. I moved on shortly after that."

"You're a traveling man by nature, then."

He didn't respond right away and he was afraid she might take that to mean she was prying, which was not his intention. "I suppose so, yes. It's not something I think much about."

She nodded. "Would you like more tea, Mr. Gage?"

"No, thank you, ma'am." He stood. "But it was just right. The soup and bread as well. I'll need to check in on my horse; then, if you don't mind, I'll return and get everything set for tomorrow."

"Tomorrow?" she said.

"Yes, I'd like to make that run to Clabberville. No sense losing our momentum now. Word will get out that we, that is to say *you,* are back in business, and we won't want to disappoint your clients."

Mrs. Shierson was quiet for a moment, then said, "Do you really think there's the possibility of success?"

"I do. And I would not say that otherwise."

"Well, Mr. Gage, I do appreciate your frankness—if you really think you can do it. But I'm afraid I won't be able to leave Mr. Cooley. He's ill enough that he will need attention for a few days, I suspect."

"That's fine. I have made the run before, as you know. So it should work out well."

He did not dare tell her that they were hunted on their run to Bewley. But he did debate as to whether he should leave her and Cooley alone, especially with him in his weakened state, suspecting ill intent from Delano and his hired brutes.

But if he stayed on and did not make the run, Delano would be getting what he wanted, which was a lack of competition. If he made the run, on the other hand, perhaps he might be the hunted one. Which suited him fine.

And then Cooley muttered again in his delirium. "Blue devil! Killer!"

Mrs. Shierson looked at Cooley and then to Gage. "There's no need to hide your concern, Mr. Gage. I know to whom he is referring. One of the beasts who killed my husband wore a blue shirt."

"How did you know?"

She looked at him as if she knew that he already knew the answer to that. "This is a small town, Mr. Gage. Nothing is kept a secret for long, even if the holder is a good man, such as Mr. Cooley. I pray that Blue Boy, as

Mr. Cooley calls him, has long since passed from this earth." She turned back to the worktable. "And writhed in agony the entire time."

This admission of anger did not surprise him. She was, after all, an intelligent woman and deserved to feel such rage toward those who killed her husband. His only surprise was that she had not yet left the town, but chose to remain, and in such close proximity to Patrick Delano, the obvious man behind her husband's untimely death.

Gage watched her tend to the clutter on the worktable; then he made for the door. There seemed nothing more to say.

"Mr. Gage."

He stopped. "Ma'am?"

"Make the run to Clabberville if you want, but don't take unnecessary risks. It really is not worth it."

He nodded. "I will make the run, ma'am. But with all due respect to yourself, it is worth the effort."

He left by the back door, grateful for the glow of the nearly full moon lighting enough of the backyard and side alleyways that he was able to cut cross-lots and emerge onto the main street across from the stable.

Gage decided he would check on Rig, then make for the Shierson lot once more and bed down at the small Shierson stable for a few hours of needed rest before dawn. He wanted to be nearby tonight, in case he was needed. He figured he could rig up the same wagon— it was a solid one and in decent condition.

He'd hitch up the team, which he knew would consist of the other two horses in the paddock. Cooley had assured him they were the equal, in temperament anyway, of the pair they'd used to get to Bewley and back.

As plans went, it wasn't much of one, but it was all he had. And he knew from long experience that even a scant plan was a good one if it was thought through and followed. Gage trusted in that notion and proceeded to set it all in motion.

Chapter 19

He'd returned to Shierson's, after having spent an hour or so with Rig and Charles at the stable, during which time he'd sampled the old gent's home brew, a fiery concoction that left him gasping for a few seconds.

Charles was bothered to hear his old chum Cooley was on the raw side of a fever, and vowed he'd make his way there the following day to pay him a visit and to offer whatever help he might to Mrs. Shierson. Gage learned that she was well liked and had a small, loyal group of friends in town, among them Charles, Gerty, and the silent blacksmith, as well as a few others.

On his return to Shierson's, despite his intention to keep the sounds of his prep work to a minimum, Mrs. Shierson emerged with a lantern, and did not seem surprised to see him. With a kind, brief greeting, she left the lantern with him and returned to the warehouse.

A short while later, she reemerged with food for his

journey, as well as a spare blanket for him to use. And she would not hear of him leaving in the early hours without first stopping in for hot tea and biscuits, which, she assured him, were Mr. Cooley's favorites.

"How is he?"

"The fever has lowered and he is sleeping soundly. The nostrum seems to have helped."

"That's good to hear."

"In your brief absence to visit Charles and your horse, Mr. Sawtell, a friend from the mercantile at the east end of town, handed me this list of goods left with him by a rider departing from Clabberville for the winter and making for points east. His is the only store I frequent, namely because it is not in the grip of Delano."

She handed Gage a modest list that included sizable quantities of flour, beans, coffee beans, cornmeal, and such. She let him read it through, then said, with the bare hint of a smile, "He has it ready and waiting. The orders the rider gave were that Shierson Freight Haulage, and only Shierson Freight Haulage, was to deliver the goods to Clabberville."

"Oh, that is good news, ma'am. I will leave a pinch early and load up. Can I make it back there from behind the buildings?"

She nodded. "You can, but it's a tight little roadway. You might have to cut wide at Sawtell's end and come back at him from the east."

"It'll be worth it, then, so as to keep off Main Street."

"Why is that important to you, Mr. Gage?"

"Because I don't want to tip off Delano to our plans just yet."

"I should think we would want him to know what we are up to. Unless there is something you're not telling me." She looked at him hard with narrowed eyes.

"No, ma'am. That is to say—"

"Mr. Gage." She shook her head, and again he thought he caught a hint of a smile. "Don't ever play poker." She left him then in the small stable and returned to the warehouse.

Gage smirked in the quiet stable and scratched the forelock of the nearest horse. "That's the second person in as many days who has told me to stay away from gambling. I reckon that's what I'll have to do, eh, boy?"

A few short hours later, Gage once again found himself piloting a freight wagon, heading for Clabberville, but this time around, it was more than half loaded with goods on behalf of Shierson Freight Haulage.

His first visit to Clabberville seemed to him a hundred years in the past. The primary difference this time out was that he was not driving for Delano. Plus, he now knew that he was marked for death by that dirty, fat little man.

He hated leaving Mrs. Shierson alone with the ailing Cooley, but there was nothing for it. There were townsfolk who were her friends, but none, it seemed, dared cross Delano and risk the tightening of his control on the town.

What Gage wondered, as he rolled northward into the hills, was how, if Delano was so hard up for cash, could he continue to hold Newel in such a death grip? Surely, folks could see through his thin schemes, see the threadbare ways of his business.

The entire long run up and into Clabberville was smooth, even if the roadway was anything but. The section before and after the lightning-struck tree was the worst, with the residue of the landslide not having changed much, due in no small part to the lack of rainy weather. Still, unless more of the roadway was cleared, future passage into and out of the remote little mine camp would no doubt be hindered. But that, Gage decided, was not his problem.

Snow would soon drop down, in increasing and heavy amounts, leaving the roadway impassable for months. These folks needed their goods, and he hoped, if they needed, to be able to deliver another load of goods to them, and to Bewley, before the winter weather rendered freight wagon traffic impossible.

After that, it would be up to men on bold, strong horses, and then men on snowshoes, dragging sledges. No wonder they wanted to lay in as many goods as they could before the inevitable blizzards struck.

"Good luck to them," muttered Gage as he maneuvered the wagon slowly around the last of the gravel-narrowed landslide.

He hated to do it, but by the time they unloaded the wagon, a return run to Newel, or at least a start on it, would be impossible that day. He'd have to bunk at the town's stable, and then make an early start.

As he drifted off, his belly full of Mrs. Reilly's toothsome stew, heavy on the "critter meats," as Morton called it, with a wink, and light on the vegetables, Gage knew he had been in a whole lot worse situations come nightfall on the trail.

His thoughts turned to Mrs. Shierson and Cooley, and he hoped they were safe, and that she was on guard. Gage had let the fiery Charles know that they had been stirring up things on the Delano front. He had tapped his nose, in a manner reminiscent of Cooley, and nodded. "I'll be watchful, don't you fret. Others too."

Gage had taken that to mean there would be some sort of vigilance in town in keeping Mrs. Shierson and Cooley somewhat safe. It wasn't much, really, but it was something.

He readjusted himself, resting as he was on a lumpy mound of stale, dusty hay and twigs, topped with a couple of smelly horse blankets that were now more hole than blanket. He was beginning to think that he might avoid freighting jobs in the future. Even punching cattle was starting to feel better than this.

Gage's final thoughts for the day drifted to the notion of holing up somewhere at a line camp for the winter. Such cold-season ranch work was appealing to him, had been for some time, and when he'd done so, he found he was suited to it.

The problem came when some of the larger ranches wanted to put two men together in one of those remote camps, tending the cattle at their winter stomping grounds. He knew by now that he was best suited to working alone, and he liked his own company just fine.

The next day dawned gray, and with a tinge of bitter chill to the air that he'd felt before. It portended ice and snow and he didn't want any part of that. He made his excuses, and after accepting two hot biscuits and two cups of hastily downed coffee, he rolled on out of Clabberville on the long, up-and-down journey back to Newel.

The folks in the little mine camp all watched him leave and he had a feeling they were watching a lifeline stretch thin, and then, when he finally rolled out of sight, snap, leaving them isolated and losing hope by the day.

He sure hoped he was wrong, but their sorrowful looks and lingering handshakes were difficult to part with. He'd told them he was certain he'd make another run, not to worry. He'd do his best, but he knew, and they knew, they were hollow words. Winter was on its way.

Gage was a good couple of hours into his journey, and busy with maneuvering the horses to avoid anything that might fetch them up or damage a wheel. He could take no chances, for so many reasons—he was alone, he had limited tools and replacement parts with him, he was miles from other folks who might help, and he sure as heck didn't want to let down Mrs. Shierson and Cooley.

As he concentrated on his task, something, a slight movement, tensed him from his already watchful state.

The blue-shirted man emerged as if conjured, stepping out into the roadway like a startling mirage, his notable garment partially covered with a black wool vest. But the rifle he held tight to his shoulder, the deadly snout end aimed right at Gage's body, was anything but a spectral vision.

Gage also noted that the steely curl of the hammer was ratcheted back to the set-to-kill position.

Gage bit back the instant rage he felt for himself for letting down his guard even for a few moments. It mattered little to him that the scrubby, thick gray rabbit brush, and even thicker ponderosa pine from which the man had emerged, would have prevented Gage from seeing him until it was too late. He had blundered into this obvious setup, much as a novice would have.

"Here now," said the blue-shirted man, smiling and not lowering his rifle. "I expect you have grown tired of seeing me out here. Or anywhere, for that matter."

Gage had drawn up on the reins and held them that way, but only with his left hand. His right, he let trail down to rest on his thigh. If there was any hope of surviving this preventable mess, it would lie in him somehow snatching up the shotgun he had resting in a divot carved for that purpose, cradled against the seat. It was ready, or so he hoped, for quick action.

The man in blue walked slowly toward him, feeling the terrain with his leading foot. He kept that rifle leveled on Gage as he advanced, and he kept on, with his wide and annoying smile.

"What do you think about that?" said the man.

"About what?"

"Oh, so you can talk. Okay, what do you think about what I said? About you getting tired of seeing me out here."

Gage did not answer for a moment, but used the opportunity to shift his position on the seat, as if he were sore and needed to move.

"No, no, now! No pretending you are restless. You know better and I know better. Also, I ain't blind, Gage. I can see your shotgun, plain as day." Blue Shirt chuckled.

A soft, scuffing noise close behind him, and to his left, caused Gage, out of reflex, to jerk and look over his left shoulder. As he did so, he saw, nearly in his face, a brown blur close in on him. At the same time, he smelled the rank tang of man sweat and woodsmoke.

Instinct drove his left arm up, loosening the lines to the horses. The brown blur was too close, but Gage knew what it was, all right. In that blink of time, he knew it was the buckskin-clad compadre of Blue Shirt, and he also knew he'd been hoodwinked. Blue Shirt had kept him distracted while Buckskin attacked from behind. And he'd fallen for it.

It was one of the oldest tricks known to man, and he, Jon Gage, had walked right into it. Or rather he'd driven.

And even as the man's smelly, soiled, rough tunic slammed into the left side of his head, Gage recoiled, grasping for the lines that were no longer in his hand. He scrabbled for them, shouting low, angry, hot sounds, not even words. But it was no use—that was all he had time for, and it was not nearly enough of a reaction to provoke the horses into action.

And then, within seconds of his realizing he'd been fooled, something hard smacked into his temple and he felt hotness bloom like a volcano up the side of his head. His hat flew off, and landed somewhere in the distance. The wash of pain flowed fast, up and over his scalp. His head whipped to the right, his eyes angling upward.

Then came the sky, filling his eyes. Something inside his neck felt as though it had popped, and added a new thumb-size clot to the growing mass of pain filling his world, his vision, his hearing, which now seemed to thin, narrow into a funnel, along with his eyesight.

The edges of all he saw darkened and yet dazzled with pinpricks of light. The sounds he heard then— horses champing and stomping, the laughter of two odd men, chains sliding, the squawking of the hubs as the horses jerked in the traces, all of it added up to a feeling he had experienced several times before.

And none of those times had it been a pleasant experience. They'd come about when he'd been attacked, clubbed in bar fights or some such, and he was nearing the edge of unconsciousness.

But Gage, though he knew he was down, also knew he wasn't yet out of the fight. Even as he'd been skunked from behind, he had rounded on the brown, smelly shape closing in. With his last slivers of waning effort, he lashed upward with his left arm. His big knuckled hand had connected with something firm, yet yielding, and the blow produced a shriek and a growled curse.

Then the brown blur smacked him hard once more and anything Jon Gage knew tailed off in a sickening, dizzying swirl of growing blackness and hot, thudding pain. And he knew no more.

"Nob! Did I, or did I not, say to hit him once, and only once! Now, didn't I tell you that, you oaf?"

"Aw, look what he done to me!" The speaker, he of the buckskin tunic, was bent at the waist and holding his face with both hands. Through his grubby, stubby fingers, blood welled and leached. He looked up at Pierce. "You got a rag?"

"Yes, but you're not getting it."

"Aw, come on! I need a rag, a shirt, something."

"Yes, yes, you do." Pierce strode that last few feet to the wagon, thumbed the rifle off full cock, and leaned it against the front wheel. He reached up and set the wagon's brake, then unfastened the neck kerchief the unconscious man wore. "Here." He tossed it to Nob, who dropped it.

"Look," said Pierce. "You need to clean yourself up. We have work to do, and if I end up doing it all, I will take all the money and leave you to fend for yourself."

"Oh no, Pierce, don't do that. I'll clean up, just give me a minute."

"That's all you get. One minute. Starting now." Pierce smiled as he slid his watch back into his vest pocket.

Nob grabbed Gage by the lapels of his work jacket and dragged him to the edge of the seat, then readjusted his grip and, walking backward, dragged the sloppy form with him, letting Gage fall to the ground with a hard thud. The man lay on his back, his legs bent at uncomfortable angles, one arm behind him.

Nob snatched the man's shoulders and dragged him back, away from the wagon, and left him there, along the roadside.

"Now tie him up," said Pierce. "And do a good job. Arms behind his back, and boots together."

"It ain't been a minute."

"I don't care. Do it now or die poor."

"Aw." Nob finished stuffing twisted corners of the kerchief up his nostril and touched his big nose gingerly with his fingertips. "Ow! Ow!"

He growled and kicked the still form on the ground hard, low on its right side. "Take that! Bust up my nose, you!"

"I don't think it really is broken," said Pierce. "Now stop kicking that man and get to work. I'm going to go through his pockets, and then I'll get that cashbox down here."

Pierce rummaged in Gage's pockets and found what he was looking for—a small skeleton key tucked well inside the bottom of a buttoned inner coat pocket. He smiled and held it up.

Nob saw it and nodded, smiling as he set about trussing the man's boots together, tight at the ankle.

Pierce climbed up into the wagon, casting a downward look at his longtime trail mate, who had moved on to half rolling Gage on his side and was struggling in tugging the unconscious man's arms behind him.

If anyone could be said to be Pierce's friend, it was Nob, the smelliest, homeliest little Mexican–whatever-tribe Indian he'd ever seen in all his days. Also the only one of such a lineage that he knew of.

Pierce was tempted to chuckle at the man, just for fun, but he didn't want the fool to look up at him and ask what he was laughing about. As long as he treated Nob with a firm hand, the swarthy giant was solid. Sure, he had to walk him through every blamed thing in a day's time, but that's just the way the man was. If he could think for himself, he'd not be of any use to Pierce.

He unlocked the strongbox, which was tucked beneath the seat, and bolted from the bottom, inside, through the floor of the wagon. Pierce knew from those previous attempts, it would be fruitless to try to remove the box, for beneath the floor, on the underside of the wagon, the bolts were formed in a U shape and secured through a thick steel plate. Then they poked up into the box itself, where they were nutted tight.

But the key clicked the mechanism open nicely, and he lifted the lid to see a small sack. He hoped it contained plenty of gold nuggets and dust. As he untied it and peered in, he was not disappointed.

"You about done down there?"

"Yep, he's all tied."

"Good man." That was all Pierce needed to tell Nob, he knew, for the little savage would feast off that one compliment for the rest of the day. It puffed up the chesty little man and took his mind off his swelling, bloodied nose.

Pierce had to hand it to Gage, the man, even when clubbed in the bean, still swung a hefty, hard fist.

The outlaw jumped down out of the wagon, dust rising from around his boots. He held the sack in his hand and gazed down at the flopped form. "So that's what a famous gunfighter looks like, huh?"

"Yeah," said Nob. "Huh."

Pierce shook his head and, smiling once more as he eyed the sack in his hand, he strode into the woods to where three horses stood waiting, tied to trees. He thumbed open one of his saddlebags and slid the sack in.

Then he buckled the bag and pulled in a deep breath. He was, he had to admit, getting long in the tooth for this sort of work. Maybe this would be their last job. Then he'd have to figure out where to go, what to do with Nob, and such. But those would be solid topics to chew on once they dealt with the little troll Delano.

He made it back to the wagon and to Nob, and the still-unconscious Gage. Somehow, even though he was not among the land of the wakeful, Pierce thought that Jon Gage looked as though he'd been freshly kicked and punched. His face was puffing more and in a different spot than it had been but a few minutes ago.

"Odd, Nob, but it seems to me that this Gage fellow must have gotten up off the ground and rammed his mangy head into a tree or two, maybe even a rock, in between the time I went to the horses and came back here. Don't you find that odd?"

Nob looked at Gage, then up at Pierce, his brows drawn tight in the middle. Then he said, "Oh no, I—" He stopped himself with a hand over his mouth, his eyes wide. "What I mean is, sure, yeah, must have been something like that, yeah."

"That's what I thought. I sure hope it doesn't happen again, because if it does, I am liable to lose my temper. And when that happens, hoo-boy, you know what that means."

"Do I?" Nob looked at him with that confused face he pulled when he knew he'd have to do some thinking, but didn't like the notion of it.

Pierce sighed. "Nob, drag him up there to the horses. I'll deal with this team, and then it's your turn."

"You mean I get to . . ." The man was far too excited to even finish his sentence.

"Yeah, Nob. But don't get too nutty with it. You know what almost happened last time. Nearly lost the entire woods."

"Sure I remember. It was beautiful."

Nob jerked the unconscious man's arms hard and quick until they were raised above Gage's head. Then the fiend set off up the hill, upslope and into the trees, dragging Gage by the rope binding his wrists.

Pierce shook his head and retrieved his rifle from where he'd leaned it, then he cocked it and, without breaking stride, placed the snout up snug to the little hollow above the left-side horse's left eye. He pulled the trigger and the horse collapsed with a high-pitched, quick whinny that pinched off as quickly as it had burst out.

The other horse, as Pierce had expected, jerked and danced and lunged, grinding its teeth and shaking its head, its eyes wide and white-seeming. But once Pierce moved around to its outside flank, it eased up on its fidgeting.

Once again, in a fluid motion, he raised the rifle, cocked it, and aimed it. The horse jerked and shrieked. The snout of the barrel nested in that little hollow above the eye, and Pierce pulled the trigger. The big beast collapsed, though it dropped to its knees and stayed that way. Pierce sighed and, with a boot, shoved the nearly dead horse over onto its side.

"There," he said, wincing as he heard the horse groan and then do no more.

Just then, Nob appeared before him, his hand outstretched. "Can I have them matches now?"

"Naw, I had me a think on it and we'll just shove the wagon off the edge there to the right. It's steep enough the thing will tumble nicely. If we're lucky, it'll hit those boulders. Won't that be a sight?" This last utterance was Pierce's weak attempt to placate the visibly disappointed Nob.

In truth, Pierce did feel a little bad about promising the swine he could set fire to the wagon, but he didn't want to have to stand around with the fool and watch it burn. Nob was a right pain to drag away from a fire once he got settled in to watching the flames.

Besides, thought Pierce, he didn't want any of those mining fools from Clabberville or Bewley to come running. He wanted to keep their back trail clean. At least until he got closer to Newel, and to the little pig Delano.

"Let's get to it, Nob. Lots to do today. Money to be made."

"Oh, all right. Might as well," said Nob, already shoving the wagon from the front, even before Pierce slashed free the traces.

Chapter 20

He'd heard of such things happening, had even seen a man draped over the back of a horse a few times in the past, but each time those men had been dead, and each time they were being towed back to civilization, so called, on a horse led behind a bounty man.

But to find himself in just that position made Gage wonder, not for the first time that day, if he really was dead. Heck, if he wasn't, he figured he might as well ought to be. He felt as rough as he had ever felt.

It had begun with a sudden, hard, sharp jarring sensation, as if someone had lifted his head up off the ground as if it were a rock, and then lobbed it off the side of a cliff. And then it proceeded to bounce and tumble, banging into other rocks all the way down.

Somehow he had managed to force open an eye. It was nearly the worst feeling he'd ever had, for it forced the meager bites of breakfast he'd bolted down that morning to rise up his gorge and burst out of his mouth as if he were a mountain freshet in springtime.

Trouble was, he found himself lashed face down atop a saddle-less horse's back. His wrists were bound tight with hemp rope, and given that he could not move his legs, he figured they were, too. Heck, even if he wanted to move, to slide backward off the beast and make a dash for the trees that appeared to be all around them, he could not do it.

In addition to his bouncing, his head was muddied, and it pounded with a cannonade inside. With each step the horse took, it threatened to burst right out through his eyeballs. It felt as if there were a couple of tiny men inside his skull, sitting back and wedging their bootheels against the back sides of his eyeballs.

One step and they pushed, another and they pushed more. He pictured them in there, half grinning and half sneering at what they were doing, as they worked harder than ever to shove his eyeballs out of his head.

He vomited again, and his chin, resting against the horse blanket, bounced slightly with the effort. Somehow the bile and gut juices and chunks of half-chewed biscuit came up and out, clogging his nose. It ran down his cheeks, from bottom to top, and streamed into his eyes, no matter how hard he tried to squeeze them shut.

He coughed and gagged and tried to force the glutting, clogging goop out of his packed nose.

The stink was awful—dead animals and vomit and horsehair and hide and sweat all mingled—and he wished he did not have the ability to smell.

The pain wracking his body, he presumed from having forced it to endure this lashed-down, unmoving, unnatural position, was beyond his ability to endure. He had never felt such agony in his limbs; his muscles felt as though they were being torn apart with each jarring step the horse took.

He must have passed out because when he came around once more, he found himself squinting harder than ever. It was a brightness that blinded him, seemed to sear into his pulsing eyes, and threatened to ignite his head with heat and pain.

"Unhhh" was all he could manage to say, even though he had intended to shout, *What happened? Where am I?*

"What did you say?"

The voice was familiar to him. Gage tried to recall where he'd heard it. And then he remembered. Blue Shirt. Blue Shirt and the brutish little black-haired half-breed in buckskins.

"All right, let's stop here."

They stopped, a small mercy, thought Gage.

"But we ain't but halfway there yet."

The first voice, Gage knew, was the man in the blue shirt. The voice sighed, then said, "How many times have I told you, Nob, that if you back-talk or question me, there's going to be bad consequences."

"Sure, Pierce, I remember. Only . . ."

Another sigh. "Only what?"

"Only, I never do know what you mean by 'consa-whatevers.'"

"*Consequences.* The things that will happen to you if you don't do as I say."

"Oh, like what?"

"My word, man! Shut up your questions and ride that horse on over to the left there where that stream is. After they drink, let the horses crop that grass, whatever is left of it this late in the season."

"What you gonna do, Pierce?"

Gage heard a man make a sliding sound, then stomping and groaning.

"I am going to set this killer free from the horse and give his aching bones a rest. Heck, if he feels half as sore as I do, even a death dealer like this man deserves a break from the saddle."

"But he ain't in a saddle, Pierce."

Another sigh. "True, Nob. I stand corrected. You happy?"

The other man said, "I guess. I been happier, I do know that much."

To Gage's surprise, Blue Shirt laughed. "I swear, Nob. Just when I am about to shoot you in the back of the head for your impertinence, you make me stay my hand. You are a born clown."

"Thank you, Pierce. I appreciate that."

Gage felt some small amount of satisfaction at learning their names. Blue Shirt was Pierce, and the half-breed was Nob.

Okay, then. Now, he asked himself, *what are you going to do with that information, Gage?*

He heard rustling. Then through his snake-slit eyes, which was about all he could muster, lest the light burn him right through, he saw dark legs in dark, dusty trousers, tucked into tall, equally dusty leather boots, silver conchos lining the outer legs, the boots' dog-eared flaps jostling with each step the legs took, drawing closer. Finally they stood before him.

"Well, now. Hello there, Mr. Jonathan Gage, or should I say . . . Texas Lightning?" The man made a wheezing, sniggering sound that tailed off in a cough. "Curse this dust!"

"You . . ." Gage tried to speak, but he, too, lost his voice to a cough. He gave up and wondered what was coming next. He didn't have long to wonder.

The man fumbled and fidgeted beside him, then above him, and Gage felt the tension holding him down to the horse lessening. A sigh slid from his mouth, leaking out as a small, almost mewling sound. Even in his awful condition, he hated hearing such a sound coming from himself.

Then the man grasped both of Gage's shoulders and shoved him upward, hard. All it took was the one mighty shove for Gage's world once more to turn upside down. His head dizzied anew, and then, through fluttering eyelids, he saw first the man's body before him, the cursed blue shirt a quick blur of a leering, tired-looking face topped with a black hat. And then he saw sky, high up and blue with clouds, not white clouds, but dark.

Snow, he thought. It might snow.

That was all he had time for, because he kept right on sliding, and soon felt himself descending, falling backward.

Time felt for a moment as if it had slowed, he was falling, nothing holding him down any longer. It was, if not wholly pleasant, owing to all the other woes his head and body endured, at least a minor moment of relief.

And then it was over.

He hit the earth hard, his back slamming first; then

his head caromed off the hard-packed ground, and came to rest with the too-bright sky above glaring down at him. Something else entered his narrow eye-line. It was dark and then moved closer, darkening what little he could see.

"Mr. Gage, I do believe you have run into hard times."

Gage recognized the voice as Blue Shirt, aka Pierce.

"Yes, yes, I do believe so," continued the man. "I'd like to show you something."

A moment later, Gage felt a fresh wash of pain as the man bent and then lifted what felt to Gage as brands of fire attached to his own body.

"Just look at these!" The man's voice was full of wonder and awe.

Gage struggled through the pain to crack open his eyes once again. What he saw was a bloated, mottled pink-and-red-and-purpling mass that bore little resemblance to much of anything he'd ever seen before.

"Recognize those? No? Why, Mr. Gage, those are your very own hands!" The man brayed and chuckled and let the things drop. Then he sighed. "Aw, like it or not, I can't let that happen to you for much longer. Else we might lose you to sheer pain and exhaustion before we get you back to civilization. And that would be a shame, because alive you are worth more than dead, believe it or not.

"Usually, most folks such as yourself, vicious murderers, I mean, will often fetch top dollar alive or dead. In which case, I do not care much one way or the other about them. Never have, never will. But Delano wants you alive, and I wish to humor him for a spell longer, for personal reasons. So here we be.

"Now I am going to tie a fresh rope to your hands before I cut away this old one, provided I can find the rope to cut. It's in there, I can see it, just barely, though. Nested behind your fat hands. Heck, Gage, your fingers are even fatter than Delano's, and that's saying something!"

The devil jerked the hands upward once more and Gage moaned and whimpered, pitiful sounds.

Pierce threaded fresh rope around Gage's wrists, up above the first, and wrapped and snugged and tied it. Then he slicked out his big sheath knife and probed for the half-hidden rope with the pointed tip.

All the while, Gage watched, his eyes grew wider than they had been since the savages had waylaid and clubbed him.

"Oops! I see blood. Sorry about that. Though I admit, it might be far easier to poke about a dozen holes in these inflated hands of yours and let them ooze and drain out. I am tempted."

He poked a fingertip with the knife's tip, and though Gage could not feel it, he could see the blood bubble, then spurt upward.

"What do you say to that notion?"

"N-n-no! No . . . don't!"

"*Don't?* Oh, okay, then, we'll do it the hard way."

Pierce probed more, grimacing, and when Gage grunted or gasped, he grinned. "Nearly there, stop your whining."

Finally he stepped back, regarded his now-bloody

blade, and wiped it on Gage's trousers. He looked over at the exhausted Gage's face. "The swelling should go down some soon."

He regarded Gage a moment longer, then walked off, shaking his head.

Gage heard the two men speaking, low mumbles, but he could not bring himself to raise his head. The cannons in his head had subsided a pinch, but they still thundered, as though he were hearing and feeling a battle a half mile away, instead of right before him.

His hands began to ache, and though he knew this was a good sign, for it meant the blood was beginning to flow back into his fingers, they hurt more than if the fool had just cut them off. One thing he might be able to do for himself was to beg for water.

The very thought that he was completely in the power of these two men was something he'd accepted hours before, drifting in and out of wakefulness while slamming and bouncing on the horse's back. But he needed water badly, and the only way he figured he was going to get any was to ask.

If the goons wouldn't comply, he'd resort to begging. He realized it was a fine line he was asking of himself, but there it was. He was still alive; therefore he was still a man. A man proud enough to not beg, if he didn't have to.

Then they walked closer, and Gage heard what they said.

"Still wish you'd let me kill him. He broke my nose."

"No, he did not break your nose, Nob, but I am going to, if you don't shut your mouth."

"But what about killing him? You said I could at least stomp on him some."

Pierce said nothing, but looked down at Gage. "Reckon you'd like some water, huh?"

Gage tried to look the man in the eye and nod. He succeeded in half squinting upward and looking at the dim shapes above him. "Yes . . . please."

"You heard that, Nob? We got ourselves a polite fellow. Who knew killers could be so blamed nice?" He stared down at Gage a few moments more, then said, "Nob, go and fetch my canteen."

"But, Pierce."

Before Gage knew what had happened, Pierce had swung his left arm upward from where it had hung down by his side. It caught his grubby chum on the right side of the face and spun his head, snapping it so that even from Gage's muted, fuzzy perspective, it looked as if the man's neck had snapped.

Gage watched as the buckskin-wearing ogre staggered hard to his left and fell against a nearby boulder.

It was then that Gage recognized the spot as the place he and Cooley had stopped not too many days before to rest the horses and brew up coffee. Something else came to him then: the image of a flapping feather in a clump of grass stalks.

It had made no sense to him, but the memory helped him think of something other than his own agony. His thoughts turned to Cooley and to the pretty Mrs. Shierson. He'd let them down.

All this was a fleeting thought and had already drifted once more from Gage's mind by the time Nob regained himself and looked up at Pierce from where he leaned on the rock.

"Why'd you do that, Pierce?"

"Because, you fool, I warned you to shut your mouth or I'd do it to you. Apparently, that didn't even work."

The smaller man held his face once more. "You didn't break my nose, at least."

"See? I could have, but I chose not to. Now, then, are you going to go fetch my canteen without more back talk, or do I have to shoot you next?"

"I'll go, I'll go, Pierce. Just don't shoot m—" Too late, the runty man realized he'd once more spoken, when he ought not to have, another violation of the man's oaths. Nob cringed and covered his mouth with his hands.

Both men looked at each other, and then in a low voice, Pierce said, "Go get the water."

Nob nodded fast and scampered, his hands still covering his mouth.

Pierce turned back to looking at Gage, his head shaking slowly. "My word, I honestly do not know how I have put up with that idiot for so long." He leaned closer. "How those hands doing?" He reached down and rapped them hard with a backhand and laughed. "Oh, boy, they're still fat, but I reckon you'll live."

Gage sucked in a tight breath and promised himself that if he lived through this, he was going to beat the tar out of this blue-shirted fool. But between now and then, he knew he had to play it quiet, do whatever it took to stay alive; and whenever possible, he would have to take the opportunity, any opportunity, to escape. No sense waiting around to die.

He darn sure knew these two weren't about to show him any human kindness.

They covered Gage's head with burlap sacking and cinched it tight around his neck. Then they dragged him once more from the horse. It was getting to be a tired routine, but one that didn't seem any less painful with each dragging he endured. How long had it been since he'd been nabbed? He felt it had been less than a day, but time was playing funny tricks with him.

The two men emitted the usual grunts and groans, and Pierce commented once more that it felt as though Gage was eating too well.

Gage was heartened, if only a bit, to discover he was feeling just as much pain as ever, but less of the swimming, dizzied head sensations of earlier. Time, he knew, was the only thing that might ease him out of this mess. And it was the one thing he had none of.

"Tell you, Nob. This is getting old."

"What do you mean, Pierce? He ain't that heavy."

"Huh? No, wait, what do you think, that when people get old, they get heavier?"

"I don't know. All I know is I am hungry."

Pierce sighed. "Nob, you are always hungry. You might well be the one to prove your point."

"How's that?"

"That folks get fat when they get old."

"Oh."

Gage heard a low squeaking, a sound familiar to him, but one he'd not heard in a couple of days. Then boots on boards. A door had opened and a voice said, "I hate to interrupt you two geniuses."

This third voice set Gage's aching jaws together tight. He recognized it as the man behind this mess.

"Oh, it's you, Delano," said Pierce. "Didn't see your buggy out front."

"That's because I parked it around back. Now get him on in here and close that door. I don't want any prying eyes, if you see what I mean."

Pierce snorted. "Ain't likely out here, Delano. We're a couple miles from town. Who do you think is going to be sniffing around here?"

They dragged him inside and the door squeaked and clunked shut.

All this was most interesting to Gage, and he hoped they'd take the sacking from his head soon. It itched and he kept threatening to sneeze. So far, he hadn't, but he didn't want to attract any attention to himself yet. Let them think he was still addled. He was, but, hopefully, less than they might think.

"Throw him over there. No, no, in that chair in the corner. I don't want any surprises. Lash his arms behind him and tie his feet to the chair. And take off his boots, too. I don't want him thinking he can escape."

"You sure?" said Nob. "Man without boots can be a smelly thing."

Pierce chuckled, actually chuckled.

Heck, thought Gage. If he wasn't the one who was about to die at any minute, he might also find the grubby little sidekick's comment humorous, too.

"Never mind about the boots, Nob."

Delano's eyes narrowed. "I told you I am the boss of this situation!"

Then Pierce grew serious once more. "See here, Delano, if you want to go around pretending you're the boss of this outfit, that's fine with me. Just so you know, and I know, you aren't my boss, or Nob's."

"That's right!"

"Shut up, Nob."

"Okay, Pierce."

Pierce sighed.

"Now you look here," said Delano. "Just because you went out and fetched him don't give you the right to think you run things. That's not how I built a freighting empire—"

Gage heard Pierce laughing.

"What's so funny?" said Delano.

"You haven't got anything close to an empire, Delano. You have half the people in Newel hoodwinked into thinking you own their half of the town, and you are down to those two idiots, Trigg and Axel, who drive your wagons for you. You don't have any other freight offices in any other town anymore. I know, I checked into it. You owe so much money all over the West that you've about run out of places to hide. It's a wonder you've been able to hang on in Newel as long as you have."

Gage heard the little fat man spluttering, and wished they'd take the cursed burlap sacking off his head so he could see the puffy red face for himself.

As if they'd heard his thoughts, Pierce slipped the bag from Gage's head and kept right on ignoring him.

All of them did, in fact. It was fine with him, for he had to readjust his sight to the interior of the cabin.

Thankfully, Delano had built a fire in the fireplace, and while it was not throwing off much heat, they had placed him in a corner but a few feet from the stone hearth. The heat he did receive from it felt as good as a first bite of hot cherry pie after a long day on the trail.

"None of what you're saying is true! It just ain't, I tell you!"

Gage looked at Delano through his half-closed eyes. The portly little man looked worse than the last time Gage had seen him. He was unshaven and his clothes appeared to be as far from laundering as Gage's. And it looked as if the front of his shirt and coat bore old, dried food stains.

"Oh, Delano, believe what you need to. It makes no never mind to me or to Nob. What does interest me is knowing when we are going to collect on this growing pile of money you owe us."

"But . . . like I told you, I will pay you when I get the cash for this sorry fool. I have got a few other things to do first."

"Such as?" Pierce asked.

"Such as they ain't *none* of your business!"

Gage had noticed that Delano had been abandoning any attempt at speaking well whenever he grew frustrated. And he was most certainly frustrated right now.

"What are you looking at, Gage? You killer!"

Gage continued to regard Delano for a few moments more, watching as the pudgy man crossed the room toward him and stopped—his face, indeed, bright red.

He looked at Gage, whose features were warring over whether to smile or sneer.

"I expect you know that you are a wanted man, Gage. Or should I say . . . Texas Lightning!"

Delano stepped back, a smile pulling his portly features wide. He glanced to either side of himself, as if to acknowledge the two other men in the cabin with him.

"Too late," said Gage, his voice rough, craggy, but loud enough for the man to hear him.

"What?" said Delano, his smile drooping. "What's that mean?"

Gage half smiled. "It means these two already used up that joke."

It took Delano a moment to understand what Gage meant. Then he turned to Pierce. "You already told him—"

"What? Who he is? I think Gage is well aware of who and what he is, Delano." Pierce glanced at Gage as if to commiserate with him.

It was an odd moment, thought Gage. Almost one of comradeship, though with no urge for such in either man.

"Yeah, he's a paid killer, that's what he is!"

My word, thought Gage. This man truly was a dolt.

"Now, see, that's where I will take issue with you there, Delano." Pierce was smirking.

"How's that?" said the freight boss.

"Me and Nob, we're killers for hire. Might as well just out and say it. You know it, seeing as how you've hired us to do your killing for you. But Gage here, he's just a gunfighter. Quick with the draw, sure, but so what? Like as not, the most he made out of it is the price of a drink, maybe some time with a cooing dove, ain't that about right, Texas Lightning?"

Gage held a moment, then said, "You're telling it, not me."

Pierce nodded. "I'll take that as a yes, then."

Delano shook his head. "Ain't none of this matters. What does matter is that he is my prisoner and I aim to cash in on his hide. But I got a use for him first. A job of his own, you might say."

Gage figured Delano had some sort of fool plan for him; otherwise, why not just turn him over to the law right away, or shoot him or lynch him, and then turn him in for the reward money?

"What is it you figure on doing with the man, Delano?"

Gage noticed a tinge of concern, perhaps, in Pierce's tone and expression. Delano did, too.

The chubby man smiled. "Just you wait a minute. First off, I don't think we're treating my guest all that well, do you?" He looked about and his eyes settled on a wooden crate on a shelf on the far wall. He walked over to it and lifted out a loaf of bread, something weighty wrapped in waxed cotton, and a bottle of whiskey. "Nob, free up his wrists. I want to see if those puffy hands can hold some food and a drink."

At this, Gage was at once hungry, thirsty, and annoyed with himself for feeling a flash of gratitude, however brief and misguided, for Delano's offer. But, boy, was he feeling starved and parched like never before.

"Water," he said. "I'd like water, please."

"*Please?* Did you hear that? The mighty killer man wants water." Delano smiled and nodded in accord with his newfound benevolence.

Pierce chuckled.

"Of course, of course. I can do that. Nob, why don't you scare up a cup off that shelf there. This place isn't much," said Delano, "but it's tidy and not too dusty. I dare say it will be comfortable for you for the duration of your stay."

Gage was confused, but not surprised. Delano was playing a game with him and he knew better than to give in to his urge to shout at the man to shut up and bring him water. He'd waited this long, he could hold out a little longer.

He had to, or he'd show these fiends he was weaker than they thought he might be. He had to show strength. Whatever their intentions for him, he knew they weren't going to end with him being alive.

Sooner or later, someone was going to lay him low. And wasn't that part of the deal he made with himself when he parted ways with life by the gun?

As he rode away from the town that mourned the death of that beautiful blond young woman, who had a life of promise and grace before her, he'd told himself in the stormy, confused days that followed, that if he could not bring himself to kill himself, he could at least live as true a life as he was able. If someone asked if he was Jon Gage, also known as Texas Lightning, he would not lie.

If someone recognized him for what he was, what he had been, he would acknowledge it. If they chose to kill him for it, for whatever reasons they felt they had, then he would die, provided he was unable to defend himself without resorting to shooting his accuser with a six-gun. And never in a street fight. Never again would that happen.

Gage had told himself that the only way he would use a gun again, other than to make meat for camp or perhaps to lay low a hydrophobic beast, was to defend himself for being a person on whom others relied.

He'd also do so in the defense of someone else, someone who was being molested by others, and especially by someone intent on doing the innocents harm.

This plan had served him well these past years. But that entire time, he knew he might well be gunned down either for his past or for whatever fight he might be waging in the present, on behalf of the innocents.

And as he sat there, trussed and parched and starving, he knew this situation was unlike others he had been in of recent years, in that he was both found out and reviled for helping the downtrodden Mrs. Shierson and Cooley.

Chapter 21

"The plan, Nob, is nothing you need to know about." Delano looked over his shoulder before he continued speaking. "Good thing Pierce ain't here just now. See, you and Pierce need to do as you are hired to do. And what I need you to do is to do what I tell you, when I tell you, and nothing but that."

Gage saw Nob's grimy face wrinkle up in confusion. "I don't think that makes any sense."

Delano sighed as if he had been saddled with dolts his entire life and he was plumb tired of it. "Look, now. Pierce might be your boss or your pard or whatever you call yourselves, but he's a menace. And he can't be trusted.

"That is why me and Trigg and Axel here, such as they are, are about the only honest folks you're likely to find. You want to stay alive and keep your scalp, you start paying attention to me and ignoring ol' Pierce." Delano nodded as if agreeing with himself.

As he spoke, the pudgy man rewrapped the rope binding Gage's wrists. After the quick sip of water

Delano had given him when they'd first arrived at the cabin, the fat man had, unexpectedly, tied his hands in front of Gage, on his lap, instead of jerking them tight around behind his back.

Gage feigned fatigue—which he did not have to work hard at—and did his best to widen his hands, in the thin hope that Delano would not know he had allowed slack in the wrappings.

Gage was assisted in this by Delano's chatter. The man had an audience and was plainly not intimidated by Trigg or Axel, and not even by Nob, who, it appeared to Gage, was only useful when Pierce was around.

"Now, Nob, I am going to leave you here in charge of Gage, you got that?"

Nob nodded. "Pierce is coming back before too long. He said he had things to do. Hey, you know what? I think he was looking for you, Delano. Though sometimes when he says he has things to tend to, it means he's got to find himself a outhouse."

"I know," said Delano, trying not to smirk. "Sorry we missed him. We'll see you both later, though. You bet. Just now, Nob, me and the boys are off to do the job him and you are too weak to do."

"We ain't weak. What job is that?"

"We're going to go take care of that nosy woman and that fool old man, once and for all. That's what the job is! And I won't have to pay you two to do it, neither!"

Gage's head was swimming, both from the beatings he'd taken and from the news that Delano was going to leave here with Trigg and Axel and go kill Mrs. Shierson and Cooley. This could not be—not so soon, not like this.

But Nob was still standing there with his gun aimed right on Gage. The little grubby man might be an idiot capable of very little, save for following Pierce's orders, but Gage knew that Nob was good with a gun, and as much a killer as was Pierce. That was the biggest reason Gage had not made a play for freedom earlier. He had no desire to get a bullet to the face or the gut for his ill-fated troubles.

But he cursed himself now, wondering if he'd wasted the only real chance he'd had up until now to escape. Pierce had been gone and then Delano and Trigg and Axel had shown up. Now they were leaving Gage alone with Nob again. But Pierce couldn't stay gone forever.

Time for a plan, Gage, he told himself.

Delano finished fidgeting with the knot he was tying—something a child might do when he was learning to make a knot—and eyeing Gage's face once with narrowed eyes, as if that might appear menacing.

Delano turned from him and stood between Gage and Nob. He blathered a moment more about how he needed Nob to stay there and keep a hard eye on Gage, while he and his two drivers made for town, presumably to kill Mrs. Shierson and Cooley.

This moment was all that Gage needed. He flexed his bound wrists and felt the rope cut into his sore and swollen flesh. The wrappings were loose, though—just loose enough that with a few moments more of working them, he might free his hands. He had only to pick his time. If he freed himself now, there were four men there, all armed.

He'd wait until Delano and his two dim barbarians left.

And that moment came quickly.

The three men departed, with Delano casting one last, withering glance his way. Gage looked down as if chastened. As soon as the door closed, Nob looked back to him.

"May I have water, please?" said Gage, trying to sound pathetic and desperate. It wasn't much of a stretch for him. He felt awful, but he knew that while water would do him a world of good, what he needed most was to free himself and get to town. All before Pierce returned, which could be any moment.

"You got to be kidding me," said Nob, but he was grinning. "So you think I am going to get you a drink of water, when you busted my nose? Only thing I want to do to you now that Pierce ain't here to stop me is to beat your nose in with this gun." The thought of it flashed a smile wide on the grimy, stubbled face.

Gage had expected this and said, "What about that whiskey? It's right over there. I don't even have to have my hands untied. You could just hold the bottle. I just need a drink, Nob. Then you can hit me all you want."

This seemed to appeal to the grubby half-breed, as Gage suspected it might. The dolt had forgotten about the whiskey bottles standing there on the table beside the bread and cheese.

He liked his whiskey, this filthy man did, and Gage knew it. He could always tell a whiskey hound by sight—the lip licking, the red, wet eyes, the veining on the nose—for he had been one himself at one time. And he had known one of the most devoted whiskey hounds of all, his own father, Jasper Gage.

Nob sneered at him and began walking sideways toward the table to his left. He had trouble with it, and then he caught sight of the bottles of promising liquid. He ignored Gage then and reached for the nearest bottle, flashing a quick glance back at Gage, then turned his back on Gage and popped the cork.

Nob sighed and upended the bottle. All this time, Gage worked the ropes binding his wrists and fought through the tear-inducing pain of it. His wrists were rubbed raw, chafed to bleeding, and his fingers were still swollen, but he had to get his hands free.

Then Nob lowered the bottle and smacked his lips, and began to turn, a wide smile on his mouth and his revolver rising once more to bear on Gage.

Gage held his hands still in his lap and did not look down at them. No need to draw attention to them. Especially as they were all but free. He just needed Nob to come close with the bottle. Close enough for him to grab the gun . . .

"I expect you are thinking you will get me to hold this here bottle while you suckle like a piglet on the teat. Ha!" Nob grinned at his own wit. He swung the bottle up again, glugging back a goodly portion.

It was obvious to Gage that the man was enjoying his brief moment of power and freedom from the oppressive rule of both Pierce and Delano. And anybody else in his life, Gage suspected.

"Nob," said Gage. He licked his lips and looked at

the bottle. He'd gladly kill a man for anything wet just then, but he reminded himself that it was just the thirst goading him on. "Look, Nob, I have money, real money. Good amount of it. Stashed. I just need a drink and then I'll tell you where. We can split it."

That held the scruffy man's attention and his hand. The bottle, half full, sloshed in midair. "You got money?"

Gage nodded. "Just a drink, Nob. That's all I ask."

Nob looked at the bottle. "I guess you're pretty serious, then. 'Cause I know I wouldn't never give anybody money. Not for a drink."

Gage didn't want to mention that the idiot did that every time he went to a bar. "One drink. Okay?"

The man shrugged. "Okay." He shambled over to Gage and even wiped the rim of the bottle on his grimy cuff before he proffered it. "Oh, I ain't never held a bottle for no one before. Except me."

"Pretend I'm you, then." Gage wanted the grubby man to lean a little closer. And he did.

Nob scrunched his eyes and cheeks as if in deep concentration. Gage reached forward as if to drink from the bottle. A little closer, he thought, trying not to look at the man's gun, the snout of which was now mere inches from his chest.

"Hold on," said Nob. "This is too tricky. I got to . . ." He didn't finish his sentence, but he thrust the revolver back into its holster. Gage couldn't believe his good fortune.

"Okay, now, one drink, and then you'll tell me where the money is."

"Yep." Gage nodded his head and the bottle closed

in once more. He waited a moment longer; then, as the smelly fellow was crouched before him, Gage rammed both hands upward, still held together as if bound, but the rope fell away as if sprung from a trap.

Gage's puffed hands slammed as hard as he could drive them, upward under Nob's sweaty, whiskered chin.

It worked, at least for a moment. The blow rattled the half-breed so that his eyes rolled back in their sockets, the bloodshot whites showing. Then the bottle whipped from the man's grasp and smacked against something behind them, to one side of the door.

Nob jerked upright, and though he was not a tall man, he stood higher than Gage sat. As he stiffened, a high-pitched whine leaked from him and a thin jet of blood spumed from the man's mouth. His lips sagged open and Gage saw that the man's tongue tip was missing. Blood quickly drooled out of the open mouth.

Then Nob's left knee buckled and he began to fall backward. Gage had not planned very far ahead, but he knew that if he did not grab hold of that gun, and quick, he was going to be in trouble. And then there was the fact that Pierce would return to the cabin at any moment.

As Nob flopped on his left side on the plank floor, emitting mewling, grunting sounds, his eyes bulged and rolled, and he snatched with clawing fingers at nothing and everything all at once. The man was in the foggy, hazy place between consciousness and oblivion, but Gage doubted it would last long.

He began rocking his body, fore and aft, trying to topple the chair forward. His legs were tied tight around his ankles, lashed separately to chair legs, and though they already ached, the motion began to saw the rough rope against his ankle and lower shinbones. He gritted his teeth and kept jerking the chair forward.

There was a moment when he worked it too hard and almost fell backward. That would have been bad, a slowdown at best, but a surefire way to promote his own death if the man regained enough of his consciousness to grab for his gun.

Gage had seen men in much worse condition than this man still behave as if they knew what they were doing.

One last shove and he pitched with a slowness that made it seem to him as if time had drawn to a crawl. But he finally toppled flat against the still-scrabbling form of Nob. He snatched at the holstered gun with his left hand, while his right slipped off the man's gut and hit the floor, giving Gage leverage to push away from the slowly reviving Nob.

He hesitated in punching the side of the grubby man's face a moment too long. It was enough time for the buckskinned buffoon to realize what was happening. Even if he was now covered in his own blood, and more blood was still drizzling from his gasping mouth, he knew enough to claw at his right side for his gun.

"Don't do it!" growled Gage.

A lucky kick by Nob smacked Gage's left forearm and the revolver slipped from his grasp, already a weak effort, given his puffy, nerve-deadened hands. But he saw it happen and tried to grab the thing right away. So did Nob.

With Gage half incapacitated due to being lashed to

a chair, and with Nob still fighting to regain his senses after the driving blow Gage delivered to his chin, both men were somewhat well matched. Then Nob lunged at him, his bloodied mouth open as if about to take a bite of Gage's face.

Gage jerked his head to the left in time, then whipped it back hard, slamming his own temple into Nob's. The effect was less impressive than his first blow had been, but it dizzied up the sidewinder enough that Gage was able to once more shove away from him.

This time, he was able to get his left knee beneath him and, balancing on this, forced his right leg up, hoping the effort would snap the chair leg before the rope, which felt like a knife made out of fire, sliced right through his flesh and bone.

He felt the chair weakening, and heard cracking sounds in the wood. Or at least he hoped it was the wood and not his own bones. He pressed on, and then Nob swung a thick, ham hand around with a wild punch that clipped Gage high on his right cheek.

The blow worked two ways, one against Gage, for he lost his balance and felt himself flopping backward and to his left side. And yet the blow worked in his favor, too, for the toppling served to force his right leg into an extreme pose as he fought for his balance. In doing so, the chair leg snapped. Wriggling, despite his predicament, Gage knew what that sound had meant.

He jerked his right leg a last time and got the boot beneath him. He also managed to snag hold of the revolver a finger snap quicker than Nob. No matter how bloated and pained his hands felt, Gage vowed he would not let go of the gun this time.

He had grabbed it by the barrel, and as Nob was now sitting up and reaching for his big sheath knife and squirming at the same time, Gage swung that revolver up, to his left, then downward, to his right in a hard arc, and connected the flat of the gun's butt with that soft spot just behind Nob's right eye.

The result was as if Gage had huffed out a big breath at a guttering candle. Nob jerked, wheezed, and once more his eyes rolled. He sloped backward with a groan.

Gage wasted no time, but shoved backward from the sloped man and set down the gun close by himself on the floor. He worked to untie the ropes binding his feet to the chair legs, one of them a snapped, raw-wood thing, and the other still attached to the rest of the chair.

Despite his cautious efforts, as he fumbled with numb fingers to untie his left leg, Gage's swollen and sore limbs and addled, fatigued brain were unable to maintain the last of his balance and he collapsed to his left, pinning his arm and leg on that side for the moment. He grunted and righted himself with as much speed, if not grace, as he was able.

But he was not quick enough, for in the time he had taken to regain himself, Nob had roused and had managed, without Gage noticing, to slide his big knife from its sheath. By then, Gage had freed his lower leg, but a jerking motion he hadn't intended as he yanked his pinned arm free knocked the revolver, spinning it just beyond his easy grasp.

He growled a curse and lunged for it, but he knew he was too late, for by then, Nob's big blade arced and drove down at him. It was shinier and keener-looking than Gage expected a tool might be from such a slovenly fellow; though at that moment, his primary concern was how to evade the gleaming steel fang.

He wasn't able to, and it plunged downward at his raised right shoulder. The only thing Gage could do was drop down lower and hope he could roll with it, in an effort to lessen the deadly swing.

And then the world as Gage knew it exploded, and everything changed.

The knife still drove down at him, but before it made it to his shoulder, the grubby hand wielding it stiffened and jerked backward; then as quickly, the fingers released their tight grip and the hand opened wide, setting free the knife, which spun away, then hit the near wall and clattered to the plank floor.

But following all this was not something Gage could do well, as Nob's body, inches above his staring face, stiffened, and, as did his hand, the man's gut and chest spasmed, and seemed to pulse outward, then draw back in, just beneath the stained, filthy buckskin tunic.

Without warning, Nob pitched forward, flopping right down atop Gage, who had managed to jerk and roll away enough to avoid most of the burly man's lifeless mass.

The stink of gunpowder and a rank cloud of smoke clung to everything, along with the buzzing, whistling sounds of hearing suddenly rattled and pinched in and out.

"Gage? Gage! Where you at?"

He could have been mistaken, must have been, for who could be shouting his name. Unless he'd been shot and this was how it felt. Maybe a fusillade of gunfire blasted right through the dirty leather tunic of Nob and found its way into his own body.

Maybe this was the end of it all, no more worry, no more fear, no more trying to remain aloof and not look over his shoulder. None of it would matter anymore.

As suddenly as it came to him, he decided this prospect did not make him happy. He wanted to live— plain and simple. He had to, for he had far too much to do. To atone for . . . somehow.

"Gage, blast it, get yourself up!"

The former gunfighter struggled to get the last of the flopped man's torso off his head and shoulder and looked up.

Chapter 22

"Now look here, you two." Delano glared at Trigg and Axel and shook his head. "I can't afford to let anything go amiss tonight. You hear me?"

"Sure thing, boss." It was Trigg, the smarter of the two, though that was slicing the pie pretty thin, thought Delano. As far as he was concerned, they both had more in common with tree stumps or piles of rocks than they did with humans, especially those that spent their time thinking and accomplishing things. Like making money.

"Do you even know what I'm asking you to keep from making a mess of, Trigg?"

The big man looked at his boots and shrugged.

"That's what I thought. Now look here," said Delano again. He waited for them to crowd in a bit closer. They smelled like sweat and stale beer and tobacco smoke and grease, so he didn't dare let them much closer. But he did need to keep from raising his voice, lest someone hear him.

"I need you two to make for Shierson's freighting office and—"

"Why?" said Axel.

Delano gritted his teeth. "If you didn't interrupt me, you'd know that by now, you moron."

"Huh," said Axel.

"I need you to go there because we have to deal with Mrs. Shierson and that pesky old man, Cooley."

"What do you mean by 'deal' with them?" said Trigg.

Delano indulged in a long sigh. "I need you to make certain they are dead and gone, to be plain about it."

"But ain't that why you hired Nob and Pierce?"

"It is, yes, but look, Pierce has gone odd on me. He wants all the money for himself, and that is not going to happen. I need to take care of those two myself, by way of you two, and then I need to get back to the cabin before he dispenses with Gage himself and ruins everything. If I know Pierce at all, and I believe I do, he will just kill Gage and saw off the man's head, tie it in a burlap sack, and take that grisly prize to the nearest law office with an active sheriff."

"I don't know, boss," said Trigg. He rubbed thick, grimy fingers through his greasy, stringy hair, his mouth drawn into a frown.

"I dare say there are a good many things you do not know, Trigg. That is why you and Axel will be paid very well for your troubles."

"But why kill the woman? She's right pretty, she is."

"Really?" said Delano. He looked skyward. "I had not noticed."

"Oh yeah." Axel nodded with enthusiasm, looking

to Delano like a donkey scratching his neck on a fence post. "She's something else."

"Good," said Delano. "She will perish looking pretty then."

"Beating on ol' Cooley was one thing. He's a tough old bean, I don't mind saying," said Trigg. "And that Gage fella didn't help matters none. But beatin' on Mrs. Shierson? She'd just see us, and then she could tell the lawdogs who done it to her."

Delano smiled. "This is why you have to use care. Oh, and don't just beat on her—as I said, I need her dead and gone. You understand that, don't you?"

"Why don't you do it yourself?"

"Look, you two!" Delano stuck out his jaw, ground his molars, and shoved hard toward them. He was shorter than Trigg, but about the same height as Axel. But somehow he'd been able to maintain the upper hand over both men for years now. They were good and afraid of him, and he had to keep that edge maintained or all was lost. They had proven time and again to be idiots, but reliable to conduct the most basic, as he thought of them, tricky deeds that needed doing in order for him to stay in business. And now was no exception.

"Enough of this talk. You each are armed, yes?"

They both nodded.

"A gun each and a knife each, good. In addition, I want at least one of you to have a rifle. Stop by the warehouse and fetch whatever you'll need. But there will be no dawdling. I need you to deal with the two of them within the next half hour. Is that clear?"

"What's in it for us, then?" Trigg asked, but instead of the narrowed eyes of someone who felt he's in a position of bargaining power, Delano saw raised eyebrows and a lost look on the brute's face.

"Why, I thought I mentioned that," said Delano, smiling a winning grin. "You will both, of course, receive half of the reward money."

"Oh, is Mrs. Shierson and Cooley wanted folks, too, then?"

Delano growled in disgust. "Gage is." Then he thought better of this and quickly said, "But now that you mention it, Mrs. Shierson and Cooley both are part of a ring of thieves who have been stealing the folks blind in the far-up mine camps."

"Really?" Axel's raised eyebrows rivaled those of his chum Trigg.

"Oh yes," said Delano, pulling a long, disappointed look on his pink, fleshy face. "It's been bad. Trigg, you remember the marshal from down country. Portins was his name?" Delano leaned in even closer to the two men. "I'll take you both into my confidence, but don't tell anyone else, you see?"

They both nodded again.

"He's been asking me for some time to keep an eye on them two. But now things have gotten out of hand and they've gone and killed folks up there. And Portins has deputized me to do what I can with them. He said not to bother bringing them to him alive—that would only be a waste of citizen money, you see. So I have the sad duty to pass judgment on them myself."

"But you're the one deputized, not us," said Trigg.

"That's true, that's true, but Portins also gave me

special permission to deputize whoever I felt I needed to, in order to bring those two to the ultimate justice."

"Who all else has been deputized?" said Trigg.

"Why, nobody. The first and only folks I had in mind for the task were you two men, Trigg and Axel. I didn't mention it before now because I was waiting for the exact right moment." Delano held his hands up, as if that explained it all.

"Now, if that isn't to your liking, well, you just tell me and I'll not deputize you two men, and justice will have to wait for two other men with the hearts and minds willing to take on the mighty task. And it is a task, I will admit, that not just any man is capable of. That's why, again, I thought of the two of you, as my longtime, most trusted confidants. I thought you were up to it. But maybe I was wrong. You two just talk among yourselves and I'll wait on over here. But don't take too long. Justice won't wait. Remember that, justice won't wait."

By the time Delano glanced at their two slack-jawed faces and turned around, he was fighting to suppress a grin. He knew at that moment that he had them right where he wanted them. They would not only say yes, but they would be honored in the process. As if they were doing him—and all humanity—a favor. Well, weren't they, after all? For him, at least.

"Hey, boss?"

It was Trigg.

Delano faced them fully once more. "Yes, men? Come to a decision, have you?"

"Sure thing we have," said Axel.

He looked to Delano as if he were a green boy and

was about to be given a sweet treat at the confectioner's shop.

"Good, good. I can count on you two men. Shall I deputize you, then?"

"You bet, boss," said Trigg.

Both men stood tall and puff-chested.

Great, thought Delano. *And now I have to come up with some sort of little ceremony to deputize these two idiots.*

"Hey, boss?"

"Yes, Axel?"

"We gonna get shiny pins for our chests?"

"Oh, well, now, see, that's the thing about being a special deputy. That means you are operative in a way that nobody else can know. You see? Secret, as if you were on a mission, because that's what you will be doing.

"If you wore a pin," Delano hastened to add, because he saw the glint in the eyes of the two men wane just a pinch, "then everybody will see that you are deputies, and then what happens?" Delano let that question hang in the air.

Neither man answered him, but their scrunched eyebrows told him all he needed to know.

"Nothing will happen. That's precisely correct of you two. You see, justice will be ignored and killers will rove among us once more."

"But ain't Pierce and Nob killers?" said Trigg.

Delano did his best to tamp down the urge to slap the oaf across his sweaty, hairy jowls. "They are, indeed. Which is why I will personally take care of them while you two are dealing with Mrs. Shierson and

Cooley. I decided, as the senior deputy among us, it should be me to handle the difficult and more dangerous job of dispensing with Pierce and Nob. You see?"

Both men nodded, eyes wide. And Delano proceeded to conjure up a quick, somewhat-impressive-sounding, if he said so himself, deputizing ceremony.

He sent them on their way and he climbed back into his buggy and made for the cabin once more, not quite succeeding at suppressing a giggle of glee. This mess might turn out all right, after all.

"Mother Delano didn't raise no fool!" He cackled and laid the whip across the hindquarters of the nag pulling the buggy.

Chapter 23

"Cooley—what are you doing here?"

"Good to see you, too, Gage." The old man didn't sound miffed, but ready to chuckle. "Ain't had to unload on a man in some time. It gives me no pleasure, but that beast was about to try something foul."

Gage, still dazed by the blast of sound and the stink of gunfire and smoke, shook his head and welcomed the help given by the wily old rascal standing over him with that sawed-off single-barrel shotgun of his. A curl of smoke rose from the business end of the barrel.

"You want to point that thing away from me, Cooley?"

"Oh yeah, well, no worries there, I ain't slid in a fresh shell yet. But that don't mean I won't. All it takes is one twitch from that fool there and you'll see!"

"I thank you. Could you lend me a hand now?"

Cooley sighed. "I got to do everything for you, Gage?" He winked and leaned his shotgun against the broken chair, which was, in part, still attached to Gage. Then he reached down and extended his good arm to Gage.

Gage noticed that the old-timer's wounded wing,

still in a sling, was newly wrapped. He wondered how long it would be before the man had use of the limb once more. Broken arms didn't heal quickly, and when someone was older, Gage knew that bones tended to knit back together even slower.

Still, it was Cooley he was looking at, and for a man who'd looked to be knocking on death's front door a couple of times in the past week or so, the old gent looked surprisingly spry.

With the man's help, Gage got his feet under him and watched, steadying himself from dizziness, as Cooley slid his own belt knife free and sliced the remaining ropes attaching Gage to the chair.

"There, now ain't you glad I come along?"

"Well, you did save me just in time, and for that, I thank you very much." They both looked down at Nob's hunched, bloodied body.

"You're welcome. That beast"—Cooley nudged the dead man with a toe—"was about to slice you open like a prize bird."

"I know it," said Gage. "I was having a time of it myself, got tangled, and before I knew it, he was on me."

"Well, never was a shotgun shell better spent. Now let's get out of here." Cooley retrieved his shotgun and cradled it in the crook of his good arm.

Gage walked with a bit of caution at first, then with more boldness, to the table and snatched up the canteen resting there. He popped the cork out and glugged back most of the water. Never had anything wet tasted so blamed good, he thought.

For the flicker of a moment, he understood his father's gasped, relieved sounds when he knocked back a few swallows of whiskey after having been without it for a few days, depending on their slim financial situation when Gage was a kid.

And never had he felt so revived with such speed. He saw Cooley looking at him with a serious gaze. "You have looked better, Gage."

"Thanks. I've felt better, too. Say, how did you know I was here?"

"Oh"—Cooley tapped the side of his nose—"I have my ways. Naw, not really. I just had enough of Mrs. Shierson mothering me, so I slipped out, needing a walk. I took the shotgun with me, always do when it's wartime, if you catch my meaning, and it's been wartime hereabouts in Newel pretty near since Delano, that pig, rumbled into town."

Gage nodded, slicing himself some cheese and ripping off a hunk of the dried-out bread with shaky, aching hands. It could have been a rock shaped like a hunk of bread and he would not have cared. He'd never been so hungry in all his days. He held out some to Cooley, but the old man shook his head and kept right on talking.

"So I was out there, making my way along the north side of Main Street, might be I was edging my way down toward Delano's little rathole, see what I could find out."

"About what?" said Gage.

"About you! You was overdue by near two days!"

"Oh." Gage knew he had lost some track of time after being clunked on the head, but he hadn't known it was nearly two days that he could not account for. He felt so fuzzy in the head, and knew he wasn't thinking right just yet.

"I made my way on down there, and crossed the street before I saw way up back where I'd come from, Mrs. Shierson, standing on the loading dock and looking around, one hand above her eyes. I knew she was trying to find me."

Cooley laughed. "But I outfoxed her. Oh, she's got nothing but good intentions in mind, but I ain't a child, been a long time since I was, and a lot longer before I will be again."

Gage wasn't certain he knew what that meant, but right then, something was perplexing him. Something he had to do, on top of everything else he knew he needed to do. But Cooley kept right on with his yarn.

"So I sneaked on over and, heck, before I made it across the street, I heard Delano's big fat face shouting and lobbing out blue oaths at those two saps who work for him, Trigg and Axel. My word, how they put up with that abuse is something I will never understand. But then again, they deserve every letter he growls their way.

"So I kept moving on in, closer all the time, and pretty soon I heard Delano telling them that he had to go meet two men named Pierce and Nob, because he had to make certain that the delivery they were going to make to him was not harmed in any way. That there got my attention."

"Why's that?" said Gage, chewing and sipping and trying to recall what it was he needed to do.

"Why, because I figured *you* was the delivery! Don't ask me why, even though you just did. I just had a hunch.

Good one, too. I wasn't certain I knew where they was headed to meet up with those two killers, but I kept my ears cleaned. Then they made for their back lot, and I kept up, took some doing, because I had to go around the end of the building, but I did it.

"And all the time, Delano was smacking his fat pink hands together and yammering about all the things he was going to do with the reward money they were going to get for the special delivery that this Pierce and Nob were making to him."

Gage had been half listening, and then he looked about him at the cabin, at the mess, and realized with a jolt and a chill up his spine what it was that had been bothering him—Pierce was not here. But he was darn sure going to be there soon!

And maybe even sooner than that, given that a shotgun blast louder than it had any right to be had gone off inside the building. Pierce would surely have heard it, had he been on his way back to the cabin.

Wherever that was, thought Gage. He had no idea where the cabin was located.

"Where are we, by the way?" he asked Cooley, moving to the door to close it tight.

"Why, that's what I was about to tell you, if you'd let a man tell his story straight out without all your interrupting."

Gage flung open the window at the back of the cabin and did his best to usher out the smoke and stink of gunpowder. "Sorry, Cooley. And I understand, believe me, but there'll be time for chatter later. Listen to me now, Delano left here making for Mrs. Shierson's."

"He what? See, I couldn't get close enough to hear that bit."

"Yeah," said Gage. "And he thinks you're incapacitated and she'll be an easy one to kill."

"Don't bet on that!" sneered Cooley, already making for the door.

"He wants to pin her death and yours on me," said Gage.

"You? Why would you want to kill her? I seen the way you two looked at each other. Nobody in their right mind would believe that."

What Cooley said shocked Gage a bit, but he shook it off. "Plenty of folks are looking for my skin, Cooley. Look, I don't have time to explain right now, but I'm not what you think I am."

"Oh, you mean the Texas Lightning business? I figured that out some time back. Told you I've been around. Bah, I say to that. Ain't nobody need judge a man based on his past. If that was the case, I'd have been swinging from a rope many a year ago. Why, I could tell you stories—"

"No time, Cooley. Delano's making for her depot right now."

"Why didn't you say so?"

"I don't think Delano has the guts to kill anyone himself, let alone a woman, but those two animals of his might. And then again, Delano has surprised me."

"He's as ruthless as they come. Born bad, as my old mama used to say. Come on, son, you and me, we can stop him. We have more guns there, but why don't you take this one and I'll use my knife."

Gage shook his head. "No, you go and I'll slow down Pierce. That's Blue Boy's name. He's due back at any time."

Cooley's wide eyes roved from the door to the dead man on the floor. He seemed to be in the grip of indecision. Gage grabbed the old man by the good arm and jerked him away from the door.

"Cooley, get going! Out that back window. Hurry—I'll be right behind you. Now go!"

The old man snapped out of his reverie and allowed himself to be hustled to the window.

"Mrs. Shierson, Cooley. You have to stop Delano and those two idiots who drive for him. I don't care how good a shot she is, they'll be too many for her to face alone."

That seemed to convince the old man, for Gage knew, above all else, even more so than getting revenge on Blue Boy, that Cooley was devoted to Mrs. Shierson. And the fact that she was in mortal danger was unacceptable. He stepped to a chair, then slung a leg over the windowsill.

"Heck with that Blue Boy fool. You come, too, Gage. I need your help!"

"I'll be right behind you. I need to slow him down, Cooley. Believe me, it'll be easier now than to have him follow us there. He's ruthless."

"But—"

"No! Now go!"

Cooley dropped the ten or so inches to the ground and Gage handed him down the shotgun. "You're going to need this."

At the same time, Gage was thinking how much he was going to need it. But he didn't want to turn Cooley loose without a gun. The old man was operating with one wing, as it was. Then he remembered Nob's revolver. He'd go for it in a moment.

Cooley accepted the shotgun without comment and was about to say something else, when Gage cocked his head. "Hush—I think he's coming. Go now, go and save Mrs. Shierson!"

At the mention of her name once more, Cooley spun and loped off, making straight for town. Gage hoped the old man wouldn't run into any trouble on the way.

But then he had no time for any more thought. He eased the window down and was about to make for the revolver on the floor to his far left, but he heard boots crunching gravel. The sound grew louder; then it became boots on wooden planking. And then the cabin door burst open.

Chapter 24

When Gage heard boots on the gravel outside the cabin, he had just enough time to pull back into the corner before the door slammed open and clunked against the upended chair. Pierce stood framed in the doorway, lit from behind by the day's waning light and from the front by the dim glow of the lantern in the cabin.

"What's going on in here?" Pierce said it to no one in particular as he eyed the room before him.

Pierce stepped inside, and though the light was dim inside the cabin, his sight fell right away on Gage, who had only been able to half conceal himself in the shadowed corner.

For a brief moment, Gage cursed himself for not following Cooley's advice and climbing through the window, the same as the old man had. But he knew he had to buy Cooley and Mrs. Shierson time by slowing down Pierce.

Then the blue-shirted man looked down at the dark mass at his feet. He did not understand what it was—

that much was plain to Gage, who saw the killer's eyebrows pull together in confusion. Pierce shoved the door open wider, allowing more light from without to reveal the horror at his feet.

"What did you do?" He stood over the hunched body of his pard, the buckskin-covered mass of the man's back now a ragged eruption of meat and bone. The stink of blood and the muck of a man's innards filled the small, close room.

Gage stood still, watching the man from the half-shadowed corner. He knew he was caught in a bad spot this time, to be sure. He was unarmed, and in one of the few times since his abandonment of gunfighting, Jon Gage had to admit he was a little afraid. This blue-shirted devil was a singular fellow who could not help but to command respect and awe and fear from others about him, begrudging or not.

Not since he was a boy, and suffering under his father's frequent bouts of dark rage, had Jonathan Gage felt this way, so uncertain and not confident in his abilities. The feeling was brief, but real enough. Yet somehow it gave him the confidence oddly enough to take on this bullying madman.

For anyone who killed for profit, targeting whoever he had been hired to kill, regardless of their kindness or worth, was truly mad in the head, a hydrophobic dog roving through civilized society, winding between the innocents of the world, barely containing his lunges and gnashing fangs. And now here Gage was, facing this man, unarmed and close to death himself, this much he was convinced of.

But at least the woman was, if but for the moment,

safe. Safe, that is, if Cooley was able to get to her in time, to make it to her before Delano did.

Gage had no intention of dying right there and then, but he did know if that should happen, he had done what he could do to protect them. And to rid the world of Delano and Pierce and Nob.

No, he corrected himself. He had done certain things, but he had not succeeded, for Delano still roved free and so did this blue-shirted fool. He had to best this man.

"I spoke to you." The man stared at the half-lit face of Gage, his voice low and cold and even, like steel slowly dragging on steel. "And you have not answered me."

Gage pulled in a deep, long breath, then let it out slowly. "I answer to one man, and he isn't you."

"He wasn't yours to kill! He was mine or no one's! That's what friends are for!"

The man's sudden shout shocked Gage, who had been expecting more of the same measured tones. And then Pierce followed his barked words with a grab for his revolver.

Instinct, deeply buried in the tarry pit of buried memory, forced Gage's left hand to snatch for his revolver. A gun that hadn't ridden on that hip in so many years.

Pierce had his own gun slicked out, hammered back, and leveled on Gage's chest, while Gage came up with a hand holding nothing but crabbing fingers.

Pierce barked a laugh. "Imagine that! In a showdown with Texas Lightning and he ain't even got the good sense to wear a gun! What say we fix that, you foul murderer!"

"I could say the same thing to you."

"You killed my friend, let alone all the other folks you laid low in your past!"

"Who says I killed that unfortunate mess at your feet?" As he spoke, Gage took a step forward and out of the shadows. He knew this was pushing his luck, but he had to get closer to that table to his right, where a small knife sat partially hidden by Delano's wedge of cheese.

The table sat snugged to the wall and held bread, the cheese, the empty canteen, a blunt little knife, and an empty bottle of whiskey.

But the thing that interested him was the short, keen-edged knife that Delano had used to slice the cheese. It was not much, as knives went, but it had appeared to be sharp when the fat man had sliced the cheese, and besides, it was better than any weapon he now had.

Pierce looked at Gage with narrowed eyes and his head tilted to one side, as if assessing the man. Finally he said, "You know, for a famous gunfighter, you sure aren't much to look at."

"I'll try not to be too offended by your comment. But I have to say . . ." Gage spoke slowly and, he hoped, hypnotically as he made his slow, steady way toward the table and the wee knife.

That's when Pierce's eyes flocked in that direction. "Don't tell me you're hungry."

He sidestepped on over, closer to the table. He managed to do so without really ever taking his eyes from Gage for more than a finger snap of time.

Gage still progressed toward the table, too, but knew he would not make it there before Pierce. And he was correct.

The hired killer reached out with his left hand and snagged the hunk of cheese and was about to lob it to Gage, when his eyesight settled on the little knife sitting there, mostly hidden behind the cheese.

"Oh, don't tell me that is what you were making your way over here for."

Pierce's mocking tone continued and he swung his head side to side in a schoolmarm look intending shame.

"That is one of the more pathetic things I have seen in a long, ol' time, I can tell you true." He looked again at the little knife, then smiled. "Here." He snatched it up and stabbed it into the lump of cheese; then he tossed them both to Gage.

Much to his shame, Gage fumbled the catch, dropping the cheese with its feeble knife, but he bent and snatched them up quickly. He could not resist, and as he yanked the little knife out with his left hand, he thumbed away dirt from the cheese with his right thumb and bit into the cheese, all the while keeping a sharp eye on the man in the blue shirt.

The man regarded him with that same half-squinty, adderlike look.

Finally Pierce said, "I expect you are so pathetic-looking because you have been kept trussed like an animal for a while now."

"Is that a question or an observation?" Gage felt dog-tired and in no mood for this silliness. He needed something to happen, something that would get rid of this fool once and for all. But he was caught like a rabbit in a snare.

No, he thought, not quite. His thinking was still muddied, that much he knew. But if he could get more water and could buy himself more time to get his hands and feet back into somewhat decent condition to grip and hold something, he might stand some sort of chance here.

Trouble was, there was no time for such frivolities as feeling in fine fettle.

"You are still spunky, I'll grant you that, Gage."

"What are your plans, Pierce?"

"My plans? That's rich. Okay, I'll play your game. Let's see, first off, I'm going to kill you. Then I'm going to wait right here for that idiot, Delano. I reckon he'll meander back here before too long. He wants to collect your hide, so he'll be back. Or I guess I could wait to dispatch you. Either way won't make a difference to me. I'll take the reward money all for myself in the end anyway."

A skimpy idea had come to Gage, and while it was rather thin in the odds department, he had nothing else to try. "Good plan, except that Delano isn't coming back, Pierce."

"Course he is. The only thing that stands between him and financial ruin—well, deeper ruin—is you. Or rather the cash money capturing you will bring."

"Won't be that easy, Pierce."

"No? Tell me why, then, Texas Lightning."

Gage saw a slight slipping in what he had come to realize was nothing more than a thin skin of confidence.

"Because, unlike you, I am not an outlaw. Which means I am not actually wanted by the law. Oh, I don't doubt there's a bounty on my head, but that's posted by irate family folks seeking revenge. And I can't blame them. But looking at me as a lucky strike with a big reward? Not going to work. Delano realized this and took himself on out of here. Yes, he was cursing you for lying to him. Claimed you told him I was worth a fortune."

"That's because you are, Gage. No amount of your blathering is going to change that. I know what I know."

Gage nodded, wondering how long he could play this out. He was heartened only by the slight flicker of something, and he hoped it was doubt, flash across the killer's face. "I don't doubt that, Pierce. But that doesn't change the fact that Delano is in the act of clearing clean out of Newel with all the gold he has in that secret safe of his."

"Ha! What secret safe would that be? Man has but one and I saw inside it. It's threadbare."

"That's because you saw his business safe. Don't forget, Delano's no fool. Well, he is, but he was also, at one time, a successful businessman. I saw his other safe, a pinch smaller, and tucked around back in that small room behind his desk. You know the space."

"That's where he sleeps."

Gage nodded. "That's what he told you, sure. Anyway, he's there now and those two fools who work for him were given strict orders to finish what they started."

"Just what is it they are supposed to have started?"

Gage nodded toward the slumped, bloodied lump that had been Nob. "Told me himself he's scared enough of you he's going to kill you and be done with it. Of course, he didn't say 'kill.' He said he'd 'deal with you' in a similar manner as he did to Nob. Oh, I don't think he's the man for it, but that's why he has Trigg and Axel. They might not be the sharpest knives in the kitchen, but they will do most anything Delano says. Always have."

"What's that mean?" Pierce kept staring hard at Gage, his eyes narrowed.

"I expect it means they are under orders from Delano to lay in wait for you somewhere out there, ready to do for you as they did for poor ol' Nob here." Gage nodded toward the dead man.

Gage thought for certain he was making gains with Pierce. All he felt he had to do was introduce a bit of doubt. That, and slow down the man from making for the Shierson depot. And then Pierce chuckled and shook his head.

"Oh, I see it all clear now. And I know Delano's plan. True, he's not the clever type he thinks he is, but sometimes he hits the nail square." Pierce chuckled and wagged the revolver.

Gage watched the man's face and he thought he detected a twitch in the man's right eye.

"Now, Gage. Where's Delano? Tell me the truth and I won't kill you slow and hard. Otherwise, it ain't going to be pretty."

Gage looked at Pierce for a bit; then with a sigh, he said, "All right, all right. He's been, shall we say, dispatched by my friend. You know ol' Cooley?"

"Now, see, I know you're lying to me again. Rumor has told me the old hound is about done in, knocking on death's door himself."

"Nope. Who do you think dealt with your dumb friend here?" Gage nodded to the dead man slumped and bleeding out on the floor between them.

Gage thought his caustic, cold words might provoke Pierce. But the man merely snorted and hauled back a boot toe, then kicked the dead man hard on the rib cage. "He's done me a favor, then. It means I won't have to do for him myself. You ever shoot a friend, Gage? It's a hard shine, I tell you. Oh, what am I saying? Of course, you've shot friends. Why, I've heard you have laid low just about any critter that's ever walked, crawled, slithered, or swam on this earth. And I reckon that includes children and women, too. Ain't that right, killer man?"

It was Gage's turn to offer a cool smile. He knew the man was goading him, but he also knew he could only take so much. Especially that part about women. And one in particular. Did Pierce know about her? Maybe he was guessing. Didn't much matter, for the truth had a way of pricking holes in a man's soul, come what may.

"Oh, did I nibble at something you didn't want to hear, Gage? Yeah, I know a whole lot more about you than you care to admit, killer man."

Gage ground his teeth together, suddenly feeling the fool for chewing cheese and palming a joke of a knife that, at best, would bounce off the man's guts, should he get close enough to lunge.

What now, Jon Gage? he asked himself. *Are you going to cry like a bairn, as Cooley might say, or are you going to figure out a way to get a leg up and over this latest headache?*

Pierce was just one of a handful of problems to be dealt with. But he was the one most immediate.

"Looks to me like you're putting far too much thought into how you are going to kill me, killer man. I can save you the trouble. Ain't going to happen. Leastwise not today." The blue-shirted man wagged the revolver that he'd shucked and palmed when Gage was busy fumbling the lump of cheese.

"You are not as impressive as I had expected a man of your reputation to be, Gage. Frankly, I'm a little disappointed."

"Me too," said Gage. He sighed and looked, he hoped, as if he were about to collapse into a crying ruin of a man. He even slumped his shoulders, but he was tensing, too, for he had to try the only idea he had left to him. At least it was the only plan he was able to conjure in his slightly dizzy and aching head.

Just as he was about to whip the wad of cheese into Pierce's face, in what he hoped would be a direct blow, a voice from outside shouted, "Hey! Hey, in there!"

It was Patrick Delano.

Gage and Pierce looked at each other, sharing a moment of confusion. Pierce was the first to recover. He began to grin as Delano shoved through the doorway.

"What is going on in here? What's he doing untied?"

Beyond him, Gage saw through the open doorway that late dusk had descended on them, and night was about to settle in for the duration.

The fat man pointed at Gage, then looked down at Nob. "And what's he doing dead?"

"Never mind that, this fool here told me you were on your way back to town," said Pierce.

"I was, sent Trigg and Axel on ahead to deal with that pesky woman and the old man Cooley. This time, it's for good."

"Then, why come back?" asked Gage, hoping to introduce a bit of a distraction.

"Not that it's your business, but I didn't trust Nob to watch over you. And I certainly didn't trust you, Pierce, with my investment."

Pierce chuckled. "Wise man."

"You mean you weren't emptying out your safe?" Gage inquired.

"The empty one?" said Delano, smiling.

"No, the other one, your secret safe in the back room," Gage countered.

"My what?" Delano seemed confused, a look of surprise and concern on his face.

Gage thought for a moment that he must have guessed correctly and the little fat man really did have a stash of money hidden away somewhere at his shambles of a depot.

Pierce met Gage's gaze with a narrowed look. That's when Gage knew he had succeeded in wedging in some doubt.

Pierce rounded on Delano. "I have had about enough of this foolishness, Delano. Gage is coming with me, and you are going"—Pierce swung the revolver on the fat man—"to the same place Nob's at. Right now."

Delano screamed like a little boy who just saw his kitten stomped by a rogue bull. He dropped to his knees, his pudgy pink fingers clasped before him, raised, begging. His words rushed out in a tearful, stuttering jumble.

Gage paid no more attention, but grabbed this one thin opportunity and, pivoting on his left foot, spun and dove for the open window behind him, expecting a bullet to drive right on into his retreating body as it disappeared through the window.

He almost made it through the square space, but his numb legs slammed the sill as he slipped out and his shins clunked hard. Fresh jags of hot pain shot through his legs, but he clawed at the sill and the planked side of the shack from the outside, attempting to shove himself through.

It felt as if it took him an hour of grunting effort, but he knew it was mere seconds. But that was time he did not have. For within the cabin, he heard shouts and then a gunshot, followed by another. The first whizzed right over him and the second plowed a furrow in the wood beside his right hand.

Gage yelped and slipped through the space, and he did the thing he had decided to do before he turned and bolted—he did not run. That would have made him an easy target. He scrambled close to the shack's wall, with his back to it, stepping quickly, trying to see where he was placing his feet next and looking ahead at the same time.

He made it past the rocky mass of the fireplace's chimney and hugged the wall, then saw what he didn't know he needed—an arm-thick four-foot length of unchopped firewood. He hefted it and continued on, aware of the sounds of boots on boards inside, then the squawk of the front door opening, and more boots on the porch puncheons.

"Go left, I'll go right and chase after him!"

The voice was Pierce's, and Gage felt a flutter of hope. He knew he hadn't much time, but if what he heard was true, Delano would be the one he came upon first. He hustled around the far side of the house and emerged beside the porch on the left side, just as a short, wide shape emerged. Delano.

One, two steps closer, and Gage, with the short log already raised, brought it down, in a swing from left to right, against the man's head. The fat man didn't have time to do much more than grunt and drop. Perfect. Gage wasted no time, but stepped over the fallen lump of a man and peered into the dimly lit yard beyond the porch.

He saw nothing but three single horses, one of which was saddled. That had to be Pierce's mount. Beyond that, a two-wheeled buggy sat behind a fidgety horse.

Gage held tight to the branch and bolted for the single saddled horse.

He hoped his guess was correct and Pierce had taken the right side of the house. But Pierce was no fool. He'd not waste his time roving in the dark, looking for an escaped man. He'd come back for his horse and make for town.

Not if Gage had the horse, instead. And even if Pierce commandeered Delano's buggy, he wouldn't be able to catch up or keep up with Gage.

He untied the reins from the rail, hoisted his sore body into the saddle, and, laying the log across his lap, jerked the reins and heeled the beast at the same time. He ducked low and cut west, threading through the thin trees, hoping to loop northward, then eastward, toward Newel, once he was out of sight and within easy shooting range of the cabin.

He'd not ridden fifty feet before he heard Pierce's voice bellowing behind.

"You come back here now! Now!"

A shot ripped the air twenty feet to his right and Gage knew Pierce couldn't see him. Gage smiled and shook his head as he kept low in the saddle and urged the horse into a faster run, his heels drumming the beast's big rib cage.

He wanted to laugh out loud at Pierce, but he wasn't out of danger yet. Pierce was angry enough to hop on one of the other horses bareback and give chase.

Gage heard no sign of pursuit. But that didn't mean he slowed the horse one bit. There would be no sparing this beast until he got to Newel and the Shierson depot.

Chapter 25

"Mrs. Shierson? You in here?" Cooley whispered the query and did not repeat it. He also jerked his head back and waited, keeping his right ear and the side of his face pressed to the sun-puckered gray planking of the door.

He had a hard, dry lump in his throat that he had had a tough time swallowing back. It had crept up on him as he nosed his way, or barreled his way, with the sniffer of the shotgun poking in first, through the back door, a smaller hinged affair set into the larger left-side sliding door.

He still felt the grip of the hotness about his head and neck. The woman had called it a fever, but ever since he'd been a child, Cooley had always thought of that peculiar sensation of sickness as a hotness, usually about the head, that lingered for far too long, always far too long.

And so it was now, though he could not tell anyone how awful he felt. For if there ever was a time when ol'

Cooley, as he thought of himself, had to rise up and make believe like a kiddie playing at being a sailor or woodsman, it was now.

The gunfighter Gage—and Cooley had come to regard him as a solid fellow, and maybe even a friend—was in hard shape, but Cooley believed that when he'd left him back there at Delano's mine camp, Gage was about to skedaddle out of there himself. Good man that he was, Gage had said he was going to slow down that blue-shirted killer man.

And that meant it was up to Cooley to make certain the rest of the meager plan worked out. He had to save Mrs. Shierson from sure death at the hands of the vicious little pig Delano. Not to mention the two brutes Axel and Trigg, who'd put Cooley in this busted-wing situation in the first place.

Had he gotten here in time? He knew it was unlikely he'd beaten Delano and the two louts back here, but maybe, just maybe, they'd stopped at Delano's depot first.

He nudged his way in, a pinch more, peering with one eye into the darkness. It was a foolhardy move, but Cooley felt he knew something that the attackers didn't. He knew that Mrs. Shierson often sat alone in the dark these days, just inside that depot room, which had become her home, too.

Sat there like an old widow woman and stared at nothing. He pitied her mighty, but Cooley had never been able to shake her out of her somber ways.

He held there, scarcely breathing, his trusty short shotgun held tight in his good hand, and the butt wedged a little painfully in the crux of his wounded arm. But the pain kept him focused on the task at hand, so there was that.

He sniffed and tried to detect any smell other than the usual depot scents of the mustiness of old grains, burlap sacking, dry wood, and woodsmoke from the small stove Mrs. Shierson used for heat and cooking. He smelled nothing that might alarm him.

Cooley knew that his sniffer wasn't what it used to be—heck, what part of him was? Still, he prided himself on having what he thought was, for his age, keen hearing. He also knew that he was at best possessed of average hearing for his age, but a man had to have a pinch of pride about something, didn't he? At any rate, he thought, in this moment he would choose the former.

He cupped his right ear, which he considered to be capable of slightly better hearing than the left, close by the door's crack, knowing full well that as it was still daylight out, anyone inside the warehouse would be able to see that there was someone standing there. But he had no other choice, there was no other entry into the place, save for the front door, and that seemed an even poorer choice for lurking and listening.

He was almost ready to give up on trying to detect oddness about the inside, when he heard a slight sound from within. It was a quick, dry, dragging sound, as if by a shoe sole.

Cooley held his breath and remained rigid. He heard nothing else. Somebody was in there, all right. And they had likely heard and perhaps even seen him lurking out here. What to do? He was no doubt visible somehow to whoever was in there, or why else would they keep themselves hidden?

Hadn't he already whispered to her, and thus revealed himself?

And then he had no more time for self-doubt, because he heard boots on gravel behind, to his right, and approaching this way.

He'd only been on the back dock, before the doors, for less than what he guessed was five minutes. But could it have been possible that he had indeed beat Delano and Trigg and Axel to the depot?

But what to do—there were noises behind, footsteps of . . . one man, that was all. But he was in plain sight, or soon would be, and he had no time to scamper off the dock in any direction, save for one.

Cooley gulped and ducked low. He brought the shotgun to bear before him, cocked and ready, and low-walked, fast as he was able, through that little doorway.

His belt knife snagged on the doorframe and he froze a moment. Then, still hearing the footsteps outside, he crouched even lower, low as he was able without dropping to his knees.

As he freed up his knife, he heard two things at once that startled him and kept him from moving deeper into the unlit space. The first was the sound of the boots outside. They had switched from the harsh grating-gravel and crunchy-earth sounds to the softer sound of soles on wood planking, the steps leading up to the loading dock.

He guessed that whoever it was had not seen him; if

they had, they would have seized in place and maybe even opened fire on him. He'd made it in, just in time. But that led him to the second thing that had happened— he heard a voice, a man's voice, whispering as he had done, but it was hoarse and ragged. And it came from inside. And because he'd been on the move and had not lingered in the dim light of the doorway, he'd not been shot at by that person, either.

But that didn't mean he wouldn't soon feel a bullet pierce his old buckskins. But Cooley's real concern was for Mrs. Shierson. If there was a man inside, then that meant she was likely in trouble.

He strained his ears and soon he heard a voice say, "Boss? That you?"

Then another man's voice, deeper, whisper-growled, "Shut up, fool! Don't know that it is the boss!"

And, Cooley thought, it dang sure was not the boss. Because if that meant it was those two drunken brutes— Trigg and Axel—inside the warehouse, then that might well be Delano behind him. Mere feet behind him.

The best thing he could do was take one, two steps backward and hug the wall behind him, just to the left of the left-side door, which led to the dock. At least he was inside, ready for whatever might come his way.

Oddly enough, Cooley felt that same old wash of calmness that always came over him whenever he found himself in a risky setup. This time, as always, it dipped down from his head and seemed to slow him, and it gave him a good, clear notion of the situation and how he had to think about it.

He took stock of what he had going for him—he had

his hip knife, and he strained the fingers on his wounded arm to grasp the forestock of the shotgun a quick moment so he could unlace the thong holding his knife in place. No need to waste time in a close-in fight tugging on that blasted thing.

Next he grasped the shotgun once more, mainly with his good hand, and lightly ran his wide thumb over the hammer. It was slicked back, all right. No worries there. He could open up on anyone he needed to. Just had to make darn sure he was certain who it was that he was ripping into first.

He could not live with himself if he were to catch Mrs. Shierson with a stray blast. The thought made him shudder.

All this took place within three or four seconds of him hearing that second scolding voice. Trigg and Axel, he thought with a sneer. And then he had no time for more thought, because to his right, not but six feet away, the little loading-dock door opened wider and in stepped someone.

He saw the person's profile before he heard them speak.

"Molly, yoo-hoo! You home?"

Cooley's eyes widened. It was Gerty.

Oh, my word, she is going to get herself shot. Or someone else.

Cooley dithered, not certain if he should reveal himself and get her to safety, or take a chance that Trigg and Axel wouldn't harm the woman. Then they decided for him.

He heard a woman, not Gerty, shout.

"Hush up, woman!" one of them growled.

It was Mrs. Shierson who'd tried to shout, and it sure sounded as if she was trying to say, "Help!" only the rascals had shut her up quick with a slapping sound. Oh, but his blood was boiling, and if he wasn't careful, ol' Cooley would grind his old worn-down molars right into powder.

He stiffened. "Who is that? Mr. Cooley? And what did you say to me? Nobody talks to me like that, mister! Show yourself or get ready, because I'm about to teach you a lesson!"

Cooley swallowed and whispered, "Gerty! It wasn't me! Come over here and keep yourself quiet!"

That last bit he knew was a risky thing to say to the old bird, because she was a fiery sort and not prone to taking directives from anyone, save herself. He saw her stiffen and swing her bulk in his direction.

"Mr. Cooley? Come out and show yourself!"

"Hush up and get over here!" he growled, louder than he intended. He was really going to pay for this, he just knew it. And he didn't have long to wait.

A revolver shot cracked from the darkness of the warehouse. Cooley had already stepped a couple of paces backward and ducked down, lower than standing height, a simple maneuver that had served him well in the past.

For whatever reason, he knew it certainly wasn't because she wanted to do a thing he told her to—had to be the convincing, persuasive powers of the gunshot— Gerty bustled straight for him. Cooley could just see her in the dim light of the vast, unlit room.

It was her white shirt and once-white apron, both sizable garments, that gave her away. Cooley tensed, but kept from returning fire. It was far too risky, what with Mrs. Shierson somewhere back there and Gerty barreling toward him like a big, soft freight train.

And she did just that, quicker than he'd expected, because she, no doubt, couldn't see him and he was too busy squinting into the darkness, wishing for a little more light to let them have a return dose. But he couldn't do it—he had a shotgun, and if those savages had a hand clamped on Mrs. Shierson's mouth, surely his shot would harm her, too.

But none of that mattered, because Gerty slammed right into him and knocked him sideways, to his left, and onto the floor. His shotgun hit the planking and, despite the fact that it was cocked, it did not blast off. But that did him little good, because he couldn't see where it had ended up.

Cooley growled and squirmed and tried to get out from under her. She smelled of woodsmoke and sweat and . . . *Is that berries? Might be, if she'd been busy making one of her famous pies. This woman could sure cook.*

All these little foolish thoughts flurried in and out of his mind with speed, and when he finally squirmed out from beneath her, she was sitting upright, patting her sleeves and gasping. He knew any second she'd start to blabbing, because she was a talker.

He did the one thing he knew might get him in big trouble, sooner rather than later, but there was nothing for it—he clamped his good hand over her mouth, his wounded arm throbbing like a hammer-smacked thumb.

"Hush yourself, woman!" He growled the words low and close to the side of her face. He hoped she wouldn't commence to squirming again, because he had but the one useful arm and she was a mighty big woman, and could smack him silly for a week, as his mama used to say. She didn't move.

She was breathing hard through her nose and he felt mighty bad about it, but he didn't remove his hand from her mouth. This close up, he saw her eyes were wide and she was nothing but frightened, no matter her usual overpowering demeanor.

This lady is scared. Good, he thought. *Keep it that way and we might live through this.*

He leaned in again and whispered, quick and low, "It's me, Cooley. Delano and his men have Mrs. Shierson somewhere in there and they know we're over here. Any second, they're going to gun for us again and then we'll be done for. We got to move. To your left, you keep on going that way, there's a pile of sacking and straw in that corner. You stay there. You hear me? No talking now!"

She nodded her head and he pulled his hand away. "Now get going. Crawl low to that corner!"

He had just finished saying that, when his good hand, helping to keep him from falling over, rapped against something on the floor. He shifted to his right haunch and touched the thing with his fingertips. It was the stock of his shotgun. Never had a gun felt so welcome to him.

He cast a glance toward the darkness to his left at the retreating form of the big woman. He'd give her this much, she was game. And a heck of a cook.

Cooley shoved thoughts of food—how long since he'd had a hot meal?—out of his mind and scrabbled to his left, angling with as much quiet and care as he dared into the dark. He had the advantage of knowing where everything in the warehouse sat, from the low partitions he'd built to help keep stored goods separated to the stacked empty barrels, far fewer than in years past. Pity none of them had any more whiskey. He knew, because he'd checked. Twice.

Despite his caution, he heard every little scrape and drag his boots made, and with a gimped arm still in a sling—and after the beatings he'd taken today, it would be in there a long, ol' time yet—he figured that it wasn't but a matter of moments before those rascals figured out just where he was.

He also heard a couple of whimpers from a woman and just knew they were from Gerty, somewhere in the dark behind him. He was too far away to shush her this time, though. That would be asking for a bullet.

And just why weren't they shooting at him yet? It's not that he was disappointed, but it worried him. Might mean they were waiting him out, might mean they had flown the coop. Nah, he'd have seen the daylight from the front door when they swung it open.

He paused and listened again. He'd sworn it was Gerty, but now he heard it again, coupled with a scuffling, as if folks were struggling. Suddenly, from ahead, perhaps thirty feet, and to his right, toward the living space Mrs. Shierson had set up for herself, he heard a man's voice, low and coarse, growling words Cooley could not make out.

But they were not words uttered in kindness, that much he knew. He heard other sounds, then, more sounds of struggle, and a woman's voice, as if released in midword, growled back, "No!"

That was Mrs. Shierson and whoever the man was, Trigg or Axel, no matter to Cooley at that moment, for whoever he was, he was about to feel something awful. Cooley could not creep about in the shadows of the warehouse any longer. He wasn't the swiftest runner, never had been, truth be told, but he was determined, and he was already on the move.

He said not a word, but yanked that shotgun up to his new cradled firing position and made straight for the woman's little sleeping quarters, right where the sounds were coming from.

He knew his boots clumping on the puncheons were giving him away, and soon he would pass before the gappy front door, where much of the only light, dusky and barely brighter than indoors, was still slanting in, revealing motes of dust floating in the air and then slits of lit floorboards beneath.

But he had no choice.

As soon as he passed before one, a shot cracked from his far right, from the back door, where he'd begun his journey.

One of the men might well have circled around that way. Or another one had come along, and now that he'd given his position away, there was no turning back or giving in.

Cooley made it the remaining dozen feet to the wall to the left of the bedchamber door and hit it with a thud, not intended, to his wounded arm's shoulder. He slid to his right a foot, checked the shotgun cradled there, it was still cocked and ready, and stepped once more to the door, but he was now bent low and creeping.

Whoever was in there had heard both him and the shot and had hushed up.

He pulled in a quick breath, then spun, shotgun at the ready, and dropped low to his right knee. It popped and he knew he was going to pay later for all this slamming around.

But what he saw, or thought he saw—it was somewhat dark in there—boiled his blood anew. Trigg or Axel, one of those demons, looked to be struggling with someone else, someone weaker and beneath him. But someone who was now making growling, angry sounds that weren't words. Someone who sounded an awful lot like a woman, and who also sounded as if she was wearing a gag on her mouth.

"Hold, I say! Hold right there, you vermin!"

The man paused in his struggles and said, "Axel?"

"Nope!" growled Cooley. "Get up off her now!"

The man began to comply, and Mrs. Shierson, for that's who Cooley knew it was, thrashed and kicked and landed a good one, just as the man began to rise up and draw down on Cooley.

The wiry old man dropped and scuttled inside, low and to his right.

Two shots went off, one a hard, close crack! The other, the booming report of Cooley's shotgun.

Trigg's bullet parted the air a foot to Cooley's left, then punched into wood in the warehouse beyond. A woman's yelp sounded from out there.

Because Cooley shifted his position at the last moment, his shot caught Trigg square in the chest and face. He had no time to scream, but he slammed backward and hit the wall beyond the woman's cot.

Boards puckered and splintered and Trigg made a mewling sound as he flopped forward. His thick body smacked hard to the floor, and he thrashed and bled and then was still.

Mrs. Shierson screamed, a muffled sound given the rag or kerchief wrapped tight around her face. She jerked backward, shoving herself into the corner and huddled there.

Cooley shook his head to dispel the ringing and then rushed for his friend and employer.

"Hush now, hush now, Mrs. Shierson. It's ol' Cooley. You're all right now, all right." He thumbed free the kerchief, sliding it down her chin to her neck, and then, seeing and feeling that her arms were tied behind her, he made quick work of the rope binding her wrists.

"Oh, Mr. Cooley!" Mrs. Shierson hugged him about the neck. "Thank you—that savage man was—"

"Yes, ma'am," he whispered. "I expect we know what he was on about. No worries now, ma'am. Let's get out of here. But we need to keep low—Axel and Delano are here somewhere."

Before either of them could speak again, they heard shouting voices from the front loading dock. They both held still in the doorway.

"What's happening in there? Cooley? Mrs. Shierson?"

It was a voice familiar to Cooley. "It's old Charlie from the stable!" He wanted to go to the front door and let him in, but Axel, at least, and likely Delano, and maybe even Blue Boy, were somewhere lurking in the dark of the warehouse.

"Mr. Cooley!"

This time, the voice came from the back of the warehouse. And it was a woman's.

"Oh, boy, I forgot about Gerty!" Cooley turned to Mrs. Shierson. "Ma'am, stay low right here a moment. I got to check on her."

"Mr. Cooley!" shouted Gerty. "One of those beasts has escaped!"

Cooley didn't wait for his employer to reply, but ran low and straight for the back door, where he'd heard Gerty yell.

"You all right, Gerty?" he said, fumbling for another shell.

"Yes, of course, but one of those men, Axel or Trigg, one of those two menaces, shoved right by me and bolted. He ran across the loading dock and then went left, I think toward the west end of town."

"Okay, I'll find him. But get yourself back from that door, lest him or Delano sees you and shoots."

From the front of the building, Cooley heard a familiar sound—the drawn-out squeak and squawk of hinges that needed oil. He turned to the sound, then said, "Gerty, Mrs. Shierson's up by her room. I'd be obliged if you take her out of here, someplace safe."

"Of course, right behind you." And she stuck close

behind Cooley as he made for the front of the warehouse once more, feeling as if he were playing some sort of kiddie game, with all this back-and-forth nonsense.

Cooley had covered half the distance, when he saw a familiar shape in the doorway, with another couple of shapes close by.

"Gage?"

"Cooley, everything all right here?"

"Yes, Mr. Gage. Mr. Cooley saved our lives, but had to gun down a man in the process," Mrs. Shierson answered.

"A worthy trade," said Gage. "Who?"

"It was Trigg," Cooley replied.

"Where's Axel?"

Gerty piped up. "He ran off, out the back door, like the useless fool he is."

Cooley turned, looking into the dark of the warehouse. "Still don't know where Delano is, or that foul Blue Boy."

"I knocked Delano cold at the cabin," said Gage. "And then I took Pierce's horse. But he'll be close behind. And he'll be angry. We don't have much time. Cooley, you get the women to safety. It's me that Delano and Pierce want most. But they're not above taking hostages to get what they want. Let me deal with them."

"Not so fast," said a voice from the shadows beside Gage.

"Charlie?" said Cooley. "Who else is there with you?"

"Oh, it's Joe, the blacksmith. We come running when we heard the shots."

"Good," said Gage. "Maybe you two can keep an eye out, let one of us know if you see Pierce or Delano come into town."

"Who's Pierce?" said the stableman.

Cooley said, "You know him, he's that fancy man with the conchos and blue shirt who works for Delano sometimes."

"Ah, that nasty killer." Charlie nodded to Mrs. Shierson. "Pardon me, ma'am."

"That's quite all right, Charles."

Charles and the big, silent blacksmith, Joe, departed with nods and toting their long guns. They split up and took positions at opposite ends of the street.

"Okay, now we still have to find Delano and Pierce and Axel. Unless you think you hit Delano hard enough to keep him shut for good, Gage?"

"No, that might be too much to wish for."

"All right, then. We've got to hunt them down like rats!" growled Cooley, adjusting his arm sling with a grimace.

"Mr. Cooley," said Mrs. Shierson, "I hardly think likening them to vermin is appropriate. They are men, after all."

His eyes widened and his mouth dropped open. "But . . . But . . ."

"What I think Cooley is trying to say, ma'am," said Gage, "is that those men are killers and thieves and are bent on doing you harm."

"I am well aware of what they are, Mr. Gage. And

dare I say that it's rich that a man with your past has the audacity to call others killers." Her fine jaw and clear eyes marked her face with determination as she glared at him in the dim glow of the lamplight.

If he had been in doubt before, Gage knew now that she was well aware of his past as a gunfighter. And no amount of explaining would or could ever lessen the sting of that knowledge.

And for such a comment to come from her made the sting doubly painful. Yes, he'd earned every moment of it because of his past, but that didn't mean it needled less. And that bothered him, because he had to admit he'd taken quite a shine to her.

She was a comely woman and, in a different life, if he had ever had the ability to attract a woman, she would be the very model of that person. But not with the life he'd led trailing behind him like a ribby, slavering cur. Surely not. And so in that stinging moment, Jon Gage kept his mouth shut.

But not Cooley. He regained his wind and said, "I am sorry, Mrs. Shierson, if this rubs your fur the wrong way, but those men are nothing but vermin. I don't care if you disagree with me or not. They were trying to do—well, you know what they were trying to do! They are bad men with bad things in mind and I can't let that stand!"

Gage winced and said, "Cooley, keep it down."

"Oh, right. Anyway, I'm sorry, ma'am, but it's all decided. We got to go. You and Gerty, you head somewhere safe. And Gage here will do what he needs to. I can't let any more time pass before I slip on out of here and track that Axel rogue. He's—"

"I know, Mr. Cooley. He is, as you say, a verminous character. I take your meaning quite well." Mrs. Shierson smiled. "And I am far more grateful to you for your concern than I am dedicated to preserving the dignity of human life, no matter the bearer."

A cloud of confusion passed over the old man's face, and then he nodded. "Well, all right, then. Now . . . you take care, Mrs. Shierson. I vowed to your husband that I'd always be here for you and I don't intend to stop now. But, well, just in case—"

"Oh, Mr. Cooley," she said, closing the three feet between them in a stride and engulfing him in her arms. "I cherish you."

He patted her back with his good arm and nodded. "Well, me too, ma'am. Now"—he backed from her and cleared his throat—"I best get going before I get all snuffy." He tugged his hat brim, nodded to her, then to Gage, and slipped toward the back door.

Before he'd covered a half-dozen feet, Gerty bustled toward him from the shadows, where she'd been rummaging in the basket she'd brought. Now she was stuffing cheese and cold sliced chicken between slices of bread. "Don't you go leaving without taking some sort of sustenance with you, little man."

Cooley had spun when he heard her to his left. "What? Oh, hey now, Gerty. I got to go."

"Fine. You go, but you give me ten seconds and then I'm going with you."

"What? No, no! You're going to take Mrs. Shierson to safety."

But she ignored him and walked quickly over to Gage and Mrs. Shierson. She handed them a tin plate with food on it and said, "Eat. You don't take in some sort of strength that only food can give you, why, you'll end up dead. And that's not acceptable. I am going with Mr. Cooley, who needs help. Look at the state of him! I dare say, Molly, that you will be safer with Mr. Gage than with me."

She hugged Mrs. Shierson quickly; then before anyone could argue, she walked back to Cooley. The codger stood and watched the scene with an open jaw and his good hand clutching a big wad of bread and cheese and chicken, his shotgun cradled in the crook of the same arm.

"But—"

"Don't 'but' me, mister. You ain't got but one good wing and I have two. I can be of use to you. Besides, I know this town better than most folks."

"But I can't be bogged down by a woman! I'm fixing to move light and fast!"

"We'll talk about what you just said later. Right now, I'll pretend I didn't hear it. Now eat your food and let's go! You're wasting time."

"But look here, Gerty, you ain't even got a gun!"

"Who says I don't?" She whipped back one hanging side of her shawl to reveal a sizable six-gun in a well-oiled holster strapped around her ample waist, just below her ample bosom, all atop her stained, but clean, apron.

"Oh." Cooley regarded this woman a moment, then stuffed his mouth full of food and walked toward the door, muttering something.

Gerty was right beside him, and the last thing Gage

and Mrs. Shierson heard was Gerty saying, "Don't talk with your mouth full, Mr. Cooley. It ain't proper."

Even in the teeth of the grim moment in which they all found themselves, Gage had to smile. He sure didn't envy Cooley, but somehow he was relieved, too, to know the old man would have the formidable cook with him. He only hoped she was as capable in a fight as she seemed.

Chapter 26

Gage and Mrs. Shierson watched the single small inset door open. It squeaked slightly, and Gage thought that if ever there was a moment when another gunshot might be heard, it was right then. It was likely that someone would be poised and lying in wait for them, but there was no other way out of the drafty warehouse.

The door widened a pinch more, then one set of boots scurried out, followed by a second set of softer-treaded footsteps. The door closed once more, dimming the scant light from the ending day. Soon, even their footsteps vanished from hearing.

A brief moment of silence followed; then Mrs. Shierson said, "How long before you leave to find Delano or the killer Pierce?"

Gage pulled in a deep breath and let it out through his nose, his eyes all but closed. He could sense more than see her standing not but two feet to his left. Even now that he knew she reviled him—and he could scarcely blame her—he felt an attraction to her that he was ashamed of, and a little saddened by. He didn't want her with him, because he knew what he was headed for wasn't going to be a Sunday riverside picnic, but likely a bloody mess.

But he couldn't leave her here, knowing what Trigg had just tried to do to her, and what a brutal scene her home was now. Sure, she was tough, but he bet that at her core she was rattled and frightened.

"I can't leave you here, Mrs. Shierson."

She began to protest, but he held up a hand, between them, in what he hoped she'd take as a gentle gesture. "Ma'am, please. I was not raised with much in the way of guidance or manners, but I do know that leaving a lady, especially one such as yourself, alone in a dire situation, is unacceptable. No, we'll go at this together or not at all."

"Fine, Mr. Gage. What do we do, then?"

"Well . . ." He rasped a hand over his bristly face.

"You remind me much of my husband, Roger. I imagine Mr. Cooley has told you of him."

"Yes, ma'am." In fact, Gage was actually a little confused. "What they did to your husband, ma'am, goes a long way toward why I'm here, helping. Pierce, that animal, isn't a good man. Some folks are born raw or become that way. The test is if they work to correct that about themselves.

"If they don't, they stay bad and never get better. I think he not only never intended to change himself, I think that blue-shirted devil enjoys hurting other people. All for money. I lost out to him once, but luck was with me and I escaped his grasp. I won't give him the chance to nab me a second time."

As he spoke, Gage checked the rifle Cooley had given him on his arrival at the depot. "I know you can shoot, Mrs. Shierson."

"Molly, please. Just call me Molly."

"Okay, then, Molly. All right."

"And I can shoot. But I prefer not to."

"There are a whole lot of things in life most of us would prefer, ma'am. And not being in this situation is one of them."

"But here we are, nonetheless, eh, Mr. Gage?" she asked, a half smile on her pretty face as she emptied the last of a box of cartridges into the gun belt she had about her shoulder.

He noticed the revolver and nodded. "A solid gun rig," he said.

"If a gun can be praised, then, yes, I suppose it is that. Solid, I mean. It belonged to my husband." She paused and looked at him. "In truth, Mr. Gage, I don't know how to wield it very well. I believe I am a better shot with the rifle or a shotgun."

She slid the belt off her shoulder and held it out to him. "You use it. I expect you are more adept with it than I am."

"Oh, ma'am, I . . ."

What was he going to tell her? That he'd sworn off using handguns after he killed that girl? In fact, he'd sworn off using guns of any sort for the longest time after that awful day. And he'd nearly starved to death because of it.

He'd finally bought himself a beat-up old rifle purely for making meat, as the old-timers called shooting beasts to feed themselves. But it had taken him the better part of a year afterward to not feel as if he was going to throw up every time he laid his hands on the thing.

Eventually he got to the point where he could raise it to his shoulder, aim, and squeeze the trigger without succumbing to a case of the shakes. Of course, then, after he'd brought down his quarry, he'd doubled over with a horrible case of the dry heaves. Nothing seemed to help, but time. And his need for food. A man could only live for so long, he'd decided, on badly cooked beans and poorly cooked biscuits.

Over time, he improved his campfire cooking skills and now he realized he didn't need to make meat nearly as much as he'd thought. He could get by on fresh vegetables grown by farmers as he passed through the various fertile valleys he explored in his travels. At least for part of the year. He tended, as many folks in cold climates, to eat more meat in the winter months.

He also appreciated the many and fine and varied home-cooked meals he'd been invited to share at the tables of families, large and small, from all over the world.

He'd had indescribably tasty foods, which he could not begin to make himself, nor did he much recognize the flavors or ingredients or spices at the tables of the Chinese, Mexican, German, Italian, French, Polish, and various other families. And not once had he gone away from the table wanting or disappointed. All for the exchange of a few hours of honest labor.

Sometimes he'd find himself hunkered at a farmstead for a week or more, depending on what crops needed more man power. He was grateful for the work, and the farmers and their families always seemed grateful for the help. He refused money, but never went away from their places with empty saddlebags.

He was paid with potatoes, carrots, onions, greens, fresh-baked breads, cookies, biscuits, coffee beans, and even boiled sweets, which he always saved for the children of future families with which he bunked for a spell.

And his horse, Rig, had always fared well, too, grazing and nibbling at whatever toothsome treats the farmers fed their own horses, usually teams of burly work beasts. Yes, while he could not say it had been a grand life, or one he could have imagined for himself, these past years on the trail had had their rewarding moments. And he had thus far not been displeased with his efforts to not rely on the use of a handgun. Until now.

Looking at Molly's face, Gage saw obvious and logical fear warring with the strong woman's urge to remain calm and in control, if not of the odd situation in which they found themselves, but at least of herself. He also detected hopefulness there, a knowledge, if he had to bet, of his past as a gunman. And though this disgusted her, he suspected that she was also hoping he was someone she could rely on in this mess. No, he could not, would not, let her down.

"All right," he said, accepting the offered gun belt. "If that's your preference."

"It is," she said, letting go of it.

As soon as he felt the full weight of the belt with its filled bullet loops, and the holster and the gun within it, Gage's gut tightened and he felt a prickling swarm on his scalp and cold sweat stippling his forehead and upper lip, flecking his whisker stubble.

"Are you okay, Mr. Gage?"

He blinked hard, then nodded. "Yes, I'll be fine."

"Is it the gun?" Her voice was low and quiet.

"Ma'am?" He tried to sound calm and not at all how he really felt—about to throw up.

"You know, Mr. Gage, on second thought, I feel confident enough with the handgun."

"No, no, Mrs. Shierson. I assure you, I'm fine. Just fine." He held his breath and pulled on the gun belt, buckling it on with shaking hands.

He hoped the fact that it was somewhat dim in the warehouse helped mask his nerves.

Get ahold of yourself, Gage, he told himself, gritting his teeth together hard. *If I grind them any harder, they will turn to powder.*

"All right, then," she said, hefting the rifle and checking it. He was impressed—she knew what she was doing, he could tell by the way she handled it.

"What do you suggest, Mr. Gage?"

He held his tongue for a moment, thinking.

She said, "Unless, of course, you are uncertain. In which case, I will leave you to it and go on out there myself."

"No, no. That would be a bad idea, ma'am. We must stick together. There is wisdom in this, I assure you."

"Fine," she said. "But you should know, I have nothing to lose, Mr. Gage."

The remark was filled with words unsaid, and he knew that meant she was unafraid to take risks. He had to admit that was the way he lived, too, so he was quite used to that notion. But while she was under his care, not a view he would dare tell her, she was going to be behind him, and be in as little danger from here on out as possible.

"We need to leave through the front door, ma'am. And we need to do so in about five more minutes."

"Why the front?" she asked. "And why wait any longer? We've already wasted enough time."

"No, ma'am. We're waiting to get as close to full dark out there as we can. Then we're going to leave by the door they least expect us to use."

She said nothing, but her eyes shone, and her brows rose. "Mr. Gage," she whispered.

"Yes?"

"I have just remembered, there is a third door."

"Where?"

"Over there." She pointed back beyond them, toward the rear of the building, but at the floor, in the center.

"A trapdoor. In the center of the room."

"Roger had insisted that we build in such a feature. He said that warehouses were notorious for burning, and if that should ever come to pass, we would be able to escape the conflagration with fewer injuries and burns than if we were forced to flee through the usual doors."

"Wise thinking," he said. "Which way?"

"Over here, not far from that central post." She was already on the move, low-walking and holding aloft the lantern. She had turned down the wick so that it offered low, steady light. No doubt the moving glow might well be seen from the outside through cracks and gaps in the vertical board and batten plank siding. But there was nothing for it; they had to see enough to get moving.

"Here," she said, at the same time as he heard the clunk and squeak of dusty, unused steel being moved.

Gage bent low beside her and saw she'd pried up a steel loop that had been recess cut into a corresponding groove in the floor planking. He also saw that the door was approximately three feet square, hinged at the opposite end.

He brushed away stray old bits of hay chaff. He reached for the steel ring and she let him, pulling her hand away. He began to lift it, but held off, not hefting it more than a half an inch.

"Ma'am, we'll need to douse that light, otherwise it might be seen from out front, or to the rear, as the warehouse is built up on the three-foot or so pole height."

"How will we see?"

"It's not full dark, so once our sight has adjusted, with any luck we should be able to see the dim shapes of everything around us."

She nodded and blew out the lantern. He held there

a moment, letting the darkness rise, letting their eyesight adjust to the surroundings.

"Ready?" he said, grasping tighter the steel ring in the floor.

"Yes," she said in a near whisper.

He tugged the old door upward and the hinges squawked low. He slowed his tugging and the steel groaned. It sounded as if the entire town might hear, but he knew that unless someone was less than ten feet from them, they were the only folks to hear the hinges.

Gage walked the door backward and laid it open, back on the floor; then on his knees, he worked his way back beside her and felt the edges of the newly revealed hole in the floor.

"I'll go down first," he said, pausing to check the revolver. It was loaded, as he had seen her do so, not long before.

With a quick breath, he decided to keep it in hand and lowered himself down through the hole, half expecting at any moment to hear a crack and feel the sharp, hot lance of pain a bullet delivers to flesh. But no such sting came to him.

He stood on the ground and, judging from the warehouse floor's height on his chest, he guessed the building was built up about three feet on a robust cribbing of timbers. It was an unusual setup for most businesses, save for freighting and shipping concerns. It helped in keeping the two loading docks high enough to fill and unload wagons with ease.

"Ma'am, would you like a hand?"

"No, but take the rifle for a moment, if you would."

He did so and then saw she was about to slide down into the hole as well. That would put them quite close. He ducked out of the way, and while he turned to look anywhere but at her legs as she dropped the few feet to the earth, he knocked the left side of his forehead on a beam. He winced, but said nothing.

"Okay," she said, ducking down beside him. "Which way?"

"To our right," he said. "We'll make for Delano's warehouse. He won't expect that. If he somehow made it back there, he'll think we're staying holed up, awaiting law that will not arrive in time."

"And Pierce?"

"I have a hunch that he, too, will make for Delano's. I hinted that Delano had gold stashed there and Pierce seemed keen to hear this."

"Lead the way," she said, speaking in a whisper that mimicked his own.

The route was slow going, but he wanted to get to the alley that separated them from the next business eastward of them. Two more structures beyond the Shierson freighting building, and he knew this would put them across from Delano's place of business.

They reached the alleyway, not without a couple of knocks to the head on timbers for each of them, and then they were each looking out, left then right, into the near darkness for any sign of someone lying in wait.

They saw no one. By mutual unspoken consent, neither made a sound other than the occasional scuff of their boots on gravel.

Gage led the way and they crossed the narrow alleyway and tucked behind the next building, a hardware concern, as Gage recalled. Soon they would be behind the Big Strike Saloon, which might be trickier, since its back doors were usually busy with customers seeking relief in the outhouse out back.

He was not wrong in recalling this, because they had not yet reached that building when they heard a door swing open, boots clunk on wood, then a long, loud belch.

Beside him, closer than he expected, he heard Mrs. Shierson whisper, "Honestly."

He turned to her, as if to shush her, but she was looking ahead with squinted eyes, as if that might help her vision in this low light.

The belcher stomped down three steps to the back gravel and crate-filled space. He clunked into a stack of crates filled with empty bottles and they emitted soft clinks as they jostled together from the mild collision.

He cursed and walked on toward his destination, a small two-door structure at the far back end of the yard, which he entered, belching again, and allowed the door to clunk behind him.

"Come on," said Gage, grabbing her wrist and leading her across the jumbled lot behind the bar. They forsook quiet and stealth in exchange for speed, and their boots crunched gravel and dirt and clunked stones.

"I'll be out in a minute," growled the belcher from inside the latrine. He then grunted and awful sounds came to them as they ran.

Gage felt shame and embarrassment color his face and his ears grew hot. He kept on, knowing she was beside him, likely scowling. He was shocked when he heard her giggle.

The back area was lit well enough, and she was close enough to him that when he glanced at her, he saw her trying to hide a smile and shake her head as if to tell him to look away, to not see her laughing in this uncouth moment.

He, too, grinned and kept moving toward the far side of the yard. The last thing he wanted at that moment was to see another drunk wander out the back door of the saloon and see them. She surprised him at every moment, it seemed. Oh, he thought, if life had been different for him somehow.

They made it across and then edged to their right, in near-dark shadow, hugging the side of the building. Across the street and up a pinch, to the left, sat the bulk of Delano's warehouse. The curtains to the office were drawn, but lit from within.

At the end of the alley, before venturing across the street, they held and she whispered, "Mr. Gage, I hope you have a plan. Because I confess I do not have much of one."

"Oh, you don't need a plan, pretty lady."

The voice came from behind Gage, to his right. And it was a voice he recognized. It chilled him to the core, even as he raised the revolver and thumbed back the hammer as if born to the task.

The man leaned against the front of the saloon, barely

discernible in shadow. But Gage didn't need to see the man to know who it was: Pierce, he of the blue shirt and ill regard for life.

That's a rich and hypocritical thought, mused Gage, for a man who used to exist as he had. Within a breath of time, he'd raised the gun and, out of instinct, shoved Mrs. Shierson back into the alley with his left arm.

"Tell you what," said Pierce. "I'll let you live if you do me a favor. You trot on over across the way there, kill yourself a fat man—I bet you know who I'm talking about."

"Delano's back?" said Gage.

"Oh yeah, he's over there, all right. Got himself a sore head from a rap to the bean he took. Wonder how that happened? He's dizzied up and as riled as a rooster, but not so bad he can't get his safes open and emptied. I'll leave him to that, then go on over and collect the fees he owes me.

"But back to my proposition. See, you go on over and do for him, and then I reckon you'll have to skedaddle. But that's all right. I know you have a horse and such at the stable down the street a ways. Me and him, we had a nice chat not but a few minutes ago at the end of the street, yonder. Come to an agreement, we did. And your horse will be waiting for you, Gage."

"You kill Charles?" said Gage.

"Naw, naw, just pressed him for information. Old men tend to fold easy when you threaten them. He's breathing and dandy, last I saw."

"And the lady?" growled Gage, trying to think this through, to buy time.

"Oh," Pierce said, chuckling. "She's not part of the deal. No. At least not a part you need concern yourself with. You see, she's staying with me."

"I will do no such thing!" snapped Mrs. Shierson.

"Oh! A spirited little vixen. That's good, that's good. Just how I like 'em."

Before he could stop her, Mrs. Shierson had shoved her way past Gage and rounded the edge of the board-walk, resting one boot on the step. She'd also raised her rifle and had it aimed at the shadowed man.

"Oh, ma'am, I do like a fiery lass." He shifted from his position of leaning against the vertical plank wall.

"You killed my husband, you . . . you verminous man!"

"Could be, could be," said Pierce.

Gage tensed, ready to shove her to one side and slick out his own gun.

"Well, look here, pretty thing," Pierce continued.

"Shut your mouth, vermin!"

Gage raised his arm as he saw Pierce's right arm move and his left leg bend, turning to shoot the woman.

But both men were too late.

Molly Shierson's rifle cracked and coughed flame, and her bullet cored the smarmy killer, high up on his chest, in the center of his pretty blue shirt.

Pierce looked down at the thumb-size smoking hole as blood welled out. His eyes, as wide as any man's Gage had ever seen, looked up at them both. He opened his mouth to speak and his words came out, trapped in a bubble of blood that grew, hung, quivered, and popped.

He pitched forward slowly, as doors up and down the main street clunked open, and shadowy figures scurried out, then sought cover. The saloon emptied of the three people within.

But Mrs. Shierson didn't see any of them. She had already turned and was making for Delano's depot. With Gage one step behind.

Chapter 27

"Gerty, I can't do what I need to do with you yammering and stomping on my heels. I got to move fast. And—"

"Oh, hush now, Mr. Cooley. Did you eat that food I put in your hand?"

"Well, yes, ma'am, but—"

"Good. That will give you the strength to endure whatever is coming."

Cooley was about to respond, when a hurried clunking of boots on planks reached him from somewhere ahead in the darkness. He held up his good arm, the forestock of the shotgun gripped in his thick fingers. He expected Gerty to comply, but she kept on yammering and walking.

He turned on her, not for the first time that evening, and within inches from her face, he said, in a growled whisper, "Hush now, woman! He's up ahead of us!"

That did it. The old warhorse felt her heavy breathing on his face stop, as if she had held her breath. And then he felt her lips on his, or rather on his whiskers, planting a light kiss there.

"Good luck, Mr. Cooley."

He was too stunned to do much more than say, "Oh . . . okay . . . um, thank you, Gerty."

Then, from ahead, once more he heard the scuffing of boots grinding on sand and gravel, and then the sound ceased.

Cooley also held his spot, waiting. They had reached the end of the street anchored by Gerty's establishment. He could almost make it out in the darkness to his left.

Beyond it, the roadway bent westward, then north from town, into the foothills and the mine camps beyond.

Does Axel, that fool, have a horse hidden there? What is he doing?

Before Cooley could do much more speculating, he heard a voice, thin and trembling, but clear, emerging from the darkness to the north, just ahead of them.

"I told Trigg not to do it! I told him! I don't want any troubles! I'm going, I swear it. Right now. I'm laying down my gun! There, on the ground! And I'm going now—you won't see me ever again. I promise it! Please just let me go, I don't want no troubles!"

The frightened words stopped and the last of them hung in the frigid air of the darkened night.

Cooley waited five, ten, twenty seconds without moving. Then he and Gerty heard boots crunching at a loping pace, moving away from them, from town. The sounds quickly receded, growing faint as they traveled into the north.

"Can you trust him?" Gerty asked in a small whisper in Cooley's left ear, much closer than he expected her to be.

Cooley flinched. "You scared me. But I reckon I do believe I can trust him," the old man whispered. "Far as I know, Axel didn't do no killing for Delano. Oh, he's a right idiot, but he's no killer. Somehow I believe we can let him be and he'll be true to his word." He turned to face the woman standing beside him. "I'd like to believe that."

"Me too," said Gerty, looking into the dark night, northward.

Chapter 28

Molly Shierson mounted the loading dock stairs fronting Delano's warehouse with quick steps, but Gage was faster and grabbed her left arm, pulling her to the side. She began to protest, but he held a long finger up before his own lips, his face close to hers.

"Quiet," he whispered, glancing toward the half-open front door leading to Delano's office. He saw no movement within, but he knew that meant little. "You were lucky once, ma'am, but that won't happen again. Now stay behind me and do as I say!"

"Mr. Gage—"

He moved his face even closer to hers and spoke in a low, steely, whispering growl. "I have been in situations that have equipped me for this sort of mess, ma'am." He looked at her pretty face from inches away. "And you have not."

"Molly," she finally said, answering back in an equally low whisper.

He was hypnotized by the moment. Then he said, "You will have to trust me, Molly."

She stiffened and the moment popped like a bubble of soap on a breeze. Then she nodded. "Understood, Mr. Gage."

He returned the nod, then, hugging the wall, he led the way into the office, nosing in first with a boot. He toed the door open wider and waited, hearing a rustling, then a low murmuring sound.

Gage leaned his head into the frame and looked beyond Delano's desk toward the dark shape of the door back there. He knew that was the small room where Delano slept and stored his ledgers.

But there was a sliver of light peeking out from beneath the door. Delano was in there. He looked at her and once more held his finger to his lips, then ventured inside.

They made it behind the desk and he continued to the right. The door to the warehouse was open. "Wait in there," he whispered over his right shoulder, pointing toward the darkness of the warehouse.

He was about to confront Delano in that little room, and if the little fat man proved quicker to shoot than Gage expected, he did not want her behind him, or anywhere near him, in fact.

Gage moved forward and listened. He heard a quick scuffing, then more mumbling sounds. That told him Delano had no notion that anyone was right outside his door.

Gage pulled in a breath, felt the heft of the killing tool in his left hand, Roger Shierson's revolver, cocked and ready to do the only thing a gun was made for, and he lightly set a hand on the steel door latch.

He got ready to shove his way into the little room,

making unavoidable noises of a bootstep and the clicking and pushing of the door. Gage gritted his teeth and pushed. The door bowed, but did not yield—the blasted thing was locked from the inside.

At the same instant, he heard a similar sound from within the room, then bootsteps.

Just behind him, he heard more footsteps. Gage knew it was Mrs. Shierson, moving when he'd told her to stay put. He raised his right boot and slammed it against the door latch. The planked portal crashed open, swinging wide and shedding the soft, honeyed glow of an oil lamp outward.

The lamp sat on a small worktable in the middle of the room. The rest of the room was a mess of strewn papers. Atop the cot, to his left, a welter of blankets sat knotted and draped to the floor. But it was the small, open door to the rear of the room that concerned Gage.

He rushed for it and stomped on through, the revolver leading the way into the darkness of the warehouse.

All was quiet. He heard no sounds—no bootsteps, no labored breathing, nothing. Still, Gage held his spot, unmoving. It would be far too simple and far too foolish to shout either Delano's or Molly Shierson's name into the cold stillness of the vast space. Instead, he listened. Within moments, he was rewarded with the sound of bootsteps ahead, slightly to the left. The sounds ceased.

Then Gage heard footsteps again, two sets, one being forced, one heavier, doing the forcing. A muffled sound came to him, too, like a voice being stifled. Then he saw them, not twenty feet before him. Delano shoved Mrs. Shierson forward, ahead of him, into the dim circle of light.

Somehow the little fat man had managed to surprise her and take her hostage. That would account for the scuffling and clunking Gage had heard.

He must have found it too difficult to keep his chunky fingers clamped around her mouth, for he released her face from his grasp and snatched her gathered hair from the back, and jerked her head backward. She winced and gasped, but did not utter a sound of complaint.

Delano stood behind her, looking over her right shoulder at Gage. He smiled, showing his teeth held together tight in his fleshy mouth. Gage noticed the right side of the man's head was dark, his hair matted, but wet-looking. Blood had seeped down over his right eye and cheek, giving his visage a grotesque look.

In that moment, Gage wished he had hit Delano harder back at the cabin.

Then the fat man growled. "I will kill this woman, and no one will ever know I did it, Gage! And they will blame it all on you, because you are a foul, ruthless killer!"

"You're wrong, Delano," said Gage, guessing the distance between them to be more than fifteen feet, less than twenty. "I'll know. And you'll know. And she will know."

Delano was silent for a moment, then let out a ripple of laughter. "Ha! She'll be dead and you'll be damned, Gage. That's all you both will be!"

But Gage knew it was nothing more than a hopeful claim, and a laugh of nervousness, born of uncertainty.

The piggish little man was beginning to realize that the few strands left holding his plan together were snapping rapidly. One or two more and then he would be undone completely.

Gage pressed on, in an even, bold voice. "And besides, Delano, you can't kill me."

"What? Why ever not, killer man!" Delano laughed.

"Because," said Gage, "other men, better men than you, Delano, have tried. And to a man, they have all failed."

"You shut up! Shut up now! I'm the boss here!"

Gage ignored the fool's claim and said, "Okay, Mrs. Shierson?"

"Understood, Mr. Gage."

Gage's words did what he hoped they would do— they provoked the man into a rash move.

Delano tried to slap a hand over her mouth again, but she jerked to her left, fast and low, exposing more of Delano than the bloodied meat of his face peeking over her shoulder.

It was far more of a target than Gage required.

Delano howled "No!" loud and long into the chill, still night air.

With lightning speed, Gage's hand whipped up black in the dark, cold night and pointed a deadly steel finger. A finger that spat flame and smoke.

As it had always done, every time Gage had found himself in a gunfight, time seemed to seize in place, as if it had pulled in its breath. Then it resumed, but slower.

He fancied he could see the short trail of the bullet

as it parted the cold night air, as it collided with the greasy center of the fat man's forehead, drilling through flesh, blood, fat, bone, and brain.

Then the little death-dealing missile continued its journey as it shoved on out the back of the man's skull, before lodging in a plank somewhere in the vicious little man's echoing, frigid warehouse.

Gage saw the foul man's last, blown breath plume outward against the dull glow cast from the lamp in the other room. Then Patrick Delano wobbled and dropped, his hostage jerking and spinning away from him, half turning to see the man who had caused her so much torment, so much brutal agony in life, finally reap his rank, sown reward.

She watched as Patrick Delano collapsed in a sloppy heap, his head angled back, his eyes open, his lips sagged wide. Blood slid from one corner of his mouth, matching the narrow, but thick, trickle of the same from the perfect hole in the center of his forehead.

She looked over, to her left, at the shadowed stranger lowering his pointing arm, the slight gleam of steel glinting in his hand.

Gage turned his head slowly and regarded her, no recognition at first to alter his features from the passive mask his face had become.

Then he seemed to see Molly Shierson as if for the first time, and his angular, shadowed, chiseled features softened, and for the slightest of moments, he saw the woman so close by as his heart wished to see her. There she was, a beautiful woman who, perhaps, felt toward him as he did toward her.

And then the hard, harsh facts of the situation, of their lives, gnawed their way in and the moment was lost, popped once more like a bubble.

Gage's face clouded and settled into the familiar, tired, disappointed mask it was accustomed to being.

As if they had been given permission to speak, voices from townsfolk began moving about, gabbling, rising and falling, filling the air with excited, nervous chatter.

"Is it over?" Molly Shierson's voice sounded tired and relieved, as if saying something with finality.

Gage nodded. "Yes. Yes, it is. It's all done with here."

Epilogue

"Where do you suppose he went?" Gerty looked over the small table toward Molly. The buxom cook glanced to her left toward Mr. Cooley, who was looking toward the north.

Cooley shifted his gaze westward. "No idea," he said in a quiet voice. "But wherever it is, good luck to him. He's got a life I don't envy."

Molly Shierson said nothing, but sat gazing at the empty chair across the table from her, not really seeing it. Not really seeing much of anything, save for her husband's gun belt and guns hanging on the back of the empty chair.

for murder. His trail is getting bloodier every day. And Smoke is gearing up for the craziest showdown of his life—with a force of nature called Smoke Jensen . . .

National Bestselling Authors
William W. Johnstone
and J.A. Johnstone

BLOOD BOUNTY OF THE MOUNTAIN MAN

On sale now, wherever Pinnacle Books are sold.

Live Free. Read Hard.
www.williamjohnstone.net
Visit us at www.kensingtonbooks.com

Chapter 1

Smoke Jensen wasn't quite ready to draw his gun, but he was definitely of a mind to punch someone.

That someone happened to be an ugly hombre—wildly askew red hair, a craggy face, and broken, jagged yellow teeth—standing at the bar not far from Smoke who had just said something very ungentlemanly-like to a lady.

The lady's face glowed a bright, embarrassed red. Her eyes darted to the men who sat with her around the rough-hewn table at the stage station. They looked uncomfortable, too. Most of them dropped their gazes to the simple but filling fare spread out on the table. A couple muttered unintelligible comments. If they'd been standing, they would have been scuffing their feet on the hard-packed dirt floor.

But it was evident they weren't going to stand up to the loud, obnoxious man who had just uttered the vulgarities.

Smoke wasn't surprised. They all looked like townies. Men who were well insulated from the dangers of frontier life and unaccustomed to conflicts. He couldn't blame them for that, but still . . . no matter a man's station in life, he ought to stand up for a lady. Always.

So Smoke intervened.

He placed his coffee cup on the scarred bar top, turned to face the ugly patron, and said to the varmint, "Seems to me the lady isn't interested in your advances. If I were you, I'd stop."

The man continued to lean with his back to the bar, his elbows propped up on either side. He chuckled, but that was the only recognition he gave Smoke's words. He kept his eyes on the lady.

Smoke found that rude, too.

Equally as offensive was the man's stench. Not to mention the dirt that clung to the gray pants, tattered, brown shirt, and gray vest he wore. There were a few stains that looked to be blood.

Someone else's, more than likely, Smoke assumed.

The hombre opened his mouth to say something—no doubt something crude directed at the lady—but Smoke wasn't about to let that happen.

He decided to shift tactics.

"Friend, I'd be happy to buy you a drink. One for the road. Then you just ride on. Safe travels."

Smoke's eyes darted to the short, balding man behind the bar. Sweat beaded his forehead. It was clear he didn't want trouble in his humble establishment. It was probably a constant fear. They were in the middle of nowhere. The wild, tall uncut of Montana. The man probably saw his share of hard cases ride through.

"The d-drink is on the house," the proprietor said hoarsely.

"See? Can't beat that. I'd take the deal, friend," Smoke encouraged.

Finally, the hombre took his elbows off the bar and turned to face Smoke. He must have recognized something in Smoke's eyes because the fire temporarily dimmed in his. He recovered quickly. Or tried to appear that way, at least.

"You new to this country?" he growled.

Smoke smiled. "Not hardly."

He thought about letting the man know exactly who he was. The name Smoke Jensen carried weight around those parts, even as far from the Sugarloaf as Montana was. But he decided against it. That may only provoke the man more. Being the man who killed Smoke Jensen would make someone awfully famous. Smoke didn't want to pull iron if he could avoid it. The man before him was rude and obnoxious, no doubt about that. That didn't mean he deserved to die, though.

He just needed to learn a good lesson.

The hombre studied Smoke and sneered as if he were a bug he wanted to squash. "Well, since you seem to think we're friends, offering to buy me a drink and all, let me give you some *friendly* advice. Don't go poking your nose where it don't belong. Not around here." He tapped the chipped handle of the iron pouched on his hip. "Could get a man hurt. Maybe even worse." He chuckled.

Smoke sighed.

"What?" the man said.

"I wish you wouldn't have done that."

Smoke's Colt was out, aimed, and cocked almost quicker than the naked eye could comprehend. Everyone in the stage station froze.

A long, heavy moment passed.

Finally, the man gulped, nodded, and slowly backed away. "You best hope we don't meet up along the trail, *friend*."

Smoke smiled. "I'll be ready if we do. Can't say it bothers me much one way or the other."

"If I were you, I'd just leave this well enough alone!" the proprietor said to the redhead.

The ugly man glanced at him but didn't respond. Smoke figured he realized it was best to quit while behind.

And with that Colt pointed squarely at his forehead, the man was clearly behind.

He backed out of the stage station without another word. A minute later, the swift rataplan of hoofbeats resounded loudly through the open door, hurrying across the prairie.

"Mighty glad you were here, mister," the owner said, using a dirty cloth to mop the line of sweat from his wrinkled brow. "That could have turned into trouble mighty easy."

Smoke hoped the barkeep wasn't going to use that same cloth to clean the glasses and mugs, but he didn't voice that concern. Instead, he pouched his iron and turned his focus back to the coffee. It was a bit cooler now but still drinkable.

"My goodness! Thank you, sir," the woman said, rushing up to him.

She had long, silky brown hair, a smooth, unblemished face, and a shapely form. She was probably twenty-five or thereabouts. The blue-and-white gingham dress she wore hugged her curves in a way that could easily capture a man's imagination.

"Don't mention it. I'm just glad everything is fine now." Smoke smiled at her, raised his coffee in a slight toast, and then took a sip.

"You could have been killed!" she said.

Her British accent was heavy. Smoke guessed she hadn't been away from her homeland for very long.

"Did we watch the same ruckus?" one of the men at the table said. He was an old fellow in a dusty brown suit and matching derby hat. White muttonchops framed his face. "That was over before it even got started."

"I ain't never seen anybody draw so fast!" another man at the table said. He was a tall, lanky fellow with a bobbing Adam's apple. His gray suit hung loosely from his frame.

"I have," the old-timer said. "Saw Frank and Jesse James back in Missouri. You talk about fast! Heck, Jesse could pull and plug a man quicker'n anything you've ever seen. I saw him do it, too. Saw it with my own eyes!"

"You ain't never seen Jesse James," the lanky man said, shaking his head. "Sometimes I don't know if you really believe the yarns you tell or if you're just trying to be somebody."

The old man bristled. He mumbled something and then said loud enough for all to hear, "I seen Jesse James. Sure as shootin'. And I'm telling you, I think this feller is as fast or faster than him!" He got to his feet and walked over to Smoke. "What did you say your name was?"

"Don't think I did," Smoke said with an affable smile. "Just passing through." He took one more long swallow of his coffee, put a coin on the bar, and then tipped his hat to the lady. "Ma'am."

Smoke smiled as he strolled toward the door. He didn't know if the old man had actually ever seen the James boys. He sure had, though. Jesse, at least.

His mind raced back to when he'd been a boy. His pa away at war. His brother Luke gone, too. Young Smoke—Kirby as he'd been known back then—had tried hard to keep that Missouri farm going. But he'd only been one man. Not even a man, really. Just a boy forced to grow up too quickly. And that was a hard-scrabble life, anyway, trying to scratch out crops in those rocky Ozarks.

Then one day Jesse had ridden in with the outfit he'd joined. Smoke had heard the stories. Those raiders were responsible for their fair share of looting and killing. Jesse had been nice to him, though. Even gave him the first pistol Smoke had ever owned.

That was a lifetime ago. Or it felt that way. Smoke wasn't an old man, by any means. But he'd lived a lot in the ensuing years. More than most men do in a whole lifetime.

The group inside the station was still talking about him when Smoke closed the door. He went low, moving quickly, zigzagging to a nearby lean-to where he'd left his horse. He waited. Listened. Scanned the countryside. More than anything, he became one with it, connecting with its patterns. Breathing with it.

Being careful was a habit with him. It had kept him alive this long.

Once satisfied the ugly stranger had truly ridden away, Smoke swung up into the saddle and rode on down the trail. It was going to take him a while to get back to the Sugarloaf. The train he'd sent Pearlie, Cal, and the other hands back on after selling the herd would have been much quicker. But Smoke didn't mind the trip.

He'd chosen it.

He didn't mind the solitude, either.

He had more than enough memories to keep him company.

Chapter 2

There were a lot of things about the old days that Smoke didn't miss.

He'd ridden the vengeance trail. His first wife's murder—and his father's—had demanded he do so.

As he rode along through the beautiful Montana countryside, with the majestic, towering mountains around him, rising into the deep blue sky, his mind continued to drift . . .

Nicole had been beautiful. The first woman he'd ever loved. It had taken a while, there in that little cabin he and Preacher had built in Southwest Colorado. Neither he nor Nicole had jumped at each other the first chance they'd gotten. Smoke chuckled thinking about it. They'd both been shy about such things. Downright nervous, even.

That was back in the days after Preacher had taken him in, teaching him the ways of the mountain man. Then, one day, Preacher just up and rode away, getting one of those wild hairs he was prone to get. That's what he'd said, at least. Smoke knew the truth—he'd wanted to give Smoke and Nicole some privacy. He'd figured that once the two were alone, love would blossom.

That plan of his had worked, too.

Smoke and Nicole couldn't deny the feelings that tend to spring up between a young man and a young woman.

He chuckled as he remembered their first time. They'd both been so clumsy and awkward.

A pang of guilt stabbed at his insides. What would Sally think if she knew he was reminiscing about all this?

The guilt left as quickly as it had come. Sally wasn't particular about such things. Granted, she wouldn't like it much if Smoke was thinking about some living woman in such terms. But she understood that in a way, Smoke and Nicole would always be connected.

She'd borne him a child, after all.

The child that was ripped from him along with Nicole when vicious bounty hunters perpetrated an act of unspeakable evil.

Smoke had answered that horrible challenge. Or rather, his guns had. Every last one of those men had fallen at the barrel of his smoking irons.

They were hardly the last to do so.

Those guns had also roared with flame and death when he'd donned the alias of Buck West, pretending to be an outlaw so he could root out his father's killers.

Emmett Jensen hadn't been a perfect father by any means. He would have admitted as much. He'd left his family for the war. True, it was a cause he believed in. At first, at least. Smoke supposed like so many he'd grown disillusioned by the war's end.

Years of bloodshed will do that to a man.

Yet Emmett Jensen had still been a man of principle. Nothing would have stripped that from him. So, when men who were supposed to stand on the same principles he did had made off with a shipment of Confederate gold and apparently murdered his other son Luke in the process of committing their villainous act, Emmett had to go after them. Even after Lee's surrender.

Appomattox be damned.

Integrity meant something to the Jensens.

Yet Emmett hadn't been able to finish the job. Smoke, however, had.

As he rode along, he realized he didn't miss the violence of those days. There wasn't a chance to. His days were pretty violent still. While life had periods of relative peace with Sally there on the Sugarloaf, he still found himself involved in more than his fair share of scrapes.

Yet he wasn't a man who relished spilling blood. He took no delight in killing. He just couldn't sit back and watch evil men victimize decent folk. He feared there would come a day when men grew soft and complacent, unable to do what needed to be done in the face of evil, even making excuses for all the wrong being perpetrated on the world.

But Smoke would never abide that way. He couldn't. So, more often than not, it was that sense of justice that fueled his many adventures. In the old days, though, it had been vengeance.

And vengeance is always a heavy load to bear. No, Smoke didn't miss that at all.

But he did miss how close to nature he used to be. There was something calling to him as of late. Something about the way he'd lived off the land back in those early years, carrying on the traditions Preacher had taught him, living as the mountain men had lived.

"That's what it is," he said aloud.

He turned his head slowly, admiring the wild country. He'd been feeling nostalgic for that life of solitude, for being out where so few people were. It seemed as if the town of Big Rock was growing by leaps and bounds.

Soon, the country would be so full there wouldn't be any wide-open spaces left.

He wouldn't trade his life with Sally for anything. He'd stay on the Sugarloaf until the day he died. Yet even the happiest, most content of men could yearn for those old days every now and again.

That's all this little detour was. Sending half the money from the sale of the herd back with Pearlie, Cal, and the other hands, the rest was tucked safely in a belt that was strapped around his stomach inside his shirt. Now, he had nothing to worry about and plenty of time to enjoy the scenery, take a trip or two down memory lane, and daydream about the future.

Yet something in his gut told him trouble was just over the horizon. He wasn't afraid. But he wanted to be prepared.

Could just be my imagination, he thought. Maybe

reflecting on his time as Buck West and that vengeance trail he'd ridden just had him stirred up.

Or maybe it was something more.

His gut told him it was the latter rather than the former.

And Smoke Jensen was a man who'd learned long ago to trust his gut.